All the Flowers are Dying

All the Flowers are Dying

A MATT SCUDDER NOVEL

Lawrence Block

W F HOWES LTD

This large print edition published in 2005 by
W F Howes Ltd
Units 6/7, Victoria Mills, Fowke Street
Rothley, Leicester LE7 7PJ

1 3 5 7 9 10 8 6 4 2

First published in the United Kingdom in 2005
by Orion

ISBN 1 84505 822 4

Typeset by Palimpsest Book Production Limited,
Polmont, Stirlingshire
Printed and bound in Great Britain
by Antony Rowe Ltd, Chippenham, Wilts.

for a pair of Knockaround Guys:

BRIAN KOPPELMAN

&

DAVID LEVIEN

O Danny Boy, the pipes, the pipes are callin',
From glen to glen, and down the mountainside,
The summer's gone, the roses all are fallen,
And now 'tis you must go, and I must bide.

But come ye back when spring is in the meadow,
Or when the hills are hushed and white with snow,
Ye'll find me there, in sunshine or in shadow,
O Danny Boy, O Danny Boy, I love you so.

But if ye come, and all the flowers are dyin',
And I am dead, as dead I well may be,
Then you will find the place where I am lyin',
And kneel and say an Ave there for me.

And I will hear, though soft you tread above me,
And then my grave will warmer, softer be,
And you will bend and tell me that you love me,
And I will wait in peace until you come to me.

FREDERIC EDWARD WEATHERLY, 'Danny Boy'

Listen, O judges: here is yet another madness, and that comes *before* the deed. Alas, you have not yet crept deep enough into this soul.

Thus speaks the red judge, 'Why did this criminal murder? He wanted to rob.' But I say unto you: his soul wanted blood, not robbery; he thirsted after the bliss of the knife.

FRIEDRICH NIETZSCHE, *Thus Spake Zarathustra*
Translated by Walter Kaufmann

ACKNOWLEDGMENTS

The author is pleased to acknowledge the considerable contribution of the Ragdale Foundation, in Lake Forest, Illinois, where most of this book was written.

CHAPTER 1

When I got there, Joe Durkin was already holding down a corner table and working on a drink – vodka on the rocks, from the looks of it. I took in the room and listened to the hum of conversation at the bar, and I guess some of what I was feeling must have found its way to my face, because the first thing Joe asked me was if I was all right. I said I was fine, and why?

'Because you look like you saw a ghost,' he said.

'Be funny if I didn't,' I said. 'The room is full of them.'

'A little new for ghosts, isn't it? How long have they been open, two years?'

'Closer to three.'

'Time flies,' he said, 'whether you're having fun or not. Jake's Place, whoever Jake is. You got a history with him?'

'I don't know who he is. I had a history with the place before it was his.'

'Jimmy Armstrong's.'

'That's right.'

'He died, didn't he? Was that before or after 9/11?'

That's our watershed; everything in our lives is before or after that date. 'After,' I said, 'by five or six months. He left the place to a nephew, who tried running it for a few months and then decided it wasn't the life he wanted for himself. So I guess he sold it to Jake, whoever Jake is.'

'Whoever Jake is,' he said, 'he puts a good meal on the table. You know what they've got here? You can get an Irish breakfast all day long.'

'What's that, a cigarette and a six-pack?'

'Very funny. You must know what an Irish breakfast is, a sophisticated guy like yourself.'

I nodded. 'It's the cardiac special, right? Bacon and eggs and sausage.'

'And grilled tomato.'

'Ah, health food.'

'And black pudding,' he said, 'which is hard to find. You know what you want? Because I'll have the Irish breakfast.'

I told the waitress I'd have the same, and a cup of coffee. Joe said one vodka was enough, but she could bring him a beer. Something Irish, to go with the breakfast, but not Guinness. She suggested a Harp, and he said that would be fine.

I've known Joe for twenty years, though I don't know that ours is an intimate friendship. He's spent those years as a detective at Midtown North, working out of the old stationhouse on West Fifty-fourth Street, and we'd developed a working relationship over time. I went to him for favors, and returned them, sometimes in cash, sometimes in kind. Now and then he steered a client my way. There were times when our relations had been strained; my close friendship with a career criminal never sat well with him, while his attitude after one vodka too many didn't make me relish his company. But we'd been around long enough to know how to make it work, overlooking what we didn't like to look at and staying close but not too close.

Around the time our food arrived, he told me he'd put in his papers. I said he'd been threatening to do so for years, and he said he'd had everything filled out and ready to go a few years ago, and then the towers came down. 'That was no time to retire,' he said. 'Although guys did, and how could you blame 'em? They lost their heart for the job. Me, I'd already lost my heart for it. Shoveling shit against the tide, all we ever do. Right then, though, I managed to convince myself I was needed.'

'I can imagine.'

'So I stayed three years longer than I intended, and if I did anything useful in those three years I can't remember what it was. Anyway, I'm done. Today's what, Wednesday? A week from Friday's my last day. So all I have to do now is figure out what the hell to do with the rest of my life.'

Which was why he'd asked me to meet him for dinner, in a room full of ghosts.

★　　★　　★

3

It had been over thirty years since I put in my papers and retired from the NYPD, and shortly thereafter I'd retired as well from my role as husband and father, and moved from a comfortable suburban house in Syosset to a monastic little room at the Hotel Northwestern. I didn't spend much time in that room; Jimmy Armstrong's saloon, around the corner on Ninth between Fifty-seventh and Fifty-eighth, served as a combination of living room and office for me. I met clients there, I ate meals there, and what social life I had was centered there. I drank there, too, day in and day out, because that's what I did back then.

I kept it up for as long as I could. Then I put the plug in the jug, as the old-timers say, and began spending my idle hours not at Jimmy's joint but two blocks north of there, in the basement of St Paul the Apostle. And in other church basements and storefronts, where I looked for something to put in the empty places alcohol used to fill.

Somewhere along the way, Jimmy lost his lease and moved half a block south and a long block west, to the corner of Fifty-seventh and Tenth. I'd kept my distance from the old place after I sobered up, and I avoided the new one for a while as well. It never did become a hangout, but Elaine and I would drop in for a meal from time to time. Jimmy always served good food, and the kitchen stayed open late, which made it a good choice after an evening at the theater or Lincoln Center.

I'd been to the service, at a funeral parlor on West Forty-fourth, where someone played a favorite song of his. It was 'Last Call,' by Dave Van Ronk, and I'd first heard it when Billie Keegan played it for me after a long night of whiskey. I'd made him play the song over and over. Keegan worked for Jimmy back then, tending bar on weekday evenings; he'd long since moved out to California. And Van Ronk, who wrote the song and sang it a capella, had died a month or so before Jimmy, and so I'd sat there listening to one dead man sing a song to another dead man.

A week or two later they had a wake for Jimmy at the bar, and I went to that and didn't stay long. Some people showed up I hadn't seen for years, and it was good to see them, but it was a relief to get out of there and go home. One night in the summer, after the lease had been sold, they closed things out by letting everybody drink free. Several different people told me to be sure and show up, and I didn't even have to think about it. I stayed home and watched the Yankees game.

And here I was, in a roomful of ghosts. Manny Karesh was one of them. I'd known him in the old days on Ninth Avenue, and he'd never moved out of the neighborhood. He dropped in at Jimmy's just about every day, to drink one or two beers and chat up the nurses. He was at the wake, of course, and he'd have been there for the final night, but I don't know if he made it. He told me at the wake that he didn't have much time left. They'd offered him chemotherapy, he said, but they didn't hold out much hope that it would do any good, so he couldn't see any reason to subject himself to it. He died sometime that summer, not too long after the bar closed, but I didn't hear about it until the fall. So that's one funeral I missed, but these days there's always another funeral to go to. They're like buses. If you miss one, there'll be another coming your way in a few minutes.

'I'm fifty-eight,' Joe said. 'That's plenty old enough to retire, but too young to be retired, you know what I mean?'

'You know what you're going to do?'

'What I'm not gonna do,' he said, 'is buy a little house in fucking Florida. I don't fish, I don't play golf, and I got this County Waterford skin, I can get a sunburn from a desk lamp.'

'I don't think you'd like Florida.'

'No kidding. I could stay here and live on my pension, but I'd go nuts without something to do. I'd spend all my time in bars, which is no good, or I'd stay home and drink, which is worse. This is the best, this black pudding. There aren't many places you can get it. I suppose the old Irish neighborhoods, Woodside, Fordham Road, but who's got the time to chase out there?'

'Well, now that you're retired.'

'Yeah, I can spend a day looking for black pudding.'

'You wouldn't have to go that far,' I said. 'Any bodega can sell you all you want.'

'You're kidding. Black pudding?'

'They call it *morcilla*, but it's the same thing.'

'What is it, Puerto Rican? I bet it's spicier.'

'Spicier than Irish cuisine? Gee, do you suppose that's possible? But it's pretty much the same thing. You can call it *morcilla* or black pudding, but either way you've got sausage made from pig's blood.'

'Jesus!'

'What's the matter?'

'Do you fucking mind? I'm eating.'

'You didn't know what it was?'

'Of course I know, but that doesn't mean I want to fucking dwell on it.' He drank some beer, put the glass down, shook his head. 'Some of the guys wind up working private security. Not at the rent-a-cop level, but higher up. Guy I knew put his papers in ten years ago, went to work overseeing security at the stock exchange. Regular hours, and better money than he ever made on the job. Now he's retired from that, and he's got two pensions, plus his Social Security. And he's down in Florida, playing golf and fishing.'

'You interested in something like that?'

'Florida? I already said . . . oh, the private security thing. Well, see, I carried a gold shield for a lot of years. I was a detective, and the job he had, it's more administrative. I could do it, but I don't know that I'd love it. Probably a fair amount of chickenshit involved, too.' He picked up his empty glass, looked at it, put it down again. Without looking at me he said, 'I was thinking about a private ticket.'

I'd seen this coming.

'To do it right,' I said, 'you have to be a businessman, keeping records and filing reports and networking in order to get cases. That's if you're in business for yourself, but the other way, going to work for one of the big agencies, you're mostly doing boring work for short money, and doing it without a badge. I don't think it would suit you.'

'Neither would the reports and the record keeping. But you didn't do all that.'

'Well, I was never very good at doing things by the book,' I said. 'I worked for years without a license, and when I finally got one I didn't hang on to it very long.'

'I remember. You got by okay without it.'

'I guess. It was hand to mouth sometimes.'

'Well, I got that pension. It's a cushion.'

'True.'

'What I was thinking . . .'

And what he was thinking, of course, was that the two of us could work together. I had the experience on the private side, and he'd be bringing much fresher contacts within the department. I let him pitch the idea, and when he'd run through it I told him he was a few years too late.

'I'm pretty much retired,' I said. 'Not formally, because there's no need. But I don't go looking for business, and the phone doesn't ring very often, and when it does I usually find a reason to turn down whatever's on offer. Do that a few times and people quit calling, and that's okay with me. I don't need the dough. I've got Social Security, plus a small monthly check from the city, and we've got the income from some rental property Elaine owns, plus the profits from her shop.'

'Art and antiques,' he said. 'I pass it all the time, I never see anyone go in or out. Does she make any money there?'

'She's got a good eye, and a head for business. The rent's no bargain, and there are months she comes up short, but now and then she spots something for ten bucks at a thrift shop and sells it for a few thousand. She could probably do the same thing on eBay and save the rent, but she likes having the shop, which is why she opened it in the first place. And whenever I get tired of long walks and ESPN, I can take a turn behind the counter.'

'Oh, you do that?'

'Now and then.'

'You know enough about the business?'

'I know how to ring a sale and how to process a credit card transaction. I know when to tell them

9

to come back and see the proprietor. I know how to tell when someone's contemplating shoplifting or robbery, and how to discourage them. I can usually tell when somebody's trying to sell me stolen goods. That's about as much as I need to know to hold down the job.'

'I guess you don't need a partner in the gumshoe business.'

'No, but if you'd asked me five years ago . . .'

Five years ago the answer would still have been no, but I'd have had to find a different way to phrase it.

We ordered coffee, and he sat back and ran his eyes around the room. I sensed in him a mixture of disappointment and relief, which was about what I'd feel in his circumstances. And I felt some of it myself. The last thing I wanted was a partner, but there's something about that sort of offer that makes one want to accept it. You think it's a cure for loneliness. A lot of ill-advised partnerships start that way, and more than a few bad marriages.

The coffee came, and we talked about other things. The crime rate was still going down, and neither of us could figure out why. 'There's this moron in the state legislature,' he said, 'who claims credit for it, because he helped push the death penalty through. It's hard to figure that one out, given that the only time anybody gets a lethal injection in New York State is when he buys a bag of smack laced with rat poison. There's guys upstate on Death Row, but they'll die of old age before they get the needle.'

'You figure it's a deterrent?'

'I figure it's a pretty good deterrent against doing it again. To tell you the truth, I don't think anybody really gives a shit if it's a deterrent. There's some guys that you're just happier not having them breathe the same air as the rest of us. People who just ought to be dead. Terrorists, mass murderers. Serial killers. Fucking perverts who kill children. You can tell me they're sick people, they were abused as children themselves, di dah di dah di dah, and I won't disagree with you, but the truth is I don't care. Let 'em be dead. I'm happier when they're dead.'

'You're not going to get an argument from me.'

'There's one set to go a week from Friday. Not here, nobody gets it in this fucking state. In Virginia, that son of a bitch who killed the three little boys. Four, five years ago it was. I forget his name.'

'I know who you mean.'

'The one argument I'll even listen to is suppose you execute an innocent man. And I guess it does happen. This guy, though. You remember the case? Open and shut.'

'So I understand.'

'He fucked these kids,' he said, 'and he tortured them, and he kept souvenirs, and the cops had enough physical evidence to convict him a hundred times over. A week from Friday he gets

11

the needle. I put in my last day on the job, and I go home and pour myself a drink, and somewhere down in Virginia that cocksucker gets a hot shot. You know what? It's better than a gold watch, far as I'm concerned.'

CHAPTER 2

He'd originally suggested dinner at seven, but I'd pushed it back to six-thirty. When the waitress brought the check he grabbed it, reminding me that dinner had been his idea. 'Besides,' he said, 'I'm off the job in a matter of days. I better get in practice picking up the tab.'

All the years I'd known him, I was the one who picked up the checks.

'If you want,' he said, 'we could go somewhere else and you can buy the drinks. Or dessert, or some more coffee.'

'I've got to be someplace.'

'Oh, right, you said as much when we made the date. Taking the little woman out on the town?'

I shook my head. 'She's having dinner with a girlfriend. I've got a meeting I have to go to.'

'You're still going, huh?'

'Not as often as I used to, but once or twice a week.'

'You could miss a night.'

'I could and would,' I said, 'but the fellow who's leading the meeting is a friend of mine, and I'm the one who booked him to speak.'

'So you pretty much have to be there. Who's the guy, anybody I know?'

'Just a drunk.'

'Must be nice to have meetings to go to.'

It is, though that's not why I go.

'What they ought to have,' he said, 'is meetings for guys who drink a certain amount, and have no reason to stop.'

'That's a terrific idea, Joe.'

'You think so?'

'Absolutely. You wouldn't need to hang out in church basements, either. You could hold the meetings in a saloon.'

'My name is Joe D.,' he said, 'and I'm retired.'

The meeting was at my home group at St Paul's, and I was there in plenty of time to open it up, read the AA Preamble, and introduce the speaker. 'My name's Ray,' he said, 'and I'm an alcoholic,' and then he spent the next fifteen or twenty minutes doing what we do, telling his story, what it used to be like, what happened, and what it's like now.

Joe had asked if the speaker was anyone he knew, and I'd avoided a direct answer. If he didn't know Ray Gruliow personally, he certainly knew him by reputation, and would recognize the long Lincolnesque face and the rich raspy voice. Hard-Way Ray was a criminal lawyer who'd made a career out of representing radicals and outcasts, championing the country's least sympathetic defendants by putting the system itself on trial. The police hated him, and hardly anyone doubted that it had been a cop, some years ago, who'd fired a couple of shots through the front window of Ray's Commerce Street town house. (No one was hurt, and the resultant publicity was a bonanza for Ray. 'If I'd known I'd get that much of a bounce out of it,' he'd said, 'I might have done it myself.')

I'd run into Ray in May, at the annual dinner of the Club of Thirty-one. It had been a happy event, we hadn't lost any members since last year's gathering, and toward the end of the evening I told Ray I was booking the speaker every other Wednesday at St Paul's, and when would he like to speak?

There were forty or fifty people at the meeting that night, and at least half of them must have recognized Ray, but the tradition of anonymity runs deep among us. During the discussion that followed his lead, no one gave any indication that he knew more about him than he'd told us. 'Guess who I heard at St Paul's last night,' they might tell other members at other meetings, because we tend to do that, although we're probably not supposed to. But we don't tell friends outside of the program, as I had not told Joe Durkin, and, perhaps more to the point, we don't let it affect how we relate to one another in the rooms. Paul T., who delivers lunches for the deli on Fifty-seventh Street, and Abie, who does something arcane with computers, get as much attention and respect in that room as

15

Raymond F. Gruliow, Esq. Maybe more – they've been sober longer.

The meeting breaks at ten, and a few of us generally wind up at the Flame, a coffee shop on Ninth Avenue almost directly across the street from Jimmy's original saloon. This time there were seven of us at the big table in the corner. These days I'm often the person in the room with the longest continuous sobriety, which is the sort of thing that's apt to happen to you sooner or later if you don't drink and don't die. Tonight, though, there were two men at our table who'd been sober longer than I by several years, and one of them, Bill D., had very likely been at my first meeting. (I didn't remember him from that night, having been only peripherally aware of my own presence.) He used to share with some frequency at meetings, and I always liked what he said; I might have asked him to be my sponsor if Jim Faber hadn't emerged as the clear choice for that role. Later, after Jim was killed, I decided that if I ever felt the need of a sponsor I'd ask Bill. But so far I hadn't.

These days he didn't talk much, although he went to as many meetings as ever. He was a tall man, rail thin, with sparse white hair, and some of the newer members called him William the Silent. That was an adjective that would never be attached to Pat, who was short and stocky and sober about as long as Bill. He was a nice enough fellow, but he talked too much.

Bill had retired a while ago after fifty years as a stagehand; he'd probably seen more Broadway plays than anyone I knew. Pat, also retired, had worked downtown in one of the bureaucracies quartered in City Hall; I was never too clear on which agency he worked for, or what he did there, but whatever it was he'd stopped doing it four or five years ago.

Johnny Sidewalls had worked construction until a job-related injury left him with two bad legs and a disability pension; he got around with the help of two canes and worked from his home, carrying on some sort of Internet-based mail-order business. He'd been very sullen and embittered when he showed up at St Paul's and Fireside and other neighborhood meetings a few years ago, but his attitude leveled out over time. Like Bill, he was a neighborhood guy, who'd lived all his life in and around Hell's Kitchen and San Juan Hill. I don't know why they called him Johnny Sidewalls, and I think he may have had the name before he got sober. Some sort of sobriquet's almost inevitable when your name is John, but no one seems to know where this one came from.

When your name is Abie, on the other hand, neither a nickname nor an initial is required. Abie – short for Abraham, I supposed, but he always gave his name as Abie, and corrected you if you truncated it to Abe – was sober ten years and change, but new in New York; he'd sobered up in Oregon, then relocated to northern California. A few months ago he moved to New York and started showing up at St Paul's and a few other West Side meetings. He was in his early forties, around five-eleven, with a medium build and a clean-cut face that was hard to keep in your mind when you weren't looking at him. There were no strong features there for the memory to grab onto.

It seemed to me he had a personality to match. I'd heard his AA qualification at a noon meeting in the Sixty-third Street Y, but all I could remember of his drinking story was that he used to drink and now he doesn't. He didn't share often, but when he did it tended to be bland and unexceptionable. I figured it was probably a matter of style. The sharing tends to be less personal and more pro forma at small-town meetings, and that's what he was used to.

At one of the first meetings I went to, a gay woman talked about having realized that drinking might be a problem for her when she noticed that she kept coming out of blackouts on her knees with some guy's dick in her mouth. 'I never did that when I was sober,' she said. I have a feeling Abie never got to hear anything like that in Dogbane, Oregon.

Herb had been coming around about as long as Abie had, and he'd made ninety days the previous week. That's a benchmark of sorts; until you've put together ninety days clean and dry, you can't lead a meeting or take on a service commitment. Herb had qualified at a daytime meeting. I hadn't been there, but I'd probably get to hear his story sooner or later, if he and I both stayed sober. He was around fifty, pudgy and balding, but almost boyish with the enthusiasm that's characteristic of some members' early sobriety.

I hadn't been that way myself, nor was I as bitter about the whole thing as Johnny had been. Jim Faber, who'd watched the process, had told me I was at once dogged and fatalistic, sure I would drink again but determined not to. I couldn't tell you what I was like. I just remember dragging myself from one meeting to the next, scared it would work for me and scared it wouldn't.

I don't remember who brought up capital punishment. Somebody did, and somebody made one of the standard observations on the subject, and then Johnny Sidewalls turned to Ray and said, 'I suppose you're against it.' That could have been said with an edge, but it wasn't. It was just an observation, with the tacit implication that, given who Ray was, he'd be opposed to the death penalty.

'I'm against it for my clients,' Ray said.

'Well, you'd have to be, wouldn't you?'

'Of course. I'm against any penalty for my clients.'

'They're all innocent,' I said.

'Innocent's a stretch,' he allowed. 'I'll settle for not guilty. I've tried a few capital cases. I never lost one, and they weren't cases where the death penalty was a real possibility. Still, even the slimmest chance that your client might go to the chair concentrates an attorney's mind wonderfully. 'Go to the chair' – that dates me, doesn't it? There's no chair anymore. They let you lie down, in fact they insist on it. Strap you to a gurney, make a regular medical procedure out of it. And the odds against you are even worse than in regular surgery.'

'What I always liked,' Bill said, 'is the alcohol swab.'

Ray nodded. 'Because God forbid you might get a staph infection. You have to wonder what latter-day Mengele thought that one up. Am I against the death penalty? Well, aside from the fact that it can't be established to have any deterrent effect, and that the whole process of appeals and execution costs substantially more than feeding and housing the sonofabitch for the rest of his natural life, that it's essentially barbaric and puts us on the same side of the line as China and the Muslim dictatorships, and that, unlike the rain which falls equally upon the just and the unjust, it falls exclusively upon the poor and underprivileged. Aside from all that, there's the unfortunate fact that every once in a while we get our signals crossed and execute the wrong person. It wasn't that long ago that nobody even heard of DNA, and now it's getting a ton of convictions reversed. Who knows what the next step in forensics will be, and what percentage of the poor bastards the state of Texas is busy killing will turn out innocent?'

'That would be awful,' Herb said. 'Imagine knowing you didn't do something, and there's nothing you can do to stop it from happening to you.'

'People die all the time,' Pat said, 'for no good reason at all.'

'But the state doesn't do it to them. That's different, somehow.'

Abie said, 'But sometimes there's just no fit response short of death. Terrorists, for example. What would you do with them?'

'Shoot them out of hand,' Ray said. 'Failing that, hang the bastards.'

'But if you're against capital punishment—'

'You asked me what I would do, not what I think is right. When it comes to terrorists, home-grown or foreign, I don't care what's right. I'd hang the fuckers.'

This made for a spirited discussion, but I tuned out most of it. In the main I enjoy the company of my fellow sober alcoholics, but I have to say I like it less when they talk politics or philosophy or, indeed, anything much beyond their own immediate lives. The more abstract the conversation got, the less attention I paid to it, until I perked up a little when Abie said, 'What about Applewhite? Preston Applewhite, from Richmond, Virginia. He killed those three little boys, and he's scheduled for execution sometime next week.'

'Friday,' I said. Ray gave me a look. 'It came up in a conversation earlier tonight,' I explained. 'I gather the evidence is pretty cut-and-dried.'

'Overwhelming,' Abie said. 'And you know sex

killers will do it again if they get the chance. There's no reforming them.'

'Well, if life without parole really meant life without parole . . .'

And I tuned out again. Preston Applewhite, whose case hadn't interested me much at the time and of whose guilt or innocence I had no opinion, had unwittingly found his way into two very different conversations. That had caught my attention, but now I could forget about him.

'I had the Irish breakfast,' I told Elaine, 'complete with black pudding, which Joe is crazy about so long as he can manage to forget what it is.'

'There's probably a kosher vegetarian version,' she said, 'made out of wheat gluten. Did it feel strange going there?'

'A little, but less so as the evening wore on and I got used to it. The menu's not as interesting as Jimmy's, but what I had was pretty good.'

'It's hard to screw up an Irish breakfast.'

'We'll go sometime and you can see what you think. Of the place – I already know what you would think of the Irish breakfast. You're home early, incidentally.'

'Monica had a late date.'

'The mystery man?'

She nodded. Monica's her best friend, and her men run to type: they're all married. At first it would bother her when they'd hop out of her bed to catch the last train to Upper Saddle River, and then she realized that she liked it better that way. No bad breath in your face first thing in the morning, plus you had your weekends free. Wasn't that the best of all worlds?

Usually she showed off her married beaus. Some of them were proud and some were sheepish, but what this one was we seemed unlikely to find out, as he'd somehow impressed upon her the need for secrecy. She'd been seeing him for a few weeks now, and Elaine, her confidante in all matters, couldn't get a thing out of her beyond the admission that he was extremely intelligent and – no kidding – very secretive.

'They don't go out in public together,' she reported, 'not even for a charming little dinner in a charming little bistro. There's no way she can reach him, not by phone or e-mail, and when he calls her the conversations are brief and cryptic. He won't say her name over the phone, and doesn't want her to use his. And she's not even sure the name he gave her is his real name, but whatever it is she won't tell me.'

'It sounds as though she's getting off on the secrecy.'

'Oh, no question. It's frustrating, because she'd like to be able to talk about him, but at the same time she likes that she can't. And since she doesn't know who he is or what he does, she can make him into anything in her mind. Like a government agent, and she can't even be sure what government.'

'So he calls her and comes over and they go to bed. End of story?'

'She says it's not just sex.'

'They watch *Jeopardy* together?'

'If they do,' she said, 'I bet he knows all the answers.'

'Everybody knows the answers.'

'Smartass. The questions, then. He knows all the questions. Because he's superintelligent.'

'It's a shame we'll never get to meet him,' I said. 'He sounds like a whole lot of fun.'

CHAPTER 3

The Greensville Correctional Center is located just outside of Jarratt, Virginia, an hour's drive south of Richmond. He pulls up to the gate-house, rolls down his window, shows the guard his driver's license and the letter from the warden. His car, a white Ford Crown Victoria with a moon-roof, is immaculate; he spent the previous night in Richmond, and before he left this morning he ran it through a car wash. This car's a rental, and it hadn't gotten all that dirty in a few hundred miles of highway travel, but he likes a clean car, always has. Keep your car washed, your hair combed, and your shoes shined, he likes to say, because you never get a second chance to make a first impression.

He parks where the guard indicates, no more than thirty yards from the main entrance, over which the facade is filled with the institution's name: GREENSVILLE / CORRECTIONAL / CENTER. The name's scarcely necessary, the structure could hardly be anything else, squat and rectilinear and hinting at confinement and punishment.

There's a briefcase on the seat beside him, but he's already decided not to take it inside, to avoid the

25

nuisance of having to open it time and time again. He opens it now, takes out a small spiral-bound note-book. He doubts he'll need to take notes, but it's a useful prop.

Before leaving the car he checks himself again in the rearview mirror. Adjusts the knot of his silver tie, smoothes his mustache. Tries on a few expressions, settling on a rueful half-smile.

He locks the car. Hardly necessary, as the likelihood of someone breaking into a car in a prison parking lot in the very shadow of the guards' tower strikes him as infinitesimal. But he always locks the car upon leaving it. If you always lock it, you'll never leave it unlocked. If you're always early, you'll never be late.

He likes catchphrases like that. Pronounced with the right degree of certainty, even of solemnity, they can make a remarkable impression on others. Repeated over time, their effect can verge on the hypnotic.

He strides across the tarmac toward the entrance, a trimly built man wearing a gray suit, a crisp white shirt, an unpatterned silver tie. His black cap-toe shoes are freshly shined, and the rueful half-smile is in place upon his thin lips.

The warden, one John Humphries, is also wearing a gray suit, but there the resemblance ends. Humphries is the taller by several inches and heavier by fifty or sixty pounds. He carries the weight well and has the look of an ex-college athlete who never lost the habit of gym workouts. His handshake is firm, his authority unmistakable.

'Dr Bodinson,' he says.

'Warden.'

'Well, Applewhite's agreed to see you.'

'I'm glad of that.'

'For my part, I wish I had a better sense of your interest in him.'

He nods, grooms his mustache with his thumb and forefinger. 'I'm a psychologist,' he says.

'So I understand. Yale doctorate, undergraduate work at UVA. I was at Charlottesville myself, though that would have been before your time.'

Humphries is fifty-three, ten years his senior. He knows the man's age, just as he knew he'd graduated from the University of Virginia at Charlottesville. The Internet's wonderful, it can tell you almost anything you need to know, and this particular bit of knowledge is responsible for his having included UVA on his own résumé.

'Yale tends to impress people,' he says, 'but if I ever amount to anything in this world, the credit should go to the education I got here in Virginia.'

'Is that a fact?' Humphries looks at him, and it seems to him that his gaze is less guarded, more respectful. 'And are you a Virginian yourself?'

He shakes his head. 'Army brat. I grew up all over the place, and mostly overseas. My four years in Charlottesville was the longest I ever stayed in one spot in my whole life.'

They reminisce briefly about the old school, and it turns out that their respective fraternities were friendly rivals. He'd considered making himself a fellow member of Sigma Chi, but decided that would be pushing it. He'd picked another house, just two doors away on Fraternity Row.

They finish with their old school ties, and he explains his interest in Preston Applewhite. This interview, he tells Humphries, will be one part of an extensive study of criminals who steadfastly maintain their innocence in the face of overwhelming evidence of their guilt. He is particularly interested, he says, in murderers facing the death penalty, insisting on their lack of culpability right up to the very moment of execution.

Humphries takes this in, frowns in thought. 'In your letter to Applewhite,' he says, 'you indicate that you believe him.'

'I was attempting to give that impression.'

'What's that mean, Doctor? You think he's innocent?'

'Certainly not.'

'Because the evidence offered at his trial —'

'Was overwhelming and conclusive. It convinced the jury, and well it might have.'

'I have to say I'm relieved to hear you say that. But I don't know that I understand your motive in suggesting otherwise to Applewhite.'

'I suppose one could argue the ethics of it,' he says, and smoothes his mustache. 'I've found that, in order to win the confidence and co-operation of the men I need to interview, I have to give them something. I'm not prepared to offer them hope, or anything tangible. But it seems to me permissible to let them think that I believe in the veracity of their protestations of

28

innocence. It's easier for them to pour their revelations into a sympathetic ear, and it may even do them some good.'

'How do you figure that?'

'If I believe a man's story, it's that much easier for him to believe it himself.'

'But you don't. Believe their stories, that is.'

He shakes his head. 'If I had the slightest doubt of a man's guilt,' he says, 'I wouldn't include him in my study. I'm not investigating the unjustly accused. The men I'm looking at have been justly accused and justly convicted and, I must say, justly condemned to death.'

'You're not opposed to capital punishment.'

'Not at all. I think the social order requires it.'

'Now there,' Humphries says, 'I wish I had your certainty. I don't disagree with you, but I'm in the unfortunate position of being able to see both sides of the issue.'

'That can't make your job easier.'

'It can't and it doesn't. But it's part of my job, and only a small part, although it takes up a disproportionate amount of my time and thought. And I like my job, and like to think I'm good at it.'

He lets Humphries talk about the job, its trials and its satisfactions, providing the nods and responses and sympathetic facial expressions that would encourage the flow of words, There's no hurry. Preston Applewhite isn't going anywhere, not until Friday, when it's time for them to put the needle in his arm and send him off to wherever people go.

'Well, I didn't mean to go into all that,' Humphries says at length. 'I was wondering how you'd get Applewhite to talk to you, but I don't guess you'll have much trouble drawing him out. Look how you drew me out, and you weren't even trying.'

'I was interested in what you were saying.'

Humphries leans forward, puts his hands together on his desk blotter. 'When you talk to him,' he says, 'you're not going to offer him any false hope, are you?'

False hope? What other kind is there?

But what he says is, 'My abiding interest is in what he has to say. For my part, I'll do what I can to help him reconcile the impossible contradiction of his situation.'

'That being?'

'That he's going to be put to death in a matter of days, and that he's innocent.'

'But you don't believe he's innocent. Oh, I see. His innocence is something in which you're both pretending to believe.'

'It's pretense on my part. He may very well believe it.'

'Oh?'

He leans forward, folds his own hands, purposely mirroring the warden's own body language. 'Some of the men I've interviewed,' he confides, 'will actually admit, with a wink or a nod or in so many words, that they've done the deeds for which they're condemned to death. But there have only been a few of those. Others, probably the greater portion, know

30

they're guilty. I can see it in their eyes, I can hear it in their voices and read it in their faces, but they won't admit it to me or to anyone else. They're holding out deliberately, waiting for a stay from the Supreme Court, an eleventh-hour phone call from the governor.'

'This one's up for re-election next fall, and Applewhite's the most hated man in the state of Virginia. If there's a phone call, it'll be for the doctor, wishing him luck in finding a good vein.'

That thought seems to call for the rueful half-smile, and he supplies it. 'But what I've come to realize,' he says, 'is that a substantial minority of condemned men honestly believe they're innocent. Not that they had just cause, not that it was the victim's own fault, not that the Devil made them do it. But that they didn't do it at all. The cops must have framed them, the evidence must have been planted, and if only the real killer can turn up then the world will recognize their own abiding innocence.'

'This facility houses three thousand inmates,' Humphries says, 'and I don't know how many committed crimes they can't consciously recall. They were in a blackout, drug- or alcohol-induced. They don't necessarily deny their actions, but they don't remember them. But that's not what you mean.'

'No. There are some instances, especially in sex crimes of the sort Applewhite committed, where the perpetrator's in an altered state during the performance of the act. But that's rarely enough to keep him from being aware of what he did. No, the

31

phenomenon I'm talking about happens after the fact, and it's a case of the wish being father to the thought.'

'Oh?'

'Let me put myself in Applewhite's place for a moment. Suppose I killed three boys over a period of – what was it, two months?'

'I believe so.'

'Abducted them one by one, committed forcible sodomy, tortured them, killed them, concealed the bodies, and covered up evidence of the murders. Either I found a way to make this acceptable to my conscience or I was sufficiently sociopathic as not to be burdened with a conscience in the first place.'

'I grew up certain that everyone had a conscience,' Humphries reflects. 'That's an illusion you lose in a hurry in this line of work.'

'These people are sane. They just lack a piece of standard human equipment. They know right from wrong, but they don't feel the distinction applies to them. It strikes them as somehow beside the point.'

'And they can be quite charming.'

He nods. 'And can act convincingly normal. They know what a conscience is, they understand the concept, so they can behave as though they have one.' The rueful smile. 'Well. I've killed these boys, and it doesn't bother me in the least, but then I'm caught, and placed under arrest, and it turns out there's an abundance of evidence of my culpability. I'm in a jail cell, with the media damning me as the blackest villain of the century, and all I can do is protest my innocence.

'And I do so, with increasing conviction. I have to do more than insist I'm innocent, I have to do so with utter certainty, for how am I to convince anyone if I am not myself convincing? And how better to be convincing than to believe myself in the truth of my arguments?'

'Other words, you wind up believing your own lies.'

'That's what appears to happen. I'm not entirely certain of the mechanics of the process, but that's how it manifests itself.'

'It sounds almost like self-hypnosis.'

'Except that self-hypnosis is generally a conscious process, while what I've described is largely un-conscious. But there are elements of self-hypnosis, certainly, and elements of denial as well. 'I could not have done this, ergo I did not do it.' The mind's reality trumps the reality of the physical world.'

'Fascinating. You make me wish I'd taken more psych courses.'

'I'd say you're getting a crash course on the job.'

'I'm an administrator, Dr Bodinson, and—'

'Arne.'

'Arne. I'm an administrator, the plant manager at a factory. My job is to keep the line running and handle problems as they arise. But you're right, it's a crash course in the intricacies of the human psyche. You know, if Applewhite believes he didn't do it—'

'Which I haven't yet established, but which strikes me as likely.'

'Well, that means there won't be any last-minute confession.'

'How could there be, if in his mind he has nothing to admit to?'

'It ordinarily wouldn't matter,' Humphries says, 'because either way he gets the needle, but I was thinking of the parents of the one boy, the first victim. I don't recall his name, and I should. I've heard it often enough.'

'Jeffrey Willis, wasn't it? The one whose body was never found.'

'Yes, of course. Jeffrey Willis, and his parents are Peg and Baldwin Willis, and they're having a terrible time of it. They can't get closure. That's one good thing about capital punishment, it provides closure for the victim's family in the way a life sentence never does, but for the Willises it'll be only partial closure, because they're deprived of the opportunity to bury their son.'

'And in their minds they can't shake off the slim hope that he's alive.'

'They know he's not,' Humphries says. 'They know he's dead and they know Applewhite killed him. There was a manila envelope in a locked drawer of the man's desk, and in it were three glassine envelopes, each containing a lock of hair. One was the Willis boy's, and the others were from the other two victims.' He shakes his head. 'Of course Applewhite had no explanation. Of course someone must have planted the trophies in his desk. Of course he'd never seen them before.'

'He may believe that.'

'All anyone wants from him now, all he can do in the world on his way out of it, is tell those poor people where their son's body is buried. That might get him a call from the governor, at the very least staying his execution long enough to recover the body. But if he honestly believes he didn't do it—'

'Then he can't admit it. And couldn't locate the body, because he no longer knows where it is.'

'If that's what he believes, I don't suppose there's anything to be done in that regard. But if he's just putting on an act, and if he were somehow convinced that it's in his own best interests to provide us with the where-abouts of the body . . .'

'I'll see what I can do,' he says.

CHAPTER 4

The cell is larger than he'd expected, and more comfortably appointed. There's a built-in concrete platform to support the mattress, a built-in kneehole desk. There's a television set mounted high on the wall, out of reach, with a remote control pointed toward it and bolted to the desktop. A single molded plastic chair – white, stackable if there were another to stack upon it – is the cell's only movable furniture. After a tentative handshake, Applewhite motions him to the chair, takes a seat for himself on the bed.

He is a handsome man, is Preston Applewhite, although the years in confinement have taken a toll. He's five years older than when he was arrested, and they've been hard years, soul-deadening years. They've rounded his broad shoulders, bowed his back. They've put some gray in his dark blond hair, even as they've etched vertical lines at the sides of his full-lipped mouth. Have they washed some of the blue from his eyes? Perhaps, or it could be that it's not the color but the expression in those eyes that has faded. The thousand-yard stare, the unfocused gaze into the middle distance, and on into the abyss.

When he speaks, his voice is flat, uninflected. 'I hope this isn't a ruse, Dr Bodinson. I hope you're not from the media.'

'Certainly not.'

'I've turned down their requests. I don't want to be interviewed, I don't want a chance to tell my story. I don't have a story to tell. My only story is that I'm innocent, that I'm living in a nightmare, and that's not a story anyone wants to hear.'

'I'm not from the media.'

'Or from the boy's parents? They want to know where their son is huried, so they can dig him up and bury him again. For the love of God, don't they think I'd tell them if I knew?'

'They think you're unwilling to own up to knowing.'

'Why? Friday they're going to pump a mix of chemicals into me, and what little life I've got is going to come to an end. That's going to happen no matter what I do. I don't deserve it, I never harmed anyone in my life, but that's beside the point. Twelve men and women looked at the evidence and decided I was guilty, and then they thought it over and decided I deserved to die for it, and I can't really blame them for either of those decisions. I mean, look at the evidence.'

'Yes.'

'Child pornography on my computer hard drive. Little envelopes of hair from the dead boys in my desk drawer. A bloody handkerchief found at the burial site, and the blood's mine. There was even a file on my computer, an elaborate obscene third-person account of one of the murders. It had been erased, but they managed to recover it, and only a monster could have written it. It contained details of the crime that could only have been known to the person who committed it. If I'd been on that jury, I wouldn't have hesitated for a moment. A guilty verdict was the only verdict possible.'

'They didn't spend much time in deliberations.'

'They didn't have to. I read an account, an interview with one of the jurors. They went around the room, and everyone said guilty. Then they discussed the evidence, trying to find arguments refuting some of it, and they voted again, and it was unanimous again. And then they discussed it some more, just to make absolutely certain they were all on the same page, and then they voted formally, and it was twelve for conviction and none for acquittal, and there was really no reason to waste any more time. So they filed back into the courtroom and announced the verdict. Then my lawyer insisted the jury be polled, and one by one they said the same thing, over and over. Guilty, guilty, guilty. What else did he expect them to say?'

'And the penalty phase?'

'My lawyer wanted me to change my story. He'd never believed me, although he wouldn't come right out and say so. Well, why should he have believed me? To take my story at face value would have been evidence of incompetence on his part.'

'He thought you'd have a better chance at escaping a death sentence if you said you'd done it.'

'Which is nonsense,' he says, 'because the sentence would have been the same either way. He wanted me to express remorse. Remorse! What remorse could possibly match the enormity of those crimes? And how could I express remorse for something I hadn't done? I asked him as much and he just looked at me. He wouldn't come right out and tell me I was full of shit, but that's what he was thinking. But he didn't push it, because he knew it wouldn't make any difference. The death sentence didn't take them any more time than the guilty verdict.'

'Did it surprise you?'

'It shocked me. Later, when the judge pronounced sentence, that shocked me, too. Shock's not the same thing as surprise.'

'No.'

'The idea of it. "You're going to die." Well, everybody's going to die. But when someone sits there and tells you, well, it has an impact.'

'I can imagine.'

'Remorse. Could you express remorse by proxy? Because I couldn't be sorry that I'd killed those boys, because I hadn't, but I was damn well sorry that someone had.' He frowns, a vertical line in his forehead forming to match the ones at the sides of his mouth. 'He told me it would be a great help if I could tell them where to find the third body. But how could I do that if I'd never set eyes on the Willis boy and had no idea where he might be? I could tell him, he said, and he could say I let it slip while still maintaining my innocence. I told him I couldn't quite see the logic of that. I'd be sticking to a lie while admitting it was a lie. He hemmed and hawed, and I said it hardly mattered, because I couldn't tell what I didn't know. You know, I didn't care if he believed me, or if anyone else believed me. My wife didn't believe me, she couldn't even look at me. She's divorced me, you know.'

'So I understand.'

'I haven't seen her or my children since I was taken into custody. No, I take that back. I saw her once. She came to the jail and asked me how I could do such a thing. I said I was innocent and she had to believe me. But she didn't, and something died in me, and from that point on it didn't really matter what anyone else believed or didn't believe.'

Fascinating, just fascinating.

'You wrote that you believed me.'

'Yes.'

'I suppose that was just a way to get me to approve the visit. Well, it worked.'

'I'm glad it got me here,' he says, 'but it wasn't a ruse. I know you didn't commit those barbarities.'

'I almost think you're serious.'

'I am.'

'But how can you possibly be? You're a rational man, a scientist.'

'If psychology's a science, and there are those who'd argue that it's not.'

'What else could it be?'

'An art. A black art, some would say. There were

those, you know, who wanted to give Freud the Nobel, not in medicine but in literature. A back-handed compliment, that. I like to think there's a scientific basis to what I do, Preston, but – I'm sorry, is it all right if I call you Preston?'

'I don't mind.'

'And my name is Arne. That's A-R-N-E, the Scandinavian spelling, though it's pronounced like the diminutive for Arnold. My parents were English and Scots-Irish on both sides, I can't think why they thought to give me a Swedish name. But that's off the point, and I'm afraid I've lost track of what I was saying.'

'A scientific basis to what you do.'

'Yes, of course.' He hadn't lost track, but is pleased to note that Applewhite's been paying attention. 'But even pure science has an intuitive element. Most scientific discovery comes out of intuition, out of an inspired leap of faith that owes little to logic or scientific method. I know you're innocent. I know it with a certainty that leaves no room for doubt. I can't explain how I know it, to you or to myself, but I know it.' He treats Applewhite to a gentler version of the rueful smile. 'I'm afraid,' he says, 'that you'll have to take my word for it.'

Applewhite just looks at him, his face soft now, defenseless. And, unhidden and quite unexpected, tears begin to flow down his cheeks.

'I'm sorry. I haven't cried in, hell, I couldn't even guess how long it's been. Ages.'

41

'It's nothing to apologize for. Perhaps I'm the one who should apologize.'

'For what? For being the first person to believe me?' He laughed shortly. 'Except that's not strictly true. I've received letters from half a dozen women over the years. They just know I couldn't have done such things, and their hearts go out to me, and they want me to know how strongly they support me in my hour of need. I'm told everyone on Death Row gets letters like that, and the nastier and more publicized your crimes, the more mail you get.'

'It's a curious phenomenon.'

'Most of them sent their pictures. I didn't keep the photos, or the letters, for that matter, and I didn't even think about answering them, but a couple of them kept writing all the same. They wanted to visit me, and one just wouldn't give up. She wants to marry me. Now that my divorce is final, she explained, we can get married. And it's my constitutional right, according to her. It's a right I'm somehow not tempted to exercise.'

'No, I wouldn't think you would be.'

'And I don't really think for a moment that she or any of the others really believed I was innocent. Because they don't want a romance with some poor bastard who's going to die for no reason whatsoever. They want an affair, or the fantasy of an affair, with a man who's the very personification of evil. Each of them wants to be the one selfless woman able to see the good in this worst of men, and if there's a chance I might wring her neck, well, the danger just adds spice to the mix.'

They talk some more about the vagaries of human behavior. Applewhite is intelligent, as he'd known he would be, with an extensive vocabulary and a logical mind.

'Tell me again why you're here, Arne.'

He thinks for a moment. 'I guess because you meet the criteria for what seems to be my interest these days.'

'And that is?'

'There must be a better phrase, but what comes to mind is "doomed innocence."'

'Doomed innocence. You and I are the only two people on earth who think I'm innocent. The doomed part, that's pretty clear to everyone.'

'I'm interested,' he says, 'in how a person in your position faces the inevitable.'

'Calmly.'

'Yes, I can see that.'

'When I think about it, everybody with a pulse is under a death sentence. Some of us are under more immediate ones. People with terminal illnesses. They're as innocent as I am, but because some cell went haywire and nobody caught it in time, they're going to die ahead of schedule. They can beat themselves up, they can say they should have quit smoking, they shouldn't have put off that annual physical, they should have eaten less and exercised more, but who knows if that would have made any difference? The bottom line is they're going to die, and it's not their fault. And so am I, and it's not my fault.'

43

'And every day...'

'Every day,' he says, 'I get a day closer to the end. I told my lawyer not to bother trying for any more stays. I could drag it out for another year or two, if I pushed, but why? All I've been doing is marking time, and all it would get me is a little more time to mark.'

'So how do you get through the days, Preston?'

'There aren't that many. Friday's the day.'

'Yes.'

'Until then, I get through the hours. Three times a day they bring me something to eat. You'd think I'd have lost my taste for food, but one's appetite doesn't seem to have much to do with one's long-term prospects. They bring the food and I eat it. They bring a newspaper and I read it. They'll bring books if I ask for them. Lately I haven't felt much like reading.'

'And you have the TV.'

'There's a channel that has nothing but reruns of cop shows. *Homicide, Law & Order, NYPD Blue.* For a while I was addicted, I watched them one after another. Then I realized what I was doing.'

'Seeking escape?'

'No, that's what I'd assumed, but that wasn't it. I was looking for an answer, a solution.'

'To your own dilemma.'

'Exactly. Surely one of those programs would hold the key. I'd see something, and there'd be that aha! Moment, that instant of revelation that would enable me to save myself and pinpoint the real killer.' He shakes his head. 'Listen to me, will you? "The real killer." I sound like OJ, for Christ's sake.' He purses his lips, emits a soundless whistle. 'Once I knew why I was watching the shows, I couldn't watch them anymore. Lost my taste for them completely. There's not much I can watch, actually. Football, during the season, but that's over until the fall. I've seen my last football game.'

'Other sports? Baseball? Basketball?'

'I used to play a little basketball.' His eyes narrow for a moment, as if reaching for a memory, but it eludes him and he lets it go. 'I watched the college games. The tournament, the Final Four. When the college season ended I lost interest. I put a pro game on a few days ago but I couldn't keep my mind on it. And I never could work up an interest in baseball.'

'So you don't watch much television.'

'No. It passes the time, which is part of its appeal, but it wastes the time, and I don't have that much time left that I can afford to waste any of it. You asked how I get through the days. There's nothing to it. I just sit here, and one way or another the hours pass. And the next thing you know it's Friday, and that's as far as I have to go.'

'I'd better go,' he says, rising from the white plastic chair. 'I'm taking up all your time, and you already said you don't have that much of it left.'

'I've enjoyed this, Arne.'

'Have you?'

'This is the first time I've been in the company of anybody who thought I was innocent. I can't tell you what a difference that makes.'

'Really?'

'Oh, absolutely. There's been an element of stress in every conversation I've had since they cuffed me and read me my rights, because every single person, even the ones who've tried to help me, have believed me to be this monster. It was always there, you know? And today for the first time it wasn't, and I could have an unguarded conversation and relate to another human being. I haven't talked like this in, well, I couldn't say how long. Since I was arrested, but maybe longer than that. I'm glad you came, and I'm sorry to see you leave.'

He hesitates, then says, tentatively, 'I could come back tomorrow.'

'You could?'

'I don't have anything I have to do for the next several days. I'll come back tomorrow, if you'd like, and as often as you want after that.'

'Well, Jesus,' Applewhite says. 'Yes, I'd like that. Damn right I'd like that. Come anytime. I'm not going anywhere.'

CHAPTER 5

At a meeting over the weekend a woman whom I knew by sight came up to me and said she'd heard I was a private investigator. Was that true?

'Sort of,' I said, and explained that I was semi-retired, and didn't have a license, which meant I lacked any official standing.

'But you could investigate someone,' she said.

'Anyone in particular?'

'I have to think about this,' she said. 'Is there a number where I can reach you?'

I gave her a card, one of the new ones with my cell phone number on it, along with the phone in our apartment. I avoided a cell phone as long as I possibly could, until the realization that I was being ridiculous gradually overcame the stubbornness that seems to be an irreducible part of me. I still forget to carry it half the time, and don't always remember to turn it on when I do, but I'd done both Monday morning, and when it rang I even managed to answer it without disconnecting the caller.

'This is Louise,' she said. 'You gave me your card.

The other night, I asked if you could investigate someone, and—'

'I remember. You had to think about it.'

'I've thought all I need to, and I'd like to talk to you. Could we meet somewhere?'

I was having breakfast with TJ, who'd kept a remarkably straight face while I'd fumbled with the phone. 'I'm at the Morning Star,' I said.

'Are you really? Because I'm at the Flame.'

The Morning Star's on the northwest corner of Ninth and Fifty-seventh; the Flame's at the Fifty-eighth Street end of the same block. They're both New York-style Greek coffee shops, and neither one's a candidate for the next edition of Zagat, but they're not terrible, and God knows they're handy.

She said, 'Will you still be there in fifteen minutes? I want to finish this cup of coffee, and then I want to stand around outside long enough to smoke a cigarette, and then I'll come to the Morning Star, if you'll still be there.'

'They haven't even brought my eggs yet,' I told her. 'Take your time.'

'I feel funny about this,' she said. 'Here I'm having this romance, and it feels as though it might really go somewhere, and a relationship ought to be based on trust, and how trusting am I if I hire a detective to investigate the guy? It's like I'm sabotaging the whole process from the get-go.'

48

Louise was somewhere in her late thirties, medium height and build, with dark brown hair and light brown eyes. She'd had acne in adolescence, and its legacy was a light pitting on her cheeks and pointed chin. She was dressed for the office in a skirt and blouse, and she'd put on some cologne, a floral scent that blended imperfectly with the smell of cigarette smoke.

She'd joined us at our table, a little taken aback to discover that I wasn't alone. I introduced TJ as my assistant, and that mollified her some. He's a black man in his twenties – I don't know his exact age, but then I still don't know his last name, for all that he's a virtual member of the family – and this morning he was dressed for comfort in baggy bleached denim shorts and a black T-shirt with the sleeves and neckband cut off. He didn't look much like my assistant, or anybody else's, except perhaps a dope dealer's. I could tell she'd be more comfortable if it were just the two of us, but I'd only have to fill TJ in afterward, and I figured she could get over it, and she did.

I said, 'Trust is at the basis of most enduring relationships.'

'That's what I keep telling myself, but—'

'It's also a key component of most scams and con games. They couldn't work without it. You might have an easier time trusting this guy if you can establish that there's no abiding reason not to trust him.'

'And that's the other thing I keep telling myself,'

she said. 'It seems tacky, but I can't get past the fact that I don't really know a thing about him. It's not like my parents and his parents are friends, or I met him at a church social.'

'How did you meet?'

'On the Internet.'

'One of the dating services?'

She nodded, and gave its name. 'I don't know how the hell else people are supposed to hook up in this city,' she said. 'I work all day. In fact I'm supposed to be at my desk in twenty minutes, but Tinkerbell's not gonna die if I'm ten minutes late. I spend my days at the office and my nights at AA meetings. My last relationship was with somebody I knew from the program. That gets you past the small talk, but then when things don't work out one of you has to start going to different meetings.' She glanced at my left hand. 'You're married, right? Is she in the program?'

'No.'

'How'd you meet, if you don't mind my asking?'

We met in an after-hours gin joint, at Danny Boy Bell's table. She was a young call girl then, and I was a cop with a wife and two kids. But that was a lot more than she needed to know, and what I said was that Elaine and I had known each other years ago, that we'd met up again after having lost contact, and that this time it had worked out for us.

'That's romantic,' she said.

'I suppose it is.'

'Well, the men in my past, I hope to God they stay there. My boyfriend in high school was cute, but he never got over it when I threw up in the middle of . . . well, never mind. Jesus, I wish you could smoke in here. If you can have a cup of coffee you ought to be able to have a cigarette with it. Our tightass mayor should go fuck himself. Can you believe he wants to ban smoking outside, too? Like it's not bad enough you have to go out in the street for a smoke? I mean, who does he think he is?'

She didn't wait for an answer, which was just as well, as I didn't have one handy. 'I should get to the point, Matt. I met this guy on the Internet, and we had a lot of exchanges, first by e-mail and then with Instant Messaging. You know what that is, right? Sort of an online conversation?'

I nodded. TJ and Elaine IM back and forth regularly, like a couple of kids with two cans and a wire. He lives right across the street from us, in the hotel room I occupied for years, and he comes over a couple of nights a week for dinner, and he and Elaine are both easy enough to reach by phone, but evidently there's something irresistible about Instant Messaging. One of them will notice that the other's online, and the next thing you know they're chatting like magpies.

'It can get very intimate, or at least it seems that way. People let their guard down in e-mails, or forget to put it up in the first place. I mean, it's so easy. You type something out like you're writing in a diary, and before you have time to think about it you hit the Send button, and it's gone. You can't even check the spelling, let alone give some thought to whether you really wanted to tell him you had an abortion your senior year in high school. So it seems intimate, because you're finding out a lot about the person, but it's only what he chooses to tell you, and you're just reading it on the screen. It's just words, there's no tone of voice to go with it, no facial expressions, no body language. You fill in the rest in your mind, and you make it what you want it to be. But it may not be an accurate reflection of the real person. Sooner or later you trade jpegs, that's online photographs—'

'I know.'

'—so you know what he looks like, but that's just the visual equivalent of words on the screen. You still don't know him.'

'But you've met this man.'

'Oh, of course. I wouldn't be wasting your time if this was still just an online flirtation. I met him about a month ago and I've seen him seven or eight times since then. I didn't see him this weekend because he was out of town.'

'I gather the two of you hit it off.'

'We liked each other. The attraction was there. He's nice-looking but not handsome. Handsome puts me off. A therapist once told me it's a self-esteem issue, that I don't think I deserve a handsome boyfriend, but I don't think that's it. I just don't trust men who are too good-looking. They always turn out to be narcissists.'

'Been a real problem for me,' TJ said.

She grinned. 'But you're dealing with it.'

'Best I can.'

'I like the guy,' she said. 'He didn't rush me into bed, but we both knew that's where we were going, and it didn't take us that long to get there. And it was nice. And he likes me, and I'd love to jump up and down and tell the world I'm in love, but something holds me back.'

'What don't you know about him?'

'I don't know where to start. Well, what *do* I know about him? He's forty-one, he's divorced, he lives alone in a fifth-floor walk-up in Kips Bay. He's self-employed, he creates direct-mail advertising packages for corporate clients. Sometimes he has to work long hours and sometimes he has dry spells with no work at all. Feast or famine, he says.'

'Does he have an office?'

'A home office. That's one reason we always go to my place. His is a mess, he says, with a sofa that he sleeps on. It's not even a convertible because there's no room to open it up, with his desk and filing cabinets taking up so much floor space. There's a fax, there's a copying machine, there's his computer and printer and I don't know what else.'

'So you've never been there.'

'No. I said I'd like to see it and he just said it

was a mess, and a mess you have to climb four flights of stairs to get to. And it's plausible enough, it could certainly be true.'

'Or he could be married.'

'Or he could be married and live anywhere at all. I thought I could go to his building and at least see if his name's on the mailbox, but I don't even know the address. I have a phone number for him, but it's his cell. He could be married, he could be an ex-con, he could be a fucking axe murderer for all I know. I don't honestly think he's any of those things, but the problem is I don't know for sure, and I can't let go emotionally if I've got these worries in the back of my mind.'

'And not that far back, from the sound of it.'

'No, you're right. It's always there, and it gets in the way.' She frowned. 'I get this spam, everybody does, links to these websites where they claim you can find out the truth about anybody, I've gone to the sites, and I've been tempted, but that's as far as I've gone. I don't know how reliable those things are, anyway.'

'They probably vary,' I said. 'What they do is access various publicly available data bases.'

'You can find out anything on the Internet,' TJ put in, 'but only part of it is true.'

'His name's David Thompson,' she said. 'Or at least I think his name's David Thompson. I did a Yahoo People search, and it'd be a lot easier if his name was Hiram Weatherwax. You wouldn't believe how many David Thompsons there are.'

'Common names make it tough. You must know his e-mail address.'

'DThomps5465 at hotmail.com. Anybody can set up a free account at Hotmail, all you have to do is go to their site and register. I have a Yahoo account, FareLady315. That's F-A-R-E, as in subway fare, because I ride it to and from work every day.' She glanced at her watch. 'I'm all right. I live on Eighty-seventh Street, I rode down to Columbus Circle. Then I had a bagel and coffee, and then I came here, and my office is a five-minute walk from here. I'll smoke a cigarette on the way over there, because it goes without saying we're not allowed to smoke in the fucking office. I could keep a bottle in my desk and drink, that'd be fine, but God forbid I should smoke a cigarette. Did I mention that he smokes? David?'

'No.'

'I specified that in my ad. Not just that I smoked, but that I was looking to meet a smoker. People say they're tolerant, but then they wind up waving their hand in the air, or run around opening windows. I don't need that. I don't drink a day at a time, and I don't take drugs, I won't even take fucking Midol for cramps, so I figure I can smoke all I want, and the hell with the mayor.' She let out a sudden yelp of laughter. 'Jesus, listen to me, will you? "Hey, Louise, why don't you tell us how you really feel?" The thing is, I know one of these days I'm going to quit. I don't even like to talk about it, but one of these days when I'm good and ready it's gonna happen. And, just my luck, it'll most likely happen in the middle of a terrific relationship with a guy who smokes like a chimney, and the last thing *he'll* want to do is quit, and his cigarettes'll wind up driving *me* crazy.'

It's a hard old world. 'Does David know you're in the program?'

'Dave, he likes to be called. And yes, that was one of the first things I told him, when we were just DThomps and FareLady. He'd said something about it'd be nice to share a bottle of wine, and I wanted to let him know that wasn't gonna happen. He's a light social drinker. Or at least he is when he's around me, but that's another thing I don't know about him, because he could be controlling it when we're together and knocking back the silver bullets when we're not.'

She gave me a picture, one he'd sent her that she'd downloaded and printed. It was, she assured me, a pretty good likeness. It showed the head and shoulders of a man with the forced expression most people have when trying to smile for the camera. He looked pleasant enough, with a square jaw, a neatly trimmed mustache, and a full head of dark hair. He wasn't movie-star handsome, certainly, but he looked okay to me.

For a moment I thought she was going to ask for the photo back, but she made her decision and sat back. 'I hate doing this,' she said, 'but I'd hate myself more if I didn't. I mean, you read things.'

'Yes.'

'And I'm no heiress, but I have some investments and a few dollars in the bank. I own my apartment. I've got something to lose, you know?'

After she left I called the waiter over and got the check. She'd tried to leave a buck for her cup of coffee, but I figured I could afford to treat her. She'd given me five hundred dollars as a retainer, and all she got in return was a receipt, along with an explanation of the ground rules: I wouldn't be giving her elaborate written reports, but would let her know what I found out, and would make my inquiries in a manner designed to keep him from getting wind of their source. I'd cover my own expenses, which didn't figure to amount to much anyway, and if I wound up putting in more time than the five hundred bucks covered, I'd let her know, and she could decide whether or not to pay it. That's a little unstructured for some people, but she didn't have a problem with it. Or maybe she was just in a hurry to get outside where she could smoke.

'Glad I never got the habit,' TJ said. 'You a smoker, back in the day?'

'Once or twice a year,' I said, 'I would drink myself into the kind of mood that led me to buy a pack of cigarettes and smoke six or eight of them one right after the other. Then I'd throw the rest of the pack away, and I wouldn't want another for months.'

'Weird.'

'I guess.'

He laid a finger on the photo of the putative David Thompson. 'You want me to see what shows up online?'

'I was hoping you would.'

'You know,' he said, 'ain't nothing I can do that you couldn't do for yourself. Just get on Elaine's Mac and let yourself go. You don't even have to log on, 'cause now that she's got the DSL line you're logged on all the time. You just start with Google and poke around some and see where it takes you.'

'I'm always afraid I'll break something.'

'Won't even break a sweat, Chet. But it's cool, I'll take a shot at it. What say we go over what we know about the dude.'

That didn't take long because we didn't know much. I suggested some lines of inquiry that might lead somewhere, and we both made some notes, and he pushed back his chair and stood up. 'I'd best get back to my room,' he said. 'Market opened ten minutes ago.'

'You still doing okay?'

'Some days be better than others. Some days the whole market goes up, and you look like a genius whatever you do. 'Less you went short, in which case you look like a fool.'

I have two grown sons, Michael and Andrew. Michael and June live in Santa Cruz, California, and Andy was in Wyoming the last time I heard from him. I'm not sure of the city; he'd recently moved, but whether it was from Cheyenne to Laramie or the other way around I can't be sure, and I don't suppose it's too important, because that was around Christmas and he's probably moved again since then. I haven't seen him in four or five years, when he flew east for his mother's funeral. Michael's been back once since then, on a quick business trip the summer before last, and then last year Elaine and I flew out there shortly after their second daughter was born.

Antonia, they called her. 'We wanted to name her for Mom,' Michael told me, 'but neither of us really liked the name Anita, and Antonia has all the same letters, plus an *O* and an extra *N*. June says that means *Anita* is living *on*.'

'Your mother would like that,' I said, wondering if it was true. I'd left the woman thirty years ago, and even then I had never been too clear on what she would or wouldn't like.

'We were sort of hoping for a boy. To keep the name going, you know? But to tell you the truth we were both a little relieved when the sonogram indicated we were going to have a girl. And Melanie, well, she was very clear on the subject. She wanted a baby sister, period, end of story. A brother would not be an acceptable substitute.'

'They might have another, you know,' Elaine said on the flight home. 'To continue the Scudder name.'

'It's not that uncommon a name,' I told her. 'Last time I looked, there were hundreds scattered all over the country. Maybe thousands, for all I know, plus a whole family of mutual funds.'

'You don't mind not having a grandson?'

'Not at all, and I've got to say I think Antonia goes a lot better with Scudder than Antonio would.'

'Well,' she said, 'I've got to agree with you there.'

The point is that there's a distance between me and my sons, and geography is only a part of it. I didn't really get to watch them become the men they are today, and I can only view their continuing evolution as from across a great divide. All of which makes TJ's company especially gratifying. For all that I don't know about him – like his last name, and what, if anything, the T and the J stand for – I get to see him up close and watch at point-blank range his continuing self-realization.

A few years ago he started hanging out on the Columbia campus, apparently having mastered the art of flimflamming the campus security forces. He audited classes over a whole range of subjects, did almost all of the assigned reading, and probably got more from the enterprise than ninety percent of the kids who were taking the same courses for credit. Now and then he wrote a paper, just for the hell of it, and, when the instructor struck him as sufficiently sympathetic, he'd hand it in. One professor in the history department was desperate to have him enroll and was sure he could put together an aid package that would give TJ an Ivy League education at virtually no cost. TJ pointed out that he was already getting just that, plus he got to pick his courses. When Elaine suggested that a Columbia diploma could open a lot of doors, he countered that they led to rooms he didn't want to go into.

'Besides,' he'd say, popping his eyes, 'I's a detective, I's already gots a career.'

More recently he'd sampled some classes at the business school. He dressed the part, and left the hip-hop patter behind when he got off the train at 116th Street, but I suspect at least some of the professors knew he didn't belong there. If so, they would have to realize that they were dealing with someone who actually wanted to attend their lectures without the goal of a Columbia MBA. Why on earth would they want to discourage him?

I don't think their program focuses much on the stock market, but he got interested, and found books and magazines to read, and by the time classes broke for the summer he was set up in his room at the Northwestern as a day trader, with CNBC running all day on the little television set and his computer – a high-powered successor to the one we'd given him for Christmas some years ago – all set up for online trading. He had an Ameritrade account, though I can't imagine he had much capital to fund it with, but it was enough to get him started, and he evidently managed to keep his head above water.

'He'll probably go broke,' Elaine said, 'but so what if he does? If you're gonna go broke, that's the right age to be when it happens. And who knows? He could turn out to be a genius at it.'

He didn't talk much about his wins or losses, so it was hard to tell how he was doing. He wasn't driving a BMW or wearing bespoke suits, and neither was he missing any meals. I figured he'd do it until he didn't want to do it anymore, and that he'd get something out of it, one way or the other. He always does.

CHAPTER 6

There's a Red Roof Inn just outside of Jarratt, at the exit off I-95, but on reflection he decides that's closer than he wants to be. Twenty miles to the south is the North Carolina state line, and he drives across it and a few miles beyond, to the exit for the town of Roanoke Rapids, where he has several motels to choose among. He picks a Days Inn, gets a room. He registers as Arne Bodinson and gives the clerk a Visa card in that name, telling her he'll be checking out Friday morning.

His room's in the rear and on the top floor, as he'd requested. He parks in back and carries his brief-case and his blue canvas duffel bag up to his room. He unpacks, puts his clothes away, sets his laptop on the desk and the bottle of Scotch on the bedside table. Packing for this trip, he remembered that the South is a curious region, with unfathomable liquor laws that change every time you cross a county line. In some places you can only get beer, in others you can't get anything at all, and liquor stores, if they even exist, are apt to keep strange and limited hours. In order to drink at a bar, you might be required to purchase a nominal membership in what calls itself a private club. For a one-time charge of five or ten dollars, you are entitled to all the rights and privileges of membership, which is to say you can buy drinks there for as long as your money lasts.

None of it makes any sense to him, but that's not the point. It's the way things work, and what he has to do – what he always has to do – is determine how things work and act accordingly.

He takes the plastic bucket the hotel provided and goes down the hall for ice cubes, then frowns at the disposable plastic tumbler. You'd think they could give you a proper glass for what they charged, but they hadn't, so you do what you always do. You deal with what life deals you.

He makes himself a drink, takes a sip. It would taste better out of a glass container, but there's no point in dwelling on that fact. It will only get in the way of his enjoyment of the Scotch, and it is in fact very good Scotch indeed, full-bodied and smoky and bracing. He's had an arduous day, and it's a long hard road that has no drink at the end of it.

He takes his time with the drink, savoring it, sitting in a chair with the plastic tumbler in his hand. He closes his eyes and regulates his breathing, matching the exhale to the inhale, tuning in to the rhythms of his body. He lets himself feel the effects of the drink, of the alcohol in his bloodstream, and he chooses to imagine it as the equivalent for the human body and spirit of one of those space-age polymers you add to the engine of an old car, so that it can fill all the scrapes and pits in tired old metal, coating the inner surfaces, eliminating friction, increasing efficiency, smoothing out and cushioning the ride.

When he opens his eyes he reaches for his cell phone and makes a call. His party answers on the third ring. He says, 'Hey, Bill. It's me. Oh, nothing much, just thought I'd give a ring and check in with you. I got a deskful of work in front of me and I don't know when I'm gonna get out of here. Well, I thought I'd see you tonight but it doesn't look like it. No, I'm fine, just busy as a one-armed paper-hanger with the hives. Well, you too, my friend. Take care.'

He rings off, sits down at the desk, hooks up his laptop and gets online to check his e-mail. When he's done, he makes another phone call, then fixes himself another drink.

It's midmorning when he gets back to Greensville. Applewhite seems surprised to see him, but genuinely pleased. They shake hands, and assume their places, Applewhite on the bed, he in the white plastic chair. The conversation, tentative at first, starts with the weather and moves to the previous Super Bowl, then subsides into an awkward stillness.

Applewhite says, 'I didn't think I'd see you today.'
'I said I'd come.'
'I know. And I believed you meant it, but I thought you'd change your mind after you left. You'd want to get home to your wife and kids.'
'No wife. No kids either, as far as I know.'
'As far as you know.'

65

'Well, who's to say what fruit might have been borne of a youthful indiscretion? But there weren't so many of those, and I think I'd have been informed if I'd been the cause of any abdominal swellings. In any event, nothing to draw me home.'

'Where's home, Arne? I don't think you told me.'

'New Haven. I did my doctoral work at Yale and never managed to get away from the place.'

Which leads them to college reminiscences, always a useful topic for men who have nothing of substance to say to one another. It serves now as it served yesterday, with the warden. He talks about Charlottesville – one might as well be consistent. Applewhite is a graduate of Vanderbilt University, in Nashville, and that leads them into a discussion of country music. It's not what it used to be, they agree. It's too commercial, too polished, too Top Forty.

There's something that goes unmentioned, and it's a matter of time before someone brings it up, and a question as to who it will be. He comes close to raising the subject himself, but waits, and finally it is Applewhite who sighs and announces, 'Today's Tuesday.'

'Yes.'

'Tomorrow and tomorrow,' he intones, 'and tomorrow. Macbeth's soliloquy. 'Tomorrow and tomorrow and tomorrow / creeps in this petty pace from day to day / to the last syllable of recorded time.' Except that the petty pace runs out on the third tomorrow.'

'Do you want to talk about death, Preston?'

'What's there to talk about?' He considers his own question, shakes his head. 'I think about it all the time. I could probably find things to say about it.'

'Oh?'

'There are days when I almost look forward to it. To get it over with, you know? To get on to the next thing. Except, of course, that in this case there's not going to be a next thing.'

'Are you sure of that?'

The man's eyes narrow, and his expression turns guarded. 'Arne,' he says, 'I appreciate the friendship you've offered, but there's something I have to know. You're not here to save my fucking soul, are you?'

'I'm afraid salvation's a little out of my line.'

'Because if you're here selling fear of hell or hope of heaven, I'm not in the market. There've been a couple of clergymen who've tried to get in to see me. Fortunately the state gives a man a certain amount of control over things to compensate for the fact that they're planning to take his life. I don't have to see anyone I don't want to see, and I've been able to keep the gentlemen of the cloth out of this cell.'

'I swear I'm not a priest, minister, or rabbi,' he says, smiling gently. 'I'm not even a religious member of the laity. I might be concerned with saving your soul if I were more nearly convinced that you have one, and that souls can be saved, or need saving.'

'What do you believe happens when you die?'

'You first.'

His words brook no argument, and Applewhite

seems indisposed to offer one. 'I think it ends,' he says. 'I think it's just over, like a movie after the last reel runs out.'

'No final credits?'

'Nothing at all. I think the rest of the world goes on, the same as it does when anybody else dies. Subjectively, I think it's a resumption of the same nonexistence one had before birth. Or before conception, if you prefer. It's hard at first to accept the notion that you're not going to exist anymore, but it gets a little easier when you think of all the centuries, all the millennia, when you hadn't yet been born and the world got along just fine without you.'

'One hears of near-death experiences . . .'

'The tunnel, the white light? Some sort of hallucination, very likely with a physiological basis to it, and one that medical science will no doubt be able to explain to us at some future date. I won't get to hear the explanation, but I guess I can live without it. Or die without it, come to think of it.'

'Gallows humor.'

'There's a phrase due for an update. Hard to find a proper gallows in our enlightened age. Well, better the needle than the rope. But now it's your turn. What do you think happens when we die?'

He doesn't hesitate. 'I think we go out like a light, Preston. I think it's like going to sleep, but with no dreams and no awakening. And why should that be so hard to believe? Do we think cattle go from the abattoir straight to cow heaven? What's so special about our consciousness that it should be permitted to survive?' The rueful half-smile. 'Although I expect I'll be drawn down the tunnel to the white light. But when I pop through at the end of the tunnel I'll cease to be. I'll become part of that light, perhaps, or I won't, and what possible difference will it make either way?'

'I'd like to come again tomorrow, Preston.'

'I'll be grateful if you do. Do you think they'll let you?'

'I don't anticipate any problem. The warden thinks I might accomplish something.'

'Help me resign myself to my fate?'

He shakes his head. 'It's his hope that you'll tell me where the Willis boy's body is buried.'

'But —'

'But if I truly believe in your innocence, how can I possibly attempt that? Is that what you were going to say?'

A nod.

'I'm afraid I may have dissimulated some with Warden Humphries. I may have led him to think that I believe you believe in your innocence.'

Briefly, he sketches what he'd postulated for the warden, explained how the wish could be father to the thought, how a man, in the course of denying his crimes, could genuinely convince himself that he had not in fact committed them.

'Is that what you think?'

'Do I think it ever happens that way? I know for a fact that it does. Do I think that's what's operating in your case? Absolutely not.'

69

Applewhite ponders this. 'But how could you be sure?' he wonders. 'Even if you've got some kind of built-in lie detector, all that would tell you is that I'm speaking what I believe to be the truth. But if I've sold myself a bill of goods—'

'You haven't.'

'You sound so certain.'

'I've never been more certain of anything.'

On the way out, he gets the guard to take him to the warden's office. 'I think I'm making progress,' he tells Humphries. 'I think it's just a matter of time.'

It's raining when he leaves the prison, a light rain that's not much more than a mist. He has difficulty finding the right setting for the windshield wiper, and it makes driving less of a pleasure and more of a chore than it has been.

It's mid-afternoon when he gets to the Days Inn, and the parking lot is virtually empty. He parks in back and goes to his room. It's a little early for a drink, he decides, but not too early for a phone call.

It turns out there's a message on his voice mail. He listens to it, deletes it. He makes three calls, all to numbers on his speed dial. The third is to a woman, and now his voice is different, the tone deeper, the phrasing more deliberate.

'I've been thinking of you,' he says. 'More than I should, actually. I have challenging work to do, and I should be giving it a hundred percent of my attention, but instead I'll find myself thinking of you. God,

70

I wish I knew. Four or five days, I would think. I wish I could tell you where I am. It's a place where they have a different attitude toward privacy. I wouldn't be surprised if this phone is tapped. My cell? I left it home, it wouldn't work here. If you left me a message, it'll be waiting for me when I get home. So there are things I'd say, but I'd better not. Yes, as soon as I know. And I miss you, too. More than I can say.'

He rings off, wondering if he's made a mistake by denying that he's calling from his cell phone. It's set up to block Caller ID, so anyone with that feature should get a NUMBER UNAVAILABLE OR CALLER OUT OF AREA message, but glitches happen. Does she have Caller ID? He's never thought to check, and that, he decides, is a sin of omission. Not necessarily a grievous sin, it shouldn't matter, but he'd rather leave as little as possible to chance.

He's checking his e-mail when it strikes him that he hasn't eaten in over twenty-four hours. He's not hungry, he never gets hungry, but his body ought to have regular feedings.

Emporia's not a large town, the population's around five thousand, but it's the county seat of Greensville County, and it's got an Outback Steakhouse. He's noted the sign several times now, near the Interstate exit for U.S. 58. He drives ten miles into Virginia, finds his way to the place, and orders a rare rib eye steak with fries and salad, and a big glass of unsweetened iced tea. Everything's good, and the steak they bring him is actually rare, just as he ordered it, a welcome surprise in a part of the country where everything's overcooked, and almost everything's fried.

Driving back to his motel, he wonders what Preston Applewhite will want for his last meal.

Wednesday morning. It's getting on for noon, and Applewhite has clearly been anxiously awaiting his arrival. They shake hands, and he lets his left hand cup Applewhite's shoulder.

He's no sooner seated in the white chair than Applewhite says, 'I've been thinking about what you said yesterday.'

'I said a number of things,' he says, 'and I rather doubt any of them is worth thinking about.'

'About the theory you proposed to Humphries. That a man can be guilty but truly believe himself innocent.'

'Oh, that.'

'The one thing I've been sure of, from the first moment on, is that they were all making a horrible mistake. I knew I didn't kill those boys.'

'Of course you didn't.'

'But if what you say is true—'

'For some people. Sociopaths, men with something missing inside them. You're not like that.'

'How do you know?'

'I know.'

'Well, how do I know? Believe me, I'd like to take your word for it, but failing that, how can I be sure? You can see where logic leads. It's a conundrum. If

I'm innocent, I'd know I was innocent. But if I was guilty, and had managed to convince myself I was innocent, I'd also know I was innocent.'

'Look at yourself, Preston.'

'At myself?'

'At the sort of man you are, the sort of man you always have been. Have you ever committed a violent act?'

'If I killed those boys —'

'Before. Did you abuse your wife?'

'I shoved her away from me once. It was when we were first married, we'd argued and I was trying to leave the house. I wanted to go for a walk and clear my head, and she wouldn't let go of me, you'd have thought I was on my way to Brazil, and I pushed her to make her let go. And she fell down.'

'And?'

'And I helped her up, and we had a cup of coffee, and, well, it worked out.'

'That's the extent of your history of spousal abuse? How about your children? Did you beat them?'

'Never. We didn't believe in it, either of us. And I never felt the kind of anger toward them that you'd want to express physically.'

'Let's look at your childhood, shall we? Ever torture animals?'

'God, no. Why would anyone —'

'Ever set fires? I don't mean Boy Scout campfires. I mean anything ranging from mischief to pyromania.'

'No.'

'You wet the bed as a kid?'

'Maybe, when my parents were toilet training me. I don't honestly remember, I was, I don't know, two or three years old—'

'How about when you were ten or eleven?'

'No, but what does that have to do with anything?'

'The standard profile of the serial killer or lust murderer. Bedwetting, fire-setting, and animal abuse. You're batting oh-for-three. How about your sexual orientation? Ever have sex with young boys?'

'No.'

'Ever want to?'

'The same answer. No.'

'Young girls?'

'No.'

'Really? When you approached middle age, didn't teenagers start looking good to you?'

Applewhite thinks it over. 'I won't say I never noticed them,' he said, 'but I was never interested. All my life, the girls and women I've been attracted to have been around my own age.'

'And the males?'

'I've never had relations with a man.'

'Or a boy?'

'Or a boy.'

'Ever wanted to?'

'No.'

'Ever found a male attractive, even without having any desire to act on it?'

'Not really.'

'"Not really"? What does that mean?'

'I've never been attracted to a man myself, but

I might notice that a man is or is not generally attractive.'

'You sound awfully normal, Preston.'

'I always thought I was, but—'

'How about sexual fantasies? And don't tell me you never had any. That's too normal to be normal.'

'Some.'

Ah, he'd touched a nerve. 'If you'd rather not go there, Preston—'

'We were married a long time,' he says. 'I was faithful. Sometimes, though, when we made love—'

'You entertained fantasies.'

'Yes.'

'That's hardly unusual. Other women?'

'Yes. Women I knew, women I just . . . imagined.'

'Did you ever discuss your fantasies with your wife?'

'Of course not. I couldn't do that.'

'Were there men in the fantasies?'

'No. Well, sometimes there were men present. Sometimes the fantasy was a party, all our friends, and people would take off their clothes, and it would be sort of a free-for-all.'

'Would you have liked to transform that fantasy into reality?'

'If you knew the people,' he says, 'you'd know how inconceivable that is. It was hard enough to make them act like that in my own mind.'

'And you never had sex with another man in these fantasies?'

He shakes his head. 'There was nothing like that.

The closest was sharing a woman with another man.'

'And you never did that outside of the world of your imagination?'

'No, of course not.'

'Never suggested it to your wife?'

'Jesus, no. I wouldn't have wanted to do it, but in fantasy it was exciting.'

'Any children in those fantasies?'

'None.'

'Neither girls nor boys?'

'No.'

'Any violence? Any rape, any torture?'

'No.'

'Any forcing a woman to do something she didn't want to do?'

'Never. They didn't have to be forced. They all wanted to do everything. That's one way you could tell it was a fantasy.'

They join in laughter, perhaps more than the line calls for.

He says, 'Preston? Have you been listening to yourself? It's inconceivable that you could have done what they said you did.'

'I'd always known as much, but – well, I'm relieved, Arne. You had me worried there, or perhaps I should say that I had myself worried.' He manages a smile. 'Of course the bad news,' he says, 'is that the day after tomorrow they're still going to give me the needle.'

❋   ❋   ❋

76

'It'll be around noon,' Applewhite says. 'I always assumed midnight. I mean all my life, when I thought of executions, which wasn't something I thought about often, I must say, I thought they happened in the middle of the night. Somebody throws a switch and lights go dim all over the state. I must have seen a movie at an impressionable age. And I seem to remember newsreel footage outside a penitentiary, with one crowd there to protest the death penalty and another bunch having tailgate parties to celebrate that some poor bastard's getting the shock of his life. You can't have parties like that in the middle of the day. You need a dark sky so everyone can get a good view of the fireworks.'

The words are bitter, the tone lacking in affect. Interesting.

'The judge who sentenced me never said anything about the time, just the date. The particulars are up to the warden, and I guess Humphries doesn't want to keep anybody up late.'

'Have they told you what to expect?'

'More than once. They don't want any surprises. They'll come here sometime between eleven and eleven-thirty to collect me. They'll walk me to the chamber and strap me to the gurney. There'll be a physician in attendance, among others, and there'll be some spectators on the other side of a glass wall. I'm not sure what the purpose of the glass wall is. Not soundproofing, because there's going to be a microphone, so they can hear my last words. I get

77

to make a speech. I don't know what the hell I'm supposed to say.'

'Whatever you want.'

'Maybe I'll stand mute. 'Mr Chairman, Alabama passes.' On the other hand, why miss a chance to deliver a message? I could come out for national health insurance. Or against capital punishment, except that I'm not so sure I'm against it.'

'Oh?'

'I never was, before all this happened. And if I did what they say I did, then I ought to pay with my life. And if I didn't, and there was no death penalty, well, I could spend the rest of my life in a cell that's noisier and a lot less comfortable than this one, roundly despised by people I wouldn't want to associate with in the first place. I'd probably be killed in prison, like Jeffrey Dahmer.'

'The people behind the glass wall,' he prompts.

'Some reporters, I suppose. And relatives of the victims, looking to see justice done, looking for closure. I remember what some of them said during the penalty phase of the trial, and my immediate response was to hate them, but hell, how can I blame them for hating me? They don't know I didn't do it.'

'No.'

'If they get some relief from my death, some of that blessed commodity they call closure, well, then I could say my death won't be entirely in vain. Except it will.'

'Any other witnesses?'

Applewhite shakes his head. 'Not that I know of. They told me I could invite somebody. Isn't that rich? I tried to think who would possibly welcome an invitation like that, and if there is such a person, how could I stand to be in the same room with him? My parents are long gone – and thank God for that, incidentally – and even if my wife had stuck by me, even if I was getting regular visits with my kids, would I want their last sight of me to be with a needle in my arm?'

'Still, it strikes me as an awful time to be alone.'

'My lawyer offered to come. I guess that comes under the heading of professional noblesse oblige, something you have to do at the end of one of your less successful cases. I told him I didn't want him there and he had to work hard not to look relieved.'

Come on, he urges silently. What are you waiting for?

'Arne? Do you think—'

'Of course,' he says. 'I'm honored to be chosen.'

He's up late Wednesday night watching pay-per-view porn on the motel set. Even in the Bible Belt, money calls the tune. A man's home is his castle, even if it's a cubicle rented for the night, and within its confines you can do as you please, as long as you're willing to pay $6.95 for each XXX-rated feature.

The films don't arouse him. Pornography almost never does. But nevertheless it diverts him. Not the plots, such as they are. To those he pays no attention.

79

The dialogue is a nuisance, and he'd mute the sound if it didn't mean losing other sounds as well – the background music, the sound effects of a zipper being lowered, a vibrator humming, a slap.

He watches it all, takes it all in, and lets his mind wander at will. There's a glass of Scotch on the table beside him, and he takes a sip from time to time. There's still a little left in the glass, diluted by the now-melted ice cubes, when the last film ends. He pours it down the sink and goes to bed.

Thursday he spends several hours in Applewhite's cell. Their ritual handshake has by now become an embrace. Applewhite, in a reminiscent mood, talks at length about his childhood. It's interesting enough, for all that it's predictably ordinary.

There are interruptions. A doctor is admitted to the cell, carrying an ordinary bathroom scale, on which he duly weighs Applewhite, the weight jotted down in his notebook.

'So that he can calibrate the right dose,' Applewhite says after the man has left. 'Though wouldn't you think they'd just err on the side of caution and give everybody three or four times the lethal dose? What are they trying to do, save a few dollars on chemicals?'

'They want to maintain the illusion of scientific method.'

'That must be it. Or else they're making sure they get a gurney stout enough so it won't buckle under me. You know, they'd save themselves a lot of trouble and expense if they made it possible for a man to kill himself. You could braid a rope out of strips of bed linen, but what would you hang it from?'

'Would you kill yourself if you could?'

'I think about it. I read a book years ago, a thriller, and in it a man, I think he was Chinese, killed himself by swallowing his tongue. Do you suppose it's possible?'

'I have no idea.'

'Neither have I. I was going to try it but . . .'

'But what, Preston?'

'I didn't have the nerve. I was afraid it might work.'

'I can have whatever I want for dinner tonight. Within reason, they said. You know, I've had no trouble eating whatever's on the tray. But now that they're giving me a choice I don't know what to ask for.'

'Whatever you want.'

'The guard slipped me a wink, told me he could probably bring me a drink if I wanted. I haven't had a drink since they arrested me. I don't think I want one now. You know what I think I'll have?'

'What?'

'Ice cream. Not for dessert. A whole meal of ice cream.'

'With sauce and toppings?'

'No, just plain vanilla ice cream, but a lot of it. Cool, you know? And sweet, but not too sweet. Vanilla ice cream, that's what I'll have.'

'Do you ever think about the real killer?'

'I used to. That was the only way I could be

exonerated, if they were to find him. But they weren't looking for him, and why should they? All the evidence pointed to me.'

'It must have been maddening.'

'It was exactly that. It was driving me mad. Because it wasn't just co-incidence. Someone had to have gone to great length to plant evidence implicating me. I couldn't think of anyone who would have had reason to hate me that way. I didn't have many close friends, but I didn't have any enemies, either. None that I knew of.'

'He not only framed you, but he killed three innocent boys in a horrible fashion.'

'That's it – it's not as though he embezzled money from a company and cooked the books to implicate a co-worker. You could understand something like that, there's a rational underpinning to it. But this guy would have had to be a sociopath or a psychopath, whatever the right term is, and he'd also have to have been fixated on me, on blaming me for it. I must sound paranoid, talking about this faceless enemy, but somebody must have done all of this, and that would make him an enemy, and I can't put a face on him.'

'He won't be able to stop.'

'How's that?'

'He must have taken pleasure in the killing,' he explains. 'Destroying you was part of his plan, obviously, but he killed those boys the way he did because he's a sick bastard. He'll do it again, one way or another, and sooner or later he'll get caught. He might wind up confessing to all his crimes, that type often turns boastful once he's caught. So the day may come when you're exonerated after all.'

'It'll be too late to do me any good.'

'I'm afraid that's true.'

'But maybe the Willises will find out where their kid's buried. I suppose that's something.'

And, 'Arne? Is there something on your mind?'

'There is, actually.'

'Oh?'

'There's something I haven't told you, and I honestly don't know whether or not to mention it. Hell. Now I more or less have to, don't I?'

'I don't understand.'

'No, how could you? Here's the thing, Preston. There's a piece of information I have, and it might upset you to know it, but you might be more upset later if you don't know it.'

'After the tunnel and the white light, there's another cell just like this one.'

'God, what a thought. Actually, that helps me make the decision. Your strength, your tough-mindedness.'

'Whatever it is, Arne, let's hear it.'

'It has to do with the procedure tomorrow. The lethal injection. It's a three-part procedure, as you know. Three drugs are administered intravenously. The first is thiopental sodium, more commonly known as sodium pentothal, and popularly if in-accurately thought of as truth serum. It's classed as a hypnotic, it calms and sedates you and keeps you from feeling anything. The second, Pavulon, is derived from curare, which South American Indians use to tip their arrows. It's a paralytic, it paralyzes the lungs and brings your breathing to a halt. Finally, a massive dose of potassium chloride stops the heart.'

'And you die.'

'Yes, but there's a strong argument to the effect that the procedure is not painless as advertised, that it's actually hideously painful. Onlookers get no indication of this, as the subject's facial expression never changes, but that's because it can't, the muscles are paralyzed by the Pavulon. The subject actually feels excruciating pain, and it goes on almost to the moment of death.'

'Jesus.'

'Now I don't see how they can possibly know this,' he says. 'No one's ever returned to furnish a firsthand report. So what I'm saying, I guess, is that you should be aware of the possibility of pain. And I've told you because it seems to me it would be worse coming as a complete surprise, but maybe I've made a mistake. Maybe I've just given you something unnecessary to worry about during your final hours.'

'Except I won't,' Applewhite says. 'Pain almost seems beside the point. Once you get used to the idea of dying, what difference does it make if it hurts a little? Or even more than a little? It won't last long, no matter what it feels like.'

'That's a wonderful attitude, Preston.'

'It's not going to spoil my ice cream, Arne. I'll tell you that much.'

※　　※　　※

84

Driving south on I-95, he slows down when he sees the sign for the Outback Steakhouse, then decides to keep going. There's a Circle K near his Days Inn, and he can stop there for a pint of vanilla ice cream and bring it back to his room.

CHAPTER 7

The first thing TJ tried was the phone number. It was his cell phone, Louise had told us, and the prefix was 917, which is one of two area codes set aside for mobile phones in the New York area. There's an online reverse directory TJ knows how to use, and that's where he went, hoping to find a name and address. But there was no listing for that number.

'Might be he walked into a store, bought a phone with prepaid minutes on it. You dealing in product, that's how you do. Walk into one of those stores on Fourteenth Street, pay cash for a phone, and you in business. Don't even have to give a name, 'cause you ain't opening an account, you just buying a phone with the minutes already on it. They start to run out, you go back where you bought it and give the man more money, and they give you some more minutes.'

'And it's all off the books.'

'Far as you're concerned, it is. Whether the store declares the cash, well, we don't care about that part, do we?'

'It won't keep us up nights. I don't suppose

you have to be a dope dealer to get a phone that way.'

'Way I got mine. It's simpler and you don't get no bill every month. Don't get no telemarketers, either. Don't have to get on the Do Not Call list, 'cause you ain't on the Call list to begin with.'

'Those are definite advantages,' I had to admit. 'The only way to improve on it would be not to have a phone at all. For David Thompson, though, you wouldn't think he'd want to play hard to get. He's a freelance copywriter. If nobody knows his phone number, how does he get work?'

'His clients would have the number. Same as the dope dealers.'

'What about new business?'

'Be a problem.'

'He told Louise it's feast or famine in his line of work. During famine times, I wouldn't think you'd want to make it hard for people to get in touch with you. He's got to have more than one phone.'

''Less he stupid.'

'He'd have a land line in his office. He might not give her the number because that's his business line.'

'Or because he ain't who he says he is.'

'Always a possibility.'

'Whole lot of David Thompsons in the phone book. Plus all the D Thompsons.'

'It's a place to start,' I said.

And it didn't require computer skills, either, just

a sedentary version of the kind of doggedness I'd learned fresh out of the Police Academy. GOYAKOD was the acronym, and it stood for Get Off Your Ass and Knock On Doors. I did just that, albeit metaphorically, and made phone calls, working my way through the D and David Thompsons in the Manhattan white pages.

'I'm not sure I have the right party,' I'd tell whoever answered. 'I'm trying to reach the David Thompson who writes direct-mail advertising copy.'

One man pointed out that the one thing to be said for direct-mail advertising was that it didn't interrupt your day the way a phone call did. But most of the people I reached were polite enough, if unhelpful; they weren't the David Thompson I was looking for, nor had they heard of the fellow. I thanked them and put a check mark next to their names and moved on to the next listing.

That's how it went when I got an actual person on the phone, which didn't happen all that often. Most of the time I got a machine or a voice mail system, in which case I left a message saying essentially what I'd have said to a human being, and adding my phone number. I didn't expect a lot of callbacks, but you never know, and there was always the chance someone might be monitoring his machine, waiting to see who it was before picking up. That happened once; I was halfway through my spiel when a woman came on the line to tell me her husband was not a copywriter but an insurance agent with Vermont Life. But maybe she could help me after all, she suggested. How long had it been since I'd had a thorough review of my insurance needs?

'I suppose I had that coming,' I said. 'I'll make you a deal. I won't call you anymore, and you don't call me.'

She said that sounded fair enough, and I put a check mark next to her husband's name.

I've known a few people in advertising over the years, but if I'd met them in AA I rarely knew their last names, or where they worked. There was a fellow named Ken McCutcheon I'd known when I first got sober, but I'd long since lost touch with him, and I spent a lot of time calling people I thought might have kept track of him. Eventually one of them remembered he'd moved to Dobbs Ferry, in Westchester County. I found a listing for him, not in Dobbs Ferry but nearby in Hastings, and reached a woman who turned out to be his widow. Ken had died six, no, seven years ago, she told me. I said I was sorry to hear it. She asked my name, and how I'd known him.

He was dead, and anyway she'd been his wife, so preserving his anonymity wasn't an issue, and I've never made much of a thing out of preserving my own. I said I'd known him in AA, and she surprised me by asking if I was still sober. I said I was.

'Then you're one of the lucky ones,' she said.

'Ken had nine years, nine wonderful years, and then I guess he thought he was cured. And he just couldn't stop drinking. He was in and out of treatment, he went out to Hazelden for thirty days. He flew home, and I met him at the airport, and he got off the plane drunk. And drank for another year or two after that, and then he had a seizure and died.'

I apologized for disturbing her, and she apologized for telling me more than I may have wanted to know. 'I should change the listing,' she said. 'In the phone book. But I never get around to it.'

'They don't like to call it direct mail anymore,' Bob Ripley told me. 'Don't ask me why. Nowadays it's either direct marketing or direct-response advertising. And that's very nearly the extent of my knowledge of the subject, but I know a guy who can tell you anything you need to know, including why you get six copies of the Lands' End catalog every goddam month.'

I suppose I should have thought of Bob sooner. I'd seen him less than two months ago, the same night I'd booked Ray Gruliow to speak at St Paul's. Bob, like Ray, was a fellow member of the Club of Thirty-one, and a vice president of Fowler & Kresge. I didn't know what he did in that capacity, but I knew F&K was an advertising agency, and that was enough.

Mark Safran, the fellow he referred me to, was in a meeting, but I left my number and mentioned

Bob's name, and that got me a callback within the hour. 'I could tell you a lot about direct marketing,' he said, 'but you're looking to find a particular guy, is that right?'

'Or to find out that there is no such guy.'

'That'd be tough, because there's a ton of freelance copy guys out there, and it'd be hard to prove he's not one of them. It's not like doctors or lawyers, there's no single professional organization you have to belong to. No state or municipal licensing bureau, like I guess there is in your field.'

I let that pass.

'The thing is,' he said, 'we do almost everything in-house, and when we're in a hurry and need to go outside, we use somebody we've worked with in the past. So we've got our own list of six or eight guys, and then there are the big corporate shops, but your guy's not there because he's a freelance. You know what I'm going to do? I'm going to put you in touch with one of the guys we use.'

He gave me a name and number, and it was easy to believe the guy was a freelance because he actually answered his own phone. 'Peter Hochstein,' he said, and when I explained my quest he asked the name of my quarry. 'Never heard of him,' he said, 'but that doesn't prove anything. I don't go out and meet my colleagues. Mostly I stay home and work. And if I had heard of him, it's not a name that sticks in your mind.'

'No.'

'He might belong to the DMA, but probably not. Most of the members are corporate, because membership's expensive. But he could have a free listing in *Who's Charging What*. Or he could be the kind of guy who runs small-space ads offering his services in *DM News* or *Direct* or *Target Marketing*. You could check there, and also in the classifieds in *Adweek* and *Advertising Age*.'

He was full of suggestions, and I wrote everything down. If David Thompson had won an award or made a speech, he'd probably turn up on a Google search, but that might be tricky because his name was such a common one. 'You could find me that way,' he said, 'along with the Peter Hochstein who's serving a life sentence for a contract killing in Nebraska, not to mention Peter Hochstein the German scientist.'

There was a good chance, he said, that David Thompson might fly under the radar. 'I have a listing in *Who's Charging What*,' he said, 'because it's free, so what could it hurt? But I don't run classifieds in *Ad Age*, and I don't run ads in the direct marketing publications. I don't think it's worth the money, and I'm not the only one. Most of us who've been doing this for a while seem to feel that way. It's almost as if we've stopped believing in the power of advertising, which is funny, when you think about it. I don't belong to any trade organizations, either. The business I get is all referrals, and what kind of client is going to pick you because he saw your ad? That's as unlikely as getting business from a listing in the Yellow Pages.'

I thanked him, and the first thing I did was something I should have done earlier. I looked for Thompson in the Yellow Pages – not the consumer book but the business-to-business edition. There was no separate listing for direct marketing copywriters, but there was a section of advertising copywriters, and I wasn't surprised not to find David Thompson there.

I didn't find him in the back pages of *Advertising Age* or *Adweek*, either, which were the two publications he'd mentioned that you could find on the news stand. I bit the bullet and sat down at Elaine's computer, and I Googled my way to some of the sites he'd mentioned.

Everybody tells me what a timesaver the Internet is, and how they can't believe they ever got along without it. And I know what they mean, but every time I use it I wind up wondering what people did with their spare time before computers came along to suck it all up. I sat down at the damn thing in the middle of the afternoon, and I couldn't get away from it until Elaine was putting dinner on the table.

She said she'd wanted to check her e-mail but hadn't wanted to disturb me. I told her I'd have welcomed a disturbance, that I'd spent hours without accomplishing much of anything. 'I couldn't find the son of a bitch,' I said, 'and I couldn't find half the websites I was looking for, and I wound up

Googling Peter Hochstein, don't ask me why, and he wasn't kidding, there really is somebody with the same name doing life in Nebraska for murder for hire. He was sentenced to death originally, and the sentence was changed on appeal, and it was a pretty interesting case, though why I spent the better part of an hour reading about it is something I'd be hard put to explain.'

'You know what I think? I think we should get a second computer.'

'That's funny,' I said, 'because what I think is we should get rid of the one we've got.'

New York neighborhoods rarely have sharply delineated boundaries. They're formed by a shifting consensus of newspapermen, realtors, and local inhabitants, and it's not always possible to say with assurance where one leaves off and the next one begins. Kips Bay, where David Thompson lived – or where the man who claimed to be David Thompson claimed to be living – is that area in the immediate vicinity of Kips Bay Plaza, a housing complex that fills the three-block area bounded by Thirtieth and Thirty-third streets and First and Second avenues. The neighborhood known as Kips Bay probably runs south from Thirty-fourth Street and east from Third Avenue. Bellevue and the NYU Medical Center take up the space between First Avenue and the FDR Drive. The southern edge of Kips Bay is hardest to pinpoint, but if you occupied an apartment at Twenty-sixth Street and

Second Avenue, say, I don't think you'd tell people you lived in Kips Bay.

The overall area was pretty small no matter how you figured it, and it didn't take me much more time to cover it on foot than I'd spent learning next to nothing on the Internet the day before. It's predominantly residential, with a good sprinkling of the service businesses and neighborhood restaurants that cater to local residents, and that's where I went, showing David Thompson's photograph in bodegas and delis, dry cleaners and news stands. 'Have you seen this fellow around?' I asked Korean greengrocers and Italian shoe repairmen. 'You know this man?' I asked Dominican doormen and Greek waiters. None of them did, nor did a mail carrier in the middle of his rounds, a clerk at a copy shop, or a beat cop who started out thinking that he ought to be the one asking the questions, but who lost the attitude when he found out I'd been on the job myself, especially when it turned out I'd known his father.

'He looks like a lot of guys,' the cop said. 'What's his name?' I told him, and he shook his head and said that was a big help, wasn't it? His own name was Danaher, and I remembered his father as a backslapping gladhander who could have doubled as a ward boss. He was living in Tucson, the son said, and playing golf every day unless it rained. 'And it never rains,' he said.

★   ★   ★

95

It rained that night, in New York if not in Tucson. I stayed in and watched a lackluster fight card on ESPN. The next day dawned cool and clear, and the city felt bright with promise. TJ and I met for breakfast and compared notes, and decided we were making the kind of progress Thomas Edison described, when he asserted that he now knew twelve thousand substances that wouldn't make an effective filament for a lightbulb. We'd established about that many ways not to find David Thompson, and I was starting to wonder if he was there to be found.

I didn't have anything for TJ to do, so he went home to sit in front of his computer and I got home myself in time for a phone call from one of the David Thompsons for whom I'd left a message. He was calling to let me know that he wasn't the David Thompson I was looking for. Then why had he bothered calling? I thanked him and rang off.

Sometime in the middle of the afternoon it occurred to me that the only hook I had for Louise's David Thompson was his phone number, so why didn't I use it? I couldn't trace it, I couldn't attach a name or address to it, but the one thing I could do was dial it and see who answered. I did, and at first no one did, and then after five rings his voice mail kicked in and a computer-generated voice invited me to leave a message. I rang off instead.

I thought I might run into Louise at a meeting that night, and when I didn't I gave her a call. 'I don't know,' she said. 'Maybe I jumped the gun, hiring you when I did. I haven't heard from the guy since. I hate it when a person dumps you and doesn't even tell you.'

'Have you tried calling him?'

'If he's dumping me,' she said, 'I don't want to give him the satisfaction, you know? And if he's not, I don't want to crowd him. I'm old-fashioned when it comes to girls calling guys.'

'Okay.'

'But screw that. If I can sic a detective on him, what's so extreme about calling him? Hang on, Matt, I'll get back to you.'

She called back in no time at all. 'No answer. Just his voice mail, and no, I didn't leave a message. I didn't even ask. Did you find out anything about him?'

I said I'd put in some hours on the case, but didn't have much to show for them. I didn't tell her how close I was to inventing the lightbulb.

'Well,' she said, 'maybe you shouldn't keep the meter running, you know? Because if I never hear from him again, the whole thing becomes academic. If I'm gonna forget about a guy, It's not like I need to know a whole lot about him.'

I tend to relate to a case like a dog to a bone, and have been known to keep at it after a client has told me to let it go, but in this instance it was easy to stop. It might have been harder if I could have thought of something productive to do, but all I could come up with was waiting until he had a date with her and following him home afterward. I couldn't very well do that if he never called her again.

Late the following afternoon I was at the Donnell Library on West Fifty-third, reading a book on direct marketing. It wouldn't help me find David Thompson, but I'd grown interested enough in some aspects of the subject from what I'd encountered online to spend an hour or two skimming the subject. I walked from there to Elaine's shop on Ninth Avenue, figuring I'd keep her company and walk her home when she closed up, but she wasn't there.

Monica was, and had been for most of the afternoon. 'I just dropped in,' she explained, 'figuring we'd kill an hour with girl talk. I stopped at Starbucks for a couple of mocha lattes, and as soon as she'd finished hers she said I was an angel sent from heaven, and could I mind the store while she ran out to an auction at Tepper Galleries. And I've been stuck here ever since, and one latte only goes so far, and I've been positively jonesing for a cup of coffee.'

'Why didn't you lock up for fifteen minutes and go get one?'

'Because to do that, dear Matthew, one would have to have had the key, which your good wife didn't see fit to leave with me. I'm sure there's a spare tucked away somewhere, but I couldn't find it. You want to hold the fort while I get us both a couple of coffees?'

'No, I'll go. Did you say a mocha latte?'

'I did, but that was then and this is now. Get me something really disgusting, will you? Something along the lines of a caramel mocha frappuccino, so gooped up with sugar crap that you can't taste the coffee, but with a couple of extra shots of espresso in there to kick ass. How does that sound?'

It sounded horrible, but she was the one who was going to drink it. I repeated the order verbatim, and the ring-nosed blond barista took it in stride. I brought it back to the shop, and we found things to talk about until Elaine breezed in, reporting a successful afternoon at the auction.

Monica's reward for shop-sitting was a good dinner at Paris Green. The two of them did most of the talking, with one or the other of them periodically apologizing to me for all the girl talk. What no one talked about was Monica's mystery man.

We put her in a cab and walked home, and as we walked in the door my cell phone rang.

It was Louise. 'He called,' she said. 'Late last night, very apologetic for the hour and the long silence. Busy busy busy, and he's out of town this weekend, but we've got a date Monday night. It was too late to call you last night, and then today I was the one who was busy busy busy, and besides I wanted to think about it.'

'And?'

'Well, he's evidently not dumping me after all, and I really like him, and I think what we've got

99

might have a future. And there's a point where you have to have faith, you have to be able to let go and trust somebody.'

'So you want to call off the investigation?'

'What, are you out of your mind? I just said I have to trust him, and how can I trust the son of a bitch when I don't know for sure who he is? I called to tell you to go ahead.'

CHAPTER 8

He's up before the alarm rings. He showers, shaves, dresses. He's saved a change of clothes for this day – clean underwear, a fresh white shirt. He puts on the dark gray suit he wore on his first visit to the prison, and rejects the silver tie in favor of a textured black one. Somber, he decides. You can't go wrong with somber.

He checks himself in the mirror and is pleased with what he sees. Could his mustache use a trim? He smiles at the thought, grooms the mustache with thumb and forefinger.

His shoes aren't dirty, but they could use polishing. Is there a bootblack within fifty miles? He rather doubts it. But when he picked up the ice cream at the Circle K (and he'd bought two pints, not one, and ate them both) he'd also picked up a flat tin of Kiwi black shoe polish.

Some motel amenities include a disposable cloth for polishing your shoes, provided less for the guest's convenience than to save the hotel's towels. This Days Inn has been remiss, and it's their loss. He uses a wash-cloth to apply the polish, a hand towel to buff it to a high sheen.

Before he leaves, he uses another towel to wipe surfaces he may have touched. It's not his habit to touch things unnecessarily, and there's not going to be anyone dusting his room for prints, but this is the sort of thing he does routinely, and why not? He's got plenty of time, and it's never a mistake to take precautions. Better safe than sorry.

He boots up his computer a final time, logs on, checks his e-mail. Visits the several Usenet news-groups to which he subscribes, reads a few entries. There's been a flurry of activity in a thread dealing with the impending execution of Preston Applewhite, and he catches up on the new posts. He finds a few provocative observations, tucked in among the usual predictable cries of outrage from the diehard foes of capital punishment, balanced by the cheers of death penalty fans whose only regret is that the proceedings won't be televised.

Pay-per-view, he thinks. Just a matter of time.

He logs off, finishes packing, leaves the motel by the rear door. No need to check out, as they took an imprint of his credit card. Nor is there any need to return the plastic key card. He's read that a lot of information is automatically coded into the card, that one could in theory use it to reconstruct a guest's entrances and exits. He's not sure this is actually true, and even if it were, he knows the cards are automatically recycled, their coded data erased forever when they're reprogrammed for another guest and another room. But why leave anything to chance? He'll bring the key along and discard it in another state.

It's twenty minutes past ten when he pulls up at the penitentiary gate-house, where the guard recognizes him and welcomes him with a grim smile. He parks in what has become his usual spot, checks himself in the mirror, smoothes his mustache, and walks to the entrance. The sun is high in a virtually cloudless sky, and there's no breeze. It's going to be a hot day.

But not inside, where climate controls keep the air cool and dry year-round. He passes through the metal detector, shows his ID to men who already know him by sight, and is escorted to the little room where witnesses sit to view the application of society's ultimate sanction.

He's ushered into the room at ten-forty-five, a full hour and a quarter before the proceedings are scheduled to begin, and there are already half a dozen people present, four men and two women. One man a few years his junior, wearing a shirt and tie but no jacket, makes conversational overtures. He's sure the man is a journalist, and he doesn't want to talk to him, or indeed to anyone. He dismisses the man with a shake of his head.

There is, he's surprised to note, a refreshment table laid out for the spectators, with a coffee urn and a pitcher of iced tea, along with a plate of doughnuts and another of corn and bran muffins. He doesn't want to eat anything, the whole idea is faintly distasteful, but does help himself to a cup of coffee.

And takes a chair. There are no bad seats; the viewing gallery is long and narrow, with every chair adjacent to the big plate-glass window. He's struck immediately by how close they are to what they're going to watch. But for the intervening glass, they'd be able to smell the breath of the attending physician, and the fear of his unfortunate patient.

The equipment is in place, the gurney, the apparatus holding three suspended bottles and an array of medical equipment. He glances to his right, at a middle-aged man and woman whose eyes are fixed upon a framed photograph the woman is holding. Their son, of course. One of Applewhite's three victims.

He shifts in his seat, manages a glimpse of the photo. The shock of blond hair is an unmistakable field mark; these are the Willises, parents of the first boy slain, the one whose remains were never found.

The body's location is the secret Preston Applewhite is evidently determined to take with him to the grave.

The door opens to admit another man, who takes a seat, then sees the refreshment table and helps himself to coffee and a doughnut. 'That looks good,' someone says, and goes to the table.

And the coffee is in fact better than one might expect, weaker than he'd prefer but otherwise acceptable, and freshly made. He finishes it, sets the cup aside, and gazes through the pane of glass.

And allows the memories to come . . .

❋   ❋   ❋

Richmond, Virginia, no more than fifty miles away, but further removed in time than in distance. Years ago, when the Willis boy – Jeffrey? – is alive, when Preston Applewhite is a free man, a husband and father, a respected member of his community. And a man who still enjoys a game of basketball once or twice a week at the municipal outdoor recreation area a few blocks from his office.

And he himself, Arne Bodinson (although he has another name then, and it would take some concentration to conjure it up from his memory), happens to be passing through the grounds. He's never walked there before, he's barely arrived in Richmond, and he pauses to watch the men play a boys' game.

Two men leap for a rebound. The elbow of one collides with the face of the other, and the second man cries out in pain and crumples to the pavement, blood streaming from his nose.

Why do things happen? Why does one man live while another dies, one prosper while another fails? It seems self-evident that one of two operating principles must apply. Either everything happens for a reason or nothing happens for a reason. Either it was all coded in the molecules from the very instant of the Big Bang or every bit of it, every left or right turn, every lightning strike, every broken shoelace, is the product of nothing but random chance.

He could argue the question either way, but more often than not he leans toward the latter version. Random chance rolls the dice. Things happen because they happen. You get what you get.

Consider this, then: Anyone could have paused to watch that basketball game, but it is not just anyone, it is he himself, the future Arne Bodinson, with his particular history and personality. And, although the weather renders it superfluous, he is nevertheless wearing a sport jacket, and in its breast pocket, atypically for him, there is a neatly folded white handkerchief. He's put it there that morning, so he realizes he has it, and without conscious thought he rushes across the court to the fallen man, drawing the hanky from his pocket, using it to stanch the flow of blood from the injured (but not, it will turn out, broken) nose.

Others, team-mates and opponents, are also quick to assist Applewhite, and in no time at all they have him on his feet and are leading him away to get medical attention. And he's left there with a bloody handkerchief in his hand, and he looks at it, and, wondrous to say, he is able to foresee everything that is to follow. Another man would have disposed of the handkerchief in the nearest trashcan, but he sees it at once as an unparalleled opportunity.

He bears it carefully away. As soon as he conveniently can, he tucks it away in a plastic Ziploc bag.

A man in a brown suit, evidently a subordinate of the warden's, enters the room and clears his throat, explaining in some detail just what is going to take place shortly on the other side of the window. He's heard it all before, and suspects that's as true of the others, the bereaved, the members of the press, and whoever else has contrived to get one of these precious front-row seats.

But the fellow is not just there to refresh everybody's memory. He's the approximate equivalent of the chap whose task it is to warm up a television show's studio audience, telling jokes to heighten their spirits, exhorting them to respond enthusiastically to the promptings of the APPLAUSE sign. The man in the brown suit doesn't tell jokes, of course, and his goal is to mute and muffle emotions, not amplify them. 'Remember the solemnity of the occasion,' he urges them. 'You may feel the impulse to say something. Whatever it is, keep it to yourself until after we've finished here. The sight of this man who's brought you so much pain may move you to cry out. If you feel you won't be able to control yourself, I'm going to ask you to tell me now, and I'll have you escorted to another part of the facility.'

No one is moved to do so.

'We're going to witness the end of a man's life. The process will be as painless as we know how to make it, but even so you're going to watch a man make the transition from life to death. If that's more than you care to see, let me know now. All right. If you discover when the time comes that you don't want to watch, close your eyes. That sounds obvious, but sometimes people forget that they have the option.'

There's more, but he tunes it out. The clock, after all, is ticking, and he has more to remember . . .

❊   ❊   ❊

With the bloody handkerchief zipped in a plastic bag, all of what will follow is clear in his mind, as if the script is already written, as if he need merely follow the directions.

When he first began to kill, he did so as a means to the twin ends of money and power. Those were the two things he thought he wanted, and killing was an occasionally useful technique for acquiring them. He was not surprised to discover that it did not bother him to kill, he'd somehow expected as much, but what he had not anticipated was the pleasure and satisfaction that accompanied the act. It brought excitement and a sense of accomplishment beyond anything attainable by other means.

It is hard to say with certainty just when he turned the corner, coming to the realization that money and power were secondary, that killing itself was its own reward. But he suspects it's around the time that he bought the knife.

He holds the knife, grips it in his hand. It looks like any other bowie-type hunting knife, but he paid over two hundred dollars for it, and he can feel the value in its balance and the way it fits his hand. It was handcrafted by a man named Randall, something of a legend among the makers and collectors of bench-made knives.

He's used it several times since he bought it. It's always served its purpose admirably. And on each occasion he's cleaned it afterward, scrubbing every trace of blood from its surface. It's stainless steel, of course, and impregnable, but blood could find its way into the seam of blade and hilt, so he's taken the additional precaution of soaking his knife overnight in a dilute Clorox solution. No blood, no DNA, nothing to implicate the knife or its owner in any of the several killings it has occasioned.

Now, knowing he's soon to use it again, and knowing the how and why of it, he feels the stirrings of excitement.

That night and the following day he drives around Richmond, getting his bearings. He learns where the prostitutes gather. There's no easier quarry, and he's taken prostitutes before – off the street, in a massage parlor – when the hunger for killing has demanded quick satisfaction, and there's been no time to make the act something special. One of them scarcely seemed surprised by her imminent fate, and he wondered if she and her sisters didn't expect to end that way, wondered if serial murder might rank as an occupational illness, like black lung disease for coal miners.

He comes close to selecting a prostitute the first night, a slender thing dressed for success in red hot pants and a skimpy halter top. All he has to do is stop the car. She'll get in, and the moment he pulls away from the curb her fate will be sealed. She'll be the first unfortunate victim of the man with the bloody nose.

But he needs to know more. The course is clear, but the particulars need to be determined. One has to plan.

He learns much that he needs to know. He learns

the name and address of the man with the bloody nose, and he discovers more about him through some diligent Internet research. A husband and father, Preston Applewhite has been leading an essentially blameless life. How ironic, then that he should abduct, sodomize, and murder a string of equally blameless boys.

Because he has come to see that a prostitute is not a good choice. So many of them are infected with one thing or another that it's unappealing to contemplate close contact with them and their bodily fluids. And what if the whore he picks is a surrogate police officer?

More to the point, there's insufficient outrage attendant upon a whore's death. That fellow in Oregon had needed to kill a couple of dozen of them before anybody noticed, and even then the police didn't lose sleep hunting for him.

Then, driving slowly past the scene of yesterday's inspiration, he sees another basketball game in progress. But the players are boys. Kids, really, wearing gym shorts. Half the boys sport singlets, while the others have bare chests. No hair on those chests, no five o'clock shadow on those cheeks. Youth, innocence.

Kill a prostitute and nobody will notice. But kill a child?

Once he'd written this:

I have killed both men and women. Killing men, I would say, provides me with more

110

of a sense of accomplishment. On the other hand, for sheer pleasure, there's nothing like killing an attractive woman.

And a boy? He looks at the basketball players and is unable to perceive them as sexually desirable. Still, there's undeniable excitement at the thought of harvesting one of them. He can fake the sexual aspect, can press a suitably shaped object into service as a surrogate penis. He needn't experience lust himself in order to stage a convincing lust murder.

In the end, he surprises himself.

It's several days later that he finds his victim, by which time he's purchased several items. Most of them – tape, a blanket, a garden spade, a rubber mallet – are from the local Wal-Mart, but there are two more expensive articles, an automobile and a computer. The car's a Japanese import the same size and shape as the one Preston Applewhite drives, while the computer's a laptop, a bargain-priced IBM clone. He buys the car anonymously for cash from a private owner – it's been hit, it needs body work and has probably suffered damage to the frame. But it's fine for his purposes, and it's cheap.

He's found a place near the high school where some boys wait to hitch rides, and he manages to spot a boy standing all by himself, his thumb extended. He looks to be thirteen or fourteen. Too young to drive, at any rate.

He stops the car, lets the boy in. He's a good-looking young man, his hair blond, his face and forearms lightly tanned. There's downy hair on his arms, and his face is as smooth as a girl's.

Is the boy a hustler? That's possible, hitchhiking is a time-honored way for boys to arrange liaisons with older men. This one seems innocent, however.

He chats with the boy, asks him about sports, about school. 'How about girls?' he says. 'You like girls?'

I like men better, the boy might say, but he doesn't, he says girls are okay. He is, by all indications, entirely oblivious to what's going on.

At a stop sign, he brings the car to a halt and points to the floor on the passenger side. 'There's a glove there,' he says. 'Can you reach it?'

The boy bends forward, looking for the glove that isn't there, and he swings the rubber mallet in an easy arc and hits the boy solidly on the back of the skull. Hard enough to kill him? No, but hard enough to knock him out. In no time at all the boy's hands are taped behind his back, and another piece of duct tape covers his mouth.

Five minutes later they're at the preselected killing ground.

And, he discovers, there's no need to employ a surrogate penis. His own is more than equal to the task. The boy's skin is as soft and smooth as a woman's, and his helplessness, his utter vulnerability, is exciting. He hasn't thought to bring a condom, an absurd oversight resulting from his assumption that the boy wouldn't arouse him. Never assume, he reminds himself. Never take anything for granted. Prepare for all contingencies.

So he takes his pleasure with the boy, but stops short of orgasm. And takes up the knife, the beautiful knife that Randall made.

After the knife, a scissors, to snip a lock of hair. After the scissors, the garden spade. Not to dig the grave, he did that ahead of time, anticipating a need for it, but to fill it in. The killing ground's an abandoned farm, west of the city and just beyond the Southside Speedway. Its own private family cemetery is off to the side of the ruined old farmhouse. The grave-stones are so badly weathered you can't make out the inscriptions, and now there's one new grave among the other dozen or so, and he fills it in and presses the sod in place over it. Right now it's a fresh grave, but soon it will be indistinguishable from the others.

By nightfall he's placed the battered old Camry in the storage shed he rented the previous day. If anyone finds it there, they'll find a vehicle with no fingerprints on it. There'll be no prints on the tools in the trunk, either – the spade, the mallet, the splendid knife. The roll of duct tape.

He retrieves his own car, a beige square-back Ford Tempo with his luggage in its trunk. He drives west on I-64 and north on I-81, the cruise control set at four miles over the speed limit. He doesn't stop except for gas until he's across the Pennsylvania state line. There, in a mom-and-pop motel with a front office that smells of curry, he takes a long hot shower and makes a bundle of all the clothes he wore, to be donated to Goodwill in the morning. He slips into bed naked and lets himself relive each moment of the afternoon's entertainment, starting with the boy's getting into the car and ending with the last stroke of the knife.

This time there's no need to deny himself. His climax is fierce in its intensity, and he cries out like a girl in pain.

CHAPTER 9

It's noon, and no one has yet made an appearance on the other side of the long window. It is as if the curtain has risen upon an insistently empty stage.

Where is everybody?

Has there been a call from the governor? No, surely not, because the governor wants to go on being governor, and may even hope for higher office someday. He won't be making any calls. Nor is there a lawyer out there with a last-ditch appeal to a high court. The appeal process has long since ended for Preston Applewhite.

Is Applewhite all right? He's a young man, a man just over the threshold of middle age, but old enough for a stroke, old enough for a heart attack. He pictures the man struck down in his cell at the eleventh hour, imagines the ambulance ride, the race to save his life. And then of course the stay of execution, until he's deemed in good enough condition to be put to death.

But surely it's just his own imagination, having a field day. The other spectators aren't fidgeting in their chairs or checking their watches. Perhaps executions are like rock concerts, perhaps everyone knows they never start precisely on time.

It's not as though anyone has a train to catch. But there would seem to be time for a further stroll down Memory Lane . . .

Two days after the Willis boy's death, he rents a furnished house in York, Pennsylvania. It's a few days short of a month before he returns to Richmond.

But it's not an idle month. He has a DSL line installed for his computer, and he's often online, researching subjects on the Internet, checking his e-mail, keeping up with his news groups.

At least once a day he disconnects his own laptop and boots up the one he's bought, which he thinks of as Preston Applewhite's computer. In MS-Word, he writes out a breathless account of the boy's abduction and murder, departing from reality only in that he tells of the weeks he spends leading up to the event, how he wrestles with the impulse, how he determines he has no choice but to go through with it.

And he's deliberately vague about the killing ground:

> I took him to a fine and private place. I knew no one would disturb us there. He'll simply disappear. No one will think to look for him there.

Online, he opens an e-mail account for Applewhite, ScoutMasterBates at Hotmail.com. On the registration form, he calls himself John Smith, unimaginatively enough, but the street address he provides is 476 Elm Street. Applewhite's actual street number, while not on Elm Street, is indeed 476. For city and state he enters Los Angeles, California, but includes Applewhite's Richmond zip code.

As ScoutMasterBates, he surfs the net looking for porn sites, and they don't prove terribly elusive. It's only a matter of days before his mailbox begins to fill up with porn spam, and by visiting the sites that promise young male models, that talk of man-boy love, he increasingly becomes the target of purveyors of kiddy porn. 'All models over eighteen (wink! wink!)' one site declares.

He downloads porn, pays for it with a credit card that can't be traced back to him. Weeks ago he was in a restaurant, where he saw a patron at another table pay her check with a credit card and walk off without her receipt. He got to it before the waitress, passing the table on an unnecessary trip to the men's room, palming and pocketing the yellow scrap of paper. It shows her account number and expiration date, and that's all he needs for small online purchases. In a month or two she'll go over her statement and, if she notices, call her credit card company to complain. But he'll be done with her account by then.

Back in Richmond, he sets about getting access to Applewhite's house and car and office.

That turns out to be easy. Applewhite's a monthly client at the parking garage around the corner from his office. He goes there himself, inquires about rates and hours and access, and finds questions to ask until the attendant's attention is diverted, at which time he snatches Applewhite's keys off the numbered hook. He needs a full set for his girlfriend, he tells a locksmith, and the man grins and says he's a trusting man, that he's been married eighteen years himself and his wife still doesn't have a key to his car.

A single key opens the door and the trunk. There are other keys on the ring as well, and he has them all duplicated, knowing one will be a house key and another a key to the office. Inside of an hour he makes another visit to the parking garage, where it's a simple matter to put Applewhite's keys on a table, where they might have fallen if dislodged from the hook.

Late at night, long after the lights have been turned off in the Applewhite home, he lets himself into the unlocked garage and opens the trunk of the car. He has an old army blanket with him, purchased at the Salvation Army store in York, and he spreads it out in Applewhite's trunk, rubs it here and there in the trunk's interior, takes it out and returns it to its plastic bag.

Two days later he exchanges cars, picking up the dark Camry, leaving the beige Tempo in the storage shed. He starts cruising when school lets out and soon picks up an older, more knowledgeable boy

118

than Jeffrey Willis. Scott Sawyer is fifteen, with knowing eyes and a crooked smile. His T-shirt is too small, the worn blue jeans provocatively tight on his thighs and buttocks. When he gets in the Camry, he drapes an arm over the seatback and tries to look seductive.

The effect is comical, but he doesn't laugh.

I think you'll find something interesting in the glove compartment, he tells the boy. And, at the right moment, he swings the rubber mallet.

There's a failed country club north and west of the city, off Creighton Road on the way to Old Cold Harbor. The property's for sale, and the sign to that effect has been there long enough to have served for drive-by target practice. The nine-hole golf course is all weeds, the greens neglected, the fairways over-grown. Earlier he scouted the place, picked a spot. Halfway there the youth comes to, tries to scream through the duct tape, tries to free his hands, thrashes around within the confines of his seat belt.

He tells him to stop it, and when the thrashing continues he takes up the rubber mallet and hits the boy hard on the knee. The thrashing stops.

Out on the golf course, he drives into the rough bordering the fifth hole, hauls the boy out of the car and drags him deep into the woods. He immobilizes the boy by smashing his kneecaps with the spade, strips him, and positions him appropriately, then dons a condom and rapes him.

The younger boy, Jeffrey Willis, was more appealing. Softer, smaller, his innocence more palpable.

Too, there was the novelty of sex with a male. But for all that the experience with Scott Sawyer is savagely exciting, and there's no need to hold back his climax. Straining for it, he reaches down, picks up the knife – how sweetly it fits his hand – and strikes, and strikes again.

He wraps the body in a blanket, the one that's been in the trunk of Applewhite's car, where it could pick up fibers from the trunk lining and leave fibers of its own. Every contact involves the transfer of fibers, that's why he did what he did with the blanket, and why he jettisoned the clothes he wore when he killed the Willis boy. He'll do the same with these clothes, everything down to the sneakers on his feet. They'll pick up fibers, they'll carry grass stains and soil residue, and none of that will matter because they'll wind up in a clothing donation box in Pennsylvania and no crime lab will ever look at them.

He starts to dig a grave, but it's getting dark and he's tired, and the ground underneath is a maze of tree roots, impossible to dig in. Besides, he's going to want this body to be found.

He snips a lock of hair, tucks it into a glassine envelope. He stashes it in the trunk of the Camry, along with the tools he'll need for his next visit to Richmond.

He leaves the body shrouded in the army blanket, piles loose brush over it, and heads for the storage shed, where he switches the Camry for the Tempo. He takes I-64, then I-81. The condom he used, its end knotted to secure its contents, is on the seat beside him; when he's crossed the state line into Maryland he lowers the window, tosses it, and drives on.

After two more weeks he's had enough of York. He's paid up through the end of the month, so he keeps the keys to leave himself the option of returning, but erases all traces of his occupancy so that he need not come back. He drives to Richmond and begins setting the stage, dressing the sets.

By now the cheap laptop contains on its hard drive a description of the second murder. He's still somewhat vague concerning the location of the killing ground and dump site, but does call it a golf course, and he downloads and saves on his hard drive a MapQuest close-up map of the failed country club. There are also two drafts of an essay in which he, as Applewhite, expounds on the morality of murder, justifying his actions through a line of reasoning that, he has to admit, owes a good deal to the Marquis de Sade, for all that he dredges up supporting arguments from Nietzsche and Ayn Rand. One draft of the essay, including specific references to the killings of Willis and Sawyer, he erases, knowing it will prove recoverable; the other, which covers the same ground but is less damning, he saves on the hard drive, adding to the file the notation:

Publish this? Where???

One afternoon he drives to Applewhite's suburban neighborhood. Both cars are gone, and school's still in session. He lets himself into the house, tingling with excitement as he walks from room to room. Applewhite has a den, which his tax return no doubt identifies as a home office, and he leaves the computer in a desk drawer.

In the bedroom, he takes socks and underwear from Applewhite's dresser, a shirt and a pair of khaki trousers from his closet. The shirt has a laundry mark, he notes, and the pants, hanging on a peg, have been worn at least once since their last washing.

Shoes? He considers a pair, then remembers some ragged sneakers he spotted on an earlier visit to the garage, no doubt reserved for gardening and yard work. And ideal for his purposes.

The selection and disposal of the third victim is almost beside the point, because by now his chief concern is the web he's weaving for Preston Applewhite. Slow down, he admonishes himself. Take time to smell the flowers. And, remembering how Scott Sawyer had amused him less than Jeffrey Willis, he takes pains this time to select a boy from the younger, more innocent end of the spectrum.

The online newsgroups and bulletin boards for pedophiles (and yes, he's found his way to them, and ScoutMasterBates has contributed observations of his own to more than one) have taught him a new vocabulary. A boy on the threshold of adolescence, he has learned, is said to be in his bloom, the dew of youth still on him. That is what he seeks, and what he finds in the thirteen-year-old person of Marcus Leacock. Who is not hitchhiking at all when he finds him, but merely walking home from school.

He's driving the Camry now. And he changed clothes at the storage shed. He's rolled up the sleeves of Applewhite's shirt, turned up the cuffs of the khaki trousers. The sneakers are a little large, too, and he experimented with tissue paper in the toes, but decided against it. They're not that big, and it's not as if he's going to be walking long distance in them.

'Son? Come here a minute, will you? There's an address I'm having trouble finding.'

Delicious. He's spent enough time on the man-boy bulletin boards to have little regard for the pedophiles, but their enthusiasm is not entirely incomprehensible. Out at the abandoned golf course, he takes his time with Marcus, and, while that increases his own enjoyment of the enterprise, it perforce adds to the boy's pain and suffering. Well, sometimes it does appear to be a zero-sum universe, doesn't it? A gain for one is a loss for another, and one knows on which side of the equation one would prefer to be.

Anyway, it's soon enough over, and once it's done the boy has to endure neither pain nor the memory of pain. The boy is gone, wherever people go.

Wherever that is . . .

And the finishing touches: The body, minus a lock of hair, covered in brush and a blanket a few yards from Scott Sawyer's body. Underneath it, apparently dropped and overlooked, the handkerchief that set all of this in motion, his own handkerchief, soaked two months ago in Applewhite's blood. The mallet, the spade, the tape, the scissors, stowed first in the Camry's trunk and transferred in the dead of night to Applewhite's, where they'll be found hidden away in the spare tire well. The box of a dozen condoms, minus the two he used, stashed in Applewhite's glove compartment, so they can be matched to the residue to be found on the bodies. The clothes he wore, the sneakers and socks and underwear, the khakis, the laundry-marked shirt, all go in a Hefty bag and the bag in the trunk, as if Applewhite were planning to dispose of them.

And does he dare enter the house one more time?

He does, moving slowly and silently. There's no dog, no burglar alarm. This is a safe neighborhood, a low-crime suburb, and the sleep of all the Applewhites is deep and untroubled. Standing there in their darkened house, an alternate plan suggests itself to him. He has the knife with him; how hard would it be to murder the children in their beds, to slit the throat of the sleeping wife, and to arrange a convenient suicide for the master of the house?

No, he decides. Better to stick with the original plan, better to let the Commonwealth of Virginia handle the business of punishment.

He tapes the three glassine envelopes to the underside of a desk drawer. The knife, the magnificent knife that Randall made, wiped clean of visible blood and prints but surely bearing blood traces from all three victims, proves difficult to part with.

All the more reason to part with it. One must never

allow oneself to become too deeply attached to anything – not a place, not a person, not a possession. One's only attachment, and it must be total, should be to oneself. If thy right eye offend thee, get over it; if thy house or car or custom-made knife delight thee overmuch, cast it out.

The knife goes in a desk drawer. As he leaves the house, moving slowly and silently, he transforms the pain of losing the knife into the satisfaction of having chosen the right course of action. And it's only a knife, after all, a tool, a means to an end. In the course of time there will be other knives, and he'll like some of them as much as he's liked this one.

He's been driving the Camry, and he keeps it and takes I-95 into Washington. It's morning by the time he gets there. He runs the car through a car wash, then leaves it parked on the street a few blocks from Dupont Circle, with the key in the ignition and the windows rolled down. He takes the Metro to Union Station, confident that the car will have been stolen by the time his train departs for Richmond.

He goes to the rented storage shed, reclaims his Ford, and drives off.

Two days later, after the boy's disappearance has made the newspaper headlines and led the TV news, after an eyewitness has turned up who saw a boy fitting Marcus Leacock's description getting into a small dark sedan, he uses an untraceable phone to call the number provided for tips in the case. He reports having noticed a dark-colored car leaving the grounds of the old Fairview Country Club on the evening of the boy's disappearance, and that there was something about the incident that made him suspicious enough to jot down the first four digits of the license number, which was as much as he could get.

And of course it is enough . . .

And here's the guest of honor. Here's Preston Applewhite, the star of our little spectacle, making his belated entrance. He's wearing leg shackles and wrist restraints, so it's a less elegant entrance than it might be, but he's here now, and the show can go on.

His face is expressionless, his mood unreadable. What fills his mind now? Dread of the unknown? Fury at the failure of the system to exonerate an innocent man? Hope, however unwarranted, that some miracle may come along to save his life?

A week ago he, Arne Bodinson, could have furnished just such a miracle. He might have confessed, openly or anonymously, and proved his claim by offering up the location of the Willis boy's grave. Now, having spent so many hours with Applewhite, anything he might say would be discredited out of hand. *You say you know where the body is, Dr Bodinson? If so, it's because Applewhite told you. You're only confirming his guilt.*

The warden, his face lined with the demands of his office, recites a few pro forma words, then asks the condemned man if he has anything to say. There is an extended pause. Applegate – they've not yet strapped him to the gurney, he's evidently allowed to be on his feet while he voices his last words – has his eyes lowered in thought, then raises them to look for the first time at the faces behind the glass. He finds his new friend Arne, and his eyes brighten in recognition, but only for a moment.

When he speaks, his voice is soft, as if he doesn't intend it to reach his audience. There's a microphone, however, so it's audible in the witness chamber.

'You're all certain I did these things,' he says. 'I know otherwise, but there's no reason for anyone to believe me. I almost wish I were guilty. Then I could confess, I could beg forgiveness.' A pause, and the attendants move in, thinking he's finished, but a quick shake of his head halts them. 'I forgive you,' he says. 'All of you.'

And at the end his eyes fix on those of the one man who professes to believe in his innocence. Has he figured it out? Is that the meaning of those final three words? But no, he's looking for approval of his eloquence, and he gets it, a nod of acknowledgment from behind the glass. And Applewhite registers the nod, and seems grateful for it.

Applewhite lies down on the gurney and they adjust the straps. The physician finds a good vein in his arm, swabs the skin with alcohol-soaked cotton, gets the IV inserted on the second attempt.

And then he sits transfixed, watching, while a man dies before his eyes. There's very little to see. The first drug, the pentothal, has no apparent effect. The second, the Pavulon, induces paralysis, rendering Applewhite incapable of breathing – or of changing expression. And the final ingredient, the potassium chloride, burns or does not burn, it's impossible to tell, but what is evident, at least to those close enough to see the heart monitor, or the physician who checks the pulse, is that it does what it is supposed to do.

Preston Applewhite is dead.

And, behind the glass, the man who will soon discard forever the name Arne Bodinson is careful to maintain the expression he has worn throughout, one of somber detachment. He has an erection, but he's fairly certain no one has noticed it.

I-95, he knows, will be a nightmare on a Friday. He takes Interstates 64 and 81 instead, spends what's left of the night at a motel in Pennsylvania, then drives east on I-80 Saturday morning, aiming to hit the George Washington Bridge when traffic's likely to be light. And it works out as he'd planned.

Lately, everything's been working out as he planned.

As he'd thought it would. He'd done the hard work years ago in Richmond, made his kills, planted the incriminating evidence, fitted the frame precisely around a man whose only mistake was to sustain a bloody nose at the worst possible moment. This past week came under the heading of unfinished business.

He has unfinished business of another sort in New York.

CHAPTER 10

Monday night I was having a cup of coffee in front of the television set when my cell phone rang.

'I feel like a fucking spy,' Louise said. 'I'm in the ladies' room at the restaurant. We're about to go back to my place. You've got the address?'

I said I did.

'This is so deeply weird. I'm going to take him home and have sex with him, and meanwhile you'll be lurking outside waiting to follow him home. Tell me that's not weird.'

'If you'd prefer—'

'No, it makes sense, it's just totally weird. If he's who he says he is, then he never has to know about this. If he's not, then *I* have to know about it.'

I asked if he was likely to stay overnight.

'If he does, it'll be a first. He usually comes over and stays for three or four hours, but this time we had dinner, which we usually don't, so we're getting a late start. What time is it, eight-thirty? No, closer to nine. My guess is he won't stay past eleven-thirty.'

I asked what he was wearing, to make sure I

didn't follow the wrong guy. Designer jeans and a navy-blue polo shirt, she said. I suggested she could flick the lights on and off a half dozen times as soon as he left the apartment, and she said it was a great idea, but her apartment was in the rear of the building, so I'd never be able to see it from the street.

'But I may just do it anyway,' she said, 'because it's such a cool Mata Hari-type thing to do. Hey, wait a minute. Won't you have your cell phone with you? So why don't I just call you when he leaves? And then I'll flick the lights, too, just for fun.'

Her estimate wasn't off by much. It was twenty to twelve when my cell phone rang.

'Mata Hari speaking,' she said. 'He's all yours. I have to tell you, dinner was good but the dessert was better. Do me a favor, will you? Call me tomorrow to tell me that he's David Thompson and he's single and the only secret he's keeping from me is that he's fabulously wealthy.'

I told her I'd see what I could do, and then I rang off and the door opened and he came out. I'd probably have made him without the phone call. He was wearing jeans and a dark polo shirt, and the photo I had of him was a good likeness.

Tailing somebody is complicated enough when you've got a full team, half a dozen in cars and about as many on foot. I had TJ along for company, and an off-duty cabby named Leo whom I'd promised fifty bucks for a couple of hours of chauffeur duty.

Louise lived on the third floor of a brownstone on the uptown side of West Eighty-seventh Street between Broadway and West End. Like most odd-numbered streets, Eighty-seventh is one-way westbound. If David Thompson lived in or around Kips Bay, he'd probably take a cab home, and he'd probably walk to Broadway to catch it. The same was true if he wanted to go somewhere else by cab. If he wanted the subway, he'd catch it at Eighty-sixth and Broadway, so once again he'd be walking toward Broadway, and against the flow of traffic.

We'd set up accordingly. TJ and I were standing in the doorway of a building directly opposite Louise's, while Leo's car was parked next to a hydrant on Broadway. If a cop rousted him he'd circle the block, but it wasn't likely, not at that hour. All he had to do was say he was waiting on a fare.

When Thompson left the building, we'd tag him to Broadway, then get in Leo's car and follow whatever cab he hailed. If he walked down to Eighty-sixth and took the subway, TJ would go down into the tunnel after him. He'd try to stay in touch by cell phone, and we'd try to be there when he and Thompson got off the train.

So Thompson came out the door and down the stoop, looked at his watch, hauled out a cell phone, and made a call. At first no one answered, but then someone did, or voice mail kicked in, because he talked with animation for a moment or two before snapping it shut. He held it out, looked at it, then put it away, got out a cigarette and lit it, blew out a cloud of smoke, and started walking, but not toward Broadway. He headed the other way, toward West End Avenue.

Shit.

'Plan B,' I said, and took off after Thompson, while TJ sprinted to the corner of Broadway and around it to where Leo was waiting with the bulldog edition of the *Daily News* open on the steering wheel. He had the motor running before TJ was in his seat. New York's the one place in the country when you can't make a right turn at a red light, the traffic's just too chaotic for that to work here, but David Letterman pointed out once that New Yorkers think of traffic laws as guidelines, and Leo figures a grown man ought to be able to use his own judgment. He slid around the corner and picked me up halfway down the block.

I got in back, and Leo coasted to the corner, where the light was red against us. Thompson, when he reached the corner, could have stepped to the curb to flag a southbound taxi, or he might have crossed Eighty-seventh Street himself, or waited for the light and crossed West End and headed for Riverside Drive.

If he'd done any of those things we could have followed him with no trouble, but instead he turned right on West End and headed uptown. Leo might have been willing to push his luck and run another red light, but he'd be going the wrong way on a one-way street, and we couldn't do that.

'Son of a *bitch*,' he said with feeling.

'Shoot across to Riverside and come back on Eighty-eighth,' I said, opening the door and getting out again. 'I'll try to stay with him.'

By the time I got going he had a half-block lead on me, which shouldn't have been a problem, but I lost sight of him when he turned right at Eighty-eighth Street. I increased my pace and got to the corner where he'd turned and he was gone.

Leo, who ran us back to Ninth and Fifty-seventh, wouldn't take any money. 'I thought we was gonna have an adventure,' he said. ' "Follow that cab!" I thought I'd show off my driving skills and tail the bastard through parts of Brooklyn even Pete Hamill'd get lost in. All I did was drive around the fucking block.'

'It's not your fault I lost him.'

'No, it's his fault, for turning out to be such an elusive bastard. Put your money back in your pocket, Matt. Call me again sometime, and we'll have fun, and you can pay me double. But this one's on the house.'

He'd dropped us in front of the Morning Star, but neither of us felt like going there. We crossed the street to the Parc Vendôme and went upstairs. Elaine was on the couch with a novel Monica had recommended as a perfect guilty pleasure.

'She called it the prose equivalent of a three-handkerchief movie,' she said, 'and I have to say she was right. What's the matter?'

'The guy walked around the block and lost us,' I said.

'The nerve of the son of a bitch. You want something?'

'I wouldn't mind starting the night over,' I said, 'but that would be tricky. I don't want more coffee. I don't think I want anything. TJ?'

'Maybe a Coke,' he said, and went off to fetch it himself.

I joined him in the kitchen and the two of us tried to make sense out of what had happened to us up in the West Eighties. 'It's like he made us,' he said, 'but he didn't exactly act like it.'

'What I can't figure out,' I said, 'is how he disappeared like that.'

'Magician walks down the street and turns into a drugstore.'

'It was something like that, wasn't it? He wasn't that far ahead of me when he turned the corner. Maybe a hundred feet? Not much more than that, and I would have cut the distance some, because I walked faster once the corner building blocked my view of him. And then I got there and he was gone.'

'Even if he turns the corner and starts bookin', you'd get a look at him soon as you come round the corner yourself.'

'You would think so.'

134

''Less he ducked into that building.'

'The apartment house on the corner? I thought of that. The street door's not locked, anybody can get into the vestibule. Then you'd need a key, or for someone to buzz you in. I looked in and didn't see him, but I didn't do that right away, not until I'd spent some time trying to spot him on the street. You know, it seemed strange that he would walk to West End instead of Broadway, but if he lived there—'

'Then he just a man going home.'

'A man who lives around the corner from a woman and tells her he lives a couple of miles away in the East Thirties.'

'Maybe he don't want her coming over every other day to borrow a cup of sugar.'

'More likely a pack of cigarettes. I can see that, actually. You go fishing for a girlfriend online, hoping she doesn't live in the outer reaches of Brooklyn or Queens, some bus-and-subway combination away from you, and then you find out she's right around the corner, and you realize there's such a thing as too close.'

'I don't know,' he said. 'Wouldn't she recognize him? From seeing him in the neighborhood?'

'You'd think so. New Yorkers may not know our next-door neighbors, but we're generally able to recognize them by sight. He made a phone call, let's not forget that part.'

'Right before he lit up a cigarette.'

Elaine had come in to fix herself a cup of tea.

135

'He was phoning his wife,' she said, 'to find out if he should pick up a quart of milk on the way home.'

'Or a cup of sugar,' I said. 'Or a carton of Marlboros. If he was married, would he get himself a girlfriend around the corner?'

'Not unless he had a well-developed death wish,' she said. 'Who was he talking to on the phone, a man or a woman?'

'We couldn't even hear him,' I said.

'Couldn't you tell by his body language? Whether it was a man or a woman on the other end of the call?'

'No.'

'TJ?'

'I had to guess, I'd say a woman.'

'You would?' I said. 'Why?'

'Dunno.'

'He was just *with* a woman,' I said, 'and from what Louise said he gave a good account of himself. If he wasn't calling his wife to say he'd had to stay late at the office—'

'And he wouldn't,' TJ said, 'not if he lived five minutes away. He'd just show up.'

'You're right. So it wasn't a wife he called.'

''Less it was somebody else's wife.'

'Jesus,' I said.

'He could have called his wife,' Elaine said. 'In Scarsdale, to say he'd be late, or that he wasn't going to make it home at all. And then he went to the building around the corner.'

'Who's in the building around the corner?'

'I don't know,' she said. 'You're the detective.'

'Thanks.'

TJ said, 'Could be another woman.'

'In the corner building?'

'Everybody got to be someplace.'

'So he's two-timing Louise with somebody who lives around the corner from her?'

'Three-timing, if he got that wife in Scarsdale.'

'Maybe she's a working girl,' Elaine offered.

'Louise? I honestly don't think—'

'Not Louise. The late date, the woman around the corner. Maybe she's in the game.'

'But he was just with Louise.'

'So?'

'From what she said—'

'He screwed her brains out?'

'Not the words she used,' I said, 'but that was the general impression I got, yeah.'

'Maybe the earth moved for her but not for him. Or maybe he was going for the hat trick. That's what, hockey?'

I nodded. 'When one player scores three goals in a game.'

'I knew it was three goals, I just couldn't remember if it was hockey or soccer.'

'It's migrated into other sports, but it's a hockey term.'

'I wonder where it comes from. Anyway, if he knows a working girl right around the corner from Louise, why not drop over and see her?'

I summoned up the image of him in front of

137

Louise's brownstone, phone in hand. 'He didn't have to look up her number,' I said. 'But he'd have it on his speed dial, wouldn't he?'

'Probably. That's what people have nowadays, instead of a little black book.'

'If he was still in the mood,' I said, 'why didn't he just stay upstairs a little longer?'

'Gee, I don't know,' she said. 'Do you suppose it could be that Y chromosome he's been carrying around all his life?'

'In other words, he's a guy.'

'When I was working,' she said, 'I'd have johns who would get themselves off before they came over, so they could last longer. I had one who was the opposite, he wanted me to keep him right on the edge for like an hour or more and not let him get off at all, so he could go home and give his wife a bounce she wouldn't forget. That one baffled me, I've got to say. I felt like a picador at a bullfight.'

I glanced at TJ to see what he made of her remembrance of things past. If it had any impact on him, it didn't show on his face. He knew about her career history, he and Monica were about the only people we saw regularly who did, but she rarely talked about it in his presence as she was dong now.

TJ had never known his own mother. She'd died when he was less than a year old, and his grandmother had raised him until her own death. Things she'd told him had led TJ to speculate that his

138

mother had been a working girl, and that he himself might have been a trick baby, an unplanned bonus from an unwitting client. No way to tell, he'd said, and he seemed comfortable enough with not knowing.

But the conversation had lost its way, having essentially abandoned David Thompson for a dissertation on the Men Are Strange theme. I said, 'I'm not convinced he went into that building.'

'It might have been another one?'

'Or no building at all. Maybe he knew he was being followed.'

'He wouldn't,' TJ said, ''less he was suspicious to start with. You think he picked up something from Louise?'

'Not if he used a condom,' Elaine said.

'If he's married,' I said, 'he might have suspected his wife was having him followed. That could have made him wary enough to sense us.'

'Way he stood there lighting that cigarette,' TJ said. 'Like he wanted a minute to figure out what to do as much as he wanted that nicotine hit.'

'So he turned right instead of left,' I said, 'and turned right again at West End, turned against traffic. Then he ducked into a building, or found a doorway or an alleyway to hide in.'

'Why would he do that? To shake the two of you, obviously, but why? Wouldn't it be suspicious behavior, and wouldn't you think the last thing he'd want to do if he thinks his wife is having him followed is act suspicious?'

''Less it's more important that she don't know where he's going next.'

I said, 'Maybe there was a cab there. Around the corner on Eighty-eighth.'

'He had a cab waiting for him?'

'No, but there could have been one standing there, discharging a fare. And he could have grabbed it and been on his way by the time I turned the corner.'

'Wouldn't you have seen a cab driving away?'

'If I was looking for it. If it was already halfway down the block, and I was looking around for a man on foot, well, I might not have noticed it. Or he could have had a car parked there.'

'And started it up and pulled out without being seen? Only if you was limpin' round the corner.'

'He could have parked there,' I said, 'and got in and pulled the door shut, but not started up. Because he didn't want to be spotted.'

'Or because he had something to do first,' Elaine offered, 'like make a phone call or look up an address.'

'Or smoke another cigarette,' I said, 'or anything at all. There's too much we don't know and too many avenues for speculation.'

'Plus all the side streets,' TJ said.

We batted it back and forth a little more, and Elaine said he sounded to her like a man with something to hide, and her guess would be that he was a sex addict. That was a new term, she added, for what used to be just a guy who liked

140

to party, or what earlier generations had called a good-time Charlie, or a gentleman with an eye for the ladies.

That got us talking about how the world didn't cut you much slack anymore, how yesterday's pastimes were today's pathologies. TJ finished his Coke and went home.

'Leo wouldn't take any money,' I told Elaine, 'and neither will I. Tonight's not going to come out of Louise's retainer.'

'The $500? Didn't that get used up a while ago?'

'I've barely put a dent in it.'

'You're a real hard-nosed businessman, aren't you?'

'The money doesn't really matter.'

'I know that, baby.'

'I just want to see if I can figure it out,' I said. 'It shouldn't be that hard.'

CHAPTER 11

He holds the bronze letter opener in his hands, turns it over, runs a finger over the design in low relief on the handle. A pack of hounds are holding a stag at bay. It is, he notes, quite artfully executed.

The woman, every bit as artfully executed as the letter opener, stands patiently on the other side of the counter. He asks her what she can tell him about the piece.

'Well, it's a paper knife, of course. Art Nouveau, probably French but possibly Belgian.'

'Belgian?'

'It's signed,' she says. 'On the reverse.' He turns it over and she hands him a magnifying glass with a staghorn handle. 'It's hard to see with the naked eye, or at least with my naked eye. See?'

'DeVreese.'

'Godfrey DeVreese,' she says, 'or Godefroid, if you prefer. I'm not sure which he'd have preferred. He was Belgian. I had a bronze medallion of his for years, a gorgeous thing, a good three and a half inches in diameter. Leopold the Second on one side, with a beard that was a hell of a lot nobler than the man sporting it. You know about Leopold the Second?'

He grins easily. 'I would suppose,' he says, 'that he came between Leopold the First and Leopold the Third.'

'Actually his successor was his son, Albert. Leopold Three came a little later on. Number Two was the gentle fellow who ran the Belgian Congo as his personal fief. He treated the local residents as slaves, and he'd have had more respect for the inhabitants of an ant farm. Remember all those photos of natives with their hands chopped off?'

What can she be she talking about? 'It rings a bell,' he says.

'But he looked good,' she says, 'especially in bronze. There was a horse on the other side, and he looked even better than Leo. It was a draft horse, one of those big boys you don't see anymore outside of a Budweiser commercial. Except this one was a Percheron and the Budweiser horses are Clydesdales. The medal was an award from some sort of agricultural fair. Probably the turn-of-the-century equivalent of a tractor-pulling contest.'

'You still have the medallion?'

'I thought I was going to own it forever, but some horse collector spotted it a few months ago and away it went. I'll probably never see another one like it.'

He turns the letter opener in his hands. It's quite beautiful, and he likes the heft of it.

'You said turn-of-the-century?'

'I suppose DeVreese would have said fin de siècle. Or the equivalent in Flemish, whatever that might be. I can't date it precisely, I'm afraid, but it would have to be late nineteenth or early twentieth century.'

'So it's about a hundred years old.'

'Give or take.'

He tests the point with his thumb. It's quite sharp. The blade's edges are not. It will serve to open a letter, but you couldn't slice with it.

You could stab, however.

'May I ask the price?'

'It's two hundred dollars.'

'That seems high.'

'I know,' she says disarmingly.

'Do you suppose I could get a discount?'

She considers this. 'If you pay cash,' she says, 'I could absorb the sales tax.'

'So that would be two hundred dollars even as opposed to what, two-sixteen?'

'A few dollars more than that, actually. If you want I could look it up for you, so you'll know to the penny how much you're saving.'

'But what I'd be paying,' he says, 'is two hundred dollars.'

'And in return you'd be getting a piece of history.'

'It's always nice to get a piece' – just the slightest pause here – 'of history.' Has she even noticed the pause? This would seem to be a woman who doesn't miss much, and his sense is that she took it in and decided to overlook it, all without any of this registering on her face.

He frowns, has another look at the bas-relief, notes the steadfast determination of both the hounds and their quarry. It would be the work of a moment, he thinks, to wrap his hand around the handle, to strike without warning. He visualizes the act, the underhand thrust, the sharpened bronze tip entering just below the lowest rib and reaching up for the heart. Visualizes himself turning and moving to the door before she slips to the floor behind the counter, even before the life fades from her eyes.

But he's touched things. His prints are all over the top surface of the showcase, and nothing holds a print better than glass.

'I think I'd like to have it.'

'I don't blame you.'

Besides, it would be too quick. It would be over before she knew it, and that can be very satisfying sometimes, the quick kill, but in this instance he'd want her to see it coming, want to watch her lose that confidence, that irritating self-possession.

His loins stir at the thought of what he'll do to her, when the time comes.

But none of this shows in his face as he sighs with resignation and counts bills from his wallet. She takes the money, wraps the letter opener in tissue paper, tucks it into a paper bag. He tells her he won't need a receipt, then slips his purchase into the inside breast pocket of his jacket.

'Thanks,' she says. 'Just so you know, I don't think

you paid too much. They'd ask something like five hundred in a shop on Madison Avenue.'

He smiles, murmurs something, heads for the door. But oh, Christ, how he wants to kill her! He doesn't want to wait. He wants to kill her right now.

CHAPTER 12

I didn't much want to give my client a report of the night's proceedings, and not just because it might leave her wondering if she'd hired an incompetent. More to the point, any suggestion that her Mr Thompson had given me the slip would imply that he was not what he appeared, that he had something to hide. That's how it felt to me, but it would be premature to pass that perception to Louise.

'Nothing conclusive,' I told her. 'I should be able to tell you more in a day or so.'

I found Thompson's number in my notebook, called him on my cell phone. I hoped he wouldn't answer and felt relieved when I got his Voice Mail. 'Hey, man,' I said. 'We sent you a check, payment in full, and I've got it right here in front of me. It came back, we've got the wrong address for you. Oh, shit, I've got to take that. Listen, ring me back, if I don't answer just leave your address on my voice mail. And while you're at it – oh, hell, never mind. Later.'

I'd tried to sound rushed, like some middle-management guy with everything happening at

147

once, and I couldn't tell if I'd pulled it off. I'd know more when he did or didn't call me back.

I had my cell phone in my pocket when I left the house, but I paused on the sidewalk to turn it off. I was on my way to a meeting, and you have to turn off cell phones and pagers there; at most groups they make an announcement to that effect. But I wanted mine off, meeting or no meeting, because the last thing I wanted was to answer a call and have David Thompson on the other end of the line. The first thing he'd do was ask who I was and what company the check was from, and I'd be stuck for an answer. If he got my voice mail there'd be nobody to ask, and he'd figure somebody owed him money and he might as well collect it, and he'd leave his address.

This was assuming that at least a portion of his story was true, that he was in some sort of business in the course of which companies sent him checks. It might or might not be direct marketing, and his name might or might not be David Thompson, which was why I'd been as vague as I had in my message to him.

It ought to work. And if it failed, it would simply have succeeded in another direction. If he was that suspicious, then he really did have something to hide.

I walked up to the Y on West Sixty-third and caught the noon meeting of the Fireside group. The speaker told an abbreviated drinking story and spent most of her time talking about her current dilemma, which was whether or not to face that acting wasn't working for her, that two lines in a Rolaids commercial and a few dozen days as an extra, along with nonpaying roles in showcase productions that nobody came to, wasn't all that much to show for five years of devotion to the profession.

'I'm not an actress, I'm a waitress,' she said, 'and that's okay, there's nothing wrong with it, it's a respectable way to make a living, but I'm not sure it's what I want to do with my life. I'm not even so sure anymore that acting's what I want to do with my life, as if anyone's going to give me a chance to do it.'

Abie was there; I hadn't seen him since Ray Gruliow spoke at St Paul's, and he said he'd been mostly going to noon meetings lately, plus one night he'd been booked to speak out in Middle Village. I had lunch around the corner with him and two women, an office temp named Rachel and a sharp-faced young woman who worked as a substitute teacher when she worked at all, which I gathered wasn't very often. I never did catch her name.

Whoever she was, she didn't waste any time taking the speaker's inventory. 'The nice thing about all that theatrical training,' she said, 'is that she speaks distinctly and with expression, and you can sit in the last row and hear every word. Unfortunately, every word is me me me.'

Rachel said she looked familiar, and maybe she'd

seen her in something. Abie said she didn't look familiar to him, and that was odd, because he never missed a Rolaids commercial.

'She said she had two lines,' Rachel said, 'but maybe it was a voice-over, and she wasn't on camera at all.' It was hard to tell if she was taking him literally or matching his irony with her own.

I didn't get around to turning on my cell phone until I was back home, and there was a voice mail message waiting for me. A voice I hadn't heard before said, 'Hey, thanks, man. Here's the address.' I wrote it down: 755 Amsterdam #1217, New York NY 10025. 'Don't forget the suite number,' he said, 'or it won't get here. That's probably what happened the last time.'

In Manhattan, the numbered streets run east and west, and the numbers start at Fifth Avenue. If you know the house number, you can readily tell what avenues it lies between.

The avenues run north and south, and each one has a different numbering system, depending where it starts. But there's a key, printed in street maps and pocket atlases, and to be found in most editions of the White and Yellow Pages. There are slight variations for certain thoroughfares, but the basic idea is that you take the address, drop the last digit, divide the result by two, add the particular number listed for that particular avenue, and the result is the nearest cross street.

Some realtor had had the table printed on a wallet-sized plastic card, and it was a better give-away than a calendar, because I'd had mine five years now and used it all the time. The realtor wouldn't get much business from me, nothing was going to move us from the Parc Vendôme, but she had my thanks, whatever that was worth.

And I in turn had the knowledge that the address I had for David Thompson was a block or two north of Ninety-sixth Street. That was a little more than a half mile from the corner of West End and Eighty-eighth, and a whole lot farther from Kips Bay.

I got there on the subway, walked a block east from Broadway, and found 755 Amsterdam where Amalia Ferrante's card said it should be, right in the middle of the block between Ninety-seventh and Ninety-eighth. The building was a five-story tene-ment, not yet noticeably affected by gentrification, but something was wrong, because even if they'd chopped it up into a rabbit warren over the years, there was no way there could be an apartment numbered 1217.

Maybe it was Thompson's idea of a code; when an envelope came with #1217 on it, he'd know it was from the man who'd called him. But that didn't make sense either.

I went into the vestibule and looked at the row of buzzers. There were sixteen, which worked out to four to a floor for floors two through five, with the ground floor given over to a store. Nine or ten of the sixteen had a name in the slot provided for that purpose. The rest were empty. I checked the names, and most were Hispanic. None was Thompson.

I went outside again and took a look at the store on the ground floor. It wasn't terribly inviting, with the merchandise on display faded by time or bleached by the sun, but it tried to make up for that by offering everything a marginal neighborhood could require – check cashing, passport photos, notary public, hardware and housewares, umbrellas, shoe polish, Pampers, and assorted snacks. Three neon beer signs, one for a brand they'd stopped making ten years ago, shared window space with a Café Bustelo poster. There was so much going on that it took me a while to notice the only relevant item in the window, a yellowing sheet of paper with the hand-lettered inscription PRIVATE MAILBOXES AVAILABLE.

The inside of the store was about what you'd expect. I didn't see any mailboxes, and wondered where all twelve hundred and seventeen of them could be hiding. A woman behind the counter, with a stocky build and hair like black Brillo, was keeping an eye on me. I don't know what she thought I could possibly want to steal.

I asked if she had mailboxes for rent and she nodded. I said I didn't see them. Could she show me where they were?

'Is not a mail *box*,' she said, framing a box with her hands, the sides, the top and bottom. 'Is a mail *service*.'

'How does it work?'

'You pay for the month, an' you get a number, an' you come in an' tell me your number an' I bring you your mail.'

'How much does the service cost?'

'Not so much. Fifty dollars. You pay three months in advance, you get the fourth month free.'

I flipped open my wallet and showed her a card Joe Durkin had given me. It was a Detectives Endowment Association courtesy card, and it wouldn't keep a meter maid from tagging you for parking too close to a hydrant, but it looked official enough from a distance. 'I'm interested in one of your customers,' I said. 'His number is twelve-seventeen. That's one two one seven.'

She looked at me.

'You know his name?'

She shook her head.

'You want to look it up for me?'

She thought about it, shrugged, went in the back room. When she returned her broad forehead was creased with a deep frown. I asked her what was the matter.

'No name,' she said.

I thought she couldn't tell me, but that wasn't it. She meant she didn't have a name to go with the number, and I believed her. Her puzzlement over the situation was evident.

I said, 'If there's any mail for him—'

'That's why I take so long. If there is mail for him, there is his name on it, yes? No mail for him.

He come in one, two times a week. Sometimes mail, sometimes no mail.'

'And when he comes in he tells you his number.'

'Twelve-seventeen. An' I give him his mail.'

'And when he gets a letter, is there a name on the envelope?'

'I don't pay attention.'

'If you heard the name, would you recognize it?'

'Maybe. I don't know.'

'Is the name David Thompson?'

'I don't know. Is not José Jiménez. He's Anglo, but that's all I know.'

She excused herself, waited on another customer. She came back and said, 'You buy the service, you get a number, we write your name in the book. Next to the number.'

'And there's no name in the book next to 1217.'

'No name. Maybe he come in the first time when somebody else is working, somebody who forgets to write down the name. Is not right, but . . .' She shrugged, shook her head. I think it bothered her more than it did me.

I'd brought along the photo Louise gave me, and I took it out and showed it to her. Her eyes lit up.

'Yes!'

'It's him?'

'Is him. Twelve-seventeen.'

'But you don't know his name.'

'No.'

I gave her a card. Next time he got a letter, I told her, she should call me and read me the name off the envelope. She said she'd do that, and held my card as if it were a pearl of great price. She craned her neck, took another look at the photograph.

She said, 'He do something bad, this man?'

'Not that I know of,' I said. 'I just need to know who he is.'

I got home before Elaine did. She called ahead to say she was running a little late, could I put a pot of water on the stove? I did, and lit a fire under it, and it was boiling when she walked in the door. She tossed a salad and made pasta, and we left the dishes in the sink and walked down Ninth to a small off-Broadway house on Forty-second Street, where we had complimentary tickets for a staged reading of a play called *Riga*, about the destruction of the Latvian Jews. I knew the playwright from around the rooms, that's why we were there, and after the curtain we congratulated him and told him how powerful it was.

'Too powerful,' he said. 'Nobody wants to produce it.'

On the way home Elaine said, 'Gee, I can't imagine why anybody would pass up a chance to produce that play. Why, it just makes a person feel good all over.'

'I'm glad we saw it, though.'

'I don't know if I am or not. I'm afraid it's all going to happen again.'

'You don't mean that.'

'The hell I don't. There are whole sections of the

155

Times I can't read anymore. Anything with national or international news. I can manage the Arts section, except half the time the Book Review's as bad as a news story. The Tuesday Science section's okay, and the Wednesday one with the recipes and restaurants. I never want to go to the restaurants or try the recipes, but I can stand to read it.'

'It's a shame you're not interested in sports.'

'Yeah, it'd be something I could keep up on and not wind up thinking about Prozac. Does TJ read the business section?'

'I think so.'

'Maybe he'll support us in our old age. If we have one.'

I stepped to the curb, held up a hand. A cab pulled up.

She said, 'I thought we were walking. What's the matter, don't you feel well, baby?'

'Not well enough to walk fifty blocks.' I told the driver to go up Tenth Avenue, that we wanted Amsterdam and Ninety-third.

'Mother Blue's?'

'I was just a few blocks from there this afternoon,' I said, 'but there's no reason to go there at that hour. At night it's got music.'

'And Danny Boy.'

'Unless tonight's one of his nights at Poogan's. Either way, I think we should go listen to some music.'

'I suppose you're right,' she said. 'I suppose that's a better idea than going home and killing ourselves.'

CHAPTER 13

Downstairs, he gives his name. He gets off the elevator to find her framed in the doorway of her apartment, leaning a little against the doorjamb. She's wearing a belted silk robe with a bold floral pattern. Her slippers are open-toed, and the polish on her toenails is blood red, a match for her lipstick.

He's carrying a briefcase, and he's also brought a bouquet from the Korean greengrocer, a bottle from the liquor store. 'These will pale beside your robe,' he tells her, handing her the flowers.

'Do you like it? I can't decide whether it's elegant or trashy.'

'Why can't it be both?'

'Sometimes I ask the same question of myself. These are lovely, darling. I'll put them in water.'

She fills a vase at the sink, arranges the flowers in it, puts them on the mantel. He unwraps the bottle and shows it to her.

'Strega,' she reads. 'What is it, a cordial?'

'A postprandial libation. Italian, of course. *Strega* means witch.'

'Moi?'

'You're certainly enchanting.'

'And you're a sweetie.'

She comes into his arms and they kiss. Her body, lush and full-breasted, presses against him. She's naked under the robe, and he draws her close and runs a hand down her back, stroking her bottom.

He's hard already, in anticipation. He's been like that all day, on and off.

'This is such a nice surprise,' she says. 'Two nights in a row. You'll spoil me.'

'I have very little free time,' he says. 'I've told you that.'

'Yes.'

'And it's unpredictable. Sometimes I have to go away for months at a stretch.'

'It must be a difficult life.'

'It has its moments. When I do have time to myself, I try to spend it in the most enjoyable way possible. And that's why I'm here again tonight.'

'Believe me, I wasn't complaining. Shall we sample the Strega? I don't believe I've ever had any. Or would you rather have Scotch?'

He says he'll try the cordial, that he hasn't had it in years. She finds a pair of suitable glasses and pours drinks for both of them, and they touch glasses and sip.

'Nice. A very complicated flavor, isn't it? Herbs, but I can't tell which ones. How clever you were to bring this.'

'Perhaps we can take our drinks to the bedroom.'

'More than clever,' she says. 'The man's a genius.'

In her bedroom he embraces her, draws the robe from her shoulders. She's a few years older than he, and her body is that of a mature woman, but diet and exercise have kept her in good shape, and her skin is lovely, soft as velvet.

He removes his own clothes quickly, puts them on a chair. 'Oh, my,' she says, in mock horror. 'You're not going to put that big thing in me, are you?'

'Not right away.'

She's very responsive, has been since their first time together. He brings her to orgasm first with his fingers, then with his mouth.

'My God,' she says, after her second climax. 'My God, I think you're going to kill me.'

'Oh, not just yet,' he says.

He has her in a variety of postures, moving her from one to another, slipping out of her after each orgasm and taking her again in a new position. No effort is required for him to postpone his own climax. It will wait for the right moment.

At one point she takes him in her mouth. She's good at this, and he lets her perform for a good length of time, then rolls her onto her stomach, preps her with a lubricant from the nightstand, and eases himself into her ass. They've done this before, they did it last night, in fact, and he'd gotten her to touch herself in front and make herself come.

Tonight she does so without being told.

She learns quickly, he thinks. He could probably get her to do anything he wants, and the thought is intriguing. Should he draw this out, keep her around for a few more days or weeks?

No, it's time.

'Darling? Is there something I can do?'

'You're doing fine,' he says.

'But I want you to come.'

'You can come for both of us.'

'I never came so much in my life, but it's not fair. Now it's your turn.'

'I'm having a good time.'

'I know you are, but—'

'I don't need to have an orgasm to be satisfied.'

'That's what you said last night.'

'It was true then and it's true now.'

'But it thrills me when you come,' she says, her hand on him. 'I love it, and you seem to enjoy it yourself.'

'Well, of course.'

'So tell me if there's something I can do.'

'Well . . .'

'You're not going to shock me,' she says. 'I didn't just get out of a convent.'

'No, I don't suppose you did.'

'There's something, isn't there? Look, as long as it doesn't involve bloodshed or broken bones, I'm up for it.'

He hesitates, largely to enjoy the line she's just delivered. Then he says, 'Well, how would it be if I tied you up?'

'Oh, wow.'

160

'Of course, if it's too unsettling for you—'

'No, just the opposite. The whole idea's a turn-on.' Her hand tightens on him. 'For you, too, I can see. My God.'

'Well, it does add a little something.'

'The old je ne sais quoi, the French call it. I, uh, don't have any special equipment for it.'

'I, uh, do.'

'Well, aren't you the devil!'

He fetches the briefcase, opens it. They make a game of it, attaching the silk cuffs to her wrists and ankles, positioning her on the bed with a pillow under her bottom, fastening the cords, also silken, that secure her wrists and ankles to the bed's four corners. Her eyes widen as he shows her some of the paraphernalia he's brought. She looks excited, and he touches her, and yes, she's wet, but then she's always wet, this one, always ready and willing and able.

He flicks the riding crop across her abdomen. It hurts a little, he notes, but she likes it.

So far.

'My God,' she said, 'you must have bought out the Pleasure Chest. You really are a devil.'

He opens a condom, puts it on.

'Darling, you don't need one of those. Why would you use one now? Oh, don't tell me that's why you haven't let yourself come! That's so sweet, but the last thing you have to worry about is getting me pregnant. I'm afraid those years are over.'

He's beginning to tire of listening to her. So why

161

not put an end to her prattling? He tears off a strip of duct tape, pins her head with one hand, tapes her mouth with the other. This is unexpected, and not entirely welcome, and he watches her eyes as she begins to realize the extent of her helplessness.

But that could be part of the turn-on. She's not sure yet.

He gives her a look at the letter opener. Her eyes widen, and she'd gape if her mouth weren't taped shut.

He gets on the bed with her, grips her breast, presses firmly with the letter opener until its point breaks the skin at the outer rim of the aureole. A bead of blood flows from the spot, and he takes it on the top of his index finger and shows it to her.

Oh, my, the look in her eyes . . .

'No bloodshed, you said, and I let you believe I agreed. A lie of omission, I'm afraid. You will be shedding some blood tonight after all.'

He puts his finger in his mouth and tastes her blood, relishing it, relishing too the look on her face as she watches him do it. Did she read Dracula at an impressionable age? Did she find it erotic, as so many girls seem to do?

He uses the letter opener, enlarges the wound. He puts his mouth to it and sucks blood from her, letting it fill his mouth, letting it flow down his throat. He loves the taste of blood, loves the whole idea of drinking it. The vampire myth is a powerful one, composed largely of nonsense, of course, like all myths. Eternal life, a need to shun daylight, to sleep in a coffin – amusing, certainly, but ridiculous.

And yet the satisfactions and benefits of blood would seem to transcend myth. What could be more nourishing than this vehicle that carries the very life force of its owner? Of course it rejuvenates the person who swallows it. How could it be otherwise?

He sucks greedily, careful not to yield to the impulse to bite the soft flesh. Bundy was a biter, he left tooth marks in his victims, and might have dodged Old Sparky if he hadn't. There will be no tooth marks in this plump titty, toothsome though it unquestionably is.

She's struggling against the bonds, trying to cry out against the strip of duct tape. It's futile, of course. There's nothing she can do.

He, on the other hand, may do as he will.

He props himself up, his face close to hers. 'You never should have let me tie you up,' he says, his tone conversational. 'But don't blame yourself. The die was cast the moment you opened the door. If you'd said no, if you'd tried to resist, well, it wouldn't have done you any good. There would have been a struggle, and you'd have lost, and you'd wind up just as you are now, restrained and helpless.'

He runs a hand over her flesh. Age may have softened her some, and gravity may have had an effect, but it's left her with wonderfully soft skin.

'How many times did you come this evening? I lost count. I hope you had a good time. Because

163

I don't think you're going to enjoy the rest of this. I don't think you're going to care for it at all.'

The *coup de grace* (though it's not much of a *coup*, and a little late in the day for grace) is performed with the letter opener, of course, and it's essentially the same blow he'd wanted to deliver to the woman in the shop, a deliberate thrust from just below the rib cage arcing upward into the heart. He's inside her at the moment, and he tries to time his climax to coincide with her death, but the body insists on following its own timetable, and perhaps its wisdom is the greater.

Because this way his attention is fixed entirely upon the blade in his hand and the look in her eyes, and he feels her heart at the tip of the blade, feels it allow itself to be pierced, sees the light die in her eyes, and feels the life go out of her. And surely she's a part of him now, as are all of them, all the ones he's taken. Surely her loss is his gain, her pain his pleasure, her death his life.

And now he finishes, moving slowly now, slowly, tantalizingly, within the envelope of lifeless flesh, until at last there's no holding back, no choice but surrender, and he cries out in pain or joy as he reaches his goal.

Fortunately, there's no hurry. He's eager to get away, to put distance between himself and the dead woman, but he knows not to rush his departure. He wants to leave no traces, or at least to keep them to a minimum. The police will give his efforts their full attention, and their forensic capability is legendary. It is very much in his interest to provide them with as little to work with as possible.

He's had two orgasms, one well before her death, one in its immediate aftermath, and has consequently filled two condoms. Both are knotted now, his DNA secured within. He can flush them down the toilet, surely the plumbing in a New York apartment building will be equal to the task, but suppose one gets caught in a clogged trap? Safer to pop the pair into a Ziploc bag, which can join the wrist and ankle restraints, the silk cords, the riding crop, and the rest of the Pleasure Chest playthings in his briefcase.

There's not much blood. Her breast bled some, beyond what he sucked from it, and he has managed to get some of it on his own chest and forearms. The final wound, the piercing and stopping of her heart, never had a chance to bleed, and the letter opener is still buried in her heart.

First a shower. But, as preparation, he's brought along a five-inch square of fine-mesh screening, sold to enable a do-it-yourselfer to repair a hole in a window screen. He places this over the drain in the tub and secures it with duct tape. Any head or body hair, any trace evidence that might wind up in the trap, will now be prevented from reaching the drain in the first place.

He showers thoroughly, using her soap, her shampoo and conditioner. He uses a big blue bath towel, bagging it when he's finished for removal and safe disposal. He takes up the square of screening and the tape he used to hold it in place, and bags them as well.

In a closet he finds a vacuum cleaner. Will neighbors hear the vacuum running? Perhaps, and so what if they do? He vacuums the floors throughout the large one-bedroom apartment, then changes attachments and vacuums the bed, body and all.

Hair is the enemy, hair and sweat and other secretions. He imagines, not for the first time, how absurdly easy it must have been for a criminal a century or more ago, before DNA, before blood types, before ballistics, before forensics was a word, let alone a science. It was a wonder that anyone ever got caught.

And, really, how many did? Of the bright ones, the planners, the *Übermenschen* of murder? There must have been a multitude who got away with it, even as he gets away with it, year after year after year.

He bathed before coming here, bathed and shampooed, but one is forever losing hairs, shedding skin cells. He's just finishing the vacuuming when he remembers that he was here the previous night, and God knows what hair and skin cells he may have left behind. And she's changed the sheets since then, hasn't she?

He finds yesterday's sheets in the hamper, bundles them up, and, for good measure, adds everything else in the clothes hamper. A small detail, probably an unnecessary precaution, but why take a chance?

166

She keeps her cash, he discovers, in the drawer with her underclothes. It's not a fortune, less than a thousand dollars, but he can find a use for it, and she manifestly cannot. He's had expenses – $200 for the bronze paper knife, as much again for the erotic paraphernalia, plus the cost of the bottle and the bouquet. With her cash in his wallet, the night's work becomes a self-liquidating enterprise. Except, of course, that hers is the self that's been liquidated.

Next he wipes the place down for fingerprints. He hasn't touched much, tonight or on previous visits. He wipes the bottle of Strega, and both of their glasses. He retrieves from her liquor cabinet the bottle of Glenmorangie Scotch she bought for him, pours and downs a drink, wipes and replaces the bottle. He leaves the vase of flowers on the mantel. He never touched the vase, and flowers won't hold a print.

But paper will, and he had his hands all over the paper they were wrapped in. He finds it in the kitchen wastebasket, adds it to one of his bags of trash.

Throughout this entire process he's been naked. Now, the job done, he puts on the clothes he'd left on the chair in the bedroom. He gathers everything he means to take away with him and lines it up alongside the apartment's front door. Is he done? Can he go now?

One more thing.

He picks up a manicure scissors from the top of

her dresser, uses the wall-mounted magnifying mirror, and clips three hairs from his mustache. He leaves one on the bedsheet, alongside her right arm, and drops the other two into her nest of pubic hair. *Voilà!*

CHAPTER 14

Mother Blue's was either half full or half empty, depending I suppose on whether or not you had money in the joint. It's a rarity these days, a jazz club away from Midtown and SoHo and the Village, and not many out-of-towners find their way to it. Its clientele is an even-up mix of people who come from all over the city for the music, and neighborhood locals who don't object to the music, and find it a pleasant place to kick back and get a buzz. It was always a pretty even mix of black and white, but lately the mixture's been liberally spiced with Asians.

Danny Boy's there three or four nights a week, giving the rest of his custom to Poogan's Pub, on West Seventy-second between Columbus and Amsterdam. There's no music at Poogan's, except what sneaks out of the jukebox, and if there's any charm to it beyond a certain raffish straight-forwardness, I've never spotted it. I only go to Poogan's if I'm looking for Danny Boy, but I'll go to Mother Blue's just for the music.

Danny Boy was at a table close to the bandstand,

and he saw us before we saw him. He was smiling when my eyes picked him up, and beckoning us to his table.

He said, 'Matt and Elaine. Sit down, sit down. This is Jodie. Jodie, Matt and Elaine.'

Jodie was Chinese, with utterly straight shoulder-length black hair and small perfect features in an oval face. She looked privately amused during the introductions, and indeed throughout the evening. I couldn't decide if everything amused her or it was just her natural expression.

'They're on their break,' Danny said, with a nod at the bandstand. 'You've heard the rhythm section here.' He named the musicians. 'And there's a tenor player with them, and he's very current, but I swear there are moments when he reminds me of Ben Webster. He's a kid, I don't know if he ever even heard of Ben Webster, and he certainly never caught a live performance, but wait and see if he doesn't sound just like him.'

I've never known anyone like Danny Boy Bell, but then neither has anybody else. He's barely five feet tall, small enough to buy his clothes in the boys' department at Barneys, although for the past twenty years he's had his suits made by a visiting Hong Kong tailor, which doesn't cost any more and spares him embarrassment, along with the nuisance of leaving the house before dark. He's the albino son of black West Indian parents, and strong light is hard on his eyes and bad for his skin. He spends the daylight hours in his apartment, reading or sleeping or on the phone, and his nights at Poogan's or Mother Blue's.

His business is information. Most of his contacts have yellow sheets, but an arrest record doesn't necessarily make a criminal. They are, I suppose, of the underworld, though Elaine thinks the French word *demimonde* is more suitable, if only because it's French. Players and working girls, gamblers and grifters, people working angles or being worked by them, they all tend to turn up at Danny Boy's table or call him on the phone. Sometimes he pays out money for the information he's furnished, but this doesn't happen often, and the sums are generally small. More often he pays his sources in favors, or in other information, if at all, as many people tell him things just to get the word around.

He was a source of mine on the job, and our relationship continued after I gave back my badge. We've become good friends over the forty years I've known him, and I think I've already said that I met Elaine at his table.

Elaine told him he was looking well, and he shook his head sadly. 'The first time anybody said that to me,' he said, 'is the day I first realized I was getting older. You ever hear anybody tell a kid in his twenties he's looking well? Take Jodie here, she looks positively gorgeous, and I'll tell her that, but I wouldn't think of telling her she's looking well. Look at her, she's got skin like a China doll, you should pardon the expression. It'll be twenty years before she has to hear somebody say she's looking well.'

'I take it back, Danny.'

'No, don't do that, Elaine. I'm an *alter kocker*, that's no secret, and at my age it does my heart good to hear I'm looking well. Especially from a beautiful young thing like yourself.'

'Thanks, but I've been looking well for a few years myself.'

'You're still a sweet young thing. Ask your husband, if you don't believe me. Matt, is this just social? I hope so, but if there's any business we should get it out of the way before the band comes back.'

'Just social,' I said. 'We're hoping the music will change our mood. We went to a play about the Holocaust, and Elaine left the theater convinced it was just Act One.'

He took it in, nodded. 'I don't look at the world any more than I have to,' he said, 'but what I see I don't like much.'

Elaine asked him if he was still keeping his list.

'Oh, Jesus,' he said. 'You know about that?'

'Matt told me.'

A few years ago Danny Boy had surgery for colon cancer, and whatever they give you afterward. Chemo, I guess. He was up and about again by the time I heard about it, but it gave him a peek at mortality to which he responded in an interesting fashion: He made a list of everybody

172

he'd known who had died, starting with a kid at his school who'd been hit by a car. By the time I left his table that night it was a struggle to keep from making a mental list of my own.

Now, years later, both our lists would be longer.

'I gave it up,' he said, 'when enough time passed without a recurrence so that I actually began to believe I might beat the damn thing. But what really did it was the Trade Center. Two days after the towers came down, the guy on the corner, for twenty years now he sells me a newspaper every night on my way home, now he tells me how his kid was in the North Tower on the same fucking floor that the plane hit. If you took a deep breath that day you got some of him in your lungs. I knew the kid, when he was younger he used to spend Saturday nights helping his old man with the Sunday *Times*, putting all the sections together. Tommy, his name was. I went home, I was gonna put him on my list, and I thought, Danny, what the fuck do you think you're doing? They're dying out there faster than you can write them down.'

'I'm glad we came here,' Elaine said. 'I feel a lot better already.'

He apologized, and she told him not to be silly, and he took his bottle of vodka from the silver ice bucket and filled his glass, and the waitress finally brought the drinks Elaine and I had ordered an eternity ago, a Coke for me and a Lime Rickey for her, along with another Sea Breeze for Jodie, and

173

the band came out, not a moment too soon, and played 'Laura' and 'Epistrophy' and 'Mood Indigo' and ''Round Midnight,' among other things, and Danny Boy was right, the tenor player sounded a whole lot like Ben Webster.

Right before they took a break, the piano player, a gaunt black man with horn-rimmed glasses and a precisely trimmed goatee, announced that they'd play themselves off with a song about a French girl in England who was famous for her callipygian charms. 'Ladies and gentlemen, for your enjoyment, "London Derriere."'

There were chuckles here and there, bafflement everywhere else. He was goofing on 'Londonderry Air,' of course, the old name of the tune that most people know as 'Danny Boy,' and it's one of the world's most beautiful melodies but not often thought of as a good vehicle for jazz. They'd chosen it as a tip of the hat to Danny Boy Bell, who managed to look flattered and put upon at the same time. The tenor man played one chorus absolutely straight, and it was enough to break your heart, and then they took it up-tempo and worked changes on it, and it sounded okay to me, but it was essentially a novelty number. Except for the first tenor solo, which a man could listen to the whole night through, especially if he had a glass in his hand.

They wrapped it up, acknowledged the applause, and got off the stage. The piano player came over and told Danny Boy he hoped he didn't mind, and Danny said of course not, and that they should hang on to the tenor man. 'I wish,' the pianist said. 'He's here until a week from Thursday and then he's on a plane to Stockholm.' Danny Boy asked what the hell he was going to do in Stockholm. 'Eat blonde pussy,' the pianist said, and then he realized there were two women at our table and got all flustered, apologized profusely, and got out of there as quickly as possible.

Danny had some vodka and said, 'Christ, how I always hated that fucking song.'

'It's such a beautiful tune,' Elaine said.

'And the lyric's a lovely thing, too,' he told her. '"The summer's gone, the roses all are fallen.' But I heard it all the time when I was a little kid, I was fucking taunted with it.'

'Because of your name.'

'I was going to get taunted anyway,' he said, 'because I was the funniest-looking kid anybody ever saw, this white-haired white-faced little pickaninny who couldn't play sports and had to wear sunglasses and, on top of everything, was about ten times as bright as anyone else in the school, including the teachers. "Yo, Danny Boy! The pipes is callin'!"'

'But you kept the nickname,' Jodie said.

'It wasn't a nickname. Daniel Boyd Bell is what I was christened. That was my mother's maiden name, Boyd, *B-O-Y-D*, like a Green-pointer trying to say Bird. I answered to Danny Boyd from the time I was old enough to answer to anything, and the *D* just got lost because people didn't hear it, they assumed it was Danny Boy, *B-O-Y*, like the song.'

He frowned. 'You know,' he said, 'with all the people I know who got cornholed by their fathers and the crap kicked out of them by their mothers, I guess I got a pretty good deal. When you think about it.'

We caught one more set, and Danny wouldn't let me pay. 'You had two Coca-Colas and one glass of soda water with a piece of lime in it,' he said. 'I think I can cover it.' I said something about the cover charge, and he said nobody at his table ever had to pay a cover charge. 'They want to keep my business,' he said. 'Don't ask me why.'

Something made me pull out the photo of the elusive David Thompson. I showed it to Danny and asked him if it rang any kind of a bell.

He shook his head. 'Should it?'

'Probably not. He has a private mailbox a couple of blocks from here, so I thought he might have come in.'

'He's got a face that would be easy to miss,' he said, 'but I don't think I've ever seen it. You want to make copies and I'll show it around?'

'I don't think it's worth it.'

He shrugged. 'Whatever. Who is he, anyway?'

'Either his name's David Thompson,' I said, 'or it isn't.'

'Ah,' he said. 'You know, the same can be said for almost everybody.'

When we got home Elaine said, 'You're a genius, you know that? You took a sad evening and turned it around. Did you ever think you'd live to hear the same person in the course of a single night describe himself as an albino pickaninny and an *alter kocker*?'

'Now that you mention it, no.'

'And, but for you, we'd have missed that. You know what you're gonna get, big boy?'

'What?'

'Lucky,' she said. 'But I think you should get lucky with somebody who's clean and smells nice, so I'll go freshen up. And you might want to shave.'

'And shower.'

'And shower. So why don't you meet me in the bedroom in a half an hour or so?'

That was around twelve-thirty, and it must have been close to one-thirty when she said, 'See? What did I tell you. You got lucky.'

'The luckiest I ever got was the day I met you,' I said.

'Sweet old bear. Oh, wow.'

'Wow?'

'I was just thinking. And you know, there's not a soul I know in the business, so I couldn't even go and ask somebody.'

'Ask somebody what?'

'Well, I was just wondering what the impact of

Viagra's been on working girls. I mean, it would have to have a major effect, wouldn't you think?'

'I think you're a fruitcake.'

'What? A fruitcake? How can you say that?'

'A fruitcake's not a bad thing. Good night. I love you.'

So it turned out to be a good night, a wonderful night. What I didn't know was that there weren't going to be any more of them.

CHAPTER 15

I woke up to the smell of coffee, and when I got to the kitchen Elaine had a cup poured for me, and an English muffin in the toaster. The TV was on, tuned to the *Today* show, and Katie Couric was trying to be reasonably cheerful while her guest talked about his new book on the genocide in the Sudan.

Elaine said, 'That poor schnook. He's on national television, he's got a book out on a serious subject, and all anybody's going to notice is that he's wearing a rug.'

'And not a very good one, either.'

'If it was a good one,' she said, 'we wouldn't spot it so easily. And imagine how hot it must be under those studio lights with that thing clinging to your scalp like a dead muskrat.'

She had a cup of coffee, but no breakfast. She was on her way to the yoga class she took two or three times a week, and felt it was more effective if she did it on an empty stomach. She was out the door and on her way by a quarter after eight, and that was something to be grateful for, as it turned out.

Because she wasn't around when they broke for the local news at 8:25. I was half listening to it, and just enough got through to engage my attention. A woman had been killed in Manhattan, although they didn't say who or where. That's not rare, it's a big city and a hard world, but something made me change the channel to New York One, where they give you a steady diet of local news around the clock, and I waited through a pronouncement by the mayor and an optimistic weather report and a couple of commercials, and then an off-camera reporter was talking about the savage torture-murder of an unmarried Manhattan woman, and I got a sinking feeling.

Then a shot of the building she lived in filled the screen, and that didn't mean it had to be her, she wasn't the building's only tenant, and probably not the only single woman. It didn't have to be her. It could have been someone else who'd been found nude in her bedroom, stabbed to death after what the reporter grimly described as 'an apparent marathon session of torture and abuse.'

But I knew it was her.

The name, I was told, was being withheld pending notification of kin. Did she have any kin? I couldn't remember, and wasn't sure if it was something I'd ever known. It seemed to me that her parents were dead, and she'd never had children. Wasn't there an ex-husband, and was he someone they would need to notify? Were there brothers or sisters?

I picked up the phone and dialed a number I didn't have to look up, and a voice I didn't recognize said, 'Squad room,' and it took until then for me to remember that Friday had come and gone and Joe Durkin wasn't working at Midtown North anymore. I knew a couple of other cops there, though not terribly well. And it wasn't their case, it hadn't happened in their precinct. Joe would have helped me out, made a few phone calls, but I couldn't expect anybody else over there to take the trouble. They just knew me as a friend of Joe's, a guy who'd been off the job more years than he'd been on it, and they didn't owe me a thing.

Who else did I know? The last cop I'd worked with at all closely was Ira Wentworth, a detective in the Two-Six on West 126th Street. We'd stayed in touch for a time after the case was resolved – actually, it pretty much resolved itself – and he liked to come over to our apartment, saying that Elaine made the best coffee in the city.

But we hadn't kept up the contact, aside from cards at Christmas, and there was no point calling him now, because it hadn't happened in his precinct, either.

I had her number, though. I dialed it. If she picked up, I could think of something to say. But I pretty much knew that wasn't going to happen.

It rang until voice mail cut in, and I hung up.

Sooner or later they'd have a tip line set up, a dedicated number for people to call with information on the case, but there'd been nothing like that on the news. I knew which precinct it happened in, I'd been assigned there myself for several years, although I'd long since lost touch with the people I'd worked with there. It might not be their case, Homicide might have taken it away from them, but they'd have caught the initial squeal and somebody there ought to know something.

I looked up the number, got whoever was holding down the desk. I gave my own name and phone number before he could ask and told him I'd caught an item on the news about a woman murdered in his precinct. I'd recognized the building and a friend of mine lived in it, and I hadn't caught the name and was afraid it might be her.

He told me to hang on, came back to say they weren't giving out the name yet.

I said I could understand that, I was a retired cop myself. Suppose I gave him the name of my friend. Could he tell me whether or not it was her?

He thought about it and decided that would be okay. I told him her name, and the moment of silence was answer enough.

'I hate to say it,' he said, 'but that's the name I've got here. You want to hang on? I'll transfer you to someone connected to the case.'

I held, and I guess he briefed the guy before he put him through to me, because he came on the line knowing who I was and what I wanted. His name was Mark Sussman and he and his partner were first up on the case, so it was theirs until somebody took it away from them.

Was I by any chance a relative? I said I wasn't. Then did I have any contact information for the victim's relatives? I said I didn't, and wasn't sure she had any living kin. I didn't mention the ex-husband, since I wasn't sure of his name and had no idea where – or even if – he was living.

'We got an ID from a neighbor,' he said, 'and she looks like the photo on the passport in her drawer, so there's no real doubt of her identity. It might not be a bad idea for you to make a formal identification, if you wouldn't mind doing that.'

Was the body still at the apartment?

'No, we got her out of there once the ME had a look at her and the photographer was done taking pictures. She's at the morgue, that's . . . well, you'd know where that is.'

I would indeed. I said it might take me a while, that I had to stay put until my wife got home. He said there was no rush.

'I'll want to sit down and talk with you anyway,' he said. 'Before or after you ID the body. If you knew the woman, maybe you can point us in a useful direction.'

'If I can.'

'Because we don't even have a preliminary report from forensics, but it doesn't looks like the cocksucker left us a lot of physical evidence. You could eat off the floor, the way it looked. If you had the appetite, which you wouldn't, not after you saw what he did to her.'

I didn't know what the hell to do. Out of habit I poured myself another cup of coffee, but I already felt as though I'd been drinking coffee for days. I poured it out and turned on the TV again, as if I'd learn more from it than I had from Sussman. The announcer got on my nerves and I turned it off before they could get any further than the traffic report.

I kept picking up the phone and putting it down again. Who the hell was I going to call and what could I say? At one point I had Sussman's number half-dialed before I second-guessed myself and hung up. What could I tell him? That I had a pretty good idea who'd done it, but that I didn't know his name or where to look for him?

I looked over at the phone and a number popped into my head, one I hadn't called in years. It was Jim Faber's, and I wished to God I could dial that number and hear my late sponsor's voice on the other end of the line. What would he tell me? That was easy. He'd tell me not to drink.

I didn't want to drink, hadn't consciously thought of it, but now that I did I was just as glad that Elaine and I don't keep anything alcoholic in the house. Because why do they distill whiskey, why do they put it in bottles, if not for occasions like this one?

There were other program friends I could call,

other men and women I could count on to tell me not to drink. But I wasn't going to drink, and I didn't want to have the rest of any of those conversations.

I called TJ, brought him up to speed. He said, 'Oh, man, that's terrible news.'

'Yes, it is.'

'I had the news on, I heard what they said, but I never made the connection.'

'Well, why would you?'

'Damn, I feel bad.'

'So do I.'

'Elaine home?'

'She had a yoga class. She should be home any minute.'

''Less she go straight to the store. You want, I'll come over, sit with you until she gets there.'

'Isn't the market open?'

'They 'bout to ring the bell, but it don't matter. New York Stock Exchange get along without me.'

'No, that's all right,' I said.

'You change your mind, just call. Won't take me a minute to close down here and come over.'

I rang off and tried her number at the store. I didn't think she'd go there, she rarely opens up before eleven, but it was possible. When the machine picked up I tried to keep my voice neutral, telling her it was me and to pick up if she was there. She didn't, and I was just as glad.

A few minutes later I heard her key in the lock. I was standing a few feet from the door when

185

she opened it, and she knew something was wrong as soon as she saw my face. I told her to come in, took her gym bag from her, told her to sit down.

I don't know why we do that. *Sit down*, we say, pointing at chairs. *Are you sitting down?* we want to know, before imparting bad news over the phone. What difference does it make? Are we really afraid our words will knock the recipient off his feet? Do that many people injure themselves, falling down when they hear bad news?

Brace yourself – that's what we're saying. As if a person can. As if one can prepare oneself for such awful intelligence.

'It was on the news,' I said. 'Monica's dead. She's been murdered.'

CHAPTER 16

They weren't really set up for viewing. The autopsy wasn't finished, and a woman who looked as though she spent too much time around dead people had us wait, then took us into a large room and led us to a table on which a mound was covered with a plain white sheet. She uncovered the head, and there was no mistake. It was Monica.

'Ah, no,' Elaine said. 'No, no, no.'

Outside she said, 'My best friend. The best friend I ever had. We talked every day, there wasn't a day we didn't talk. Who am I gonna talk to now? It's not fair, I'm too fucking old to get another best friend.'

A cab came along and I flagged it.

I hadn't wanted to take her to the morgue, but then I hadn't wanted to leave her alone, either. And it wasn't my decision to make, anyway, it was hers, and she'd been adamant. She wanted to be with me, and she wanted to see her friend. At the morgue, when the woman warned us it wouldn't be pretty, I told her she didn't have to do this. She said she did.

In the cab she said, 'It makes it real. That's why they have open caskets at funerals. So you'll know, so you'll accept it. Otherwise there'd be a part of me that wouldn't really believe she was gone. I'd go on thinking that I could pick up the phone and dial her number and there she'd be.'

I didn't say anything, just held her hand. We rode another block and she said, 'I'll believe that anyway. On some level. But a little bit less than if I hadn't seen her sweet face. Oh, God, Matt.'

My first thought when we met Mark Sussman was that he was awfully young, and my second thought, a corrective to the first, was that he was within a couple of years of the age I'd been when I quit the job. He was short, with a well-developed upper body suggestive of frequent workouts with weights, and his dark brown eyes were hard to read.

He was a college graduate, which seems barely worth noting these days. I don't think there was a single man in my class at the academy who'd been to college, let alone got all the way through it. There was a general feeling in the department that college was no good for a cop, that you learned too many of the wrong things and not enough of the right ones, that it unmanned you while suffusing you with an unwarranted feeling of superiority. That was all a lot of crap, of course, but so was most of what we believed about most subjects.

He'd had a split major at Brooklyn College, history and sociology, and was accepted at a couple of graduate schools when he realized he didn't want a teaching career. He took a couple of graduate courses in criminology at John Jay and decided that was his field, but he didn't want to study it, he wanted to get out there and do it. That was ten years ago, and now he had a gold shield and a desk in the detective squad room at the Sixth Precinct, on West Tenth Street in the Village.

He sat behind that desk, and we took chairs alongside it. 'Monica Driscoll,' he said. 'Now we also found documents referring to her as Monica Wellbridge.'

'That was her ex-husband's name,' Elaine told him. 'She never used it.'

'Took her maiden name back. When was the divorce, fairly recent?'

'Oh, God, no. Fifteen years ago? At least that, maybe twenty.' And no, Monica hadn't been in touch with Derek Wellbridge, and she had no idea how to reach him, or if he was alive to be reached.

'It's an unusual name,' Sussman said. 'A computer search might turn him up, if there's any reason to look for him. I think you said she was seeing somebody.'

'Yes, and he was very secretive.'

'I don't suppose you met him.'

'No. She wouldn't even tell me his name. At first

I figured it was because he was married, although we met a few of her married boyfriends over the years.'

'She did this a lot? Dated married guys?'

It should have been an easy question to answer, but Elaine didn't want to make her friend sound easy, or undiscriminating. 'If she was dating somebody,' she said after a moment, 'he generally turned out to be married.'

'She kept making the same mistake?'

'No, she liked it that way. She didn't want to get married again, she didn't want to be all wrapped up in another person.'

'This mystery man, how long had she been seeing him?'

'Not long. Two weeks? Three? Less than a month, anyway.'

'What do you know about him?'

'Oh, gosh, let me think. He was very secretive, he would have to leave town and not be able to tell her where he was going. She had the idea that he was working for the government. Or *a* government. You know, like some kind of an agent.'

'She give you any kind of a description?'

'He dressed nicely, he was well groomed. But then I never saw her with anybody who wasn't. Oh, I know. He had a mustache.'

'Yeah, that fits.' He put down his pen, looked up at us. 'The doorman sent somebody up to her apartment last night around nine-thirty or ten. Guy gave the doorman his name and she said send him up.'

'If he gave the doorman his name—'

'Yeah, well, I think we're lucky this particular genius remembers the mustache. And the flowers.'

'Flowers?'

'Which checks out, because we found fresh flowers in a vase on the mantel. He must have had his hands full, too, because he had to set something down on the floor so he could stroke his mustache while he was waiting for the elevator.'

'He put something down so he could stroke his mustache?'

'It was more like he was grooming it. You know, like this.' He put his thumb and forefinger together in the center of his bare upper lip, then spread them apart. 'Making sure he looked all right before he went upstairs. Anyway, that's how come' – he checked his notes – 'how come Hector Ruiz noticed the mustache.' He looked at Elaine.

'That's all she mentioned about his appearance? He dressed nicely and wore a mustache?'

'That's all I can remember. She said he was a good lover. Very forceful, very imaginative.'

'More than she knew.' She looked questioningly at him, and he said, 'You're going to get this anyway from the media, as much as we'd like to keep a lid on it. There's evidence of ligatures on her wrists and ankles, and tape residue in the area of her mouth. Was she into that whole scene, would you happen to know?'

'She was a sophisticated woman of a certain age,'

she told him. 'Living alone in Greenwich Village. I mean, you do the math.'

'Okay, but—'

She stopped him. 'I don't think she was kinky,' she said. 'I don't think she was *into* anything in particular. I think, you know, if she liked a guy and he wanted to do something, she wouldn't run out of there screaming for her mother.'

'That's just a figure of speech, right? Because what I've got is both parents are deceased.'

'Yes, a long time ago.'

'And no relatives that you know of.'

'She had a brother who died. There could be, I don't know, an aunt or a cousin somewhere, but nobody I knew about. Nobody she kept in touch with.'

He said, 'As far as her not being into bondage, S & M, whatever you want to call it, that would actually fit right in with our take on it.' To me he said, 'I don't know if you ever ran into this, but you must have if you worked this precinct. Anybody who's at all serious about kink, they've got a closet full of gear, leather and rubber and masks and chains, you'd almost think the equipment's more important to them than what they do with it. She didn't have a thing, no handcuffs, no whips, none of that garbage. Not that—' He stopped short, started to laugh. 'You watch *Seinfeld*? I was starting to say 'Not that there's anything wrong with that.' You remember that episode?'

'Sure.'

'I'm sorry, I don't mean to make light. What it looks like, he brought along what he figured he'd need, and he took it away with him when he was done. Did she say he was neat? You'd have to say he was the neatest heterosexual male on the planet. There was a bottle of liquor, an Italian after-dinner drink. I've got it written down here somewhere. It doesn't matter, it's just a bottle of fancy booze. We think he brought it with him, along with the flowers, and they each had a drink out of it, and he wiped the bottle and glasses before he left. He wiped everything, he didn't leave a print in the whole damned apartment, as far as we've been able to tell. We'll probably lift a partial somewhere or other before we're done, we usually do, but I have to say I wouldn't bet on it.'

'Because he was neat.'

'He even ran the vacuum cleaner. The downstairs neighbor heard it sometime around midnight. He wasn't about to complain about it, it wasn't that noisy, it was just unexpected at that hour. It was evidently out of character for her to vacuum in the middle of the night.'

'Or ever,' Elaine said. 'She had a maid come in once a week, and vacuuming was something the maid did.'

'The maid probably didn't take the vacuum cleaner bag with her when she left, either, like this guy did. She thought he was some kind of government agent? Well, if he wasn't he could have been.

He was really professional about not leaving anything behind that could be traced back to him. You know that TV show with the forensics? And then there's another version set in Miami, but it's not as good. The original one's an excellent show, but I have to say I wish they'd take it off the air.'

'Because it gives people ideas?'

'No, the nut jobs out there, you don't have to give them ideas. They come up with plenty all on their own. What it does, it makes them harder to catch. It tells them what kind of mistakes not to make.'

'You think this man was just showing what he learned on television?'

'No, I don't. I don't know what I think about the guy. That was the spookiest crime scene I've ever seen. I don't want to go into detail, and I'm sorry Mrs Scudder has to hear this at all, but he tortured that woman a long time before he killed her. And then to leave the place immaculate, everything in apple-pie order, and her naked and dead in the middle of it, it was like that painter, that Frenchman . . .'

'Magritte,' she said.

'Yeah, that's the one. Like, what's wrong with this picture? I mean, if this is the man she's been seeing, and it would almost have to be, given that he gave his name and she told the doorman to send him up. If he's been dating her, and sleeping with her – they were sleeping together?'

'She said he was a good lover.'

'Right, you told me that. There are guys who go nuts, get hold of some poor woman and do a number on her. But they don't date her first. Usually they pick a stranger, some hooker off the street or some poor woman who just winds up in the wrong place at the wrong time. Once in a while there's one who thinks he's having a relationship with the woman, but it's only in the privacy of his own mind. Erotomania, that's what they call it. It's delusional, your perp thinks it's dating but anybody else would call it stalking.'

He was right, it didn't add up.

'It would help,' he said, 'if either of you could remember anything else she might have let slip about the guy. Anything at all, like did he have a regional accent, was he educated or uneducated, even small things like was he a baseball fan, did he smell of cologne. You think something's too trivial to mention, and then it matches up with something else and you've got a clue.'

'He drinks Scotch,' Elaine said.

'Now there's something right there. She just happened to mention it?'

'She offered him a drink, and he asked for Scotch and she didn't have any. So he had something else, but the next day she went out and bought a bottle of what I guess was really good Scotch. And she evidently made a good choice, because the next time he was over he said it was really good, but he only had one small drink, and she was saying she wondered which would last longer, the relationship or the bottle.'

'The bottle,' Sussman said. 'It's still there, Glen Something-or-other.' He made a note. 'Maybe he picked it up to pour a drink on a prior visit and forgot to wipe his prints off it last night. But I wouldn't count on it. Still, that's exactly the kind of thing to come up with. You know, I wouldn't be surprised if she let something slip having to do with his name. Give it a chance and it might come to you.'

'Maybe,' she said.

'Strega,' he said suddenly. 'Speaking of things coming to you. That's the name of the bottle he brought along. That's one way we might catch him. It's not exactly Georgi Vodka. If you're a clerk in a liquor store, how often does somebody pop in for a bottle of Strega?'

'So you'll canvass stores in the neighborhood.'

'We'll start in the neighborhood and keep going. She didn't give you any indication at all of where he lived? You can't put him in any particular part of the city? Well, somebody sold him the Strega, and maybe the guy who did will actually be in the store when somebody drops in to ask, and maybe he'll not only remember but he'll decide it's okay to co-operate with the police, that he won't be infringing on his customer's inalienable right of privacy and making himself vulnerable to a lawsuit. Maybe Mr Strega paid with a credit card, though that seems like too much to hope for. Maybe the store's got security cameras installed, and maybe they actually work, and maybe we'll actually get there before that night's tapes are automatically recycled, though that's a stretch. You don't need to keep the tapes any length of time, because all you have to be able to do is ID the dirtbag who holds you up, not somebody who bought a bottle of high-priced booze from you a couple of nights ago.'

Monica's apartment building was distinctive, which may have been why I'd recognized it right away when it showed up on New York One. It's on Jane Street in the northwest corner of the Village, a seventeen-story Art Deco building with a facade of yellow-brown brick, and elaborately sculpted lintels and cornices. We walked uptown on Hudson Street without saying much, and when Monica's building, taller than its neighbors, hove into view, Elaine's hand tightened its grip on mine. By the time we were across the street from it she was crying.

She said, 'If she ever did a bad thing I never knew it. She was never mean-spirited, she never hurt anybody. Never. She fucked some married men, big fucking deal, and she quit working once her parents died and left her enough money to live on. And sometimes she'd keep candy in her purse and eat it secretly, because she was ashamed and didn't want you to know. And she probably gave more thought to her wardrobe than Mother

Teresa ever did, which probably made her a more superficial person than Mother Teresa, and a lot more fun to hang out with. And those are the worst things I can think of to say about her, and they're not so terrible, are they? They're not bad enough to get you killed. Are they?'

'No.'

'I can't look at her building. It makes me cry.'

'I'll get us a cab.'

'No, let's walk for a while. Can we walk for a while?'

We walked north on Hudson, which becomes Ninth Avenue north of Fourteenth Street. We passed a trendy restaurant called Markt, and she said, 'René Magritte wasn't French, he was Belgian.'

'But you still knew he was the painter Sussman was talking about.'

'Because I got the same image in my mind, that surreal dissonance. It's daytime but the sky's dark. Or that one with a picture of a pipe with a curved stem, and writing that says 'This is not a pipe.' Paradox. The reason I just thought of it now—'

'Is that Markt is a Belgian restaurant.'

'Yeah, and so's the little place across the street on Fourteenth, La Petite Something-or-other. Monica liked it, they've got all these different ways to cook mussels, and she was always crazy about mussels. You know what they look like?'

'Mussels? Sort of like clams.'

'Up close,' she said, 'after you take them out of the shell. They look like pussies.'

'Oh.'

'I told her it was her latent lesbianism shining through. We were going to have lunch there but we never got around to it. And now we never will.'

'You haven't had anything to eat today,' I said.

'I don't want to go there.'

'Not there,' I agreed. 'But should we stop someplace?'

'I couldn't eat.'

'Okay.'

'It wouldn't stay down. But if you're hungry . . .'

'I'm not.'

'Well, if you decide you want something, we can stop. But I've got no appetite.'

We walked a few blocks in silence, and then she said, 'People die all the time.'

'Yes.'

'It's what happens. The longer you live the more people you lose. That's how the world works.'

I didn't say anything.

'I may be a little nuts for the next few days.'

'That's okay.'

'Or longer. I wasn't ready for this.'

'No.'

'How could I be? I figured I'd always have her. I figured we'd be cranky old ladies together. She's the only friend I have who knows I used to turn tricks. I just got the tenses wrong, didn't I? She *was* the only friend I *had* who *knew* I used to turn tricks. She's in the past tense now, isn't she? She's part of the past, she's gone forever from the present and the future. I think I have to sit down.'

There was a Latino coffee shop handy. They had Cuban sandwiches and I don't know what else, because neither of us looked at the menu. I ordered two coffees, and she told the waiter to make hers a cup of tea.

'She was never the slightest bit judgmental. She was interested but not fascinated, and she didn't see anything wrong with it, or wrong with me for having spent those years that way. Who else even knows, who else that's still in my life? You and Danny Boy, who knew me then. And TJ. I can't think of anybody else.'

'No.'

'Listen to me, will you? I'm making this all about me. My God, he tortured her. She must have been so frightened. I can't imagine it, and I can't stop imagining it. I don't think I can handle this, baby.'

'You're handling it right now.'

'This is handling it? I don't know. Maybe it is.'

I drank half my coffee, and she had a couple of sips of tea, and we went outside and walked uptown for a few more blocks. Then she said she was ready to take a cab, and I managed to flag one.

On the ride home she said one word. 'Why,' she said, and there was no question mark in her voice. She didn't sound as though she expected an answer, and God knows I didn't have one.

★   ★   ★

She sat down at her computer and spent an hour working on a paid obituary notice for the *Times*, then printed it out and brought it to me to see if I thought it was all right. Before I could read it she took it back and started tearing it up. She said, 'What am I, crazy? I don't need to run an ad to tell the people she's gone. The papers and TV'll take care of that. By this time tomorrow everybody she ever knew is going to know what happened to her, along with the rest of the world.'

She went over to the window and looked through it. We're on the fourteenth floor, and we used to be able to see the World Trade Center towers from our south window. Now, of course, they're not there to be seen, but for months afterward I'd find her at that window, looking out at their absence.

Around six the doorman called up to announce TJ. She burst into tears when she saw him and he gave her a hug. 'You must be hungry,' she told him, and turned to me. 'You, too. Have you had anything to eat since breakfast?'

I hadn't.

'We have to eat,' she announced. 'Is pasta all right? And a salad?'

We said it was fine.

'It's all I ever make. God, I'm boring. How can you stand me? I cook the same meal all the fucking time, the only thing that varies is the shape of the pasta. Maybe I should start cooking meat. Just because I decided to be a vegetarian doesn't mean the two of you can't have meat.'

I said, 'Why don't you just make us all some pasta.'

'Thank you,' she said. 'That's what I'll do.'

I hadn't intended to go to a meeting, but when the time came Elaine suggested it. I said I'd just as soon stay home. She said, 'Go. TJ and I are going to play cards. Do you know how to play gin rummy?'

'Sure.'

'How about cribbage?'

'Yeah, a little bit.'

'That's no good, then. Casino? You know how to play casino?'

'I used to play with my gran.'

'Did she let you win?'

'Are you kidding? She'd cheat if she had to.'

'I bet she didn't have to. There must be a card game you don't know. How about pinochle?'

'Takes three players, don't it?'

'I'm talking two-handed pinochle,' she said. 'It's a completely different game. You don't know how to play it?'

'I never even heard of it.'

'Perfect,' she said. 'That means I can teach you. Matt, go to a meeting.'

They've got a men's meeting on Wednesdays at St Columba's, a small church on West Twenty-ninth Street. It's specifically for men over forty, and it's almost exclusively gay men who attend, although that's not a requirement. The demographics of the neighborhood support its makeup. It's in Chelsea, where most of the male population is gay, if not over forty.

I could have gone to my regular meeting at St Paul's, five minutes from my front door, but for some reason I didn't want familiar faces, and people asking how it was going. It wasn't going well, and I didn't want to talk about it.

There's a bus that goes down Ninth Avenue, but I just missed it and took a cab, which made this a banner day for cabs, if for little else. They were reading the preamble as I got there, and had already taken the collection. I decided they could probably make the rent without my dollar, and I helped myself to a cup of coffee and found a seat. The speaker, dressed and groomed like an ad in *GQ* told a story of solitary drinking at the Four Seasons bar, where he'd try to catch the eye of another unaccompanied gentleman, then repair to a wonderfully louche establishment across the street and hope his prospect would follow. If not, he'd just stay there and get drunk. 'We were all so deep in the closet back then,' he said, 'we had marks from the coat hangers. You'd have thought Joan Crawford was our mother.'

After he'd finished, they went around the room instead of asking for a show of hands. By the time it was my turn, I'd already said everything I had to say, albeit in the privacy of my own mind. 'My name's Matt,' I said, 'and I'm an alcoholic. I really enjoyed your qualification. I think I'll just listen tonight.'

A little later a voice I knew said, 'I'm really glad I got here tonight. It's not a regular meeting of mine, but I see a few familiar faces here. And I got a lot out of your story. My name's Abie and I'm an alcoholic.'

He went on to talk about having to put in long hours lately, and missing meetings, and how he had to remember that his sobriety has to come first. 'If I lose that, then I lose everything that goes with it,' he said.

It wasn't anything I hadn't heard a few thousand times over the years, but it didn't hurt me any to hear it again.

He caught up with me on the way out. 'My first time here,' he said. 'I didn't even know it was a special-interest meeting.'

'Men over forty.'

'I knew that part from the listing in the book. What I didn't know is everybody was gay.'

'Not everybody was.'

'Except for thee and me,' he said, and grinned. 'I don't mind gay people, in fact I enjoy the energy in a room full of gay men. But I wasn't expecting it.'

Not that there's anything wrong with that, I thought.

'Matt? I was surprised when you didn't share tonight.'

'Well, I'm not in the same class with William the

Silent,' I said, 'but I don't feel compelled to say something just because it's my turn.'

'Except you looked as though you had something you wanted to get out.'

'Oh?'

'Like you had something gnawing at you.' He touched my shoulder. 'You want to go get some coffee?'

'I had two cups here tonight. I think that's enough coffee for me.'

'Something to eat, then.'

'I don't think so, Abie.'

'My first sponsor used to say we were people who couldn't afford the luxury of keeping things to ourselves.'

'It's probably a good thing he wasn't in the CIA, then.'

'I suppose, but the point—'

'I think I get the point.'

He stepped back, frowning, and pinched his upper lip, a physical tic I'd seen him make before. 'Look, I didn't mean any harm,' he said. 'I guess you'd rather be alone tonight.'

I didn't tell him otherwise.

I took another cab, and got one with loud Arab music on the radio. I told the driver to turn it down. He looked at me, and I guess he saw something on my face that kept him from arguing. He turned it down and off, and we rode home in a welcome if stony silence.

The pinochle game was still in progress when I walked in the door. I asked who was winning, and Elaine made a face and pointed across the table. 'He swears he never played the game before,' she said, 'and it hurts me to think such a sweet young man could lie like a rug.'

'Never did,' he said.

'Then how come you could sit there and beat my brains out?'

'You just a good teacher, is all.'

'That must be it.' She gathered the cards. 'Go home. You're an angel for keeping me company, even if you didn't have the decency to let me win. Wait a minute. Are you hungry? Do you want a cookie?'

He shook his head.

'You sure? I baked them myself, using the name "Mrs Fields."'

He shook his head again, and she gave him a hug and let him go. She put the cards away and went to the window again, the one that no longer had a view of the towers. She sighed and turned from it to me and said, 'I've been thinking. She had other friends besides me. No one else was as close, but there were other women she'd meet for lunch, or talk to on the phone.'

'There'd have to be.'

'She might have let something slip about this guy. I mean, she told me he drinks Scotch and has a mustache. She might have said something else to somebody else.'

'And if you gather the somethings together, a picture might emerge.'

'Well, don't you think it's possible?'

'I know it's possible,' I said, 'and so will Sussman. They'll go through her address or her Rolodex, whatever she had, and they'll check out every listing. He might be in there, as far as that goes. Just because she wouldn't say his name doesn't mean he didn't give her one. If he also gave her a number, it'll be in her book.'

'You think they'll get him that way?'

I didn't, but I said it was possible.

'All right, here's another thing I was thinking. She might have gone back to her shrink. She stopped therapy years ago, but she's been back a few times for a couple of sessions here and a couple of sessions there. And I remember having the feeling recently that she might have gone back. I don't know what triggered it, but it was a feeling I got.'

'And she might have said something about the guy to the therapist?'

'Well, you know, if she can't feel free to say anything to anybody else . . .'

'That's a point.'

'But would the shrink say anything? Isn't everything you tell your shrink privileged?'

I said it was, but that there was a gray area here. When the patient was dead and the investigation was trying to uncover the killer, that would override doctor-patient privilege for some physicians, and not for others.

'Her shrink's name is Brigitte Dufy. She's French, she's got the same last name as the painter Raoul Dufy, and she may even be a relative. I know Monica asked her but I don't remember what the answer was. As if it matters. She grew up around here, her father was a souschef at the Brittany du Soir. You remember that place?'

'Yes, of course.'

'It was terrific, I wonder what happened to it. One day it was just gone. Anyway, Brigitte grew up here with a neighborhood accent that was solid Hell's Kitchen Irish. Monica liked to call her Bridget Duffy. They'll probably find her name in Monica's address book, but maybe not. You know how when you copy an address book you don't bother transferring the names of people who've dropped out of your life? Because why bother, since you're not going to call them again? Well, if she'd stopped therapy . . .'

I said I'd mention it to Sussman in the morning.

'I can't stand that she's gone,' she said. 'But I'll get used to it. That's what life is, getting used to people dying. But I can't stand the thought of somebody doing this to her and getting away with it. And I don't want to get used to it.'

'They'll get him.'

'You promise?'

How could I promise something like that? Then again, how could I deny her?

'I promise.'

'Is there anything you can do?'

'Besides get in everybody's way? I don't know. I'll see if I can come up with anything.'

'I don't expect you to get out there and find him,' she said. 'Except, see, the thing is I do. You're my hero, you know. You always have been.'

'I think you'd be better off with Spider-man.'

'No,' she said. 'No, I'm happy with the choice I made.'

CHAPTER 17

In a Kinko's on Columbus Avenue, he sits at a computer terminal, where a small hourly fee provides him with utterly anonymous Internet access. He goes to the Yahoo website and, at no cost and in a matter of minutes, he opens an account with a user name that is just a meaningless jumble of letters and numbers. It would be difficult to remember, but he won't need to remember it because he'll never use it again. It's a one-time-only account, almost certainly untraceable, but if they trace it they won't get any farther than this computer, open to the public and used by dozens of people every day.

He remembers wondering how anyone was ever caught and convicted a century ago, in the absence of forensics. But didn't science aid the criminal with one hand while it aided the criminologist with the other? He'd come across a line somewhere that had always struck him as the perfect explanation of Darwinian evolution: If you build a better mousetrap, Nature will build a better mouse.

He meditates upon this principle for a spell, then brings himself reluctantly back to the present moment. He clicks on WRITE MAIL and begins typing:

I am writing to you because it troubles me to think of the unfortunate parents of Jeffrey Willis, for whose murder Preston Applewhite recently paid the ultimate penalty. Hard as it is to lose a son, it must be harder still when his body is never recovered. One hates the thought of one's own flesh and blood lying forever in an unmarked grave, although, on reflection, I can't see that I'd much prefer lying in a marked grave. It is, I should think, one and the same to the person lying there.

Still, it seems only right for me to tell you that the spirit of Preston Applewhite (may all curse his memory!) came to me last night in a spirit of profound contrition. 'You must tell the good people at the *Richmond Times-Dispatch*,' it said, In an appropriately spectral tone, 'that I deeply regret what I've done, and seek to make amends by telling you just where to look for all that remains of the Willis boy.'

And here is where it said to look . . .

He writes out detailed instructions, creating a perfect verbal treasure map that will lead whoever follows it to the very spot in the old family graveyard where he had such a pleasant time with young

Jeffrey, who'd not had a terribly pleasant time of it himself. It brings it all back for him, and he's tempted to add a precise description of Jeffrey's last moments, but that would be inconsistent with the letter's content and tone.

Though it would surely be fun. He's reminded of Albert Fish, the deranged cannibal who murdered young children and ate them. After killing and devouring one Grace Budd, he wrote a note to her parents describing the murder and attesting to their daughter's succulence on the dinner table. But, he swore to them, 'I never fucked her. She died a virgin.'

A Budd never forced to bloom, he thinks. How reassuring that must have been for the elder Budds!

You will think at first that this is a hoax, for how could any intelligent person think otherwise? But you can hardly fail to send out a couple of men with a couple of shovels, if there's the slightest possibility that Jeffrey's bones (for the rest of him surely has long since rotted away) are where the spirit has said they are.

When you find them, as surely you shall, you and your readers and the appropriate authorities will have much to ponder. Are you to believe in spirits and their revelations? Or has someone made a grievous error?

I trust you'll forgive my not signing this. I have

lately learned the importance of anonymity. It is, to be sure, the spiritual foundation of all our traditions.

The Richmond Times-Dispatch has a website, of course, where he'd found the city editor's e-mail address. He enters that in the appropriate space and sits for several minutes, the cursor poised over the SEND button. To send it or not, that is the question, and there is no obvious answer. The whole matter of Preston Applewhite has been resolved in a most satisfactory manner, which argues mightily for leaving well enough alone.

On the other hand, it seems to him that it would be more *interesting* to send the message, to stir the pot, to see what happens. For something will most certainly happen, whereas if he leaves well enough alone, why, nothing will happen, nothing beyond what has happened already.

And interest is everything, isn't it?

But he's not too sure of that last paragraph. It will strike a chord with some of the people who read it, and send them rushing madly off in several wrong directions, but it's really just a private joke, and would deprive him of an opportunity to sign his work. He highlights the last paragraph, hits DELETE, thinks for a moment, and replaces it with this:

I'll leave you to your work, dear friends, even as I return to my own. I'll be abandoning my present e-mail address forthwith, so I regret that you'll be unable to contact me. Should I have occasion to communicate further, I'll do so from another e-mail address, which, alas, will be as untraceable as this one. But you'll know me by my signature; I have the honor to be, sir, your most obedient servant,

Abel Baker

He smiles his rueful smile, and hits the SEND button.

He rather likes New York.

He has lived here before, for several years, and he would have stayed longer if circumstances hadn't compelled him to leave. At the time those circumstances looked like a turn of bad luck, but attitude is everything, as he often says, and he was wise enough to will himself to regard what looked like adversity as opportunity. Hasn't his exile from New York given him a chance to see something of the country? Hasn't it furnished him with any number of grand adventures, culminating so recently in the remarkable affair of Preston Applewhite?

When he left, the Twin Towers stood proudly at the foot of Manhattan. He wonders sometimes what it would have been like to be present in the city when it suffered such an unfathomable blow.

That day's loss of life has no great personal impact upon him. What he does wonder at, though, and what does inspire him, is the awesome power of the man who pulled the strings, the puppet master who convinced his followers to fly planes into buildings. It bespoke an enviable talent for manipulation.

He's done some manipulation himself. When he lived here he was no mean hand at it, although no subject of his ever did anything all that dramatic. Still, his people were bright, and success demanded his employing a sort of psychological jujitsu; he won by using their own mental strength against them.

He has been walking as he's had these thoughts, and he notes with some delight that his steps and his thoughts have brought him to the same place, a house on West Seventy-fourth Street. He was on the outside of this house on many occasions, and inside it once. There were three other people with him on that occasion, and he killed two of them right here, in this very house, one with a gun and one with a knife, and killed the third an hour later in a house several miles to the south.

He'd thought at the time that the house would be his reward, that the killings would make it his. He thought that was what he wanted, a fine brownstone house a block from Central Park.

He'd thought that was why he killed.

How much freer he is now that he knows the truth about himself!

He'd wondered, on his return to the city, if this house would even still be standing. Years ago, downtown on West Eleventh Street, one brownstone in a row of brownstones had simply disappeared. The place had been a bomb factory for student radicals, owned by the parents of one of them, and how better to fulfill their unconscious motivations than by blowing up a parental home? Wasn't that, all things considered, the underlying purpose of their politics?

By the time he first came to New York, the house had already been replaced. The new structure, sized to match its neighbors, looks to have been given a twist by its architect, with a section jutting out at an oblique angle from the rest of the facade. The ostensible purpose, he knows, was to wed the contemporary to the traditional, but he senses a deeper explanation, a desire to let the plosive force that gutted the first building express itself in its successor.

But there had been no bomb factory here on West Seventy-fourth Street, and so there is no reason for this fine house to have disappeared, merely because it has ceased to hold a place in his day-to-day consciousness. It still stands, and the same young woman still occupies it, all but the lowest floor, where the same old woman, older now, maintains the same undistinguished antique shop.

He thinks of another shop, of the letter opener he bought there. Of the woman who sold it to him, calling it a paper knife. The term itself, he thinks, could be ambiguous, meaning either a knife to cut paper or a knife made of paper. Or a knife in name only, like a paper tiger.

Gone now, whatever you called it. Oh, it still exists, even as the house still exists, but it's no longer part of his life.

Is this house part of his life? Does it, like so much

else here in this extraordinary city, come under the heading of Unfinished Business?

He'll have to think about that.

On his way home he stands for a few moments directly across the street from another much larger building, this one on the southeast corner of Fifty-seventh and Ninth. There's a doorman on duty twenty-four hours a day, and there are security cameras in the elevators and the lobby. Still, how difficult a hindrance are they likely to prove? Created and installed and maintained by men, surely they can be subverted by a man.

But it's not yet time.

He walks home. He sometimes thinks of himself as a hermit crab, taking up homes and discarding them when he outgrows them. The shelter that suits him now, his home for the present, consists of three rooms on the top floor of a tenement on Fifty-third Street west of Tenth Avenue. The building shows some of the effects of gentrification. Its brick facade has been repointed, its halls and stairways renovated, its vestibule entirely redone. Many of the apartments have been done over, too, as their occupants have moved or died off, replaced by new tenants paying full market value rents. Only a few of the old rent-controlled tenants are left, and one of them, Mrs Laskowski, probably doesn't have much time left. She's fifty pounds overweight and diabetic, and suffers as well from something that makes her joints ache in bad weather. But she's out there on the front stoop, smoking a malodorous little Italian cigar, when he mounts the steps.

'Well, hello,' she says. 'How's your uncle?'

'I was just visiting him.'

'I wish I could, I'll tell you that. You see somebody for so many years, you miss seeing them. It's a shame you couldn't get them to take him at St Clare's. My cousin Marie was at St Clare's, God rest her soul, and I was able to visit her every single day until she passed.'

And what a rare treat that must have been.

'They're taking good care of him at the VA,' he reminds her. 'The best possible, and it's all free of charge.'

'I never even knew he was in the service.'

'Oh, yes, and very proud to have served. But he didn't like to talk about those days.'

'He never said a word on the subject. The Veterans, that's up in the Bronx, isn't it?'

'Kingsbridge Road.'

'I don't even know where that is. I guess it's a long ride on the subway.'

'You have to change trains,' he says, 'and then it's a long walk when you finally do get there.' He has no idea if this is true, he's only been to the Bronx once, and that was years ago. 'And visiting him can be difficult. Today he didn't know me.'

'You went all that way and he didn't know you.'

'Well, you have to take the bitter with the sweet, Mrs L. And you know what my uncle always used to say. 'You get what you get.'''

He climbs the stairs, lets himself into the apartment, locks the door. The apartment is run-down and shabby. He'd have cheerfully hired someone to clean it, but that could have caused talk, and so he'd done it himself as best he could, scrubbing the floors and walls, spraying air freshener. But one can only do so much, and the place still holds the stench of fifty years of Joe Bohan's cigarettes, mingled with the persistent aroma of Joe Bohan himself, a man who lived alone and evidently never made too much of a thing of personal hygiene.

Still, in a city where even the shabbiest hotel room is ridiculously expensive, there's much to be said for a free apartment, especially one so close to so much of his unfinished business.

In a delicatessen on Tenth Avenue, where he'd stopped for a sandwich and a cup of coffee, he'd heard two old men talking about poor Joe Bohan, who wasn't getting out much anymore. Always kept to himself, one man said, but a nicer guy you wouldn't want to meet.

He'd found a Joseph Bohan listed in the phone book. He called the number, and a man with a scratchy voice answered. No, the man said, there was no Mary Eileen Bohan at that address. He was an old man, he lived by himself. Close relatives? No, none at all. But there were lots of Bohans, although he didn't remember hearing of a Mary Eileen.

He gave the old man a day or two to forget the phone call, then packed up and moved out of the room he'd been living in, an overpriced flophouse a few blocks from Penn Station. He mounted the stoop on West Fifty-third with a suitcase in each hand, rang the buzzer marked BOHAN, and climbed to the third floor, where an unshaven old wreck stood in the doorway, wearing a gray nightshirt and at least a week's worth of body odor.

'Uncle Joe? I'm your nephew Al, come all this way to see you.'

The old man was confused, but let him inside. He was smoking a cigarette, sucking on it as if it were a breathing tube connected to an oxygen tank, and spitting out questions between puffs. Whose son is he, then? Is he Neil's boy? And what's in the suitcases? And is he alive, Neil? He'd thought his brother was dead, thought he'd died without ever marrying.

The old man was wheezing, unsteady on his feet. There were two growths on his faced that looked cancerous, and his color was bad, and God above did he ever stink. He took hold of Bohan, one hand cupping the bristly chin, the other grasping the bony shoulder, and had little trouble snapping the old man's neck. How nice when the expedient act was humane as well!

Over the next several days he let the building's other tenants get used to him, while he made the place his own, getting rid of the old man's clothes and possessions even as he got rid of the old man himself. Every day he'd haul a few trash bags down the stairs and out the door. Cleaning up, he told the neighbors. These past few years, my uncle never threw anything out. It's hard for him, you know.

Some bags he left at the curb for the trash pickup. Others, containing pieces of the old man's body, couldn't be discarded quite so casually. He'd put the corpse in the tub, drained it of its fluids, and cut it into portable chunks with a bone saw from a Ninth Avenue kitchen supply store. Portions of Joe Bohan, wrapped up like cuts of meat, he carried a few at a time across the West Side Highway to the Hudson. If they ever surface – and that's unlikely, as there won't be any gases to lessen their specific gravity – he can't imagine that anyone will make anything of them. And, if by some forensic miracle they do, the hermit crab will have long since outgrown his shell, along with the name of Aloysius Bohan.

Once the last physical remnant of Joe Bohan was gone, except for his enduring odor, he let the word out that he'd taken his uncle to the hospital. 'I tried nursing him myself,' he told Mrs Laskowski, 'but I can't give him the care he needs. Last night I got him downstairs and into a cab and we rode clear up to the VA. Cab cost a fortune, but what are you going to do? I'm all he's got in the world. He wants me to stay here until he comes home from the hospital. I'm supposed to be in San Francisco, I've got a job offer out there, but I can't just leave him here. He's my uncle.'

And that was that.

Now he sits at the kitchen table, its top scarred by hundreds of Joe Bohan's neglected cigarettes. He touches his upper lip, then frowns, annoyed with himself. Habits, he thinks, take so little time to form, so much longer to break. He boots up his computer, which has sole claim on Joe Bohan's phone line. The dial-up connection is slow today, and he'd love to install a DSL line, but that's out of the question.

Well, perhaps he won't need to be here too much longer.

CHAPTER 18

TJ said, 'You already thought of this, and it don't make sense anyway, but if I don't say it I ain't never gonna get it out of my head.'

'Okay.'

'You most likely know what's coming.'

We were at the Morning Star. He'd called and asked me to meet him there, and I'd walked away from a much better cup of coffee than the one I was drinking now.

'I might,' I said.

'Gonna make me say it all the same. 'Kay. There any chance at all that David Thompson and Monica's killer are the same person?'

'The chief thing they've got in common,' I said, 'is that you and I don't know who they are or how to find them.'

'More'n that.'

'Oh?'

'Both got a mustache.'

'Maybe they're both Hitler, and he didn't die in the bunker after all. Look at the timing and you'll see they're not the same person. Thompson – that's probably not his name, but we've got to call him something. Thompson was with Louise Monday night from the time she met him at the restaurant until he got away from us a little before midnight.'

'And?'

'And it was around nine-thirty or ten when he showed up in the lobby of Monica's building, according to Sussman, who got it from the doorman.'

'That was Tuesday. Night before last, right?'

'Jesus, you're right.'

'Wouldn't be much of a stretch to get downtown in what, twenty-two hours?'

I shook my head. 'He was there Monday night, too,' I said. 'With Monica. She told Elaine.'

'He saw her Monday and Tuesday, then. We sure of that?'

'We can't call Monica and ask her. But yes, we're sure.'

'But we don't know what time. We got a time check for Tuesday, him comin' and goin', but not for Monday.'

I thought about it, nodded slowly.

'So he leaves Louise at a quarter of twelve, an' we know the first thing he does is whip out his cell an' make a call.'

'To Monica, inviting himself over. But if I remember what Elaine said, he already had a date planned for Monday with Monica.'

'"Sorry, honey, but I'm running a little late. Be over soon's I can."'

'He was a sharp dresser, according to Monica. Did David Thompson look like he fit Monica's definition of a sharp dresser?'

'Was jeans an' a polo shirt, wasn't it?'

'Personally,' I said, 'I can't quite see our guy showing up on Jane Street with flowers and a bottle of Strega.' I pictured him coming out of Louise's building. 'He lit a cigarette,' I remembered. 'That was one thing she established online, before she met the guy. That he was a smoker, because if he wasn't she didn't want any part of him.'

'So?'

'Monica was an ex-smoker, and she hated to be in the same room with a lit cigarette. She had that heightened sensitivity people seem to develop when they've been away from tobacco for a few years. If he was a heavy smoker—'

'We don't know about the heavy part. Maybe he just made sure to light one up when he was around Louise, to keep her happy.'

'And the minute he walks out of her building, he lights up another for show?'

'See what you mean. Who you callin'?'

'A cop,' I said. Sussman had given us his card, and I was punching the number into my cell phone. When I got him on the line I identified myself and said I had just one question. Was there any indication that anyone might have smoked a cigarette in Monica Driscoll's apartment?

'Why?'

I couldn't blame him. That would have been my response if our roles were reversed. Still, I'd have been happier if he hadn't asked.

'I've been looking into something for a friend,' I said. 'She's got no connection to Monica, nothing in common, except that there's a mystery man in her life. I haven't had much luck finding out anything about him, in fact he's been damned elusive, and—'

'And you thought maybe they were one and the same.'

'No,' I said, 'I thought and continue to think that they're not, but if I can make one phone call and rule it out altogether—'

'I get you. I take it you know for a fact whether or not this second guy smokes.'

'I know for a fact that he does.'

'And Ms Driscoll didn't?'

'And had strong feelings on the subject.'

He said he'd get back to me and rang off. TJ asked about Elaine. I said she'd been out the door that morning before I'd made it to the kitchen, that it was one of her gym days. I said I figured it was a good sign that she went, because I was pretty sure she hadn't felt like it.

Something like that, he said, that was the secret to it. You had to do it all the time, not just on the days you felt like it. I told him staying sober was like that.

'Last night,' he said, 'she'd be sad an' cry from time to time, and then it'd pass, you know, and

226

her mind'd be on the card game. You know how to play pinochle?'

'No.'

'Well, she could teach you. She can teach a game real good. It's an okay game. All you got in the world is two people an' a deck of cards, you could get by with it. Course it'd have to be a pinochle deck, so you'd need two decks of cards to make it. You take two decks, an' you don't use from deuce through eight, just nine on up to ace.'

'I'm really glad you're telling me all this.'

'Yeah, well, it be just the two of us an' we ain't even got a deck of cards, and we's waiting for the damn phone to ring. But I guess you don't need to hear all this shit about pinochle.'

'No, it's all right.'

'Thing is, even when she was fine, playing cards and joking, it was there, you know? This deep-down sadness, kind that runs clear to the bone.'

Sussman said, 'You'd think it would be a simple question to answer. This age of science we live in, where you can multiply your date of birth by the change in your pocket and feed the result into a computer, and it tells you what you ate for break-fast. *Did anybody smoke a cigarette in the apartment where the murder took place?* What's so tricky about that?'

'I gather it wasn't that simple.'

'First of all,' he said, 'the son of a bitch was a neatnik. I believe I told you he vacuumed, in addition to wiping every surface but the ceiling. So there wouldn't be any cigarette butts lying around, or any ashes in the ashtrays. Something I didn't notice at the time, but I can tell you now, is there weren't any ashtrays in the place, period. So it's pretty clear *she* wasn't a smoker, and didn't have regular company that smoked.'

'She wasn't and didn't.'

'Now he could have been a smoker and not smoked in her apartment, out of respect for her wishes.'

'I suppose,' I said, 'but when he had her tied up and started torturing her, I wouldn't think respect would play much of a role.'

'No, you're absolutely right. She's tied up with tape on her mouth, first thing he'd do is light one up. And most likely use her for an ashtray, far as that goes, and that's one thing I can tell you we didn't find.'

'Burn marks.'

'He worked her over pretty good. I didn't want to go into detail in front of your wife, but this guy was a fucking animal. If he'd had a cigarette going, we'd have seen evidence on the corpse.'

'You don't smoke yourself.'

'No, I never started.'

'When you walked into the crime scene—'

'I've been asking myself the same question. Did I smell smoke? I didn't notice, but would I? I can't answer that. Plus my partner and I weren't the first people there. A pair of uniforms responded

228

to the 911 call and were first on the scene. She hadn't been dead that long, so there wasn't the intense odor of advanced decomposition that develops over time, but you know the things that happen. The bowels let go, the bladder lets go. You know right away you're not in a perfume factory.'

'So one of the blues might have lit a cigarette.'

'They're not supposed to,' he said, 'but people do it. To mask the smell and just because you're standing around and there's a dead body there and it's the middle of the night and you're a smoker and you want a cigarette so you light one up. But I didn't notice the smell of smoke, and neither did my partner, and I've got a call in to ask the two uniforms if *they* noticed the smell of smoke when they went in, but if they're smokers all bets are off.'

'If they say no, they're too used to it to notice. If they say yes, they might be lying to cover up their own smoking.'

'You know how a cop thinks,' he said with approval. 'Long and short of it, strongest argument is he's not a smoker because he didn't put out his cigarettes on her. And now that we've ruled your guy out, suppose you tell me who he is and how to get ahold of him.'

'Now that we've ruled him out.'

'Right.'

I told him I had a problem with that. I'd be compromising my client's interests. She'd wanted a confidential investigation of a new boyfriend, just to make sure he didn't have an arrest record or a wife in Mamaroneck, and the last thing she'd want me to do was put the guy front and center in a murder investigation.

He said, 'I thought you were looking into something for a friend. Now she's a client. You licensed? You working for an attorney? If not, there's no privilege here.'

'I never said there was. If I thought for a minute there was a possible connection—'

'You must have, or you wouldn't have raised the issue. You had enough of a feeling about the guy to call me, and I spent the better part of an hour on it, so where do you get off holding out?'

'You're right,' I said, 'but I haven't got anything to give you. His name is David Thompson, except that may not be his name. Now you know everything I know.'

'Not everything. Who's your client?'

'No,' I said. 'Privilege or no, I'm not giving you that. I'll talk to her, and if it's okay with her I'll give you the name. But do you really want to send the investigation in this direction? If you want to start checking out every guy who may have lied to a woman . . .'

'Let's leave it that you'll talk to her.'

That's where we left it, but as soon as I'd rung off I remembered something that had been sticking in the back of my mind. I called him right back. 'The 911 call,' I said. 'You said middle of the night?'

'Well, not quite. Four in the morning. Close enough to the middle of the night, although I guess it would have been ten or eleven in the morning in Prague.'

'The call came from Prague?'

'It might as well have. Didn't show up on Caller ID, and when we checked the LUDS we got an unregistered cell phone.'

'They record the 911 calls, don't they?'

'Oh, absolutely, and it's all on tape. Or digital, I guess. Everything's digital nowadays.'

Even fingers and toes. 'Somebody called in at four in the morning. You said "he." The caller was male?'

'Probably. It's hard to tell too much from a whisper.'

'He whispered? Unless they refined the technology, that means no voiceprint ID.'

'That's true, as far as I know.'

'So it was him. He phoned it in himself.'

'That's the working assumption,' he said. 'Whispered to prevent identification. Or he just didn't want to wake his wife by talking loud, but somehow I don't think that was it.'

'What did he say?'

'"There's a woman who's been murdered," plus the address and apartment number. Operator tried to keep him on the line but he slipped the hook and swam away. Calls like that, it's usually mischief, some drunk wants to send a cop on a wild goose chase, or he's looking to wake up some

231

schmuck he's got a beef with. But you got to check it out, so the two uniforms went and got the doorman to ring the apartment, and got a key from him when there was no answer. And walked in on more than they expected to find.'

'He wanted the body found,' I said.

'It does look that way, doesn't it?'

'He wanted it found right away. He knocked himself out to get rid of the evidence, he ran the vacuum cleaner. If you were him, wouldn't you want her to lie there undiscovered for as long as possible?'

'If I were him I'd do the world a favor and cut my fucking throat. But I had the same thought myself. The guy's not all of a piece. He's inconsistent.'

'Like a Magritte painting,' I remembered.

'Well, kind of. This part wouldn't show up in a painting, it's not visual, but it's the same kind of inconsistency. It clashes.'

Elaine had called it dissonance.

'I don't know, maybe you can't expect consistency from a crazy man, but this guy's off the chart. It's somewhere between Magritte and a turd in a punch bowl, which was an image I thought of yesterday and decided to keep to myself.'

'Thanks for sharing.'

'Yeah, right. I don't know why he called it in. Unless he was proud of his work and didn't want it to go unnoticed.'

'And four in the morning, well, he can't sleep, he's got nothing else to do . . .'

'It may be a mistake trying to figure him out. Still, how can you keep from trying? I don't know if it's enough to call it a pattern, but you could almost say the bastard's consistently inconsistent. Like with the murder weapon.'

'I don't follow you.'

'Taking everything else,' he said, 'and leaving behind the one thing most killers would take along. Didn't I tell you? He left the knife sticking in her chest. He stabbed her in the heart and left it there.'

'Jesus. No, you didn't mention this yesterday.'

'Again, probably out of deference to your wife. You don't want to be too graphic. It's something, though, wouldn't you say?'

'It seems completely out of character. Any chance you'll be able to trace it?'

'Well, I think that's why he didn't mind leaving it. We can trace it all we want and all it's going to lead is right back to her apartment. I called it a knife just now, but it's more along the lines of a dagger, and probably a ceremonial one. It's decorative, and to look at it you wouldn't think of it as a weapon, not until you saw what he did with it. I guess he must have liked the looks of it. Either he forgot to bring a weapon or he figured he'd pick something out of her knife drawer, and he saw this on the desk or coffee table, wherever she kept it. It's nice looking, if you owned it you'd leave it out where people could see it. And he certainly did that. He left it sticking straight up in the air with the tip in her heart.'

CHAPTER 19

'I guess you'll want to get upstairs,' I said. 'Don't you have to see how your stocks are doing?'

'Got no stocks.'

'You got wiped out?'

'Wiped myself out,' he said. 'Do that once a day. Way the game is played.'

He explained it for me. Ideally, a day trader started and ended the day with nothing in his account but cash. Whatever he bought during the day's trading, he sold before the closing bell. Whatever stocks he'd shorted, he covered. Win or lose, plus or minus, he faced a fresh slate each morning. I told him it's a shame the rest of life's not like that.

'There's stocks I keep an eye on,' he said. 'Charts I study. Make a dollar here, lose a dollar there. Commission be the same on each transaction, whether you a high roller or playing with nickels and dimes. Ten ninety-nine a trade. You betting basketball games, they never give you that good a line.'

'And you do okay?'

He shrugged. 'What's that thing you like to say? Woman falls off the Empire State Building, passes the thirty-fourth floor, what's she holler out?'

'"So far, so good."'

'Only the last half-inch you got to worry about.'

'That's it,' I agreed.

'So far so good. I got more'n I started with, and time to time I been drawing some cash for expenses.'

'It must be nerve-racking.'

'Not too. Worst that happens, day's a minus 'stead of a plus. You guess wrong on Lucent Technology, guy who guessed right don't show up with a nine and start bustin' caps at you. Lose a few dollars, is all.'

'You're saying it beats selling product.'

'No comparison, Harrison.' He grinned, enjoying the rhyme. 'Plus you're not out on the street corner on rainy days. Big difference right there.' He called the waiter over, said he guessed he'd have another bagel. To me he said, 'This David Thompson. Cops likely to find him?'

'I don't think they're going to make much of an effort. Sussman didn't spell it out, but in his position I'd run a computer check of yellow sheets. I'd sort all the David Thompsons, screen for age and color, toss the ones that are currently locked up, and save the rest for some night when there's nothing on TV.'

'You gonna give him Louise?'

'My guess is he'll forget to ask. And what am I

holding out? We know damn well they're two different guys.'

'Ever since Monica got killed,' he said, 'it don't seem all that important finding out about David Thompson. Like is he married or not.'

'I know. What do we care?'

'But ain't nothing changed far as Louise is concerned.'

'No,' I said, 'and if he's running a game, she ought to know about it. And if he's kosher she ought to know that, too, so she can relax and enjoy herself. I don't want to give up on Thompson, but I can't think of much we can do besides wait. Next time Louise sees him, we can take another shot at shadowing him. Or the mailbox lady could call me and give me a name.'

'I was thinking 'bout that last part. Seems like we ought to be able to hurry the process some.'

'How?'

'Say we sent him a letter, with the suite number on it and all. Soon as it gets there, she's gonna call you.'

'If she remembers.'

'If she don't, maybe you give her a call to remind her. Even run up there and remind her in person.'

'And?'

'And she looks at the letter, and—' He broke off, closed his eyes, put his head in his hands. 'And nothing,' he said. ''Cause only way she gets the name is off the envelope, an' we'd need to know it ourselves to put it down there. Good thing I ain't in front of my computer, way my mind's working today.'

The day trader grabbed the check, insisting he'd saved money by lingering in the Morning Star. I told him what he'd proposed wasn't so bad. It showed he was thinking, if not very clearly. 'And it would work fine,' I added, 'if all we wanted to do was send him a letter bomb.'

'Solve our problems that way,' he said. 'Until Louise goes and pulls another nicotine addict off of Craig's List.'

I went across the street. Elaine wasn't there, but I found her gym clothes in the hamper and deduced that she'd come home to shower and change. It was the sharpest detection work I'd done in a while and I was proud of myself. I called her at the shop and the machine answered. I didn't leave a message, and while I was trying to decide whether to try her again in ten minutes or walk over there myself, the door opened and she came in.

'I opened up,' she said, 'and I looked around, and I said the hell with it. I locked up again and came home.'

'And here you are.'

'And here I am.' She caught me looking at her and said, 'I look like hell, don't I? Tell the truth.'

'In all the years I've known you, you've never looked like hell. Not once.'

'Until now.'

'And not now, either.'

'You want to try telling me I've never looked better? I didn't think so.'

'You look fine.'

I followed her as she walked to the mirror in the foyer and put her forefingers high on her cheeks. She pressed upward, then let go. 'Fucking gravity,' she said. 'Who the hell asked for it? God damn it, I was going to be the one woman who never aged. Guess what? I'm the same as everybody else.' She turned to face me. 'My God, will you listen to me? The only thing worse than the little lines around my mouth are the words coming out of it. Me me me, all the fucking time. Who cares if I show my age, and why the hell shouldn't I, anyway? Just because I don't act it.'

'It's a rough day,' I said.

'I guess. I didn't get much sleep last night. I could lie down now but I'd just be setting myself up for another night of staring out the window. Guess what? The Towers aren't coming back, and neither is Monica.'

'No.'

'It's not a dream. Waking up won't fix it.'

'No.'

'It's gonna take time. It's what, twenty-four hours since we heard? If I was all better I'd be disgusted with myself. Time takes time, isn't that what they say?'

'That's what they say.'

'I wish I could take a pill and wake up six months from now. Except I'd still feel the same way, because I wouldn't have spent those six months dealing with it. Anyway, nobody's invented a six-month pill yet.'

'Not that I've heard of.'

'They've got a permanent pill. You take it and you don't wake up at all. I'm not ready for that yet.'

'Good.'

'Sometimes,' she said, 'it's not all that hard to understand why you used to drink.'

'It did shut things down.'

'I can see the appeal, I have to admit it. But the hell with all that, and the hell with me me me, as far as that goes. Did you talk to Sussman?'

'They haven't made any progress,' I said, 'or if they have he didn't bother to report it to me.' I told her about TJ's wild hunch, and how I'd tried it out on Sussman even though neither of us thought it stood much of a chance of being true.

'If he smoked,' she said, 'she'd have told me about it. She never would have hooked up with him in the first place, she didn't even like to be around people with the smell of smoke on their clothes, but if he just plain charmed her so much she was willing to overlook the smoking, the one thing she'd have done is mention it. "I can't tell you anything about him, but he smokes, can you believe it, and I still like him." Whatever. She'd have found a way to say something about it.'

'Eventually,' she said, 'they're going to rebuild. First everybody in the city gets to voice an opinion, and the relatives of the victims get to vote twice, and finally they'll build something. And I wonder what it's going to be like, standing here and looking out at it.'

She was at the window, of course.

'I wish something would happen,' she said, and my cell phone rang.

It was the woman I'd given my card to, the mailbox lady. She was calling to tell me that the morning's mail had held a letter for the holder of box 1217. 'An' I write down the name,' she said. 'I think is the same name you say. David Thompson.'

'That's the name,' I agreed. 'Who sent the letter?'

'Who send it? How I know who send it?'

'In the upper-left corner of the envelope,' I said, 'there's usually a return address.'

'Maybe. I don't remember.'

Jesus, it was like pulling teeth. 'Could you get the envelope now and take a look?'

'Is gone.'

'It's gone?'

'He come an' pick it up. Same man as the picture you show me.'

'He came and picked it up.'

'Is his letter. He ask for it, I give it to him. You never say not to do this.'

Nor had I asked her to note the return address. It wasn't her fault, it was mine, but knowing this somehow failed to make me feel better about the whole thing.

I asked her if she remembered anything about the envelope. It was, she said, a long envelope, not the smaller kind that bills come in. And the address was typed or printed, not handwritten.

'An' he was disappointed,' she volunteered.

'Disappointed?'

'He open it an' look inside an' he make a face.'

Because there was no check in there, I thought. That's why he'd turned up, to look for the check he thought I was going to send him, and he got some other letter instead, probably some relentless credit card issuer telling him he'd been preapproved, and he was understandably disheartened.

I thanked her, and she said next time she would write down whatever it said on the envelope. In fact she would make a photocopy. I hadn't noticed a copying machine, but now that she mentioned it I re-called another hand-lettered sign in the window, offering copies at fifteen cents apiece. That would be good, I told her, and I thanked her again and hung up.

'He'll be back tomorrow or the next day,' I told Elaine, 'because he wants the check he thinks I'm going to send him. He's sounding increasingly legit. Whatever today's letter was, the name on it was the same one he gave Louise. And he wouldn't

241

have to know who the mythical check was from in order to go pick it up. The business he's in, there's probably a long list of companies that take their time paying him. He figures he'll find out which one it is when he's got the check in hand. It's a shame she didn't note the return address, but she's not a mind reader.'

'It sounds like that's the only service they don't offer there.'

'Just about. He'll be back tomorrow, but that's no help. Not unless someone else sends him a letter.'

I made a trip to the dry cleaner's for her, and picked up sandwiches at the deli on my way back. Neither of us wanted them, but we ate anyway.

Then we were talking again about the view from the window, and how it would seem when towers in one form or another began to rise into our field of vision. I don't remember how, but that led to Magritte or dissonance or paradox, whatever, and I told her about the startling dissonance Sussman had forgotten to mention a day ago, the presence of the murder weapon at the crime scene.

She said, 'A dagger.'

'Well, some kind of decorative knife. I don't know that Sussman's an authority on edged weapons.'

'And he thinks he found it lying around? I've been in that apartment a few hundred times and I never saw a dagger there.'

'It may not have been a dagger. It may have been, I don't know . . .'

'A letter opener.'

'Something like that, sure.'

'I never saw one of those, either.'

'Well, would you notice it if you did? As far as—'

She didn't let me finish. 'Call him,' she said.

'Call him?'

'Sussman, Mark Sussman. Call him.'

It took a while, but I finally got through to him. She held out her hand for the phone and I gave it to her.

She said, 'This is Elaine Scudder. I'm fine, thank you, but that's not the point. I'd like you to describe the murder weapon for me. Was it bronze? Well, was it bronze colored? And was it sharp at the tip but not along the edges of the blade? Do you have it in front of you? Well, could you get it? Yes, of course it's important. If it wasn't important I wouldn't ask you to do it, would I? I'm sorry, I didn't mean to snap. Yes, I'll wait.'

I started to say something but she held up a hand and stopped me. 'All right,' she said, 'let me describe it to you, okay? And we'll see if it's what I think it is. It's a bronze letter opener or paper knife, ten to twelve inches long. On one side there's a scene in low relief of two hunting dogs holding a stag at bay. On the other side, you'll find the name of the sculptor in incused block capitals. The name is DeVreese, that's spelled

D-E-V-R-E-E-S-E. You may need a magnifying glass to make it out.'

She held the phone, listened. Then she said, 'Mark? Don't go anywhere. I saw him, I saw the man who killed her. I sold him the murder weapon. Oh my God. Don't go anywhere, we'll be right down.'

CHAPTER 20

The letter opener was sealed in a clear plastic evidence bag. Sussman held it out to her, and I could sense her reluctance to touch it, even wrapped in plastic. She took it gingerly in both hands and looked at it, and a tear flowed out of the corner of her eye and down her cheek. I don't think she noticed it.

'Yes, this is it,' she said. 'You see that little nick there? This is the one I had in the shop. It would almost have to be. I don't know how many of these they made, but this is the only one I've ever seen, and I never came across it in any catalogs.' She handed it back. 'He came into my shop. He stood there and he talked to me, he paid what I asked and walked off with it in his pocket. And then he killed my friend with it.'

'And this was Tuesday?'

'The day before yesterday. It didn't take him long to use it, did it? He bought it from me that afternoon and killed her that night. I think I'm going to be sick.'

Sussman told her there was a bathroom down the hall, while another detective hurried to provide

245

a wastebasket. Somebody else turned up with a glass of water. She decided she wasn't going to be sick after all, took a sip of the water, and steadied herself with a couple of deep breaths.

Sussman asked if he'd used a credit card.

She said, 'No, dammit. I had to go and offer him a discount if he paid cash. I said I'd knock off the sales tax. I pay the tax anyway, it's hardly worth breaking the law to save a few dollars, but I save the credit card commission, and it's a way to give a small discount. If I hadn't opened my big mouth—'

'He'd have paid cash anyway,' I said. 'Or used a fake card. You didn't screw anything up.'

'Why did I have to sell him the damn thing? Why didn't I tell him it wasn't for sale?' No one had an answer for that, but she answered it herself. 'I'm being irrational, aren't I? I just want to rewrite the past, or at least see how it could have been rewritten. Never mind. He came into my shop and picked it out and I sold it to him.'

'How much did you charge him?'

'Two hundred dollars. There's no book price because it's not in the book, but he didn't overpay.'

'Remember the denomination of the bills?'

'Twenties, I think. I think he counted out ten twenties.'

Someone speculated that the bills might hold a print. She remembered that she'd given some of the twenties in change later that same day to a customer who'd bought a small china dog for twelve dollars and paid for it with a hundred-dollar bill. And she'd taken a couple of twenties out of the register and spent them shopping. But there might be one of the killer's twenties in the register, and it might have prints on it, some of which might be his, and—

It sounded like a long shot to me. But someone would have to check it out, because we were down to long shots.

She said, 'He gave me the creeps.'

'Now, when you think about it?' Sussman asked. 'Or at the time?'

'At the time. There was something about him. At the time I thought he was hitting on me, which I get a certain amount of, any woman does. Sometimes it's flirting and sometimes it's more exploratory.'

'Which was this?'

'It was somewhere in the middle, or at least that's what it felt like, but it was distinctly creepy. It wasn't anything he did, just the way he looked at me.' A light came into her eyes, and she shuddered. 'He wanted to kill me,' she said. 'There was a moment there when he was considering something, I could see it in his eyes, and I thought it was, you know, making a pass. But he had the paper knife in his hand, and he was thinking about stabbing me with it.'

Sussman told her she couldn't know that.

'Fine,' she said. 'So don't write it down. But that's what he was doing. You think he just happened to buy the murder weapon from somebody who just happened to be the victim's best friend?'

'No, I didn't say that.'

'He was stalking you,' I said.

'Yes, that's exactly what he was doing.'

'Had you seen him before?'

'I don't think so. It's possible. He was, well, pretty ordinary looking.'

'But you can picture him in your mind?'

'I think so. You want me to sit down with a police artist?'

'If you don't mind,' Sussman said, and she looked at him like he was crazy. Mind? Why should she mind?

The artist was of the new breed. He never picked up a pencil, just sat at a computer terminal loaded with a dedicated software program that had made sketches obsolete. He worked with her the same way a more traditional police artist would have worked, asking her were the eyebrows bushier, was there more definition in the jawline, and morphing the onscreen image accordingly. She sat next to him while he worked, answering his questions, occasionally reaching out to touch an area on the screen that seemed to her not to be right. A couple of us stood around watching and kept our mouths shut while the process continued.

When she decided that was as close as they were going to get, he saved the image and printed out half a dozen copies, and we each took one and stared long and hard at it. I certainly couldn't recognize the son of a bitch. He looked like everybody and nobody.

One of the cops said, 'There must be a million guys out there look like this.'

'Not a million,' Sussman said, 'but I know what you mean.'

'He didn't have any strong features,' Elaine said. 'Or especially weak ones, either. There was something about his eyes, but I think that was a matter of the look in them, and how are you going to get that out of a computer?'

'But the sketch resembles him?'

She frowned. 'It doesn't not resemble him,' she said.

'Meaning what exactly?'

'I don't know. Maybe I didn't use my eyes right, maybe I didn't want to look at him. Maybe all I saw was the mustache, and I locked in on that and didn't pay enough attention to the rest of his face.'

'It suits him, the mustache. I mean, you can see why he'd grow one. Makes his face look a little less generic.'

'I say thank God for the mustache,' Sussman said, 'because we're gonna braid a rope out of it and hang him with it. You did really well, Mrs Scudder.'

'Elaine,' she said.

'Elaine, then. You did good work. The sketch may look, I don't know, sketchy, to you, but you know how to use your eyes, and my guess is it's closer than you think. You should see some of the sketches people come up with. We had this guy, committed a string of rapes in and around the Morris Park section of the Bronx. They put three sketches of him on the news, all in a row, and I swear you thought you were looking at three different guys. They didn't even look like brothers.'

'They damn well looked like brothers,' one of the cops said.

'I'm gonna file on you,' Sussman told him. 'Have you cited for racial insensitivity. I suppose you think you can get away with saying shit like that just because you're black. They didn't look like members of the same family, is that better?'

'I say arrest all three of them,' someone else said. 'How can you go wrong?'

CHAPTER 21

The Canarsie line runs east from Eighth Avenue and Fourteenth Street to the Rockaway Parkway stop at the corner of Rockaway and Glenwood, in the Canarsie section of Brooklyn. Officially it's the L train. Not too long ago it was the LL, or Double-L. Then someone in a position of authority (though not, I shouldn't think, a whole lot of authority) decided to do away with all the double letters. The GG train became the G and the LL became the L. Meanwhile the AA became the K, because there already was an A, and eventually disappeared entirely. I don't know who makes these decisions, or what he could possibly do for a living if he ever lost that job.

I don't often have occasion to take the L, and when I do I invariably think of my father, who died riding it. He stood on the platform between two cars, probably to sneak a smoke, and he fell, and the wheels passed over him. He was probably drunk when it happened, so you could blame the drink for it, or the tobacco, if you wanted to stretch a point. When I was a boy, of course, I blamed the train.

The L train runs along Fourteenth Street and under the East River into Brooklyn. Eventually it comes up above ground and runs as an elevated line, as do most trains when they reach the outer boroughs, but we didn't stay on it that long. We got off at the first stop in Brooklyn, which is Bedford Avenue in Williamsburg. We walked north on Bedford past several numbered streets until we came to an attractive three-story house in a row of attractive three-story houses. Once they'd all been covered up with asphalt or aluminum siding, but in recent years they'd all been restored, and Elaine thought they were adorable and the whole neighborhood charming.

'I could live here,' she said.

She hadn't been out here before. I had, though not recently, and I was able to pick out Ray and Bitsy's house without having to look up the number in my book. Ray must have seen us coming; the door opened before I could knock on it, and as we followed him into the living room his wife, Bitsy, emerged from the kitchen with a plate of cookies and a carafe of coffee. It was Puerto Rican coffee, dark and rich, and I'd had a yen for a cup ever since I saw the Café Bustelo sign in the shop window on Amsterdam Avenue.

Ray told us we were both looking terrific, and Elaine asked about their kids, and Elaine and I each took a cookie, although she could only manage a bite of hers. Ray said, 'Well, we could sit and talk for hours, but I guess we should get down to it, huh?' and Elaine nodded and stood up and went to the room on the third floor where he had his studio.

I sat down and reached for another cookie, and Bitsy said, 'There's more in the kitchen. First time I tried this recipe. I have to say I think they came out pretty good, and they couldn't be simpler to make. That coffee okay?'

'It's a lot more than okay.'

'Matt? Is she all right?'

'Her best friend was killed yesterday.'

'Aw, gee, that's terrible. But, you know, I'm kind of relieved to hear it, in a way, because I was afraid, you know, that she might be ill.'

'When she feels something it shows in her face.'

'Well, besides that. Her energy's way off. Like her aura's a mess.'

'You can see people's auras?'

'Not exactly see,' she said. 'It's more I get a feeling. My mother was the same way. I don't know, it's hard to explain. Maybe it's a load of crap. But losing a best friend, and you say she was murdered? That would do it, all right. That's a terrible thing.'

We had turned right when we left the stationhouse, but before we'd gone ten steps she stopped in her tracks and said, 'Ray.' We know a few Rays, including Ray Gruliow, whose house is right there in the Sixth Precinct, but I didn't need a last name to know which one she meant.

Ray Galindez was a kid from El Barrio who became a cop and then discovered his true calling when they found out he could draw and made a police artist out of him. The IdentiKit software didn't take his job away, because they'd have been happy to train him to use it, but it took the joy out of it for him.

Elaine thought his ability amounted to far more than a knack or a job skill, that he was in fact a talented artist who possessed the ability to bond with his subjects and channel their visions into black-and-white reality. Working together, the two of them had produced a portrait of her long-dead father, and she went on to get him assignments drawing other people's dead relatives, including those of a Holocaust survivor who'd lost her whole family in the camps. It had been a remarkably cathartic experience for Elaine, who'd called the process the equivalent of a year or two of therapy. I don't know what it was like for the others who tried it, but nobody ever asked for a refund.

Because Elaine took him seriously, Ray began to take his art seriously himself. She showed his work at her shop, sold a few pieces, and managed to get a neighborhood paper, the *Chelsea-Clinton News*, to run a review. That got him some more work, and with Bitsy's encouragement he quit the NYPD and set up shop as an artist. They already had a house they were renovating in Williamsburg, which by then was becoming the ideal place for an artist to live, and he managed to pick up some commercial work that helped pay the mortgage each month. Bitsy, a trained bookkeeper, built a practice in the neighborhood, crunching numbers for people who were better at mixing colors, and that kept the lights and phone on and the freezer stocked, and let her work at home and be a full-time mother in the bargain, with plenty of time for baking cookies.

The IdentiKit software is pretty decent, and enables anyone with a decent eye and a brief course of instruction to function competently as a police artist. But Ray did something no amount of training or programming could achieve, somehow making his drawing hand function as an extension of his subject's mind. Elaine wasn't satisfied with what had come out of the squad room computer, and if there was a way to improve on it, we'd find it in Williamsburg.

I was thinking about another cookie and telling myself I didn't really want it when Ray and Elaine came downstairs. 'Show Ray what their artist came up with,' she said, and I got out our copy of their sketch and unfolded it. Ray arranged the two sketches side by side on the coffee table, and Elaine said, 'You see? All the difference in the world.'

That was a stretch. Considered together, the two pictures looked like two different views of the same man. I hadn't seen the fellow, so I couldn't say which was a better likeness. Elaine had, and as far as she was concerned there was no comparison.

'Ray's drawing looks less generic,' I allowed. 'It's hard to point to anything and say it's different, but something's different.'

'The affect is different,' Elaine said. 'The other one feel's like something you could put together with an advanced version of that kid's toy.'

'Mr Potato Head,' Bitsy said.

'I used to love Mr Potato Head,' Elaine said. 'I couldn't understand why my mother wanted the potato back so she could fix it for dinner. I started crying. My father took me on his lap and told me there would always be another potato.'

'There always will,' I said.

'Somehow I used to find that reassuring. This sketch looks just like him, Ray. You know how I can tell? Because I can't stand to look at it. I get sick to my stomach.'

My reaction was less extreme, but I did get a funny feeling looking at Ray's drawing. He'd managed to convey not just what Elaine had seen in the face but how she felt about it now that she knew what the man had done. It was in the eyes, I guess, but whatever it was there was something chilling about it.

I said, 'He looks familiar.'

'Maybe because of the time you spent staring at the other sketch.'

'Maybe.'

She turned to me. 'Are you serious? Do you know him?'

'The best I can do is say he looks familiar. Maybe I saw him on the street, or in the subway. Him or somebody with a similar look to him. You see so many people in this town, so many glancing images.'

'But you're pretty good at paying attention to what you see.'

Cop training, I suppose. I told Ray we'd want to make copies of the drawing, and was there a place in the neighborhood? He gave me a look and went upstairs, drawing in hand, and returned with a folder holding a dozen copies, plus the original pencil sketch in a manila envelope.

As we prepared to go, he took me aside. 'I've never seen her like this,' he said. 'She's scared to death of this guy.'

We'd have taken the subway home, the L and the A, but Ray called a car service. A good thing about living in Brooklyn is that you can do that, while the downside is that you have to, as you're not often able to flag a cruising taxi. Our driver was cheerful and talkative, but when we didn't respond he took the hint and lapsed into a wounded silence. When he pulled up in front of the Parc Vendôme I got out first and looked around before I helped Elaine out of the cab.

The doorman on duty was one of the regular crew, his service there dating back almost to the year we moved in. I established that no one had come around looking for us since he came on duty, and told him not to send anybody up to our apartment.

'Unless it's TJ,' Elaine said.

I amended my instructions. But no one else, I said, no matter what credentials the person might show. He could have a badge, I said. He could wear a blue uniform. That didn't mean he was a cop.

We went upstairs, and I said, 'I just realized what I'm doing. I'm like a general, preparing for the previous war.'

'Motley,' she said.

She meant not the garb jesters wear but a man named James Leo Motley, who got past her doorman wearing the uniform and carrying the badge and baton of an auxiliary policeman he'd murdered. He was a cop, so why would the doorman think to turn him away? He'd stabbed Elaine, and she'd come close to dying.

That was – Christ, it was fifteen years ago, and Motley, who'd menaced us both, had served too to bring us together after about that many years apart. I suppose that meant we owed him something, but I was glad we'd never be able to pay it, grateful beyond measure that the son of a bitch was dead.

Now we had a new one on our hands, resourceful enough to come in uniform, resourceful enough to think of something else.

When we got off the elevator I checked the hallway, then left her standing in it while I checked the apartment. I told her she could come in, and once she did I locked the door.

She said, 'I guess I won't go to the shop again until this is over.'

'No kidding.'

'I've got someone coming tomorrow afternoon. A Russian woman, or maybe she's Ukrainian. As if it makes a difference. She's got some icons she'd like to sell, and I wouldn't mind buying them if they're authentic. Or even if they're not, if the price is right and they look good. I could tell her to come here instead.'

'You could tell her to come next month.'

'Is it going to take that long?'

'To find this guy? There's no telling. They could pick him up tonight or he could stay out there for weeks.'

'God. You really don't think it's safe to have her come here? She's a little old lady in a babushka.'

'The staff here's pretty good,' I said, 'but they're not Marines guarding an embassy. If the rule's ironclad, they might get the idea that it's important. Every time you make an exception, they take the whole business a little less seriously.'

She opened her mouth to debate the point, then changed her mind and told me I was right. 'If he's really stalking me,' she said.

'What else would you call it?'

'He really did want to kill me. I don't read minds,

259

but you pick things up. That's what I was picking up. He had this weapon in his hand, and there I was, and the thought went through his mind. But maybe it was just an opportunity, you know? He had a weapon and I was there, and he's a nut who likes to kill women, and . . .'

'And?'

'And why was he there? Why my shop? It had to be because I was Monica's friend, and he had to know that. From something she said, or from following her around.'

'Or from following you around, and that's how he found his way to Monica.'

'You think?'

'I think either's equally possible.'

'I guess. Matt, he wouldn't come into my shop looking to buy a murder weapon. It's this little chichi art and antiques shop, not Macho Toys for Butch Boys. The letter opener was probably the only thing in the shop you could use to kill somebody, unless you smothered them with a hooked rug or beat them to death with one of the marble bookends. He came in because he wanted an up-close look at me.'

'That sounds right.'

'The hell with the icons. I'm Jewish, you couldn't even bury them with me. I hate for her to make the trip for nothing, though.'

'Where is she, out in Brighton Beach?'

'No, I think she's in the neighborhood some-where, but even so she shouldn't have to schlep icons there and back. I've got her number at the store.'

'I'll go over there later and get it.'

'Will you? And I'll call her and tell her what? That the shop is closed until further notice. You know what you could do while you're at it—'

'I'll put a sign in the window.'

'I'll print it out. I print neater than you.'

'You're a girl.'

'That must be it. Who are you calling?'

'Sussman,' I said. 'I want to give him something he doesn't know he needs, and save myself a trip while I'm at it.'

I was waiting at the shop when Sussman got there, a lab technician in tow. I let them in, and the techie gave us each a pair of gloves, then went around collecting fingerprints from all the likely surfaces, concentrating on the glass countertops. I opened the cash box and took out the three twenty-dollar bills it contained and gave them to Sussman. He bagged them and made a point of writing out a receipt for me. I didn't care about the sixty bucks, which was just as well for all the good the receipt would do. If the past was anything to go by, those bills were destined to spend eternity in an NYPD evidence locker.

'Now where's this sketch I've heard so much about?' Sussman asked, and I showed it to him. He said it didn't look a whole lot different to him, and

I said he'd see the difference when he looked at the two sketches side by side.

He said, 'This one's more artistic, I can see that much. It looks like it was drawn by a human being and not by a machine. That wouldn't necessarily make it a better likeness.'

'Elaine says it is.'

'Well, she should know. She's the only one who's seen the original. Who'd you say did it?'

I told him a little bit about Ray, and pointed to a framed drawing he'd done. It showed the profile of a middle-aged man sitting in a chair with a book. He was an uncle of Bitsy's who was finishing out his days in a nursing home in Santurce. This was how she remembered him, but she'd told Ray to sell the drawing if anyone wanted to buy it. 'We don't need my whole damn family all over the walls,' she'd said. 'You know how many cousins I got?'

'Guy's very good,' Sussman said. 'What would something like that go for, you happen to know?'

'I'd have to ask Elaine.'

'When this is over,' he said, 'I might be interested. The more you look at it, the more you see. I could definitely find wall space for something like that. Plus the fact that he's a former cop adds something to it for me. I don't know why it should but it does. She have other work of his?'

'In back, but—'

'No, don't drag 'em out now, just for future reference. I really like that one.' He turned to the sketch

Ray had done a couple of hours ago. 'This one too,' he said, 'but not to hang on the wall. This one I'd like to hang by the balls. I'll take this along, call in the other sketch, get this one out there. Even without seeing the original I can tell this one's a better likeness. You know how? Because you get a sense of the guy.'

CHAPTER 22

After they left I checked Elaine's appointment book. I started to copy down the name and number of a Mrs Federenko, then simplified things by calling the woman myself. I told her I was calling for Mrs Scudder, who wouldn't be able to look at the icons tomorrow because the shop was closed until further notice.

That's what it said, too, on the sheet of paper she'd given me, which I taped to the inside of the window. I left a new message on the shop's answering machine: *'Thank you for calling Elaine Scudder Art and Antiques. The shop is closed until further notice.'*

I pulled the gates shut and headed uptown. When I got to Fifty-seventh Street I called TJ and said I wanted to talk to him. He offered to come down, and I said to stay where he was, that I'd be right up. I crossed the street and went into the lobby of the old hotel. Vinnie was still working there, he'd had that job for thirty years that I knew about, and he just gave me a nod and didn't even bother calling to let TJ know I was coming. For all I know, he may have been under the impression that I still

264

lived there. God knows I'd put in enough time in that little room.

'You didn't have to come up,' TJ told me. A game of computer solitaire filled the screen, and he saw what I was looking at and turned it off. 'Wall Street's been closed since four o'clock,' he said, 'and I dumped everything before three. Had a wild ride.'

'Oh?'

'When did I get up here this morning? Whenever it was, there's this stock I been watching, an' it made a move, you know, it broke through this particular price point, so I bought some. An' it went up.'

'Isn't that what it was supposed to do?'

'Yeah, well, they don't always be doin' what they supposed to do. So it's movin' up an' movin' up, an' I pop in this trailing stop-loss order, so if it goes down I'll be out of it, but each time it goes up a notch the stop-loss order goes up a notch with it, an' you don't know what the hell I'm talking about, do you?'

'I get a general idea.'

'Well, it kept runnin' up like that for, I don't know, two hours? An' then it came back down a bit, an' when it hit my stop-loss order I didn't have to do nothin', I was out of it automatically. They already had my order an' they sold me out. An' then of course the stock turns around an' heads back up, an' I'm like, wha'd I do that for? An' then I'm like, should I buy more?'

'You're talking like a Valley Girl.'

'I am?' He frowned. 'Don't want to do that. What I did, I told myself to be cool, and it was a good thing, because it turned around and went all the way back down, an' it finished the day two whole points below where I bought it at in the first place.'

'So you did all right.'

'I did real good. They want to print up a list of contented stock-holders, they can put my name on it.'

'What's the company?'

'I dunno. Trading symbol's NFI. I never did find out the name of it.'

'Do you know what they do?'

'No.'

'Doesn't any of that matter?'

'Not if you ain't gonna own it for more'n two hours. But we can have a look.' He picked up a newspaper, ran his eyes down the stock table. 'Name's Novastar. Pays a nice dividend, must be a REIT or a MLP. Course you got to own it a little longer'n I did to collect the dividend. Who's that there? That ain't Louise's boyfriend, is it?'

'You don't think it's a good likeness?'

'Don't look like the man I saw.'

'This is someone else,' I said. 'This is the man who killed Monica.'

After I'd brought him up to speed, the two of us went across the street. It seemed to me that at least one of us should be with Elaine whenever possible. I couldn't be sure she was his primary target, and for all I knew he'd killed Monica and got on the next plane to Las Vegas, but until they ran him down and caught him I wasn't taking any chances. The way it looked to me, the man was the worst possible combination, an off-the-page homicidal maniac with an incisive, methodical mind. You couldn't wait for him to do something stupid, nor could you expect him to behave logically. He was crazy like a rabid fox, and all you could do was hope he ran out in front of a car.

Around seven I went around the corner and picked up dinner from the Chinese restaurant. We usually call down and have them deliver, but deliveries weren't part of the new regimen. No one was getting upstairs but the three of us, and if that meant a little extra coming and going, I figured I could live with that.

I ordered more food than we were likely to eat, and I guess that too was part of the siege mentality we were operating under. 'I guess I won't be going out of the house much,' Elaine said, wielding her chopsticks, and I told her she wouldn't be going out of the house at all. She let herself get used to the idea, then picked up another piece of the coconut beef.

I asked TJ if he owned a gun. He didn't, and neither did I. A few years ago Mick Ballou and I had been at war with a gang that had taken up residence at his farm upstate in Sullivan County, and we'd gone out there armed and did a decade's worth of shooting in a matter of minutes. I hadn't had a gun in my hand since that night.

'If you had a gun,' I said, 'would you know how to use it?'

'Learning curve can't be too steep,' he said. 'Some of the stupidest dudes I ever met did just fine at it.'

'What about you?' I asked Elaine. 'Would you use a gun?'

'Would I use one?'

'If he got up here,' I said, 'and you were alone, or he got past whoever was here with you. Could you pick up a gun and shoot him?'

'It's like a no-brainer camera, right? Point and shoot? I'd point it and shoot it.'

'If he was just standing here, say. No weapon in his hands and an explanation on his lips, telling you how it wasn't his doing, some other man stole the letter opener from him, and—'

'In other words, he's not coming at me. He's acting like a gentleman. Could I shoot him anyway? I swear I don't know where you got the idea that I'm some kind of shrinking violet. We're talking about the prick that killed my friend. Would I shoot him? He could be lying on this couch taking a nap and if I had a gun I'd blow his fucking brains out. You're gonna go get some guns?'

'I'm going to try.'

'Get three,' she said. 'One for each of us. No more Mr Nice Guy.'

CHAPTER 23

Knives are beautiful.

Take this one, for instance. It is ten and three-quarters inches long, a bowie type, similar to that beautiful Randall-made knife he'd had to leave in Richmond. This knife, though, had been made not by the legendary Randall, but by a young Idahoan named Reinhold Messer. He'd bought the knife from Messer himself, a long-haired full-bearded bear of a man who'd sat behind his table at a knife show in Provo, Utah, and showed off his creations with hands as gently expressive as an orchestra conductor's.

All of Messer's knives were beautiful, but he'd liked this one the best. It is heavy, you could hammer nails with the butt end, but its balance is so perfect it feels weightless in the hand. More, it feels like part of the hand itself.

Its grips, the half-round slabs on either side of the handle, are made of Micarta, a resin-based material favored by knife makers because they deem it superior to natural materials like wood and stone, ivory and oosik. (They use these materials, too, and he has seen grips of rosewood and rare tropical hardwoods,

269

of malachite and lapis lazuli, of elephant and walrus and mastodon ivory, and of oosik, which is the name, Inuit in origin, for the bone in the penis of the walrus. Who even knew such a thing existed? Investigate any area thoroughly, he is delighted to observe, and you will acquire all manner of arcane knowledge.)

A knife like this, he believes, is artisanship of the highest order, with form always following function, and beauty growing out of the synthesis of the two. The blade itself continues past the hilt to the very butt of the knife, a single piece of steel, with the part above the hilt known as the tang. (Who would guess there was a word for it, and a lovely word at that.) This particular blade is made of Damascus steel, which means not that it was imported from Syria – it was made right here in the good old U. S. of A. – but that it was produced by a venerable process that probably originated in Damascus, of bending a piece of steel back upon itself, hammering it flat, bending and hammering, over and over, until the resulting blade is almost infinitely layered, with the layers showing in the finished knife like the wood grain on a hardwood tabletop. Each Damascus blade is unique and each is beautiful, but the purpose of the process is not beauty but strength; every time the piece of steel is hammered and hardened and folded and hammered again, it grows stronger and more durable. The beauty grows out of the functionality, and who wouldn't want to own that sort of beauty? Who wouldn't want to wield it like a baton in his hand, to wave it like a wand, like the épée of a fencing master? Who wouldn't be proud to wear it on his belt and stride down the street with it?

Who wouldn't yearn to draw it smoothly from its sheath and across a throat?

He's used it twice, and one time he did in fact cut a throat with it. It was surprising, too, because it was as if it happened without his willing it, as if the knife acted on its own.

He remembers the occasion well, although it's sometimes difficult to place events in a time frame. This was in southern Colorado, in a town called Durango, and he never lived there, never even spent an entire night there. He was passing through, and he stopped for dinner, and the waitress, who brought him first a welcome glass of Scotch on the rocks and then an equally welcome blood-rare steak, flirted with him in a manner that seemed aimed at more than a good tip. He flirted back, and told her she looked a little like a movie star, if only he could remember the name. It was, he assured her, right on the tip of his tongue. Stick out your tongue, she said, and maybe I'll be able to see it.

He asked her what time she got off work. Ten-thirty, she said, and told him to wait for her at the far end of the parking lot, because she didn't want anyone knowing her business.

He was in cowboy mode, dressed in boots and jeans and a western shirt with snaps instead of buttons, and it seemed natural to wear the knife on his belt. He waited for her in his car and followed her back to her trailer, where he fucked her to their mutual satisfaction and fell asleep at her side. He woke up after an hour and found her sleeping, her bottle-blonde hair spread out on the pillow, her jaw slack. She was snoring, and her breath smelled. He'd never told her the name of the actress she reminded him of – of course there was no such actress – and he thought now that she wasn't very pretty, although she'd been a good enough sexual partner. He could stick around for a while, if only to find out what she would and wouldn't do. He had no place to go, and this town was probably as good a one as the next to spend a few days or a week or a month.

He reached for his pants, and his hand brushed the sheathed knife, and it was as if the knife decided. Because the next thing he knew the knife was in his hand, its unsheathed blade resplendent in the light of the bedside lamp. If she'd turned off the light before she passed out, if he hadn't seen the light glinting off the beautiful knife blade, if she weren't lying on her back, giving him such a good look at her pale throat . . .

Did she even feel the knife? He drew it across her throat in one fluid motion and the flesh offered no resistance at all. It was like cutting warm butter. Her eyes fell open, but never saw anything. The light was already gone from them.

He dressed and left, and by the time the sun cleared the horizon he was a hundred miles from Durango. He'd cleaned up after himself in a limited fashion. He'd left his seed in her, so there was nothing to be done about that, and no point in worrying about hairs and trace evidence when he'd already provided them with a good DNA sample. Much luck to them, a small-town police force with the nearest competent lab where, in Denver? They were welcome to his DNA, they could store it in a test tube on a shelf in some back room, and what harm could it do him? None unless they arrested him, and that wasn't going to happen.

He wiped away his fingerprints. That was enough. No one even knew he'd been to Durango, much less that he'd picked up the waitress. Anyone who'd watched her would have seen her get in her own car and drive off. No one could have noticed him pull out and drive off in her wake.

He'd paid cash for his meal. He hadn't even bought gas in Durango. No trace of him in the town, except for a few cc's of semen in a dead girl's vagina.

Besides, he had an alibi. It wasn't he who did it. It was the knife.

Online, he visits his newsgroups. There is, he's pleased to note, a flurry of activity on the subject of Preston Applewhite. Several of the newsgroup's more devoted participants have been following the coverage in the Richmond paper. Human remains have been unearthed from the private cemetery of an abandoned farmhouse, and preliminary evidence suggests strongly that the Willis boy has indeed been found.

There's no end of speculation. Did Applewhite, unwilling to admit his crimes, arrange for someone to speak for him from beyond the grave? Did he have a confederate – one theorist calls him an unindicted co-conspirator – who'd participated in his crimes? Was Applewhite in fact part of a long-rumored satanic cult?

The newspaper has reproduced a portion of the e-mail he'd sent them, along with his signature, and one newsgroup member has been quick to pick up on Abel Baker. 'You younger types won't know this,' he writes, 'but these are the first two letters of the old phonetic alphabet. Able Baker Charlie Dog Easy Fox . . . Can anyone remember the rest?'

Someone of course can and does, and someone else chimes in with the modern replacement, beginning with Alpha and Bravo. And another party wonders when exactly Alpha Bravo etc. replaced Able Baker, and someone supplies a date which someone else challenges, and the thread rapidly degenerates into a discussion of the relative merits of the two alphabets, and the implication of the change in terms of the evolving role of the military.

He exits the newsgroup, Googles his way to the *Times-Dispatch's* website. He reads everything he can find on the story, including an editorial calling for a review of the whole notion of capital punishment, and an op-ed piece taking an opposite tack and arguing that the process should be streamlined, so that less 'time for mischief' separate the imposition of sentence and its execution. Neither piece, it seems to him, is a masterpiece of rational thinking.

He reads on, and yes, some enterprising reporter

has determined that Applewhite had a visitor before he died, that he spent more than a few hours during the several days before his death with one Arnold Bodinson. They've gone and anglicized the first name, he notes, probably having heard Arnie for Arne and opted for a more formal version, but surely they'll correct that in the days to come. Dr Bodinson is identified as a prominent psychologist affiliated with Yale University, and the coincidence of his initials matching those of Abel Baker has not escaped attention. No doubt the earnest chaps in the news-group will have something to say on the subject as well.

Efforts to reach Dr Bodinson have thus far been unsuccessful, the reporter states. And are doomed to remain so, he thinks, but tomorrow's paper should hold the revelation that Yale University has never heard of Arne Bodinson, or Arnold either.

Now won't that be interesting?

He thinks of Reinhold Messer and wonders if that, like Arne Bodinson, is a nom de guerre. It seems almost too good to be true, as *Messer* is the German word for *knife*. Messer certainly conformed to the militia-Aryan Brotherhood archetype, and if his name at birth had been, say, Cuthbert Lavender, a name change would seem inevitable.

He has looked for Messer on the Internet, but the man doesn't have a website, and hadn't even provided a business card. You can look for me at shows, he'd said, which suggested a life lived off the books. Not so with the man who made the other knife he owns, an owlish boy-man named Thad Jenkins, called Thaddy by his colleagues. Jenkins specialized in folding knives, finding their manufacture more of an engineering challenge. 'Sides, he'd drawled, wasn't anybody couldn't find a use for a pocketknife.

From Thaddy's array of folders, he'd selected a beauty, almost six inches long when closed, and about the same length as Messer's bowie when open. While it was neither a gravity knife nor a switchblade, its mechanism and balance were such that a simple flick of the wrist, quickly learned, would open it, whereupon the extended blade would lock securely in place.

He turns it over in his hands. The grips are a tropical hardwood of exceptional density, with a color like pecan and a very close grain. It's as smooth as glass, and quite beautiful, and over time the oils from his hand will burnish the wood and only make it more beautiful.

Of course he may not own it long enough to see that happen. Things come in and out of his life. *I came like water and like wind I go,* he wrote once, on a basement wall, quoting Omar Khayyám but attributing the line to Aubrey Beardsley. And didn't most things come like water, and go like wind? For some time he'd worn a disc of mottled pink rhodochrosite, for clarity, but he'd had to leave that behind in that very basement. But by then he'd internalized the mineral's properties and didn't need it anymore. Then he'd taken to wearing an amethyst crystal, for immortality, and it too was long gone, and he couldn't even recall what had become of it. But he'd internalized the special properties of the amethyst as well.

Would he live forever? Well, really, who was to say? But look at all the people he's already outlived . . .

He flicks the knife and the blade leaps from its casing and locks into place. The blade is slender, half the width of the bowie's, and the knife overall weighs no more than a third of its bulkier fellow. Do knives have gender? In a sense they're all masculine, all sharpened phalli. But if one were to regard some as male and others as female, it's easy to see Messer's creation as bluntly masculine, Jenkins's folder as graceful in its femininity.

The man, Scudder, the more difficult quarry, would fall to the sturdier weapon. It is Scudder who deprived him of the house on Seventy-fourth Street. He has long ceased to care about the house, he knows he never really wanted it in the first place, but that's beside the point. It is Scudder, too, who made him leave New York. He'd had a thriving practice, he'd had a house full of people who loved and revered and, yes, needed him, and he'd had to stab them all dead and burn the house down around them. And yes, it was thrilling, sacrificing those men and women, but that too was beside the point, for it was Scudder who'd left him no choice but murder and flight, and Scudder who would pay for it.

Scudder was an ox, a brute. A bull, really, and he'd fight him as one would fight a bull, tricking him with a flourish of the cape, then dispatching him with a single thrust of the Damascus steel blade.

The folder will do for the woman.

And a far more serviceable tool it will be than the elegant bit of bronze he'd left behind on Jane Street. It had been poetic, surely, to buy from one woman what he'd used to kill the other, and it had done what he'd required of it, opening a hole to let out life as efficiently as it had ever opened an envelope. But this folding knife of Jenkins will do more, and do it with grace.

And she knows, he's sure she knows. Not how or when, but only that he's coming for her. Her shop, a sign in her window proclaims, is closed until further notice. Her answering machine carries the same message. Closed until further notice.

Closed for All Time, it might better say. Closed until Grand Opening under New Management.

Her knowledge will make her wary. Thus she'll be a more elusive quarry than her friend Monica (who was really almost too easy) but she won't elude him forever. He'll find a way. And he has worlds of time.

He holds the knife, so light, so graceful, so feminine in its supple elegance. He works the catch that allows the blade to close, then flicks it open. Supple indeed, elegant indeed, but sturdy. According to the man who made it, it is more than equal to the task of skinning out big game.

There's a thought. Perhaps he'll flay her. Skin her alive, with her eyelids taped open and a mirror positioned so that she can watch, and her mouth taped shut to stifle her screams.

The image delights him, so much so that he can't sit still. Before he leaves Joe Bohan's apartment, he folds the knife shut and drops it in a pocket. It is, after all, a dangerous city. One would be well advised not to walk its streets unarmed.

CHAPTER 24

I went first to Grogan's, the uncompromising old Irish bar at Fiftieth and Tenth. There was nothing in its appearance to suggest that it had been the scene of a massacre a few years ago, a bomb hurled against the back bar, the room's interior sprayed with a burst from an updated version of the tommy gun. But most of the crowd would know this, and some of them could tell you the death toll. Grogan's had drawn a good crowd ever since it opened, as the new upscale residents of Hell's Kitchen began to discover the place and treasure it for its old-time authenticity, even as their patronage eroded the very quality that pulled them in.

Gangster chic, always in good supply in this town, at least since Jimmy Walker was mayor, got a boost from *The Sopranos*, and young lawyers and account execs liked to be able to tell their co-workers that they'd spent the previous night drinking whiskey alongside Mick Ballou.

Tonight's crowd wouldn't be able to make that claim, however, because the proprietor of Grogan's wasn't on the premises. I learned as much from the tight-lipped bartender, the latest lad to come straight from County Antrim to Grogan's, looking to Mick for sanctuary and a job. I suspect I wasn't the first to inquire, and I got the same answer as everybody else – he wasn't in, and as to whether he'd be in later, why, who was to say?

'It's Matt Scudder who's looking for him,' I said. I lowered my voice when I said this, not because it would mean anything to anyone else, but to impress the guy behind the stick. It wouldn't get an answer out of him, but if Mick was in the back room, the fellow would find an unobtrusive way to ring him on the house phone. When that didn't happen I knocked back the rest of my Coke and left.

I could have spent an hour in a meeting, and it might even have done me good, but I didn't feel like it. If I was going to kill time I'd sooner kill it in a bar. That's not recommended, and I can understand why, but I didn't give a damn.

I called the apartment and the machine picked up, which was as we'd arranged; Elaine would screen her calls, picking up only when she recognized the caller. I said a few words and she took the call, and I said I'd be a while. She said that would be fine.

I rang off and took a cab to Poogan's.

They keep the place dimly lit, which is part of its appeal for Danny Boy, who has occasionally observed that what the world needs most is a volume control and a dimmer switch, that the damn

281

place is always too loud and too bright. I let my eyes accustom themselves to the dark, and I didn't see Danny Boy but I did see his table. Poogan's, like Mother Blue's, sells him his vodka by the bottle, and lets him keep it close at hand in an ice bucket. I think there's a state law against that, but so far nobody's turned up to enforce it.

I stood at the bar with a glass of soda water and ice – I didn't want any more Coke yet – and one record finished its play on the jukebox and another replaced it, and I looked over to see Danny Boy returning from the men's room. It struck me that he looked old, but I decided it must be my eyes, because lately I was starting to see age in every face I looked at, and I didn't need a mirror to know I'd be able to spot it in mine.

He sat down heavily, took a glass, held it at a tilt the way you do when you pour a beer, and filled it halfway with iced Stolichnaya. He held it up and looked at it, and I remembered doing that with bourbon, and remembered too how the bourbon tasted when I quit just looking at it and did with it what one was meant to do.

My thoughts bothered me, and so did my actions, which felt oddly like spying. I carried my drink to his table, and he looked up as I pulled over a chair for myself. He said, 'Well, this is a treat, Matthew. I don't see you for months and then I have the pleasure of your company twice in a single week. You're alone tonight?'

'Not anymore.'

'No, now you're with an old friend, and so am I.' He started to look for the waitress, then saw I already had a drink. He hadn't done anything with his Stoli but pour it and look at it, and now he raised it and said, 'Old friends.' I raised my own glass and sipped my soda water, and he drank half of his vodka.

He asked what had brought me, and I said I had a little time to kill, and he laughed and said we'd kill it together.

'But I was going to get here sooner or later anyway,' I said, and showed him a copy of Ray's drawing.

'You showed me the other night,' he said. 'At Mother's. Wait a minute. Is this the same guy?'

'No, a different one entirely.'

'That's what I was thinking, although I can't say I have the other chap's features engraved on my heart. This one looks menacing.'

'Part of that may be the sensibilities of the person who told the artist what to draw. This is the man who murdered a woman in the Village the night before last.'

'All over the TV,' he said. 'Give me a minute and I'll tell you her name.'

I supplied it myself, along with the fact that she'd been Elaine's best friend, and Elaine had sold him the murder weapon. With Danny Boy, you could give him the first sentence and he had the whole page; what he said was, 'I hope you put her on a plane.'

'It might come to that. I don't know.' I detailed the security precautions we were taking, and that I was going to pick up a gun for her. He asked if she'd know what to do with it, and I said there, wasn't too much you had to know to shoot someone at close range.

He said, 'All my life, all the players and hard cases I've known, I've never once fired a gun, Matthew. I'm trying to think if I ever even had one in my hand. You know, I don't think I did.'

'Well, you're still a young man, Danny.'

'That's what the Yellow Peril tells me. Jodie, you met her the other night. "Danny, you are so amazing!" For a man my age, she means. And as long as they keep making those little blue pills, I can go on amazing her.'

'Science is wonderful.'

'Yeah.'

Something made me ask about his health. It had been more than five years, and he hadn't had a recurrence. So he was out of the woods, wasn't he?

'Out of the woods? Matthew, you can't even see a tree from where I'm sitting.'

'That's great.'

'I beat colon cancer. That's a funny expression, don't you think? Like I got in the ring with it and kicked the shit out of it. Cancer of the colon, off its feet and down for the count. I didn't have much to do with it, to tell you the truth. They cut me up and stitched me back together and filled me full of chemicals, and when they quit I was alive and the cancer wasn't. "I beat colon cancer." It's like saying you beat a slot machine, when all you did was pick the right time to drop your quarter in it.'

'The point is you're okay.'

'That's the good news,' he said, and waited for me to ask what the bad news was. But I'd heard too much bad news lately to seek it out.

When I didn't ask he told me.

'Prostate cancer,' he said, 'and there's good news there, too, because I've got a low Gleason score. Gleason, all I could think of was *The Honeymooners*. A low Gleason means it's slow-growing. I can treat it and risk impotence and incontinence, or I can live with it and, according to the doctor, almost certainly die of something else before the prostate cancer can get me. "If you keep on drinking like you do," he said, and I swear he was smiling while he said it, "your liver's likely to give out long before your prostate can kill you." Guess what I had as soon as I got out of his office.'

'A glass of Stoli.'

'As a matter of fact it was Absolut, but you've got the right idea. Doctor's orders, the way I look at it. Let me tell you something, put this in perspective, before you start feeling sorry for me. It's a complete fucking miracle I've lived this long. When I was born the obstetrician told my parents I would probably die within the week. Then I wasn't supposed to survive childhood. "Give him all the love you can now," the pediatrician told them, "because you're not going to have him long. The Lord's likely to want him back." That was great for me, because they took me home and spoiled me rotten. And the Lord evidently took a good long look at me and decided he didn't want me all that much.'

'Well, you can't really blame him, can you?'

'I don't blame anybody,' he said, 'for anything. I've had a good life, and I figure everything past the first week of it's been a bonus. I listen to music whenever I want, and I drink as much as I want, and I get all the pussy I want, and when little Jodie gets sick of me I'll find somebody else, because there's always one there to be found. So don't feel sorry for me.'

I told him I wouldn't dream of it.

When I got down to Grogan's, Mick said I'd just missed him by a few minutes. 'We were busy earlier,' he said. 'Busy enough for me to join Con behind the wood. I don't mind it. It's honest work, pouring an honest drink.'

Most of what he did wouldn't fit most people's definition of honest work. A few years back, when the loosely allied Irish mob the press called the Westies was in full force, Mick Ballou led a faction of it, and led it with brutal efficiency. He was a career criminal and he had become my best friend, and Joe Durkin wasn't the only man who found this puzzling. I didn't really understand it myself.

'It's thinned out some,' he said, 'though it's always busier than it used to be. The afternoons are still slow. That's the nicest time in a bar, I'd say, when your only customers are men who want to sit quietly with a drink. Or late at night, when there's no one there at all but two old friends talking the night away.'

'We've had our share of nights like that.'

'And never a one but I was glad of it. We've not had a late night in a while, but that's not what brings you here this evening, is it?'

'No, it's not.'

I told him about it. He'd met Monica, although I had to refresh his memory. We'd brought her there once after the three of us saw a Brian Friel play at the Irish Arts Centre, and he'd joined us at our table, and Monica had teased him about having poetry readings, which she assured him would be good for business at Grogan's. Yeats would be perfect, she'd said, and he'd topped her by nodding judiciously and reciting 'An Irish Airman Foresees His Death' with a flair and cadence that would not have been out of place on the stage of the Abbey.

'She had a lovely sense of humor,' he recalled. 'And she liked my poem.'

'She did.'

'Killing's terrible enough when it's done for a reason. Oh, it's an awful thing. And yet there's joy in it, you know.'

'I know.'

'But the joy can never be the reason. If I let that happen what would I be? By God, I'm bad enough as I am.'

We went into his office and he opened the big old Mosler safe and sorted through an array of handguns. I picked out a pair of nine-millimeter pistols for TJ and myself and a .38-special revolver for Elaine. It had less stopping power than the nines, but it struck me as simpler for her to operate; there was no safety catch to mess with, it was less likely to jam, and all she had to do was keep squeezing the trigger until she ran out of bullets.

Back at our table, with the guns and two boxes of shells in an old gym bag at my feet, he said I was welcome to the weapons, but that he hoped I'd have no need for them.

'The police'll pick him up tomorrow,' I said, 'and I'll bring them back as good as new.'

'Would you need a hand, do you think?'

'I'll let you know if I do, but I don't think so, Mick. All I'm going to do is keep her where he can't get at her. And we're not going to leave her alone. If I'm not there, TJ'll be.'

'I'd stand a shift anytime. Just let me know.'

'Thank you.'

He took another look at the drawing. 'The dirty man,' he said, and it sounded far worse than a curse. 'By God, he looks familiar.'

'I said the same thing, and so did Danny Boy. He sends regards, I'm supposed to tell you.'

'Does he, then. And how is the young fellow?'

'He's fine, but I don't know about the "young fellow" part. He's our age.'

'Is he indeed? I guess he would have to be, wouldn't he? It's his size makes me think him younger than he is. Ah, Jaysus, man, we're all of us getting old.'

'Tell me about it.'

'I complain about all my customers, these lawyers and stockbrokers who want to come in here and drink with the devil, but 'tis their custom that supports me. I'm making my living from this place, can you believe it? This and the few little businesses I own. I have to walk outside and spit in the street once a week so I won't forget what it's like to break a law. By God, I'm a toothless old lion, and it's a nerve I have to resent the keeper who slips food through the bars of my cage.'

'Bread soaked in milk,' I said, 'so you can handle it.'

'And yourself, waiting for the police to do what once you'd have tried to do on your own.'

'They have the resources.'

'Of course they do.'

'I don't even know who he is. I wouldn't know where to start looking for him.'

'You'll keep herself safe and sound. That's all you need to do.' He touched a forefinger to Ray's sketch. 'I could swear he's been in here. Or is there an actor he looks like?'

'There's probably a dozen.'

'You could look at him and never see him. Your eyes could glide right over him, for there's nothing there to hold you. But I'll now remember him if

I see him. That poor woman. Did you say he gave her a hard death?'

'It couldn't have been an easy one. He tortured her.'

'There's never a call for that,' he said. 'Isn't there enough suffering in the world without making a point of creating more of it? I'd kill him in an instant, should God give me the chance, but I'd not make him suffer. I'd just kill him and be done with it.'

CHAPTER 25

I took the long way home from Grogan's, up Tenth Avenue to Fifty-eighth Street, east two long blocks to Eighth Avenue, then back to Fifty-seventh Street, where I stayed on the north side and made my way to the corner of Ninth. I guess I was looking for him, looking for someone who might be lurking in my neighborhood and keeping an eye on the entrance to our building. I saw a drunk peeing in a doorway, I saw a man with an aluminum walker making his painfully slow way to the Chaldean deli, I saw a man and woman I recognized having an argument I'd watched them have a dozen times before. I saw any number of my fellow citizens, waiting for buses, descending into subway tunnels, getting in or out of taxis, or going someplace on foot, some of them taking their time, others in a New York hurry. But I didn't see the one man I was looking for, and in due course it struck me that I might be behaving in a manner likely to call attention to myself, not a good idea when I was carrying three unregistered handguns and enough ammo to start a gang war. I quit while I was ahead and went upstairs.

Elaine was dozing lightly in the big armchair. TJ was doing something with her computer. I gave him one of the nines and a loaded clip, and he checked it out as if he'd done this before. He asked if I wanted him to stay over. He could sleep on the couch, he suggested. I sent him home, roused Elaine enough to put her back to sleep in our bed, and went and stood by the south window myself.

The Towers were still absent, even as more gaps seemed to be forming in my own personal skyline. I went on looking for a while, and when nothing changed I went to bed.

TJ called while we were having breakfast. Did we need him? Because he thought he might go out for a while. I told him to go, and he reminded me that he'd be carrying his cell phone. If we needed him, all we had to do was call him.

After a second cup of coffee I put the two guns on the kitchen table, the nine and the .38. Elaine picked them up in turn, held them gingerly in her hand, and announced she liked the nine better. It wasn't as heavy, she said, and she liked the way it fit her hand. I told her I'd picked out the revolver for her, and why I thought it might suit her better. She said that was okay, but seemed disappointed.

Her disappointment abated as she became more familiar with the thing. I taught her to load it and unload it, had her aim it and dry-fire it. I'd learned to shoot one-handed, that was the way they taught you back when I joined the department, but nowadays everybody holds a gun in two hands. I think it started around the time Chris Evert taught the world there was nothing sissy about a two-handed backhand, though I can't see the connection. I don't know that a second hand improves your aim, but it does lessen the effect of recoil, and that alone was reason enough to teach her to use both hands.

The thing to remember, I told her, was to keep firing. Recoil would probably elevate the muzzle, so she'd have to take aim again, and pull the trigger again, and keep it up until the gun was empty. If she hit him the first time and dropped him, if he fell down and lay there dead, that was no reason to stop. If he's face up, shoot him in the chest. If he's face down, shoot him in the back. And then shoot him in the head.

And then cut his head off, I thought, and put it on a stick, and we'll carry it all through the town.

TJ called around ten, to make sure we were okay. He might be a while, he said. I told him everything was fine. He called again an hour later to say he was on his way, and was there anything we needed? I told him to pick up a couple of newspapers, and he brought the *Times* and the *Post* when he showed up a little before noon.

'I know it ain't high priority,' he said, 'but I didn't know what else to do. So I decided to check out David Thompson.'

'How?'

'Well, he be waitin' on that check you said you'd send him, right? So I went up to Amsterdam Avenue an' hung out there. Be good if there was a place right across the street where you could have something to eat and watch through the window, but there wasn't, so I just stood up against a building.'

'That must have gotten old in a hurry,' Elaine said.

'Legs was feeling it,' he admitted. 'I got to wishing there was a way for me to sit down, but you sit yourself down in the middle of the side-walk and people apt to look at you.'

'It's no way to avoid attention,' I agreed.

'And if you sitting down, you might miss what's happening on the other side of the street, 'specially a wide street like Amsterdam. So what I did, I crossed the street and I sat down on the sidewalk right next to the place with the mailboxes.'

'To avoid calling attention to yourself.'

He grinned. 'I's wearing this,' he said, taking off a peaked cap of pieced denim, 'in case the sun was to get in my eyes. And 'cause a hat be a good disguise. You put it on, you take it off, you changing your 'pearance. Older dude taught me that.'

'I didn't know you were paying attention.'

'Man, I always listen to the voice of experience. How else I gone learn? What I did, I put the cap on the ground in front of me, dropped all my loose change in it, an' sat with one leg sort of folded back under me. Anybody look at me, they think I be a cripple.'

'And if they saw you trot across the street and set up?'

'Then they think I's a fake cripple. Man, you think a beggar's got an easy gig, but it ain't so. People just pass you by, don't even want to look at you.'

'Day trading's probably a better deal,' Elaine said.

''Cept with begging, you not likely to end the day with less than you started with. Now and then, somebody stop an' give you something. Had one dude put in a dollar an' take change.'

'You're kidding.'

'Just took a quarter,' he said. ''Pologized to me, said he needed it for a parking meter. Leaves me seventy-five cents ahead, so why he be 'pologizing? People are strange sometimes.'

Elaine said, 'See? Look what you learned this morning.'

'Already knew that. What I learned is you just wait in the right place, you get what you lookin' for.'

'He turned up?'

He nodded. 'Came for his mail. Walked in lookin' hopeful an' came out lookin' disgusted. Guess he still waitin' on that check. And he ain't the guy in that drawing, case there was any question. He's the dude came out of Louise's building, the one lost us around the block.'

'Did you have any luck following him?'

'Didn't even try. He drove up in a big old Chevy Caprice, pulled up by the hydrant, was in and out in a couple of minutes. Hopped back in the car and drove off. I got the plate number. That do us any good?'

Joe Durkin said, 'Didn't I tell you? I'm a private citizen, I put in my last day for the City of New York. I'm officially retired.'

'I'll bet they haven't got the word yet at the DMV.'

'I'd be breaking the law,' he said. 'Impersonating a police officer.'

'Gee, I didn't think of that.'

'Yeah, I bet. Why can't you do it yourself? You've been breaking laws right and left for years.'

'You know the procedure. It's changed in the past thirty years.'

'Thirty years,' he said. 'Jesus, I guess it has. Did they even have license plates thirty years ago?'

'They did, but they kept falling off the horses.'

'Off the horses' asses, you mean. And speaking of horses' asses, I thought you were the next thing to retired yourself.'

'Something came up.'

'As the bishop said to the actress. Give me the fucking plate number, I'll see what I can do.'

It didn't take him long. He called back fifteen minutes later and said, 'Next time we have dinner, it's on you. And it won't be any cheap joint like the one I took you to, either. Write this down:

David Joel Thompson, 118 Manhattan Avenue, Apartment 4-C for Charlie. Zip is 10025. Phone number—'

'They have a phone number listed?'

'They could probably tell you his favorite color, if you knew how to ask for it.' He gave me Thompson's phone number and his date of birth, which made him forty-one. 'And a Sagittarius,' he added, 'in case Elaine wants to try doing his chart. Five-nine, a hundred sixty pounds, color of hair brown, color of eyes brown. That help?'

'You're a prince, Joe.'

'A retired prince,' he said. 'A prince with a pension.'

The name was the one he had given Louise, and the address was a five-minute walk from his mail drop. The phone number had a 212 prefix, so it would be a land line, not his cell phone. I dialed it and it rang five times before a mechanical voice informed me that the number I had reached had been disconnected.

It didn't matter, David Thompson didn't matter, but I was interested in spite of myself. If I'd had anything better to do I'd have done it, but I didn't. I could sit around waiting for Sussman to call, or I could get out of the house and do something.

I asked TJ to stick around, and made sure he had the gun with him. He'd been carrying it in the small of his back, held there by his belt and covered by the baggy blue chambray workshirt he'd neglected to tuck in. 'New York is a tough town, Myrtle,' he said, his accent suitably midwestern. 'Even the beggars carry guns.'

It was overcast, and by the time I got out of the subway the sky had darkened and I was sorry I hadn't brought an umbrella. I'd taken the One train and stayed on a stop past Ninety-sixth Street, to 103rd and Broadway. Manhattan Avenue runs north and south a short block west of Central Park, extending from 100th Street up to just below 125th. I walked there and found 118. There was no Thompson nameplate on the row of buzzers, and both the buzzer and the mailbox for Apartment 4-C for Charlie bore small plastic inserts imprinted with the name KOSTAKIS.

I rang the bell and waited and rang it again, and nobody answered. I rang the super's bell and nobody answered that, either, and I was on my way out the door when the door from the hallway opened and a man with a voice thick with phlegm asked me what I wanted.

I told him, and he frowned and scratched his head. 'David Thompson,' he said. 'He don't live here. I got a Greek couple in there now, been with me the better part of a year now. Very nice people. Guy who was in there before them, tell the truth, I don't remember his name. It's funny, 'cause I can picture him.'

I showed him the photo and he didn't hesitate. 'That's him,' he said. 'Moved, no forwarding. And I remember the name now, because the first week or two he'd get mail here, and I'd have to give it back to the postman. Then that stopped, and I could forget him, which I did.'

'He didn't pay his rent,' I told TJ and Elaine. 'He got a couple of months behind and ignored the notices they sent him. Eviction proceedings can take a while, but the super's not a man who does everything by the book. He made sure Thompson was out of the house, then changed the locks and got a friend to help him put all of Thompson's stuff on the street. The stuff disappeared gradually, he said. People would come by and take what they wanted, and eventually the sanitation men carted off the rest.'

'Thompson never showed up?'

'If he did, the super never noticed, but I'm not sure how much he notices. Thompson may have moved out on his own before the locks were changed, and not bothered to tell anybody.'

'And just left everything.'

'Everything that the super wound up tossing. We don't know what he may have taken with him.'

TJ said, 'We got a plan?'

'No,' I said. 'Not really.'

CHAPTER 26

That was Friday, and according to the *Times* it was the longest day of the year. I could have told them as much myself, but I wouldn't have been talking about the relative proportion of daylight and darkness. The hours crawled, and there seemed to be more of them than usual.

We sat around, the three of us, and we read the papers and watched TV, and for a while TJ and Elaine played canasta, which didn't work too well because neither of them was too clear on the rules. Eventually he went home and we went to bed, and when we got up it was Saturday and nothing had changed but the weather. The rain that had threatened to fall yesterday was falling now, and it contiunued off and on throughout the day.

'I keep thinking I should call Monica,' Elaine said.

I kept thinking I should call Sussman, and eventually I did. He had some progress to report, though it didn't seem to me as though it led anywhere. They'd found the liquor store where he'd bought the bottle of Strega, paying cash for it, and the clerk had given a firm positive ID of the sketch. Assuming you could get it admitted as evidence, it was no more than circumstantial, the sort of thing Ray Gruliow, liked to call 'a mere feather on the scales of Justice.'

Sussman admitted it was light. 'It means we can stop sending guys to check out liquor stores,' he said, 'and I guess that's a plus. How are you and your wife holding up?'

I told him we were all right, but we'd be a lot happier when the case was wrapped up.

'As would I,' he said. 'What I've been doing is going through all the Unsolveds, trying to find something that matches up just a little bit. You have to figure he's done this before, wouldn't you say?'

I hadn't thought about that, but of course he was right. Monica's murder was too well staged, too carefully worked out, to be anybody's maiden effort.

'But there's not a thing with his prints on it. Not literally his prints, you know what I mean.'

'Sure.'

'I've been running the MO through NCIC, and I've got a call in to an FBI field agent, one of the few I know who doubles as a human being. Because I had the thought that maybe our guy's from somewhere else. So he won't fit any of our Unsolveds, but he might fit just fine in Oshkosh or Kokomo.'

'Maybe he's like lightning and never strikes twice in the same place.'

'Then he'd be as hard to catch as lightning, because nobody'd be in a position to see a pattern develop. Unless the individual murders are rubber stamp affairs, so similar that the feds' computer can't help picking up on it. Otherwise, you know, he just crisscrosses the country, kills one person here and one person there, and there's never a full-scale manhunt because nobody realizes they're dealing with a one-man crime wave.'

'Wasn't there somebody like that a few years ago? Turned out to be a long-haul trucker?'

'Rings a bell. I can't see our guy behind the wheel of a Peterbilt, somehow.'

'No.'

'Maybe he's filled his New York quota,' he said, 'and he's off to bring his own special brand of joy to El Paso. That would put him out of our reach, but he'd also be out of our hair, and your wife could open up her store and sell me that sketch. I really liked it, you know.'

'Get this son of a bitch and she'll give it to you.'

'I would just plain love to take you up on that,' he said. 'But if he's gone and we never hear from him again? Right now I have to say that'd be fine with me.'

I hung up feeling as though I'd missed something, that he'd said something I should have picked up on. There's a way to use the answering machine as a recorder, although I've never had occasion to do so and would have to consult the manual for instructions. I'd never considered it, but it occurred to me now that it would be handy to have it on tape so I could play it back and puzzle it out.

And there was something else he'd said the other day, something that had gone right by me and I'd only thought of later on, when it was too late to ask him what he'd meant. But what the hell was it?

My memory's always been good, except for all those things I've chosen to forget. Just as Elaine had secretly believed age would never make visible inroads upon her looks, so I'd managed to tell myself I was somehow immune to the erosion of memory that comes with the years. I suppose it's pride that makes us think things will be different for us, that the universe will grant us a special dispensation. And she did, God knows, look young for her years, and was still as beautiful a woman as I'd ever known. And my memory was still pretty sharp.

But every once in a while something would come along to remind me that it wasn't as sharp as it used to be.

I said as much to Elaine, and she said, 'That reminds me. The one thing Monica always dreaded was Alzheimer's. There's some of it in her family, and she was terrified she'd get it if she lived long enough.' She winced at that. 'She made me promise I wouldn't let her live like that. She had a living will, but that's no help with Alzheimer's, not until the late stages, because there's no plug to pull.

You're perfectly healthy, you just don't have a mind anymore.

'So what I had to promise was that I'd find some way to put her out of her misery. Get her to take sleeping pills, I suppose. We didn't get into the details. And God knows what I would have done if it came to that, but at any rate I promised her.

'And she said, "Yeah, right, and a fat lot of good that's gonna do me. Because there I'll be, gaga, with my eyes looking in different directions and drool running down the corner of my mouth, and you'll stand there saying, 'Gosh, let me think now. There's something I was supposed to do for Monica and I can't for the life of me remember what the hell it was.'"'

Sunday morning TJ showed up early with a bag of lox and bagels and cream cheese. I ate quickly and left the two of them at the breakfast table and rode down to the Village for the eleven o'clock at Perry Street. A lot of old-timers tend to go to that meeting, and I always run into a few old friends there.

It was raining when I left the house, dry by the time I got to the meeting, raining again at 12:30 when it ended. I picked up the Sunday *Times* on the way home and the three of us sat around reading sections of it. It was the perfect picture of domestic tranquility, except that Elaine would lapse periodically into troughs of deep sadness. And, of course, there was someone out there trying to kill her.

I had the Sports section and was reading a story about golf, a pastime in which I have not the slightest interest, when she said, 'I think you should read this.'

'Me?'

'Uh-huh. Or maybe you already did. About that man who killed the three boys in Richmond, and earlier this month he was executed.'

'I saw it.'

'Today?'

'Yesterday, or it might have been Friday.' The days sort of run together when you're not doing anything. 'I noticed it because I had two conversations about the case just a couple of days before they put him down. Somebody tipped them off as to the location of the missing body, isn't that it?'

'There's a little more in today's paper.'

'And people are jumping up and down and saying they executed an innocent man,' I said. 'That sort of thing's been tried before, you know. Say I'm on Death Row, awaiting execution for a murder that I damn well did commit. What I do, I slip some details of the crime to you, and you have a great crisis of conscience and confess to it, supplying details that have been withheld by the police and could only be known by the actual killer. Well, right, and the actual killer told them to you. It's an old game, and when it's worked right it clouds the issue, and sometimes you'll even see a temporary stay of execution come out of it. But it can't hold up, and it doesn't.'

'This seems a little different.'

'Because the information didn't come to light until the guy got the needle. And didn't the tip come to them by untraceable e-mail? You have to wonder why the tipster bothered. He'd held off too long to save his buddy, not that it would have worked anyway.'

'Maybe he sent the message in time,' TJ suggested, 'but it got hung up in cyberspace somewhere. There's days when some of the service providers are as slow as the post office.'

'You know,' Elaine said, 'there's a lot more information in today's paper. Would it kill you to read the fucking article?'

'Probably not,' I said. 'Where is it?'

'Never mind. I'm sorry, I didn't mean to snap.'

'Can I see the article?'

'It's probably not gonna be that interesting.'

'Elaine—'

TJ, his eyes rolling, got to his feet, walked over to her, took the paper out of her hand, and came over to present it to me. 'It's nice having a family,' he said, 'even if it is what you call dysfunctional.'

I read the article.

One or two paragraphs in, I said, 'I see what you mean.'

'It's weird, isn't it?'

'And complicated,' I said. 'Let me finish.'

A *Times-Dispatch* reporter had thought to contact the authorities at Greensville, where the execution of Preston Applewhite had taken place. The warden

306

there recalled several visits by a Yale professor of psychology named Arne Bodinson. Bodinson's initials were the same as those of the rather transparent pseudonym of the e-mail tipster, which might or might not be purely coincidental.

This was where I'd come in, as all of the foregoing had been in the story I read yesterday or the day before – except for Bodinson's first name, which had originally been erroneously reported as Arnold. Since then, the reporter had established conclusively that no one at Yale had ever heard of Bodinson, Arne or Arnold, that he was not a member of the Yale faculty, nor had he, as his résumé claimed, earned a doctorate from that institution. This prompted the reporter to check with the University of Virginia in Charlottesville, where Bodinson had allegedly done his undergraduate work, and where they too had no record of his ever having attended, let alone having been awarded a degree.

'This is fascinating,' I said. 'Did you see where this Bodinson actually attended the execution? As an invited guest of Applewhite?'

'Isn't that something? The best thing we ever get invited to is the Mostly Mozart patrons' dinner.'

'Least they gave you a T-shirt,' TJ put in. 'Bet you Bodinson didn't get one.'

' "My Friend Just Got a Lethal Injection," ' Elaine said, ' "and All I Got Was This Fucking Shirt." '

I said, 'It's hard to figure this out. There doesn't seem to be any trace of Bodinson. He was in the

307

area for several days, he kept visiting Applewhite in his cell, but none of the local motels remember him. There's a picture.'

'Where? I didn't see it.'

'Not in the paper. Everyone who passes through security at Greensville walks in front of a security camera. They don't have a photo in hand, but they will, once they run through all the stored tapes. Of course, if Bodinson was savvy enough to fake credentials that got him into Applewhite's cell, he probably didn't give the security camera a very good look at him. They'll have shots with his hand in front of his face, or his head turned away. They'll probably be in tomorrow's paper, because this story's going to get a lot of national play.'

'I can see why.'

'According to the warden, Bodinson told Applewhite he believed his claim of innocence. Of course we don't know that's what he told Applewhite, because nobody heard him but Applewhite, and he's not talking. But that's what he said he was going to tell him. But in the meantime he told the warden that he'd be lying to Applewhite for the sake of the study he was doing, that it was obvious to him the man was guilty as charged. How can you figure the son of a bitch?'

'I suppose more will be revealed.'

'I wonder. If he knew Applewhite from before, why not just visit him in the normal fashion? You're allowed to have friends visit. If he was a stranger, what was the point?'

Elaine suggested the man might be a kindred spirit, part of an underground network of predatory pedophiles.

'Offering aid and comfort to a fallen comrade,' I said, 'and keeping it anonymous. He promised the warden he'd try to find out where the missing boy was buried. And evidently did find out, but instead of telling the warden what he'd learned he waited and tipped off the Richmond paper. I don't get it.'

'Maybe Applewhite told him, but swore him to secrecy until after his death. Maybe he wanted to be able to die proclaiming his innocence.'

'It's all so damn convoluted,' I said. 'Applewhite's just a pervert and a murderer, but Arne Bodinson a/k/a Abel Baker is something else again. You've got to wonder where he'll turn up next.'

CHAPTER 27

It is, he has to admit, a disturbingly good likeness. It's in the papers and on television, a full-face drawing of himself, the eyes gazing intently out at one, as in a photograph for which the subject has stared directly into the camera lens. But this is no photo, and must have been produced by a police artist, working in concert with a witness.

But what witness? Surely not the doorman in the building on Jane Street. The man had barely opened his eyes, let alone had the wit to use them. And the other doorman, the one who'd been on duty when he left, had scarcely spared him a glance. It was his job to vet persons on their way in, not those headed out.

Then who?

Oh, of course. The woman in the shop. Elaine Scudder, dealer in art and antiques. The wife of the detective. The friend of the late Monica.

Yes, he will definitely skin her. Start with her hands and feet, then work his way to the good parts.

But first there is the problem of the drawing. He can't move about effectively, can't do what he has

310

to do, if any passerby is apt to glance at him and sound the alarm. How can he give his full attention to the hunt if he's at the same time cast in the role of quarry?

He has a copy of the sketch before him, torn from this morning's Daily News. How the eyes blaze! He's only beginning to realize what a sense of strength and purpose emanates from them. Surely this ocular intensity is a continuing development, an ongoing part of his evolution. Aren't the eyes said to be the windows of the soul? The soul is a myth, surely, but substitute *spirit* or *essence* for it and you got the idea. His eyes reflect the person he is, and as he has grown in power, the look in his eyes has evolved accordingly.

He studies his reflection in the bathroom mirror, where the late Joseph Bohan must have viewed himself on those infrequent occasions when he remembered to shave. Yes, his eyes really do burn like the eyes in the drawing.

This pleases him.

He's also pleased to note the prominence of the mustache in the drawing. It is a dominant feature, it draws the eye, and a casual viewer will remember the mustache and forget the face's other features.

And he doesn't have the mustache anymore.

That's a help, but he's not sure it's enough. With eight million people out there in the city, it's not unlikely that one of them will look beyond the portcullis of the mustache and see the face plain.

His task, then, is to alter his appearance so that he looks less like the drawing. And hasn't he a long history of reinventing himself? Isn't his life an unending process of reinvention?

It would be easy, he thinks, simply to shave his head. He did this once years ago, with no purpose beyond experimentation, and was pleased if not greatly surprised to discover that he has a nicely shaped head, with none of those bumps or craters best left covered.

Shaving one's head brings about an instantaneous radical transformation, but nevertheless he knows it's a bad idea. A man with a shaved head has a commanding presence. The bald pate draws the eye. And the viewer can hardly help but wonder what the shaven head would look like without the razor's intervention.

No, the object is to avoid drawing glances. One wants to look different from one's picture, but still to blend in with one's fellows. One seeks not to stand out from the crowd but to fade into it, to be perfectly ordinary, invisible in one's mundanity.

He's been to the drugstore, and now he lines up his purchases on the bathroom shelf. He strips to the waist and gets to work.

First, the hairline. He's been blessed with a full head of hair, and it's every bit as full in the drawing as in reality. Eyes that would be drawn to a shaved head won't look twice at a receding hairline. He uses the little scissors first, clearing a path for the razor, which he then wields with the precision of a plastic surgeon, carefully delineating a new hairline. It begins an inch and a half higher on his forehead, and the recession is more pronounced on the temples. The result, when he's finished, is a textbook case of male-pattern baldness, lacking only a nascent bald spot at the crown. A bald spot, alas, is not something one can convincingly create on one's own.

Keep it simple, he tells himself.

Nice phrase, that. Keep it simple, easy does it, first things first. He's been associating with a great gathering of simpletons lately, people he won't be seeing anymore, but he does like some of their catchphrases, and when he dropped one or two of his own into their midst they generally seemed to like them as well.

You get what you get, he said on one occasion, and watched their little puppet heads bob up and down in agreement.

He keeps it simple, and is done with his hairline. Next the eyebrows, and for this operation he will need the little scissors and the pair of tweezers.

His own eyebrows are by no means bushy, but are nevertheless somewhat prominent. Trimming and plucking reduces their prominence, and it's remarkable how the change alters the whole appearance of his eyes. Looking out from beneath thinner, wispier brows, his gaze is somehow gentler, less unsettling.

Next, hair dye. His own medium-brown hair has the advantage of near invisibility; it might draw a glance in Asia or Scandinavia, but in America it is utterly ordinary. That's a good argument for leaving it alone, but after due reflection he follows the instructions on the package and renders it a shade or two darker. He knows not to dye it black – black hair, even when it's natural, somehow always looks dyed – and the color he's selected is very nearly as pedestrian as his own, yet undeniably different.

He leaves his eyebrows undyed, so that they'll appear even less distinct.

His new hairline has exposed skin heretofore untouched by the sun, and consequently lighter than the rest. The contrast is slight, but noticeable all the same, like evidence of the former presence of a ring or wristwatch. He's allowed for this, however, and he applies a small amount of sunless tanning lotion to the pale areas, and to the rest of his face as well. He's naturally light-complected, and avoids the sun, so a little color in his face will make him just a little more ordinary.

And, finally, a pair of glasses.

Not sunglasses. While they do a wonderful job of hiding the eyes and masking the face, they have the disadvantage of looking like a disguise. Ordinary eyeglasses, on the other hand, are almost as good at concealing the eyes and changing the shape of the face without looking as though that's what they're doing.

His distance vision is perfect, better than 20–20, and, while he's reached an age when presbyopia could be expected to show itself, his close vision is equally good. He doesn't even need glasses for reading.

He wanted real glasses, not a stage prop or a drug-store special. And yesterday he went to a LensCrafters shop and let the resident optometrist examine his eyes. He feigned difficulty with one of the chart's lower lines, then let the man find a lens that 'improved' his vision. It does no such thing, but it is mild enough so that it doesn't greatly interfere with it. He won't see any better with his new glasses, but he won't see all that much worse, and he doesn't think they will give him a headache.

And he'll only wear them when he's out in public.

With the glasses on, he stands at the bathroom mirror and shifts his gaze back and forth, from his reflection to the sketch to the reflection again.

Why, his own mother wouldn't recognize him.

But that's something he doesn't want to think about, not now, not ever, and he quickly wills the thought away. No one will recognize him, that's the point. Not the readers of the *Daily News*, not the viewers of *Live at Five*. The cops, fumbling about in the manner of their tribe, won't give him a second glance. Matthew Scudder won't recognize him until the Messer bowie is planted in his guts, opening him up, carving him from asshole to appetite. And as for Elaine . . .

Yes, he'll definitely skin her.

A problem, of course, lies in the fact that the other residents in his building, Joe Bohan's neighbors, have seen him as he appeared earlier – without the mustache, he has never worn that here, but with his full head of lighter hair, his paler skin, his fuller eyebrows, his unspectacled eyes. Few of them, to be sure, have had more than a glimpse of him, passing him on the stairs, perhaps. But he's had several chats with Mrs Laskowski and passed the time of day with one or two others.

So it will be best to avoid them, best to minimize his own comings and goings. It might even be prudent to quit the premises and take up residence elsewhere. Not another transient hotel, though. That's just the sort of place the police check first.

Perhaps he'll be able to stay where he is. Time is on his side; after the first fruitless days, the cops, having lost the scent, will lose their zeal as well. The press will tire of showing his picture, and the public, bombarded with new images and new horrors, will begin to forget what he looks like.

Time takes time. And you get what you get.

But he waits until dark to leave the building, waits until Mrs Laskowski will surely have given up the glory of the front stoop for the comfort of her television set. Then, the Jenkins folding knife in his pocket, he descends into the night.

At another Kinko's, this one over on the East Side, he logs on and visits one of his newsgroups. He scans the new posts, gives a few of them a thorough reading, then starts a new thread of his own.

He types:

The experts, self-styled and otherwise, the criminologists and psychologists and journalists, see those of us who kill for pleasure as driven men, essentially helpless in the grip of our own overpowering compulsions. No doubt it is more comforting to believe a man *has* to kill than that he simply *loves* to kill.

We kill, they tell us, according to the calendar, our behavior often dictated by phases of the moon. Much was made of the fact that our late brother Preston Applewhite dispatched his young friends at one-month intervals. Of course if one wished to establish a pattern, to draw public attention to the idea that a serial killer was operating, mightn't one deliberately wait a month between incidents? But no one seems to have considered this possibility.

There are, to be sure, those of us who are at the effect of our compulsions. But there are also those of us who are not. We can wait, if need be, no matter how the moon draws tides in our blood. And, when it is expedient, we can act in an instant in the absence of any inner prompting. We are much more dangerous and far less predictable than you find it comforting to believe.

He reads it over, ponders a signature, decides none is required. And hits SEND.

Back at the apartment, he thinks about what he has posted. The one thing he must do, he knows, is give himself time. Time for the Scudders to let their guard down. Time for the police to lose interest. Time for the public to forget.

But earlier, walking across town, he looked up and caught a glimpse of the moon. And it told him of what his very own blood has already informed him. That in a day, two at the most, it will be full.

He is not an automaton. He does not simply react to stimuli. He does not exist at the whim of fate. He makes his own fate, carves out his own destiny.

Yet how can he argue that the full moon is without influence?

It draws up the very seas, for heaven's sake. No one denies its role as the source of the tides. How then deny its pull upon the blood in one's veins?

Was the moon full that night in Durango? Along with the glow of the bedside lamp, did moonlight fall upon the throat and lead the bowie to it?

He rather thinks so.

Tomorrow, he knows, the pull will be at its strongest. Will it be irresistible? No, certainly not. His will is stronger than the tides, stronger than the moon.

But it might influence him to hurry things, to take needless chances. The longer he delays resolving matters with the Scudders, the more certain he can be of success. So must he stifle the moon-driven urges? Must he put them aside, perhaps until the next full moon, perhaps even longer?

Often, counseling patients, he's stressed the impor-tance of getting away from binary thinking. Beware the trap of the two alternatives, he advised them. So often, if you but look for it, you discover a third choice.

For him, the third choice, the only real choice, is obvious. All he has to do is take the pressure off.

Late Monday afternoon, at the peak of rush hour, he's crammed into a subway car on the southbound E train. As the train pulls out of the Fiftieth Street station, he draws the knife from his pocket, opens it with a practiced flick of the wrist. The bodies of his fellow passengers screen his actions from view, and no one can see him slip the knife between two ribs of the woman he's pressed against.

He's aware of the sudden intake of breath that stops when the blade finds her heart. For an instant she seems to be dancing on the end of his knife. Then the dance is over. He feels the life go out of her and breathes it in along with her scent.

The train pulls into Times Square. The doors open. He's one of many heading out the doors, and he's on the platform before the woman he's just killed has room enough to fall down. By the time they clear enough space to attempt to help her, he's up the stairs. He's out on the street long before anyone has the slightest suspicion she's dead.

There.

It's so easy. Because the moon is full, or simply because he likes to do what gives him pleasure, he's felt the need to kill. But he hasn't allowed that need to hurry his plan or expose him to unnecessary risk. He's found a simple risk-free way to act on it, and has done so with great success.

Now he can wait. Now he can bide his time, cocooned in Joe Bohan's cozy apartment, keeping up with his newsgroups, surfing the Internet, watching the Applewhite story (which is fast becoming the Bodinson story) unfold in fascinating fashion in Richmond.

The moon won't be full for another four weeks. And, should he feel the urge before then, how hard will it be to find and dispatch someone else? This city has human beings in great abundance. It won't miss a few here and there.

You can go to the ocean with a teaspoon or a bucket, he used to tell his clients. The ocean does not care.

A useful image, getting across the notion of the infinite abundance of the Universe. He's always liked it.

Indeed. With a teaspoon or a bucket. Or a knife.

CHAPTER 28

'I see your wife's shop is closed until further notice,' Sussman said. 'Until all of this is over, I take that to mean.'

'And I hope it's soon.'

'She's staying close to home?'

'She's staying home,' I said. 'Period.'

'Because I had a thought.'

'Oh?'

'It can't be much fun for her, sitting home every day. And I don't know what kind of business she does there, little shop like that, but you can't do any at all when you're not open.'

'I think I see where this is going.'

'Well, I figured you would. We can protect her, you know. I'd have two men in that back office, I'd park a panel truck in front with another two men in it, I'd have the place wired for sound. He couldn't get anywhere near her.'

'No,' I said.

'Take a minute and think about it, why don't you? We've got a chance to take a proactive stance here. Isn't that better than just sitting around waiting for something to happen?'

'Send a cop to college,' I said, 'and he comes out using words like *proactive*.'

'What's the matter with proactive? We've got a chance to quit sitting around with our thumbs up our asses. You like that better?'

'What I don't like,' I said, 'is staking my wife out like a sacrificial goat.'

There was more, and both our voices got a little louder toward the end. When I hung up, Elaine asked me just what the role of sacrificial goat consisted of. I told her to forget it.

'They want me to open the store?'

'It's a bad idea. Sussman likes it because it gives him a chance to do something.'

'That must be where proactive came in.'

'He can station men here and there and have them all stay in touch with walkie-talkies. He gets to be the general, he gets to direct the movie. But you're the one who'd be taking the risk, and to no purpose, because this guy's not stupid.'

'So you're saying it wouldn't work?'

'Not in a million years. You think he'll just waltz into the shop? They can have two guys in a Con Ed truck, looking like they're working in a manhole, and they can have another guy dressed like a bum and collecting coins in a paper cup—'

'Like TJ, with his denim cap.'

'—and two cops in the back room, and one in the basement and another on the roof, for all I know. The guy'll spot 'em in a hot second, and he'll stay away.'

'Say he does. Nobody gets hurt, and at least I'm out there doing something instead of just sitting here like a piece of Wedgwood that's too delicate to put on the table. What's the downside?'

'They put you out there,' I said. 'They bait the hook and he doesn't bite.'

'They bait the hook with a goat? Never mind. So he doesn't bite. Does that mean it wasn't worth trying?'

'It does if it means they lose their edge,' I said. 'They keep preparing for something that keeps not happening, and they start taking it for granted that nothing's going to happen. And they get sloppy, and they let their guard down. And he sits back and waits and watches, and when he finally makes his move nobody notices until it's too late.'

'You really think that would happen?'

'Yes.'

'Oh.'

'And you wouldn't just be standing there behind the counter for six or seven hours a day. You'd have to get there and back. They'd give you a police escort, and don't you think he'd spot it? And figure out a way around it?'

'I see what you mean,' she said. 'You can only take precautions so long and then you start loosening up. But won't the same thing happen to us here? I'm already getting a fierce case of cabin fever. We've got a nice roomy apartment, so I've got more than four walls to stare at, but I'm getting pretty tired of them just the same. I've been good, I do my yoga in the living room, but I don't know how long I can take it.'

'We'll take it a day at a time.'

'Like staying sober, huh?'

'Like getting through anything. Even guys in prison figure that much out. You take it a day at a time and you wait it out.'

'I know you're right,' she said. She was silent for a moment, and then she said, 'Suppose it was you.'

'Suppose what was me?'

'Suppose it was you on this asshole's shit list. And as far as that goes, how do we know it isn't? Maybe I'm not the only one he wants to kill, did you ever think of that?'

'If he makes a move on me, I hope he doesn't bring me a bottle of Strega.'

'I'm serious.'

'I guess the flowers would be okay, though. But no Strega.'

A little later she said, 'You take risks. You've even let yourself be the bait in the trap. What about the time that Colombian came at you with a machete?'

'That was more than twenty years ago. I was young and reckless then.'

'You still take risks. When you and Mick went out to his farm after those men—'

'There was nothing else to do, honey.'

'I know.'

'There was no way to bring the cops in, and we were in no position to hang back and wait it out. It was a different situation.'

She nodded. She said, 'I've been thinking a lot lately about the time I was stabbed. It must have hurt, don't you think? But it's funny, the only pain I remember is post-op, waiting to heal. I almost died, didn't I?'

'It was touch and go.'

'They had to take out my spleen.'

'They did,' I said, 'though anyone who knows you would find that hard to believe.'

'Thanks a lot. He was trying to kill you, too. Me first, but then you. I think this is the same idea.'

'Why do you say that?'

'I just have a feeling. He may not be too fussy about the order, either. I'm staying inside, I've been cooped up here for days, but you get to go out.'

'What's your point?'

'Well, you have to be careful. I don't know what I'd do if anything happened to you.'

'If I lost you,' I said, 'I really wouldn't want to go on.'

'Don't say that.'

'I'm not saying I'd kill myself. I just wouldn't want to live anymore. You reach a certain age and it can get pretty grim, you spend all your time going to other people's funerals and waiting around for your own. Your body and your mind both start giving up ground, and the best you can hope for is that they both quit on you at the same time. I can handle all that if I've got you keeping me company, but without you, well, I don't know that there'd be much point. So I realize it's a pain in the ass staying inside twenty-four hours a day, but do it anyway, okay? Humor me.'

'Okay,' she said.

A little after noon I got a phone call. It was the woman in the shop on Amsterdam Avenue. Number 1217 had come in again, wanting to pick up his mail, and there was no mail. So she'd thought of something. Tell me your name, she said, and I'll look and see if any mail for you got in the wrong box.

'So he told me, and his name is David Thompson.'

I thanked her, and was careful not to let on that we'd learned as much a couple of days ago. It was useful confirmation, anyway, and told us that David Thompson was not only the name on his driver's license but also the one under which he was receiving his mail.

All of this made him look increasingly legitimate. On the other hand, he'd been booted out of his apartment for not paying the rent, and if he was living in Kips Bay, what did he need with a mail drop on the Upper West Side?

I had a hunch, and then my phone rang again less than an hour later, and I wasn't really surprised when it was him.

'This is David Thompson,' he said. 'I never did get that check.'

'I know,' I said, 'and I'm sorry as hell. You wouldn't believe what's been going on here.'

'Oh?'

'Listen,' I said, 'I've got your check right here in front of me, and what I want to do is hand it to you personally. And while I'm at it I've got some more work for you, a bigger project that I'd prefer to discuss with you face-to-face. And I promise you won't have to wait so long to get paid this time.'

There was a pause, and he said I'd better give him the address again. The poor bastard didn't have a clue who he was talking to and didn't want to let on.

'No, don't come here,' I said. 'This place is a zoo. There's a coffee shop at Fifty-seventh and Ninth, the northwest corner, the Morning Star. Say half an hour? And you won't have trouble picking me out. I'll be the only guy there in a suit and a tie.'

He said he'd see me there. I went to the bedroom to pick out a suit and a tie.

He showed up wearing a suit and tie himself. I guess he'd figured he had to dress for the meeting. He saw me, knew he didn't recognize me, and scanned the room for another suit.

I said, 'David?'

He turned at the sound of my voice and made

a good show of recognizing me after all. 'I don't know how I missed you,' he said, and came over to shake hands. His hand was dry, his grip firm. He said something about the weather or the traffic, and I responded appropriately and motioned for him to sit. I already had coffee in front of me, and the waiter was right on the spot for a change. Thompson said he'd have tea, that coffee always made him want a cigarette.

He looked neat and clean. His suit was pressed and his shirt unwrinkled, and he'd shaved that morning. His hair was a little shaggy, but not unfashionably so, and his mustache was neatly trimmed.

'I'm going to start by apologizing,' I said. 'I got you here under false pretenses. There's a reason I don't look familiar. We've never met. I didn't give you any work, and I don't have a check for you.'

'I don't understand.'

'No, how could you? My name's Matthew Scudder, I'm a former police officer. A woman I know met you online. She had a bad experience once, and it led her to adopt a policy of running a check on people she was interested in, to make sure they aren't misrepresenting themselves.'

'Louise,' he said.

'You don't check out,' I said. 'Your name's so common it makes you hard to investigate, but what does come up has some pieces missing. I think I know what's going on here.'

'This is making me very uncomfortable.'

'You're free to leave. I can't hold you here. But why don't you listen to what I have to say, and then you can tell me if I'm right or wrong. Or just tell me to go to hell, whatever you want.'

CHAPTER 29

'He had a rough time,' I said. 'He had a job and a girlfriend, and he lost them both at about the same time, and he took it hard. Slept fifteen or more hours a day, watched television the rest of the time. Depression's a self-limiting state, and sooner or later you generally find your way out of it, unless you go and kill yourself first. He managed to avoid doing that, but by the time he surfaced he was broke and three months behind on the rent, and he knew it was only a question of time before they locked him out of his apartment. He took his laptop and some of his clothes and put them in his car, and he was just in time, because two days later he went back and saw everything he owned out at the curb. He just turned around and walked away.'

I could have told her this over the phone, I suppose, but it seemed to me she deserved more than that. So I'd called her at work and met her at five-thirty, in a coffee shop around the corner from her office.

'He wasn't destitute,' I said, 'but his credit cards

were maxed out and he was very low on cash. He called all his contacts in the business, looking for freelance work, and a couple of people gave him some work. But that meant waiting to get paid, sometimes for months. That's evidently the nature of the business.'

'It's the nature of every business,' she said.

'He looked for a place to live,' I said, 'and he couldn't find anything he'd want to live in for less than two thousand dollars a month. Even way out in Brooklyn or Queens everything he looked at was well over a thousand, and that meant coming up with a month's rent and one or two months' security deposit just to get in the door.'

'And he'd need furniture on top of that.'

'The rent alone was the killer. Even if he found a way to swing it, the monthly nut was going to be tough, because his prospects weren't that great and he didn't have a cash cushion to get him through the slow stretches. So he decided to hell with paying rent. He's been living in his car.'

'You're kidding. I didn't even know he had a car.'

'It's so old and beat up he can park it on the street, which is a good thing because he can't afford to garage it. And it's a Chevy Caprice, a big old four-door sedan with a roomy back seat.'

'And that's where he sleeps?'

'He says it's not that uncomfortable. He slept in it while he looked for an apartment, and he had grown used to it by the time he realized he wasn't going to be able to find anything he could afford. So he went on living in it, and the only problem is making sure he's always got a legal parking place. If he ever gets towed, he'll have to come up with a few hundred dollars to get his car back from the pound, and he can't afford to let that happen.'

'But he doesn't look like somebody who's living in his car. He shaves, he combs his hair, he wears clean clothes, he smells nice . . .'

'He belongs to a gym. It's a good one, the membership costs him over a hundred dollars a month, but that's a lot less than an apartment. He shows up every morning, pumps some iron or puts in his time on the treadmill, then showers and shaves and puts on the change of clothes he's brought with him. He keeps all his clothes in the trunk of his car and goes to a coin laundry when he has to.'

'And what about work? Is he really writing advertising copy?'

'Just like he said. He's got his laptop, which he hides under the front seat of the car in case somebody breaks in. When he wants to go online he goes to a café with wireless access. I'm not too clear on what that is.'

'I know how it works. I've got a card for it in my laptop but I've never used it. My God, do I know how to pick 'em or what? I find the man of my dreams and he's living in the back of his car.'

'He's not married,' I said, 'and he's not leading a double life.'

'How could he? It sounds as though he's barely leading a single life.'

'He's making ends meet. It's hard for him to get ahead of the game, but he's staying even, and that's no mean trick in this economy. He's a plucky guy. I have to say I liked him.'

'I liked him myself. Or at least I liked the person he was pretending to be.'

'The pretense bothered him,' I told her. 'Our conversation was an uncomfortable one—'

'I can imagine.'

'—but he seemed relieved to have it all out in the open. He wanted to tell you but he didn't know how.'

'"Honey, it so happens I'm a bum."'

'Well, he doesn't intend to spend the rest of his life living in his car. He's hoping to find full-time work, or build his freelance business into something that'll put him back on his feet again. Anyway, he wasn't sure how much you liked him, or whether the two of you had something that might last. If not, why bother embarrassing himself by coming clean?'

'When we went out for dinner,' she said, 'I offered to split the check. He wouldn't hear of it.'

'As I said, he's not impoverished. Just low on funds.'

'And homeless. You know, he could have stayed over. He could have slept in a real bed for a change.'

'I guess it was a point of honor for him not to.'

'Jesus,' she said, and drummed the tabletop with her fingers. 'He's gonna call me and I don't know what the hell I'm gonna say to him.'

'I don't think he'll be calling.'

'He's dumping me? Where did that come from?'

'He'll wait for you to call,' I said. 'And if you don't, well, he'll take that to mean you don't want to see him again.'

'Oh,' she said, and thought about it. 'That makes it easier for me, doesn't it? Saves us both the nuisance of a difficult conversation.' She thought some more. 'Except maybe that's tacky. I know how much fun it is to wait around wondering if the phone's gonna ring. Maybe it's simpler to make the call and get it over with.'

I told her that was up to her. She wanted to know how much she owed me, and I told her the retainer covered her tab in full. In fact, I said, reaching for the check, there was enough left over to cover the coffee.

'I'm glad you found out,' she said, 'even if I'm not crazy about *what* you found out. I knew there was something. He was too good to be true, with that adorable mustache. Plus he smokes.'

'The mustache,' I said.

'What? Don't tell me it's gone.'

334

'No,' I said. 'You just reminded me of something, that's all.'

I didn't wait until I got home. I found a doorway where the street noise wasn't too bad and called Sussman on my cell phone.

He said, 'You thought it over and changed your mind.'

'No, not a chance,' I said. 'This is something else entirely, something you said the other day that I keep meaning to ask you about.'

'So now's your chance. What did I say?'

'It had to do with his mustache. The subject came up, and you said something like the mustache is a good thing, because you could braid a rope out of it and hang him with it.'

'I said that?'

'Something like it, anyway.'

'I guess we can blame it on Brooklyn College,' he said. 'Colorful figures of speech, when I'm not using words like *proactive*. So?'

'What did you mean?'

'Oh, you weren't there when that came out? I guess maybe you weren't. All his vacuuming only worked up to a point. We found three little hairs, and they didn't belong to the woman. One on the sheet next to her and two in the bush, you should pardon the expression.'

'Hairs from a mustache.'

'So the lab techs tell me. Facial hair, anyway, and enough for a DNA profile. That's not gonna find him for us, but once we do it's golden. If there's one thing the DAs like it's some good hard physical evidence to put on the table.'

I walked a block and called him again. I guess he had Caller ID and I guess my phone wasn't blocking it, because his opening words were, 'Now what?'

'About the mustache,' I said.

'So?'

'One thing it tells me is he's clean-shaven.'

'Now, you mean? How do you figure that? He doesn't know he left a couple of hairs behind when he was having a snack. And even if he does, the DNA's not specific to the mustache. It's in every cell in his body.'

'He didn't shave,' I said. 'He didn't have to. He just used a little solvent and peeled it off.'

For a moment I thought the connection was broken. Then he said, 'You're saying it's a fake mustache.'

'That's exactly what I'm saying.'

'And it was no accident he left those hairs there. He placed them there on purpose so that we'd find them.'

'Right.'

'Jesus, that's convoluted.'

'We know he's a planner.'

'And a tricky bastard altogether. But this doesn't make any sense, Matthew. Giving us somebody else's DNA doesn't lead us down any primrose path. It's not like he's trying to frame somebody else for this. I mean, he knows we've got an eyewitness, a friend of the victim who sold him the murder weapon. We pull him in, we're not gonna cut him loose because the DNA's not a match.'

'It gives his lawyer something to play with in court,' I said.

' "Isn't it true that you found male facial hair at the crime scene? And isn't it true that you tried and failed to match that DNA with that of the defendant's?" '

' "And isn't it within the realm of possibility that another man visited the victim's apartment *after* my client had gone home, and how can you rule out the possibility that this other man was responsible for her death?" '

'Yeah, that sounds about right,' Sussman said. 'But what kind of psycho pervert murderer is so fucking painstaking? Listen, are you gonna be around for the next couple of hours?'

'Whether I am or not, I'll have my cell with me.'

'Good. I want to talk to the lab guys, and then I want to talk to you some more.'

I was just walking in the door when the phone rang. 'They didn't have to do anything,' he said. 'All I had to do was ask. The three hairs they recovered are male human facial hair, like I said. Facial hair is like body hair, it grows to a certain length and then it falls out, at which time the follicle sets about sprouting another hair.'

337

'And?'

'And these hairs didn't fall out. They were severed, probably by a scissors. Now what happens sometimes is you take a scissors and trim your mustache, and you don't comb it when you're done, and some of the trimmings stay in the mustache and get dislodged later. Which is why they weren't suspicious when they examined the hairs and saw they'd been cut.'

'Makes sense.'

'And the thing is it could have happened just that way. I can't prove it didn't. But I *know* it didn't, because if our Mr Neat trimmed his fucking mustache he'd have damn well combed it afterward.'

'Right.'

'He combed her crotch. Either that or he shaved his own bush, the way some of them do, to keep from leaving telltale evidence. Man, I bet every TV in every prison is tuned to *C.S.I.* when it comes on, I bet the motherfuckers sit there and take notes. Anyway, we didn't come up with any loose pubic hairs there, not his and not hers, but what we did find were those hairs from his mustache. So it was a fake.'

'Had to be.'

'And he wore it all along. When he met her, when he went to your wife's shop. Incidentally, forget what I said before about her going back to work. This prick's too fucking clever.'

'My thought exactly.'

'I don't know if we should change the sketch for TV and the papers. It might just tip him off that we know what he's doing. Besides, he could have a full beard by now.'

'If he found someone to sell it to him.'

'That's a line of inquiry I was just thinking about. Theatrical supply houses, because somebody had to sell him that mustache. Matt, I've got to thank you for this one. I never even thought of a false mustache. I'm not used to thinking that way. Maybe criminals were a shiftier lot back in the day, huh?'

'That must be it,' I said. 'The guy's a throwback.'

TJ was on the computer and Elaine was reading a magazine, but they both took a break to hear about David Thompson. Elaine was bothered by the idea that Louise was going to break up with him. 'So he hasn't got a place to live. So what?'

'I think it bothers her that he didn't tell her.'

'It's like herpes,' she said. 'You don't tell anybody until they need to know. Besides, he did tell her his place was too small for company. He just didn't tell her quite how small it was.'

'He said it was in Kips Bay.'

'Well, maybe he likes to park there, maybe there are lots of good spaces. I think she should buy a house in Montclair and let him park in her driveway.'

'You're just a sucker for happy endings.'

'Well, you're right about that.'

TJ remembered how, on the night we tried to tail him, Thompson had stopped to make a quick phone call as soon as he was out of Louise's building.

'We figured he was calling a woman,' I said, 'and we were right. He called Louise, to tell her what a good time he'd had. Then he took the route he did, over to West End and up to Eighty-eighth, because that's where his car was parked. And when he got in it, well, that was how he gave us the slip, without even knowing we were there.'

'An' he just got in it an' didn't start the engine or nothin'.'

'Why go anywhere? He had a space that was good until seven the next morning.'

Elaine said, 'That's men for you. After they make love, all they want to do is get in their car and go to sleep.'

'Least he got a car,' TJ said. 'They could go for rides.'

'He could take her to drive-in movies,' she said. 'If they still had them. Or he could park somewhere and lure her into the back seat.'

'An' he fall right asleep.'

'Out of force of habit,' she agreed. 'Oh, I love it.'

They turned more serious when I told them about the mustache hairs Monica's killer had left behind, and the inferences Sussman and I had drawn. I asked Elaine if the mustache had looked phony to her, and she said it hadn't, that she'd have said something if it had.

'But you don't expect a mustache to be a fake,' she said. 'A certain kind of hairline, you take a second glance to see if you can spot any of the standard telltale signs of a rug. Even then, like we were saying the other day, if it's a good one you can't tell. A false mustache should be easier to get away with, because no one would be looking for it.'

Something struck me, and I asked where the drawing was.

'Right there on the table, a whole stack of them.'

'I mean the original.'

'Oh,' she said. 'Just a minute, I think I know where I put it.'

'Bring an eraser, will you?'

'An eraser? Why do you – oh, I get it. Okay.'

She came back with Ray's pencil sketch and a cube of Artgum and said, 'Let me do it, okay? Now you want the mustache off but nothing else touched, am I right?'

'Right.'

'So I'll do it, because my hands are better than yours at detail work.'

'And lettering.'

'And lettering, and it's all because I'm a girl. That's the same reason I can't throw a baseball.'

'Or understand the infield fly rule.'

'Except I could throw a baseball fine if I were a lesbian. I don't know about the infield fly rule,

341

though.' She leaned forward, blew away the shreds of Art Gum detritus. 'There! What do you think?'

'Jesus Christ,' I said.

'What's the matter? Are you all right?'

'I'm fine.'

'You don't look fine. You look sick. What's the matter?'

'I think I know him,' I said. 'I think it's Abie.'

'His name's Abie. I've known him for, well, I don't know. One, two months? He's new in New York, but he's been sober something like ten years. He comes to meetings at St Paul's and Fireside, and just the other night he turned up at a gay men's meeting in Chelsea. I thought it was strange, running into him there. And there was something odd about his manner. I guess I thought he was gay but didn't want me to know it. He wanted to talk, tried to get *me* to talk, but I just wanted to be alone that night.'

'He was stalking you.'

I couldn't sit still. I was on my feet, walking around the room as I talked.

I said, 'It just doesn't make sense. He's been in the program ten years, for God's sake.'

'How do you know that?'

'Because he said so, and why would anybody lie about something like that? It's like a mustache, you don't look at it closely.' I frowned. 'I'm the one he latched on to, aren't I? I thought it was Monica and then you, or maybe the other way around, but it must have been me. He tagged me to AA and started coming to meetings. I don't know how he got to Monica.'

'She's over here a lot. *Was* over here a lot.'

'Then he found a way to meet her, which probably wouldn't have been too hard. And impressed upon her the need for secrecy, so she couldn't tell us about him. Didn't she buy Scotch for him?'

'Yes.'

'And he brought her a bottle of that Italian crap.'

'Strega.'

'Right, Strega. He came around and talked about his ten years of sobriety, he qualified at meetings, and then he went to her place and drank a little Scotch. And why shouldn't he, if he wasn't an alcoholic in the first place?'

I picked up the phone, looked up a number, made a call. It rang almost enough times for me to hang up before Bill picked up. I said, 'It's Matt, Bill. How's it going? Say, you sponsor Abie, don't you? Have you seen him at meetings lately? Well, why I'm asking, and I don't want you to breach a confidence, but I've got a reason to suspect him of something serious. Pretty damned serious, actually. I think he may be running a game, that he might not be sober at all. That's not the serious part, which I don't want to say just yet. Uh-huh. That's interesting. What's his last name, do you happen to know? Well, do you know where he's been living? I see. Yes, sure, Bill. I will, and thanks.'

I hung up and said, 'He hasn't seen him in several

days, doesn't know his last name, no idea where he lives. He smelled whiskey on him one time, and he didn't say anything, and Abie must have sensed something, because he pre-empted the subject by saying how he'd had a drink spilled on him at a restaurant and it was driving him crazy, walking around smelling the booze on himself. But thinking back, Bill has the feeling that might have been crap, and the booze was on his breath, not his clothes.'

'You want a cup of tea, baby? Or something to eat? You're all—'

'I'm all keyed up, and I damn well ought to be. Bill was his sponsor and Abie never told him his last name.'

'Abie's an odd name to pick. Short for Abraham, I suppose.'

'You would think, but he corrected you if you called him that. Or if you shortened it to Abe, come to think of it. And people are so polite in AA, so fucking accepting. He could have called himself Dolores and everybody would have gone along with it.'

'What's wrong with Dolores?'

TJ asked if he used a last initial, like Matt S. or Bill W.

I said, 'No, just Abie.' And then I stopped in my tracks, and I guess my eyes widened and my jaw dropped, because TJ gaped at me and Elaine took my arm and asked me what was the matter.

'So fucking clever,' I said. 'So goddam cute. Abie,

344

see? Just plain Abie. Those *are* his initials. *A* period *B* period. AB.'

'I don't see—'

'A fucking *B*. As in Abel Baker, or Arne Bodinson.'

'You can't think—'

'Or Arden Brill,' I said. 'Or Adam Breit. Or what did he write on the wall? Aubrey Beardsley. Always AB. Oh, sweet Jesus, it's him.'

CHAPTER 30

'You know,' Ira Wentworth said, 'I can't tell you how many times I've thought about that son of a bitch over the past few years. And each time I've tried to think of something else instead, because I didn't want him taking up space in my head. I wanted that chapter to be closed.'

Ira Wentworth was still at the Twenty-sixth Precinct. That's where he'd been a few years ago when the man with many names but a single set of initials ambushed a young woman named Lia Parkman in her residence on Claremont Avenue. Her room-mates were in the apartment at the time, but he managed to get in and out, and not incidentally drown Lia in the bathtub, without anyone noticing his presence. Lia, a student at Columbia, had been a friend of TJ's, and a cousin of another young woman named Kristin Hollander, whose parents had already been brutally murdered by two men in an apparent home invasion. AB – Lia knew him as Arden Brill, a doctoral candidate in English; Kristin had known him as Adam Breit, an unconventional psychotherapist – killed his accomplice

346

in the burglary, along with another young man. Earlier, he'd killed the owner of an apartment on Central Park West, then moved in, proclaiming himself the subtenant. Down the line he strangled a girl in a Korean massage parlor, wrung her neck and left her there. And, for a coda, he'd stabbed to death five homesteaders renovating a house in the Bushwick section of Brooklyn, disfiguring their corpses with muriatic acid before apparently dying himself in the basement, burned to death in the fire he'd set.

I wanted that chapter to be closed, Wentworth said, and it wasn't hard to figure out why.

Sussman said, 'The body in the basement. You couldn't get a positive ID?'

'Nothing that was a hundred percent. He was wearing a pendant, this pink stone identified as stolen in the Hollander burglary. He had a knife next to him, which we were able to tie to the five killings upstairs. The body was good and char-broiled, all you could say was it could be him. We could get DNA from it, but we didn't have anything to match it to. If he wasn't such a fucking trickster, such a cutie pie, there would have been no question.'

'So you closed the case.'

'I couldn't justify leaving it open. And if I had any kind of a gut feeling that maybe he staged the whole thing and disappeared, well, where were we going to go with it? Send out a nationwide BOLO, be on the lookout for some slick dude who kills people?' He picked up a copy of Ray's sketch. 'Is this what he looks like? You couldn't prove it by me. I never got to see him, or a picture of him. I never even came across a detailed description. But I know it's the same guy.'

'Because of the initials.'

'They nail it down, don't they? That's where he gets stupid, using the same initials all the time, making it his trademark. It's how he signs his work. The only thing bigger than his brain is his ego. You know, when we closed the case, I knew there was a chance he got out alive. But that meant he was out of the jurisdiction, and out of our hair.'

'You said as much at the time,' I remembered. And that was the bell that had tried to ring in a phone conversation with Mark Sussman. *Maybe he'd filled his New York quota, maybe he was on his way to El Paso. If so, he'd be out of our hair.* I'd got an echo then, but hadn't been able to hold on to it.

'Worst-case scenario, he was somebody else's headache,' Wentworth said, finishing the thought. 'One thing never even crossed my mind was he might come back.'

I'd called the two of them, Sussman and Wentworth, and we were all gathered in our living room. There was a carafe of coffee on the table, along with a little cream pitcher and a sugar bowl and a dish containing envelopes of artificial sweetener, both pink ones and blue ones. For boy babies and girl babies, I suppose. There was a plate of cookies, too. No one had touched the cookies, or used cream or sugar, but Wentworth had already had two cups of coffee.

There were other cops I could have invited to the party. There was Ed Iverson, from Brooklyn, who'd investigated the apparent murder and suicide on Coney Island Avenue. AB had staged that one, making it look as though Jason Bierman had killed first Carl Ivanko and then himself, effectively closing the book on the Hollander murders. There was Dan Schering, who'd had the Hollander case until Homicide North claimed it as their own. And I could think of a few others, cops from Homicide and from the Two-Six, along with a fire inspector out in Bushwick, but I'd have been hard-pressed to come up with their names, let alone guess where to reach them.

Wentworth said, 'What's it been, four years? Not hard to guess what he's been doing to get through the days.'

'Been killing people,' TJ said.

'Four that we know of,' Wentworth said. 'No, make that five.'

'Who besides Monica?' Elaine wanted to know.

'Your friend is one. Plus three boys in Virginia, unless there's anyone here who doesn't think our guy and Abel Baker and Arne Bodinger are one and the same.'

'Bodinson.'

'I stand corrected. Same guy, right?'

'Has to be,' I said.

Sussman agreed, but wondered how that meant he'd killed the boys in Richmond. Wasn't the evidence ironclad against Preston Applewhite?

'Evidence,' Wentworth said, 'would seem to be a specialty of this guy's. The Richmond killings were done with a knife, if I remember right. And the knife was recovered, it was part of the evidence. And our guy does seem to have a fondness for knives.'

'He strangled the Korean masseuse,' I reminded him. 'And he used a gun to kill Bierman and Ivanko and Byrne Hollander.'

'You don't think he did the three kids in Richmond?'

'I'm sure he did,' I said, 'and I agree he likes knives, but he doesn't limit himself.'

Elaine said, 'Weren't the boys molested? Sexually, I mean.'

'So?'

'So I thought he was straight, that's all. "Nothing queer about Chumley." You remember that joke?'

Wentworth said, 'About buggering an elephant, wasn't it? "Male or female elephant?" "Why, female elephant, old man, nothing queer about Chumley."'

'But those boys were killed years ago,' Sussman said. 'Virginia's quicker than most states, they move that appeal process right along, but even so he'd have had to put it all in motion way back when.'

'He's a patient man, Mark. And he probably

found other ways to pass the time. There's a whole lot of people get killed every year, and plenty of the killings go unsolved. And you don't have to limit yourself to the unsolved ones, either. I mean, the Richmond murders, the cops down there put that one in the Wins column. Case closed, right? Same as we closed the books on all the people he killed here.'

'I don't know,' Sussman said. 'What do we do now, call Richmond?'

They went back and forth on that one. On the one hand, the Richmond murders were a can of worms; on the other, the can was already open. Either way, the main thing to concentrate on was catching the son of a bitch, and if you brought in Richmond and the Bureau, were you increasing the odds of nailing him or setting yourself up for the Too Many Cooks syndrome?

There was a lull, and Elaine said, 'You said five.'

'How's that?'

'You said five killings,' she said to Wentworth. 'Monica is one, and the three boys in Richmond. That makes four. Who's the fifth?'

'Applegate, except that's not his name. I said it a minute ago. What the hell is it?'

'Applewhite.'

'There you go. Applewhite got a hot shot from the state of Virginia, but our friend was there to see him get it, and he's the one who put him on the gurney in the first place. He's not going to get indicted for that, and there's plenty of other things to hang him for instead, but wouldn't you say he was as much the cause of Applewhite's death as the chemicals they pumped into him? And wouldn't you call that murder?'

If the Richmond cops and the FBI came in, the whole thing turned into a media circus overnight.

'It seems to me we got one big edge right now,' Sussman said. 'We know who he is and where he's coming from, and he doesn't know we know. We go public with it and that's out the window.'

'I don't know,' Wentworth said. 'What's our edge amount to, anyway? First place, he might assume we know. It's not as though he's been working all that hard to disguise it. He's not using the same initials just so he can go on wearing the mono-grammed cuff links. Some level, he wants the whole world to know.'

' "Catch me before I kill more." '

'No, I'm not saying he's itching to get caught. He's doing everything he can to *keep* from getting caught, but consciously or unconsciously he damn well wants us to know just who it is we're not catching.'

'If we go public, what does he do?'

'I know what he did last time,' Wentworth said. 'He killed five people and disappeared. Six, counting the crispy critter he left behind in his place. I don't know that we'd trigger another bloodbath, but I'll bet he'd decide to get out of Dodge.'

'So what do we do? Besides quietly expanding the task force, putting more bodies on the case. How do we find him?'

'For a starter, we get serious about protecting Matt and Elaine. Next we get out there and look for him. He's got to be holed up someplace. Matt, how long did you say he's been turning up at meetings?'

'At least a month.'

'So he's living somewhere. Any idea where?'

'Be this neighborhood,' TJ said. 'Puts him close to this apartment, close to the meetings, close to Elaine's shop.'

'Say the West Fifties,' Sussman said, 'from Eighth Avenue to the river. Midtown North, in other words. Who do we know there?'

I let them toss names back and forth. One of the names they mentioned was Joe Durkin, and I chimed in to tell them he'd retired. They worked out details, figured out how to proceed. There were still quite a number of SRO hotels and rooming houses in the area, and that's where they thought they should concentrate.

I said, 'I don't think he'll be in a hotel.'

'No?'

TJ said, 'This another one gonna be sleeping in his car?'

They didn't know what he was talking about, and I didn't bother to enlighten them. 'He'll find an apartment,' I said.

'Then he's a genius, if he can find an apartment in this city.'

'It doesn't have to be an empty one,' I said, and reminded them how his neighbors on Central Park West had all been given to understand that he was subletting the apartment of a paleontologist on sabbatical in France. 'It was the perfect low-cost open-end sublet,' I said. 'All he had to do was kill the paleontologist and sink the body in the Hudson.'

'And you think he'd do it again?'

'The price is right,' I said, 'and it's not as though killing's a stretch for him.'

'No,' Sussman said. 'He seems to be developing a taste for it, doesn't he?'

When the two cops left, Elaine and TJ and I sat around with nothing much to say. Nobody felt like eating. I put on the TV, changed channels aimlessly for a few minutes, and turned the set off. I sat there and drifted into a curious sort of reverie in which I was trying to get a count of just how many people AB had killed that we knew about. I kept losing track and having to start over.

A few months earlier, when baseball season was just getting under way, I'd driven myself crazy one afternoon trying to remember the teams in the major leagues when I was a boy, when there were eight teams in each league and no divisions or playoffs, let alone exploding scoreboards and designated hitters. I wasn't using pencil and paper, I was doing it in my head, and it was harder than you'd think. I got all eight National League teams but only seven in the AL, and I couldn't seem to come up with the one I was missing. I forgot the whole thing, and then two days later the Yankees had a home stand against Detroit, and that was my answer, and one that raised another question. How the hell could I have forgotten the Detroit Tigers?

It was a very different country then. The westernmost city in the majors was St Louis, the southernmost Washington, D.C. Chicago had two teams, of course, but so did Boston and Philly and, yes, St Louis. New York had three.

Elaine asked me what I was thinking about. 'Baseball,' I said.

'See if there's a game on,' she suggested. 'Come on, it's something to do. I'll make popcorn.'

The Yankees were in Baltimore, playing a franchise that had once been the St Louis Browns. The Mets were winding up a three-game series at home with the Braves, who'd moved in my lifetime from Boston to Milwaukee to Atlanta. But you still get four balls and three strikes, three outs and nine innings, and if the hitters are stronger these days, well, the pitchers throw harder. We sat there on the couch and ate popcorn, the three of us, and watched the young men on the field play the old game.

CHAPTER 31

He sits in the coffee shop. He has a table next to the window, and he can sit here and eat his breakfast and keep an eye on the building diagonally across the street. Scudder lives there, Scudder and the fair Elaine, and there is a young black man who seems to spend a lot of time with them. Ever since he returned to New York he has seen Scudder in the young man's company, sometimes walking on the street, sometimes having a meal together in this very coffee shop.

Elaine never seems to leave the building. Scudder comes and goes, the black man comes and goes, but he never sees Scudder and the black man together anymore. It is hard to be certain, he doesn't spend twenty-four hours a day observing the building's entrance, but it seems to him as though at least one of the two men is always inside the building. Scudder never leaves until the black man has come to take his place at her side.

Which suggests to him that they're guarding her. Keeping her inside where no one can get at her, and standing by to protect her in the event that he might manage to get inside the building.

And if he were to go away?

The idea intrigues him. He wants to think about it. He pays for his meal, leaves the coffee shop, and walks.

He could just disappear. That's what he always does, sooner or later. He walks away from the life he's been living like a snake shedding its skin. He goes somewhere else, becomes someone else.

And does the things he does.

And if he were to do so now? Not, as he'd planned, after he'd finished his business with Mr and Mrs Scudder. Suppose he were to leave his business unfinished and simply vanish? He could go south or west, he could go anywhere, with his darker hair and his reshaped hairline and his eyeglasses, and no one would know him.

And the Scudders could remain here, waiting for the other shoe to drop. Keeping their guard up, with the woman afraid to leave the building and the man afraid to leave her alone, both of them chained by their terror, while he, the cause of that terror, is nowhere to be found. Gone, vanished, absent without leave, but they in their ignorance are unable to relax, unable to live their lives.

Like the whole country, he thinks. They'll have their own personal equivalent of long lines at airport security, they'll cower for the blow that never comes, while he's thousands of miles away.

He has the great advantage of patience. He's lived for years with unfinished business, ever since Scudder drove him out of this city. It's never eaten at him, never preyed on his mind. It's always been an item on the agenda, something to take care of sooner or later, when the time is right.

Suppose he returns it to the back burner. And suppose he's gone for a few more years, and the Scudders return to their ordinary lives, and time passes. Thoughts of him, unbidden and unwelcome, will trouble them from time to time. They'll know he's out there, they'll be aware that he might come back. But every month will make that threat a little less urgent, and they'll reach a point where they've relaxed entirely.

And then he'll return. Oh, he won't have this particular knife in his pocket when he does. He'll have let it go somewhere, for one reason or another. But he'll have another knife, and perhaps he'll like the new one even better.

And when the time is right he'll get to use it.

But he ought to do something before he goes. So that they don't forget him too soon.

CHAPTER 32

It was late morning when Mark Sussman called. Had I caught the item about the rush-hour subway stabbing in Queens? The victim was a male, sixteen years old, who'd earlier been in a shoving match with two other teenage males on the subway platform. The killing was assumed to have grown out of that argument, although no one had seen it occur; the bodies of the other passengers kept the youth's body upright until the train reached a station and the crowd thinned enough for him to fall down.

'They figured gang-related,' he said, 'but I thought about it, and then I thought about that woman killed a couple of days ago here in Manhattan. Miles apart, but it's the same train, and both times it's a stabbing and nobody saw it happen. Two different boroughs and two different medical examiners, so who's going to look at both of them at once, you know?'

He'd talked to the right people, and he was waiting for them to compare notes and get back to him. 'What I want to hear,' he said, 'is it's two different knives, two different kinds of wounds, two different everything. But you know what I think it is.'

He said he'd let me know as soon as he heard one way or the other. An hour or so later the phone rang and I thought it was him, but it wasn't. It was Mick Ballou.

'That picture you showed me,' he said. 'Didn't I tell you he looked familiar? I've tried to place him, and late last night it came to me.'

'You saw him at Grogan's?'

'I did not. 'Twas years ago I saw him, and then only for a moment. Do you recall when you had me go to a house on West Seventy-fourth Street? There was a girl there you thought might be in harm's way.'

'Kristin Hollander.'

'And a very nice young woman she was. He came to the door, your man in the drawing. Of course I'd no idea who he might be. I opened the door and told him to piss off, and he pissed off. I barely looked at him, but I've a fine old memory, haven't I? It was the same man.'

'Oh, God,' I said. 'I never even thought of her. I don't know what the hell's the matter with me. Listen, I'll have to get off the line so I can arrange police protection for her. Assuming she's all right, assuming he hasn't already paid her a visit. Christ, if he's got to her, if he's killed her—'

'No one's touched a hair on her head.'

'How do you know?'

360

'How do I know? Why, amn't I sitting across the table from her even now?'

'He drove over there late last night,' I told Elaine, 'but felt it was too late to show up on her doorstep, so he parked across the street and kept his eyes open. Then this morning, as soon as it seemed to him to be a decent hour, he rang her doorbell. He found it remarkable that she remembered him.'

'Has anyone ever forgotten Mick?'

'I asked him that. He said there've been some that wished they could.'

'I'll bet.'

'The house has a burglar alarm and a good set of locks, and she's got Mick in there with her. I don't know why it didn't occur to me to worry about her before, but now I don't have to. He killed her parents, you know.'

'I know.'

'She's still living there. All by herself, in that big house.'

'And now she's got Mick for company.'

'They're playing cribbage,' I said. 'They played cribbage four years ago, when he went and guarded her.'

I picked up the phone and called Ira Wentworth and told him most of it, although I don't think I mentioned that they were playing cribbage. 'I don't know how we forgot about her,' I said, 'but she'll be all right now. He's not going to get in there, and God help him if he does. Still, it might not be a bad idea to stake the place out.'

'Because he might show up,' he said. 'I talked to my captain, and we're reopening the Lia Parkman file. I can probably spring a couple of plainclothes to sit in a car and watch the block.'

I put the phone down, and the next time it rang it was Sussman. The lab evidence was preliminary, and you couldn't take it to the bank, but every indication was that the teenage male in Queens and the woman in Manhattan had been killed in the same manner – a single thrust from the rear, between two ribs and into the heart. The weapons used in the two homicides were at the very least similar, and probably identical.

'And for now,' he said, 'that's as far as it's gonna go. I don't even want to write it up, let alone go and tell somebody. Because God help us all if the media get hold of this. You want to try imagining the subway at rush hour with every passenger trying to watch his back?'

'They'd want metal detectors,' I said.

'At every turnstile. Take the coins out of your pockets, put 'em in the tray, and swipe your Metrocard. Yeah, right. We got to catch this prick in a hurry, that's all. Because you can only keep a lid on it for so long. If he does it one more time, takes out one more rush-hour straphanger, some media genius is gonna figure it out all by himself. And there goes the front page in every paper and

362

the lead slot on every TV newscast, and we've got panic in the streets. And under them.'

That evening I was sitting in a chair with a book, and Elaine came over looking concerned and asked me if I was all right. Evidently I'd set the book down and had been staring off into space for five or ten minutes. I hadn't been aware of it.

I said, 'I hate not doing anything. I hate waiting for something to happen and hoping I can react to it properly when it does. I hate feeling helpless and useless and out of the loop.'

'And old?'

'And old,' I said. 'I know there's nothing I can do other than what I'm doing already. I know all that, and I'll keep on doing it. But I don't like the way it feels.'

It felt a little better in the morning. Sussman called, and I could hear the change in his voice. 'We found him,' he said, and before I could react he corrected himself. 'Found where he's living, I should say. Way the hell west on Fifty-third Street. A woman recognized the sketch, said he was the nice young man come to take care of his Uncle Joe, who had to go to the Veterans Hospital up in the Bronx. Except the people at the VA never heard of Joe Bohan, and my guess is nobody's ever gonna see poor old Joe again.'

'I don't suppose our guy was on the premises.'

'No,' he said, 'but his laptop was. The laptop's

363

password-protected, but we've got a guy we can go to who can crack it quicker than a high school kid can break into a locked car. We don't have to get into it to know it's our guy's laptop, though, because Joe wasn't an online kind of guy. In fact you wouldn't know Joe ever lived there, because all of his things are gone. All that's left would seem to belong to the owner of the laptop, and one of the articles in question is a big old knife. Even as we speak, they're trying to match it up to the subway stabbings. And I've got a dozen men on the block, keeping an eye out, waiting for him to come back for his laptop. Or his knife.'

CHAPTER 33

Sometimes it seems to him that there truly are guardian angels, and that he has one. At more rational moments the notion of a guardian angel strikes him as essentially metaphorical, a convenient way to personify that portion of one's mind-spirit-self capable of perceiving the imperceptible.

Years ago, during his last stay in New York, he was away from his apartment on Central Park West when Scudder led a band of cops there. He was in a taxi, on his way home, ready to walk right into a lobby swarming with police officers just waiting for him to appear, and something warned him, something made him get out of the cab and approach the rest of the way on foot, cautiously, alert for any sign of danger.

Looking back, he has never been able to pinpoint anything that should have made him wary. He can recall no police sirens wailing in the distance, no discernible change in the appearance of the neighborhood as the cab neared its destination. But whatever you choose to call it, a guardian angel, a higher self, an elevated level of *ESP*, it is undeniable that something warned him and that he'd had the presence of mind to act on the warning.

Something made him turn away from that Central Park West apartment, retrieve his car from the garage where he kept it, and drive straight to Brooklyn. It hadn't taken him long to get there, nor had it taken him long to take care of his business and leave the Meserole Street house in flames, and get out of the city altogether.

All because he was able to listen to that inner prompting and not let logic overrule what it told him.

And now he experiences it again, that same sort of warning. He feels a tightness in the back of his neck, a tingling in the palms of his hands. He's walking south on Ninth Avenue when he first notices it, he's just passed Elaine's shop, and his first thought is that he's under observation, that someone is watching him.

He stops to look at the menu in a restaurant window, turns this way and that, getting a look around without making it too obvious that's what he's doing. He doesn't see anyone, and that's not what it is, this sensation he's experiencing. He's not being watched.

There's something waiting for him, that's what it is. And he remembers the sensation from four years ago, remembers stopping the cab abruptly, telling the driver he'll walk the rest of the way.

Remembers what was waiting for him a few blocks further along on Central Park West.

He walks to Fifty-third Street, turns right, walks west. And he's like a child playing a game, with others telling him *You're getting warmer* or *You're getting colder* as he turns this way and that. He's getting warmer, and he *feels* warmer, feels the increasing sense of a hostile presence in front of him.

Eventually he gets close enough to see them, on the block where he's been living. There are no blue uniforms, but all it takes is a glance and he is able to spot them for what they are. There's a car with its hood up, and the two men peering into its engine compartment might as well be dressed in blue. And there's a woman with a baby carriage, paying more attention to the street scene than to the infant – a doll, he's certain – within the carriage. Two men share the stoop next door to Joe Bohan's building, drinking from cans held in paper bags. Cops, all of them.

So much for his laptop. No point going back for it now, even if he could somehow thread his way through the maze of police. They'll have long since carried it off, along with everything else he owns.

What's on the laptop? The password will secure it for a while, but if you build a better mousetrap someone will surely build a better mouse, and that applies to his own mousetraps as well as those of others. They'll get past his password, in an hour or a day or a week, and what will they learn?

Is the matter of Preston Applewhite documented there? He rather thinks it must be.

No harm. Applewhite, poor fellow, has long since gone to glory, and if this serves to rehabilitate his reputation, well, he'd set that in motion with his tip to the Richmond newspaper. And it's a zero-sum universe, isn't it? Because any gain to Applewhite's reputation will come at the expense of the reputations of the whole criminal justice system of the state of Virginia.

Let them have the laptop. He can always get another. Meanwhile, there's always Kinko's.

And what else has he lost? Some clothing, some personal articles. A razor, a toothbrush, a comb.

And, of course, that beautiful knife. The Reinhold Messer bowie, with its blade of Damascus steel, so skillfully made, so perfectly balanced.

He slips a hand into his pocket, where the Thaddy Jenkins folder waits, smooth and cool to his touch. He can't help taking it out, opening it with a flick of his hand that has by now become purely reflexive. He tests the blade with his thumb, feels its keenness.

And then, a little reluctantly, he works the catch, closes the knife, returns it to his pocket.

The house?

He's thought of it before, that house on West Seventy-fourth Street. It seems to him that there would be some sort of poetic justice in taking it up as his next temporary residence, a larger and more comfortable shell for the hermit crab than poor old Joe Bohan's tenement flat. It was, after all, supposed to be his house, back in the time when he still thought a house was something he wanted.

Why he'd even had fantasies – they seem quite laughable now – of marrying Kristin Hollander, and helping her deal with the grief of having lost her parents. She is a pretty thing, Kristin, and she'd have been amusing company for a while. He might have convinced her, for example, of the therapeutic necessity of making love in the front room, the very place where he'd killed her mother and father.

And then, of course, when the amusement faded, the poor grief-stricken thing would take her own life – easy enough to arrange – and the house would be his, free and clear.

If not for Matthew Scudder . . .

He shakes his head, dismisses that whole train of thought. The past, he reminds himself, is called that for a reason – it has passed, it is over and done with. Someone has called it another country, and if so it's not one to live in, or even the place for an extended visit. It is the here and now that concerns him.

Should the here and now include the Hollander house?

She still lives there. He knows that much, and not merely because he's seen the listing in the phone book. He's seen her, too, leaving her house and walking to the corner to hail a taxi, and looking just as he remembers her. How old would she be? Twenty-five, twenty-six? Mid-twenties, certainly, and still quite lovely.

There was a time when he had a key to her house, and knew the code for the burglar alarm. Both the lock and the code have long since been changed. Still, there ought to be some way to get into the house.

And if he were simply to ring the bell?

She'd come to the door. Late at night she might be on her guard, but in the middle of the afternoon, why, she'd open the door to see who it might be.

And if she recognizes him?

Kristin, he'll say, it's so good to see you! And by the time she reacts, by the time that it strikes her that she has no reason to be glad to see him, why, he'll be inside, won't he? And it will no longer matter what she thinks or feels or tries to do.

When he's through with her, the house will be his for as long as he wants it. The hermit crab will have a spendid new shell.

The very moment he turns the corner onto her block, he senses an alien presence. His first impulse is to turn again and slip away, but the feeling that grips him is a little different this time, and he decides on a closer look. He'll be careful, he'll take pains to see without being seen, but he won't turn tail and withdraw, not quite yet.

At a Korean market around the corner on Columbus Avenue, he buys three loaves of white bread and two rolls of paper towels. The shopping bag they give him is full to overflowing, but weighs next to nothing. He's out the door when it occurs to him to add a bouquet of flowers, all wrapped up in green paper. With one arm clutching the bag of groceries to his chest and his free hand brandishing the bouquet, he manages to look ordinary and harmless while screening his features from any eyes turned in his direction.

He walks down her street, moving at the deliberate

pace his burdens would seem to dictate. He's able to glance into each parked vehicle, to check out stoops and doorways. And he sees no one the least bit suspicious, no one who might possibly be a watchful cop.

Why the warning from his guardian angel?

It was, he decided, an echo of the earlier warning. The mind would do that, summoning up the memory of a feeling when presented with a similar situation. And, while the alarm has turned out to be a false one, hasn't it been useful all the same? Because now he can ring her bell with a bag and a bouquet to block any view of him she might gain through a peephole. That had been a flaw in his original plan, the possibility that there might be a peephole in her front door that would allow her to recognize him before she had the door open. But now she'll have to open it to know who her visitor is, and what woman could leave the door closed on a man holding a bouquet of flowers?

Perfect.

He has passed her house and walked to the other end of the block, and now he turns to approach it again. He's two doors away, just steps from the walkway leading to her front door, when something makes him stop right where he is. He takes a moment to visualize it all in his mind, ringing the bell, positioning the groceries and the flowers just so, waiting until the door opens, then pushing hard against the door, forcing his way in, dropping everything, and hitting her once, as hard as he can, in the chest or stomach, to keep her from reacting or crying out

371

until he's had a chance to draw the door shut behind him.

And he stands there, seeing all of this as clearly as if it is actually happening, when a car drives up and pulls smoothly into a parking space at a fire hydrant directly across the street from her house.

Two men, and he knows at once that they're cops.

The driver cuts the engine. His passenger gets out of the car, walks into the middle of the street, and raises a hand to shield his eyes for a look at the house number. Satisfied, he turns and gets back in the car, rolling down the window to give him a better view of Kristin Hollander's house.

And to think he'd been ready to write off a clear warning as vestigial, a mere echo! Whatever its source, he'd been alerted not to the physical presence of police (who hadn't been there yet at the time) but to the reality of danger.

He walks at his deliberate pace, his face shielded by the bouquet, his innocence guaranteed by the bulk of his burden, until he reaches the corner and disappears from their view. He walks another block, drops both his bundles in a trash can, and picks up his pace.

If they are watching the Hollander house, they know who he is.

Or suspect it, at the very least. That he did not die in the fire in Brooklyn, that the body in the basement was somebody else's, that he who killed and ran away has lived to kill another day.

The thought excites him. It is, he knows, a paradox that he who so relishes his anonymity at the same time hungers for recognition. It seems clear that he is a genius, although not in an area much esteemed by the Nobel committee. Still, he has a human desire to be acknowledged for what he is – and a core of good sense that keeps him well aware of the danger of such acknowledgment.

He asks himself once again if it is not perhaps time to disappear. He has the clothes he is wearing, the money in his wallet, along with an ATM card that will give him access to a few thousand dollars in a bank account on the other side of the country. He no longer recalls the name he used to open the account, or the name and location of the bank, but what does it matter? He has the card and knows the PIN, and that's all he needs to know.

And what else does he have? The keenness of his mind, the strength of his will, and the promptings of his intuition.

And, of course, the knife in his pocket.

Enough to take him wherever he wants to go. Shall he leave, then?

CHAPTER 34

The phone call came a few minutes after five. I let the machine pick up, and after we'd listened to my own recorded message, there was a long enough silence for me to think the caller might have hung up.

Then he said, 'Well, hello, Matt S. This is Abie.'

Elaine was in the room with me, and the color left her face as she recognized the voice. She would, of course; she'd heard it when he'd come to her shop to buy the bronze paper knife.

I picked up the phone. I said, 'Hello,' and wondered why I was saying anything.

'I've been trying to reach my sponsor,' he said. 'I was hoping for the benefit of his strength, hope, and experience. But he's not answering his phone, so I thought I'd call you instead.'

'Really.'

'Maybe you could tell me not to drink, and to go to a meeting. That might be helpful in keeping me on the straight and narrow.'

'What do you want?'

'Why, I just wanted to talk. And you'll probably

want to keep me on the line so you can trace the call.'

We hadn't set up for that. It's not that hard to do nowadays, but in this case there hadn't seemed to be much point to it. We knew he'd called Bill several times, and a check of the LUDS on Bill's phone had established that all the calls from Abie had been made on an untraceable cell phone. If he called me he'd use the same phone, so why bother setting up a trace?

'I'll save you the trouble,' he said. 'I'm on a pay phone at Penn Station, and in approximately seven minutes I'll be on a train. I've decided it's time to disappear.'

'I wish you'd stick around.'

'Oh? Be careful what you pray for, my friend.'

'Because I might get it?'

'So they say. Or did you want to tell me that I can be helped, and that you'll see to it that they help me if only I turn myself in?'

'No,' I said, 'I don't want to tell you that.'

'Oh?'

'I don't want you to be helped. I want you to be killed.'

'Now *that's* refreshing,' he said. 'All the more reason for me to leave the stage, wouldn't you say? I'm enjoying this conversation, but it's time to catch my train. One thing, though. Will you give my sponsor a call? It's Bill, the older fellow they call William the Silent. He's even more silent than usual lately, and I'd feel better if you'd check on him.'

He broke the connection. I put the phone down and looked at Elaine.

She said, 'I feel like throwing out the answering machine and getting a new one. Or at least spraying this one with Lysol.'

'I know what you mean.'

'Maybe I should spray the whole apartment. It needs disinfecting, after that voice has had a chance to bounce off the walls.'

'The whole city needs disinfecting.'

'The whole planet. Who are you calling?'

'Bill,' I said. The phone rang and rang. I broke the connection and redialed and the same thing happened.

'Oh, Jesus,' I said.

They found Bill in his apartment, dead of multiple stab wounds to the chest. There were defensive wounds on his hands and forearms, suggesting he'd tried to fight off his killer.

Sussman checked the phone records, and it turned out the call we'd received had in fact come from a pay phone in Penn Station. I didn't know what to make of that.

'One of the things we found on Fifty-third Street,' he said, 'was a cell phone charger. I had to guess, I'd say his battery ran down. If he wanted to give you a call, he had to spend a quarter.'

'He called from Penn Station,' I said, 'and he said he was calling from Penn Station.'

'So?'

'So he wanted to make sure I knew it. Not only does he tell me, but he knows the LUDS will back him up.'

'He wants us to think he's leaving town.'

'Maybe. Or he really is leaving town, and he wants us to think he's not.'

'By telling us he is.'

'Right.'

Elaine said, '"How Could You Believe Me When I Said I Loved You When You Know I've Been A Liar All My Life?"'

'They don't write songs like that anymore,' Sussman said. 'So let's sum this up, okay? What we now know for sure is that either he's leaving town or he's not. Is that about it?'

I wound up going to the meeting at St Paul's. I didn't want to go anywhere, but someone had to tell them about Bill, and I decided it really ought to be me. I got there a little late, after the qualification but in time for the general discussion, and I got to be the bearer of bad tidings.

Beyond the fact that we'd lost a long-time member, I had to let everybody know that they might be in danger, and that it was impossible to guess with any degree of certainty just how real that danger might be. Abie – I called him that in the meeting, because that's how they knew him – was at once a coldly logical being and a homicidal maniac. Just as I couldn't say if he'd left town or pretended to leave town, neither could I tell if he'd killed his sponsor as an opening skirmish in a one-man war on New York AA or simply to send me a personal message. I felt like the goddam government, raising the Alert level from Yellow to Orange. Stop being Careful, I was saying, and start being More Careful. And rest assured that we'll let you know when it's time to be Extra Careful.

I didn't stop in at the Flame afterward. I hadn't left Elaine alone, TJ was with her, but all the same I was anxious to get home.

Walking the couple of blocks, I kept having the feeling someone was watching me. I looked around, but nothing caught my eye.

CHAPTER 35

The bastard's wary.

You can see it in his walk, see it in the way he keeps looking this way and that way. Maybe he can sense that he's being watched, followed. Maybe it's just an indication of the level of his anxiety.

And he's armed, too. You can't see the gun, but you know just where it is – tucked into his waistband on the right hip. His sport shirt, worn outside his trousers, hangs down far enough to cover it, but when you watch him it's no trick to pinpoint its location because of the way his right hand hovers nearby, ready to reach for the gun should the occasion arise.

And would he be fast enough? The man's in his middle sixties, and isn't likely to have the reflexes of a teenager. He's on edge, he's undoubtedly visualizing quick draws in his mind, but suppose you rush him, suppose you run hard at him from the rear with the knife open in your hand. How long will it take him to register the sound of approaching footsteps? How quickly will he turn, how swiftly can the left hand draw the shirt-tail aside while the right hand yanks the gun free?

There are other people on the street, but you can forget about them. By the time they figure out what's happening in front of their eyes, it will be over and done with, and you'll be around the corner while he's bleeding into the pavement.

You could do it. Care to give it a try?

No, not just yet.

Perhaps he should have bought a ticket. A reserved seat on the Metroliner to Washington, say. In a name they'll recognize, Arden Brill or Alan Breit or Arne Bodinson.

But would they even check ticket sales? And would they attach much significance to such a purchase if they even managed to spot it?

Probably a waste of time. A waste of money, too.

He has money to waste, if it comes to that. His wallet holds a fresh supply of cash, courtesy of the late William the Silent, who hadn't been so silent after all. Old Bill had given up his ATM card and the PIN number when it was clear nothing else would save his life. That didn't save it either, of course, and he couldn't have thought it would, but it's hard to think clearly when someone has you pinned to the floor and keeps on sticking a knife into you.

With the PIN revealed, he'd used the knife one last time. Then he'd withdrawn it, and shortly there-after he'd made another withdrawal, this for $500 from Bill's account. That, plus the cash Bill kept in his sock drawer, has improved his financial position considerably.

Money won't be a problem.

But he needs a place to stay. He'll want to sleep, and he could use a shower.

And he needs a way to get at the Scudders.

A smile comes to his lips, the cautious half-smile he practiced in the rear-view mirror in Virginia. Two birds, he thinks. And he knows where to find a stone.

The man's name is Tom Selwyn. He's a few inches over six feet in height, and must weigh well over 250 pounds. He carries the weight well, and is the sort of fat man who's inevitably described as being light on his feet. No doubt he's a good dancer, although one's not likely to find out. While the jukebox holds a decent selection of jazz and standards, there's no dance floor in the dimly lit Fifty-eighth Street bar.

'Alden,' Tom Selwyn says. 'Alden. As in Miles Standish's very good friend?'

Now there's a thought. 'As a matter of fact,' he says, 'my mother, who would never forgive me if I didn't at once point out her membership in the DAR—'

'I can well imagine.'

'Well, she managed to find a genealogist who was able to establish a direct line of descent from John Alden and Priscilla Mullins'—now how did he manage to summon up that name?—'to herself, and hence to me. Whom she would have liked to name John Alden Beals, but my father was already named John and felt one John in the family was plenty.'

'I'll omit any wordplay relating to Johns and lavatories.'

'That's because you're a gentleman, and I in turn will avoid any allusions to peeping Toms and doubting Thomases.'

'Fair enough.'

'She dropped the John and named me Alden.'

'Alden Beals.'

He bows his head, just the slighest bit theatrically. 'Myself,' he says.

'I've noticed you before, you know.'

'Really?'

'You've been here at Griselda's before. Two or three times I've seen you march in, order a single-malt Scotch, perhaps the same brand you've been drinking tonight —'

'Perhaps not. I'm not terribly loyal. Always looking for something better, you know.'

'Oh, indeed I do.'

'But willing to keep sampling as I search, one might say.'

'I suspect one might. You've come in, ordered one drink, took your time drinking it, and then left without a word to anyone.'

'I never thought anyone noticed me.'

'Oh, please. An attractive man like yourself? Surely you felt the eyes, mine among them. But you never seemed to be looking for company.'

He is silent for a moment. Then he says, 'I have someone at home.'

'I see.'

'But that's not always where I want to be.'

'And just where would you like to be now, Alden?'

'At the moment,' he says, 'I'd like to be precisely where I am. Right here in this congenial atmosphere, engaged in conversation with a very personable and attractive gentleman.'

'You're very kind.'

'It's no more than the truth. The only problem —'

'Oh, I hope there's not a problem.'

'Only that it's getting close to closing time.'

Selwyn looks at his watch, a Tourneau with a thin case and an oversize dial. 'It is,' he agrees. 'And where would you like to go when they close this pop stand?' And, when he hesitates, 'What was it your great-great-great-great-great-great-grand-mother said? "Why don't you speak for yourself, Alden?"'

He has lowered his eyes. Now he raises them to gaze directly and openly into Tom Selwyn's. 'I'd like to go back to your place,' he says.

The lobby attendant is seated at a desk on the left. He has anticipated this, and contrives to be on Selwyn's right as they enter the building, letting the big man screen him from the attendant's view. The two exchange greetings. ('Evening, Mr Selwyn.' 'A lovely evening, Jorge. I see Sammy hit one tonight.')

In the elevator Selwyn pushes Nine and sighs as the door closes. 'Sammy Sosa,' he explains. 'He and Jorge hail from the same village in the Dominican Republic. Although it may not be large enough to be called a village. What's smaller than a village?'

'A hamlet?'

'Perhaps. Or it may be more of a coriolanus. Do you follow baseball?'

'No.'

'Neither do I, but I contrive to find out what Sammy Sosa has done, so Jorge and I will have something to talk about. He's with the Cubs. Sosa, that is. Not Jorge. The Cubs play in Chicago, in the stadium that didn't have lights, but now it does. And here we are.'

The apartment consists of one large high-ceilinged room, perhaps thirty feet square, with a small kitchen alcove. Except for the king-size platform bed, piled high with pillows, the furnishings are antique. There's a large abstract oil on one wall, with a simple black gallery frame, and groups of prints and drawings on the other walls. It is, he decides, a very pleasing room, and a great improvement on Joe Bohan's apartment; it's a shame he won't be able to stay here very long.

'I have Scotch,' Selwyn says.

'Maybe later.'

'Ah. Someone doesn't wish to wait.'

'Someone doesn't even wish to talk,' he says, and begins taking off his clothes. His host raises an eyebrow, then unbuttons his own shirt, takes it off, steps out of his trousers. His clothes had concealed some of his bulk; naked, it's evident just how heavy he is.

'I was always shy about disrobing,' Tom Selwyn says. 'You can imagine how I hated gym class. In recent years I've learned that there are people who don't mind a Rubenesque figure. And it would appear you're one of those, wouldn't it? My word, no wonder you don't want to waste time on drink or small talk. You're fully prepared, aren't you? Not to say splendidly endowed. And speaking of preparation, the drawer there holds a supply of rubber goods. You'll find the large ones on the left. But here, let me help you get dressed. If I may?'

Selwyn offers a bit of artful oral homage before fitting him with the condom, then kneels at the side of the bed, his forearms planted on the mattress, his enormous buttocks on display. There's nothing attractive about the sight, nothing about Selwyn to make him a desirable sex object, and yet he finds himself consumed with the need to have this man.

First, though, he gets the knife from his pants pocket, concealing it in his hand. Then he does what is expected of him, bringing Selwyn to climax while holding back his own orgasm.

Selwyn's breathing returns to normal, and he starts to get up, but a hand on his shoulder keeps him where he is.

'My goodness,' he says, 'you're still hard. You haven't finished, have you? Do so, by all means. I want you to come.'

'I can't.'

'Is it physiological? A drug or something? Because if there's anything I can do—'

'I won't let myself finish,' he says. 'I'm saving it for a woman on the fourteenth floor.'

There is a pause, a rather delicious pause, and

Selwyn opens his mouth at last to say something, but he never gets the chance. The hand moves, the knife moves, and blood gouts from his slashed throat. His body bucks and heaves, twisting violently this way and that, and blood spurts everywhere.

Fortunately, the bathroom is magnificently appointed, the shower a great luxury. And afterward there's a sofa, untouched by blood spatters, and if it's not as comfortable as the king-size bed might be, well, surely it's more than satisfactory.

His sleep comes easily. It's deep, and of course untroubled.

The alarm wakes him at six. He's had four hours sleep, and he'd like one or two more. Morning, though, is the best time.

Suppose he stays here another twenty-four hours? It seems unlikely that anyone will come looking for Selwyn. On the other hand, the man's continuing presence will make the place increasingly unpleasant. The air-conditioning is doing what it can, but still the air is heavy with the sweet reek of decomposing flesh and blood. In another twenty-four hours—

No, it doesn't bear thinking about. And he'd have to stay, because once he leaves he won't be able to get back in. He would need Selwyn at his side in order to gain access to the Parc Vendôme, but Selwyn's not the buoyant companion he was a few hours ago.

Time to go.

He doesn't even make an attempt to clean up, to

erase traces of his presence. By now they're sure to have a full set of his fingerprints from Joe Bohan's apartment on West Fifty-third Street. He'd followed his usual policy of not touching surfaces unnecessarily, but his prints were all over his laptop and the table on which it had rested, and what difference does it really make? They have his prints, and now they'll get his DNA from the towel he used after his shower, and all that means is that they'll be able to identify him if they ever get their hands on him.

And they would anyway. There are too many people who've seen him and would be able to pick him out of a lineup. If they catch him, if they pick him up for drunk driving in Wisconsin or Wyoming, a routine fingerprint check is all it will take to end his career, if not his life.

But he never gets drunk, and never drinks before driving.

So it won't be that. It may be something else, sooner or later, but it's all far in the future – or near in the future, but in any event not in the present. And the present, after all, is what time it is now, and now's the only time it ever is. And when all is said and done, really, what do you get?

You get what you get.

There are staircases at either end of the building, but it seems simpler to take the elevator. It's empty when it arrives on Nine, and the only thing that concerns him is the possibility that someone who might recognize him – Scudder, Elaine, the black youth, some police officer – will be waiting for the elevator when the door opens on Fourteen. But it's early, it's not seven yet, and that reduces the likelihood substantially.

And he doesn't have much time to worry about it, because the elevator is at its destination before he can give the whole business much thought. When he rode up with Selwyn, he noted the placement of the elevator's security camera, monitored (if the fellow bothers) by the lobby attendant. He positions himself now to minimize his exposure to the camera, and makes sure his body conceals the knife, which he holds open at his side.

But of course there's no one waiting for the elevator, and indeed the entire hallway is empty. He walks to the door of Apartment 14-G, where a glance at the nameplate confirms that this is indeed the Scudder apartment.

If he had a key—

But, alas, he doesn't. And any approach he can think of is likely to prompt the apartment's male occupant to come to the door with a drawn gun, or to leave the door locked and simply call 911.

Stick to the plan, then.

He walks the length of the hallway to the rear stairwell. A few yards from the door leading to it is another door, which opens on a small room holding the chute for the trash compactor and a pair of recycling bins. A service elevator allows the hall porter to clear the bins.

There might be a security camera in the stairwell, though it seems unlikely that they'd have one for every floor. There's no camera here, in the compactor room, but tenants are apt to wander in with their trash, and how could he account for his presence?

He has a sudden vision of a stream of tenants, old ladies carrying shopping bags full of trash, and himself with no choice but to stab them each in turn, dismembering them and stuffing them piecemeal down the compactor chute, desperate to get one out of the way before the next one shows up.

He chooses the stairwell instead. There's no camera anywhere to be seen, and if he can't see it how can it see him?

He props the door open an inch or two. That's enough to provide a clear view of the entrance of 14-G without giving his own presence away.

Now all he requires is patience. And that quality is one he's always had in abundance.

CHAPTER 36

I slept poorly, and kept slipping in and out of a drinking dream. I woke up remembering none of the details, but concerned at first that it was somehow more than a dream, that I'd actually had a drink.

Elaine was still sleeping. I got out of bed quietly to keep from waking her. Our bedside tables each sported a handgun – the nine on my side, the .38 on hers. In the shower, I tried unsuccessfully to come up with some suitable version of *The family that prays together stays together*. When I got back to the bedroom the bed was empty, and so was her night table.

I got dressed and went to the kitchen. She wasn't there, but she'd made coffee, and the .38 now rested on the counter next to the coffee urn. I walked around looking for her, then returned to the kitchen when I heard the shower running. I poured myself a cup of coffee and toasted a muffin, and I was pouring a second cup by the time she joined me. She was wearing a belted silk robe, one I'd given her for Christmas a couple of years back. It had been one of my more successful presents. She hadn't put on makeup yet, and her scrubbed face looked like a girl's.

She asked if I wanted some eggs, and I thought about it and decided I didn't. She turned on the TV and got the local news, and there was nothing on it that demanded my attention. There was really only one topic of interest to either of us.

I said, 'He may have left town.'

'No. He's out there.'

'If he is, he hasn't got much time. They've got his prints.'

'That'll help a lot. "Attention – be on the lookout for a man with the following fingerprints . . ."'

'The point is the city's closing down around him. If he didn't catch a train yesterday, he'll have trouble boarding one today. They'll be looking for him at Penn Station. And Grand Central, and the bus terminal and the airports.'

'He could have a car,' she said. 'Or he could kill somebody and take theirs.'

'Possible.'

'He's still in town. I can tell.'

I'd be quicker to dismiss claims of intuitive knowledge if I hadn't learned over the years to trust them when I have them myself. And I'd have been especially hard put to argue with her this time because I agreed with her. I wasn't as certain as she was, but I didn't think he'd left.

And hadn't I felt him watching me on the way home from the meeting last night?

Maybe, and maybe not. Maybe anxiety was

sufficient explanation for the way I'd felt. God knows there was enough of it on hand to do the job.

I said, 'I think you're probably right. Right or wrong, though, we have to act as if he's here.'

'Meaning stay inside.'

'I'm afraid so.'

'I'm not going to argue with you. I've got the worst case of cabin fever I've ever had in my life, but I'm also scared to death. At this point it would be hard to get me to leave the apartment.'

'Good.'

'I hope it's not a permanent case of agoraphobia. I heard about a man once, he used to edit a science-fiction magazine, and he wouldn't leave his apartment building.'

'Afraid of aliens?'

'God knows what he was afraid of. God knows if it even happened, some john told me the story, he used to sell stories to the guy and I think played poker with him. None of that matters. The point is it started with him never leaving the Village, always finding an excuse not to go north of Fourteenth Street or south of Canal. Then he wouldn't leave the block, and then he wouldn't leave the building.'

'And then it got worse?'

'Quite a bit worse. He wouldn't set foot out of the apartment itself, and then he wouldn't leave the bedroom, and finally he wouldn't get out of bed. Except to go to the bathroom. I assume he would get out of bed to go to the bathroom.'

'Let's hope so.'

'He was editing a magazine where people walked around on the moons of Jupiter, but he couldn't get out of his own bed. And finally the men in the white coats came and took him away, and I don't think he ever did make it back.'

'I don't think that's going to happen to you.'

'Probably not. But I bet there are lots of people like that, never going out the door. You don't have to in New York, you can get everything delivered.'

'Speaking of which,' I said, 'you know how they keep trying to sell us home delivery of the *Times*?'

'"Available at no extra cost now for a limited time only."'

'I never saw the point,' I said, 'but if we're going to stay cooped up like this, maybe I ought to call them.'

'Where are you going? Oh, to get the paper? You want to bring me . . .'

I waited, but the sentence didn't come to an end. 'Bring you what?'

'Nothing,' she said. 'There's got to be something I want, but I can't think what it is.'

I gave her a kiss. She held on to me for a little longer than usual, then let go.

CHAPTER 37

He is completely tuned in, perfectly focused, and he hears the turning of the lock. There are several doors closer than 14-G, but he knows that's the one he's just heard, and without having to think about it he flicks his wrist and opens the knife. It makes a noise equal in volume to the lock, but he knows no one will hear it, because no one is listening for it.

The door opens. Scudder? Elaine?

It is Scudder, grim-faced, and he draws the door shut, then takes a moment to look this way and that, assuring himself that the hallway is empty. If he notices the slight gap between the stairwell door and its jamb, he pays it no mind.

He turns, walks to the elevator, reaches out a finger and jabs the button. He's wearing a short-sleeved sport shirt and a pair of dark trousers. His shoes are canvas slip-ons.

Is he carrying a gun? His shirt's tucked in, which suggests he's left the gun at home.

Should he take him now? The man's unarmed, with only his bare hands to defend against the knife. And he's not expecting anything, either.

He'd hear the approach, though, hear his nemesis rushing the length of the hallway at him. He'd turn, he'd prepare himself, and he'd cry out to summon help. The hue and cry would certainly alert Elaine.

Still . . .

The elevator arrives and spares him the decision. Scudder steps inside. The door closes and whisks him away.

Now.

He listens for a moment at the closed door. Then he draws back his fist and pounds on it.

Her voice: 'What is it?'

He notes the pronoun – What, not Who. Good.

He hammers on the door again, puts his other hand in front of his mouth to muffle his voice. Lowering it to a pitch close to Scudder's, infusing it with urgency, he says, 'Let me in. He's in the building, he got past the doorman. Let me in!'

Nothing but the truth, he thinks.

She's saying something, he can't make it out, but it doesn't matter, because the lock is turning. The instant it begins to open he hurls himself against it and it flies back, catching her shoulder and sending her reeling.

He flings the door shut, turns to her. She's staggering backward like a drunk in high heels. The wall stops her and she's trying to get her balance, and her face is something right out of a horror movie, a study in terror, and he holds the knife so she can see it.

Oh, this is going to be lovely . . .

She reaches into a pocket of the robe, comes up with a gun. Holds it in both hands, points it his way.

'Now put that down,' he says, his voice ringing with authority. 'You little fool, put that down this minute.'

She's shaking, trembling violently. He takes a confident step toward her, speaking gently to her, telling her to put the gun down, that her only chance is calm co-operation. It's going to work, he knows it's going to work, and—

She pulls the trigger.

He feels the punch of the bullet before his ears register the sound of the gunshot. It hits him high on the left shoulder, and he knows at once that it's broken the bone. There must be pain, and doubtless there will be eventually, but the pain hasn't come yet.

He rushes her. The gun's pointing at the ceiling, the recoil must have elevated it, but she's lowering it, bringing it to bear on him. She fires too soon, though, and the bullet passes harmlessly over his head, and before she can steady herself for a third shot he's reached her. His left hand won't work, the arm hangs at his side. He grabs her wrist in his right hand, shakes it until the gun drops to the floor, then lifts his hand and back-hands her hard across the face.

He hits her again, in the pit of the stomach, and when she doubles up he gives her a shove and sends her sprawling. She's scrabbling for the gun, but he gets to it first and grabs it, then straightens up and points it at her.

She's on her hands and knees on the floor, staring up at him. Her robe has fallen open and he can see her breasts. Her eyes look right into the muzzle of the gun. And it's odd, because there's no fear in them now. He wonders what happened to the terror.

Wherever it's gone, it'll be back soon enough.

In a little while,' he says softly, 'you'll wish I'd pulled the trigger.'

It would be easier to get the cylinder to swing out if he had both hands to work with. But he manages it, and tilts the gun so that the remaining rounds spill out onto the carpet. He kicks at them, sends them scurrying like bugs across the room.

'Now that that's out of the way,' he says, 'we can enjoy ourselves. Get up, Elaine. Come on, on your feet!'

She stays where she is until he draws back a foot and kicks her hard in the ribs. Then she gets up, and it's delicious just looking at her face, reading her thoughts in the expressions that pass over it. She's trying to think of something to do, something that will save her, and there's nothing, and the hopelessness of her situation is beginning to dawn on her.

And this is just the beginning! Oh, he's going to enjoy this. He's going to make it last as long as he can.

'Take off the robe, Elaine.'

She stands there, obdurate. He reaches out with the knife and she backs up until the wall stops her.

His shoulder is throbbing now. There's still no pain, and the throbbing is like a very strong pulse working in the area of the wound. There's no blood, either, except for a minimal amount at the very edge of the wound, and he wonders if the bullet could have cauterized the wound even as it inflicted it.

Is it possible that the wound is healing itself? He's heard of such things but always dismissed them as comic book fantasies. Still, something is shielding him from the pain, even as something is keeping him from losing blood.

He wore amethyst for months. Perhaps it worked, perhaps he's absorbed its essence. Perhaps he is in fact immortal . . .

He reaches out with the knife, and there's nowhere for her to go, nothing for her to do. She unbelts the robe, lets it fall from her shoulders.

Oh, lovely. Just lovely.

She's on her back on the living room floor. He's naked, his clothes where he dropped them, and he's on top of her, and it's good he didn't let himself reach climax earlier with that fat queen, because all that energy is at his disposal now, and he's rock-hard and enormous, and he's inside her, buried in her clear to the hilt, and her breasts are cushioning him, and he's holding the knife to her throat. And he could lie like this forever, thrusting lazily into her, gripped so perfectly by the envelope of her flesh, forever on the edge of his passion and yet entirely in control of it, able to go on this way for all eternity.

And, as he moves inside her, he talks to her. He tells her what he's going to do to her, how he'll cut her and drink her blood, how he'll scoop out her eyes like melon balls, how he'll slice her nipples off, how he'll skin her alive. His voice is conversational, almost gentle. But is she paying attention? Is she taking this all in?

With the tip of the knife blade, he draws an inch-long line on her shoulder. The left shoulder. She shot him in the left shoulder, inflicting a painless but paralyzing wound, and he's merely piercing the skin, drawing a white line that turns red as blood oozes from it.

He puts his mouth to the cut and tastes her blood.

And the door bursts open.

CHAPTER 38

Could I have heard something?

I don't think it's possible. There were two gunshots, and one or both of them might have rung out while I was in the elevator on the way down to the lobby. But it seems unlikely that I could have heard them, or paid much attention to them if I did.

I was just going out for the paper. Elevator to the lobby, a few steps to the news-stand on the corner, a few steps back. I hadn't even bothered to take my gun along. I'd thought of it, but it was on the bedside table and I was standing at the door, and it would have been silly, wouldn't it?

Maybe we were linked, she and I, and something within me could sense an attack on her. I don't know how these things work, or if they work. But when the elevator reached the lobby I had the feeling that something was wrong.

I have to get back there, I thought.

First get the paper, I told myself, so you won't look like an idiot when you burst into the apartment and she's got her feet up and the TV on.

No. Screw the paper.

I got back on the elevator. There were other people on it, and it crawled, stopping at three or four floors en route to mine. The closer I got the greater my sense of urgency grew, and by the time I got off at Fourteen I knew with absolute certainty that he was in there. I didn't know if she was alive, I was afraid he'd had enough time to kill her, but I knew he was there and I had no time to waste.

I had my key in my hand when the elevator door opened, and I rushed the length of the hall and got the key in the lock and threw the door open.

There was a chair overturned and clothes here and there on the floor, and she was on the floor and he was on top of her, and even as I registered this he was disengaging from her, getting to his feet, and she was lying there, motionless.

There was a trail of blood from her shoulder down toward her breast, and I couldn't tell if she was alive or dead, and I couldn't take time to look because he was there, facing me, and he had a knife in his hand and there was blood on the tip of it, her blood.

'Matt,' he said. 'Now this is providential, wouldn't you say? As soon as you and I have concluded our business' – he moved the knife from side to side, like a hypnotist swinging an amulet in front of a subject's eyes – 'then Elaine and I can take our time. It would be nice if you could watch me kill her, but you can't have everything, can you? You get what you get, Matthew. Don't ever forget that.'

Then she was alive. That was all that really registered from his little speech. She was alive. I was in time. If I could kill him then she could survive.

He stood leaning slightly forward with his weight balanced on the balls of his feet, moving the knife from side to side. He was naked, and he would have looked ridiculous, except for the fact that he clearly knew how to use the knife and just as clearly looked forward to using it.

There was something wrong with his left arm. It hung at his side. There was a wound, too, a hole in his shoulder, and at first I thought it was an old wound, scarred over, and then I realized she'd shot him, although he didn't seem to be bleeding.

That ought to be to my advantage, though I couldn't see how. A knife's not a gun, nobody needs two hands to use it properly.

He was saying something else but I wasn't paying attention. I'm not sure I could have heard him if I'd tried. I stood there looking at him and he took a step toward me and I couldn't think of the right way to do this and I didn't care. I ran at him and threw myself at him, and I felt the knife dig into my middle, and I knocked him sprawling and landed on top of him, and he twisted the knife and the pain was thin and high and insistent, like a scream.

I got a hand on his throat and bore down, and he tucked his chin down, and I drew back my hand and hammered at his face with both hands. He couldn't fight back, he had one hand that didn't work and another that was pinned between our two bodies, and in order to retrieve it he'd have to let go of the knife, and he wouldn't do that, not while he could twist the knife in my guts and send pain coursing through me like a jackhammer tearing up pavement.

I wanted to pull away from him, I wanted to cry out, I wanted to let go and let the curtain come down, but I couldn't, I couldn't, because I had to finish this, I had to end it forever, and the only way to do that was to kill him, and the only way to kill him was by hitting him and hitting him and hitting him until he was dead.

My hands were bloody and his mouth and nose were bloody and I hit him again and his front teeth were broken off at the gum line and I hammered him with my fists and his head thumped against the floor and I took hold of his head with my thumbs digging into his eyes and I gouged with my thumbs and I raised his head and pounded it against the floor and his blood spread on the carpet and my own blood was seeping out of me. The blood was welling up behind my eyes, filling my field of vision, and I had the sense that as soon as I could see nothing but the red tidal wave of blood it would sweep me up and I would drown in it.

And then I lost track of things, because all I seemed able to pay attention to was the rising curtain of blood, and all I could do was try to hold on to the few degrees of vision at the very top edge of it. And then there was a noise like a clap of thunder, and at first I thought *Oh it's a gunshot* and then I thought *Oh it's a crack in the universe* and, then I thought *No it's the end, the end of everything* and then the wave of blood swept me up and everything was red and red and red and the red darkened and then everything was black.

CHAPTER 39

I'm floating. I'm in empty sky, or in a sea of nothingness. I'm floating.

There are voices but I can't make out what they're saying. Some of them are familiar and some of them are not, but I can't identify any of them. By the time I've heard a word I've forgotten the words before it, and I forget it as well when I hear the next one.

Floating . . .

I'm in a room, a huge room, an enormous room. It may extend forever, this room. There may be no walls. Just people, strewn across the length and breadth of it.

And I'm somehow above them, looking down at them, but I can only bring into focus the person I am looking at, and I don't seem able to direct my gaze where I want. It just goes here and there, centering on this person for a moment, then moving elsewhere. It's as though I'm watching a movie, with someone else operating the camera.

And there's no time. The camera moves neither slowly nor rapidly. Everything somehow exists outside of time. There's all the time in the world, but there's no time at all.

A portion of the room is familiar. It's Jimmy Armstrong's saloon, the old one on Ninth Avenue. And there's Billie Keegan behind the bar, drawing a beer for Manny Karesh. And Jimmy's at a table, not heavy and bloated as he became in his later years, but the thin elfin Jimmy I first met, sitting at a table with a plate of steamed fish and bean sprouts. I want to say something to him but he drifts off to the edge of vision, and I see a fellow in a sharp suit spin a silver dollar on the tabletop, then snatch it up just as it begins to wobble. And it's Spinner Jablon, who knew he would be murdered and hired me ahead of time to catch his killer.

Spinner looks up, and I look with him, and the waitress is there with a tray of drinks, and it's Paula Wittlauer, who went out a high window. I barely knew her and she was gone, and her sister didn't believe it was suicide and hired me, and it turned out she was right. Paula turns toward me with a glass in her hand, and then she changes, and now she's a call girl named Portia Carr, and the man at her side is a crooked cop named Jerry Broadfield. He has a cocky grin on his face, and I watch it fade into sadness and regret.

And the images come and go faster now. I am barely able to register one face before it's gone and another is in its place. Skip Devoe and Bobby Ruslander, and Bobby betrayed Skip and Skip sold him out to the Morrissey brothers, who left him

406

with a black hood over his head and his hands wired behind his back and a bullet in the back of his head. And now they're friends again, they have their arms around each other as if they're posing for a picture. And they're gone, and there's Tommy Tillary and Carolyn Cheatham, and Tommy's wife, Margaret, whom I never met but recognize at once. Tommy killed Margaret, and got away with it, and Carolyn killed herself, and I framed him for it, and he went to prison and was murdered there.

So many people, all of them dead . . .

Miguelito Cruz and Angel Herrera. Martin Vanderpoel and his son Richie, and Wendy Hanniford. Henry Prager. John Lundgren. Glenn Holtzmann and Lisa Holtzmann and Jan Keane.

Estrellita Rivera. Six years old, and it was my own wayward bullet that killed her so many years ago. Her eyes meet mine, and she smiles knowingly, and she's gone.

Jim Faber, wearing the old army jacket he wore when I first met him, at the very first AA meeting I ever attended. Jim looks as though he's going to tell me something, and I strain to hear it, and then he's gone.

Roger Prysock, wearing a zoot suit. Adrian Whitfield and Richie Vollmer and Regis Kilbourne. James Leo Motley. Peter Khoury and Francine Khoury. Ray Callander. Andy Buckley. Vince Mahaffey. Gerry Billings. Moon Gafter and Paddy Dowling. And more men, passing through my field of vision faster than I can summon up their names.

And then some women. Kim Dakkinen, with an emerald ring on her finger. Sunny Hendryx. Connie Cooperman. Toni Cleary. Elizabeth Scudder, who'd died because we shared a surname. I'd never met her, but somehow I recognize her, and then she's gone.

And then Elaine. What are you doing here, I want to ask, with all these dead people?

Was I too late? Did he kill you, too?

She's floating above the others, and it's only her face, her perfect face, and she's so young. She looks like a girl now, she looks like the girl I first met at Danny Boy's table.

I look at her, and all I want to do is look at her, I want to look at her forever, I want to drown in her eyes.

And below us now there's a great sea of people, there's every person I ever knew who's gone. My first wife, Anita. My mother, my father. Aunts and uncles. Grandparents, stretching back to the beginning of time. Hundreds, thousands of people, and they fade out slowly, until there's nothing there but space, empty space.

Then everything shifts abruptly, like a fast cut in a film. I'm watching from on high, and below me men and women in surgical gowns and masks are hovering around a table. There's a figure on the table but I can't see who it is.

But I can see the others. There's Vince Edwards and Sam Jaffe from *Ben Casey*, and Richard Chamberlain and Raymond Massey from *Dr Kildare*, and Robert

Young as *Marcus Welby*. Mandy Patinkin and Adam Arkin from *Chicago Hope*, and that guy from *St Elsewhere*, and George Clooney and Anthony Edwards from *ER*. And I look at the women, and each one starts out as somebody else but they all somehow turn into Elaine. And I know that's me on the table. I can't see myself but I know that it's me.

Someone says: *Oh, fuck!*

It's so hard to watch. It's so hard to pay attention.

Someone says: *We're losing him.*

So much easier to let go . . .

Someone says: *No. No!*

And the lights dim all the way down, and everything ends.

CHAPTER 40

There may have been other times when I recovered consciousness, or at least hovered at its edge for a moment or two. But the first I retained any awareness of, after the curious vision of a roomful of television actors in surgical scrubs, was brief and indistinct. I was all at once present, after having been somewhere else for an indeterminate period of time. I was lying on my back, and I willed myself to move, and couldn't.

Someone was holding my hand. I opened an eye and confirmed what I already knew: It was Elaine.

I thought, she's alive. I squeezed her hand, or at least thought about it, and she turned her eyes toward mine.

'You're going to be all right,' she said.

It seemed to me that I already knew that. I wanted to say something, but then my eyes closed and I went away again.

I came back and went away again a few more times, but before it seemed possible a couple of nurses got me out of bed and made me walk around in the hospital corridor. I was getting enough Demerol to keep the pain manageable, but even so, walking was still no pleasure. They insist you do it, though, because that way you recover faster, so they can send you home and give your bed to somebody else.

By now I knew I was at Roosevelt Hospital, and that he'd done quite a number on me with his knife. They'd had to remove a couple of sections of small intestine and stitch the rest back together in what they hoped would be a serviceable fashion. I'd lost a lot of blood, and kept losing some of the blood they transfused into me, and it was touch and go in there for a while. The moment I seemed to recall – *We're losing him!* – had several real-life counterparts. There were several moments when they'd thought I was slipping away, and maybe I did, but each time something called me back.

'I yelled at you,' she said. 'I said, "Don't you dare leave me!"'

'Evidently I couldn't.'

'Not with the all-star medical team you had. Marcus Welby, though? I didn't think he spent much time in the operating room. I thought he pretty much confined himself to dispensing good homespun wisdom.'

'I never realized I watched that many medical shows,' I said. 'I guess they did a good job of imprinting on my consciousness.'

'Or unconsciousness,' she said.

They'd be feeding me through an IV line for a while, and it would be an indeterminate period of time before some parts of me worked as well as they used to.

One doctor advised Elaine that I might never be able to handle spicy foods again. 'And I told him he obviously doesn't know who he's dealing with,' she said. 'My man takes on killers with his bare hands, I told him. No Scotch bonnet pepper is going to lay him low.'

'The only reason I went after him with my bare hands,' I said, 'is that's all I had.'

'He had a knife and you ran right at him.'

'I'd risk anything to keep him from hurting you. And if you were already dead, well, then I didn't really care what happened to me.'

What had happened to him, meanwhile, was that he was dead. While I was smashing his head against the floor, Elaine had managed to get the pistol from my bedside table. That noise I'd heard, the last thing I was aware of before the blood-dimmed tide swept over me, was indeed a gunshot, the first of several. She'd had to figure out how to disengage the safety, and then she'd had to get up close enough to get off a shot at him without hitting me. She wound up sticking the gun in his ear and pulling the trigger, and I registered the sound of it even as I was letting go and slipping away.

'You told me if I ever used the gun I was supposed to keep on firing until it was empty,' she said, 'and that's what I did. The recoil didn't seem any worse than with the thirty-eight. Or maybe I was better at anticipating it, I don't know. When it started going *click* instead of *bang* I picked up the phone and called 911, but the cops were already on their way, and so was the ambulance.'

I told her she'd saved my life, and she repeated that the cop and ambulance had already been on their way by the time she made the call. 'Not by calling,' I said. 'By killing the bastard.'

'I don't know if I killed him.'

'He's dead,' I said, 'and you shot him seven or eight times in the head. I think it's safe to infer a cause-and-effect relationship there.'

'Except that he may have been dead already. They think you may have beaten him to death.'

'Oh. Well, I don't think I could have managed it if he'd had two hands at his disposal. You took a lot of fight out of him by putting a bullet in his shoulder.'

'I could have saved us both a lot of aggravation by putting it in his heart instead.'

'He's dead,' I said. 'It doesn't really matter who did it. We saved each other's lives.'

'That's nothing new,' she said. 'We do that every day.'

They never did pin a name to the son of a bitch. His prints weren't on file anywhere, except as an unidentified suspect in a murder somewhere out west. Name or no name, Wentworth and Sussman assured me that his death would clear a lot of cases all over the country, including some that had already been attributed to other people, like Preston Applewhite.

'God knows how many people he killed,' Sussman said. 'We pulled a lot out of his computer, but he's only had that particular laptop for a year or two. Taking out someone like him, it's not so much a win for the criminal justice system as it's a vitally important public health measure. You kill him and it's like you found a cure for cancer.'

Elaine had some bruises where he'd hit her and some more from falling and hurting herself, and there was a narrow scar about an inch long on her shoulder, where he'd cut her. She was putting Vitamin E on it, though, and she'd picked up something at the drugstore that would make scars disappear.

I said it wasn't all that much of a scar, and she said it didn't matter. 'I don't want his mark on me,' she said.

And he'd raped her.

'Aside from yours,' she said, 'it's been over a dozen years since I had anybody's dick in me. I could probably find a more graceful way of putting it—'

'But why bother?'

'My thought exactly. I was so disgusted, baby. Not while it was going on, not while he had the knife at my throat. I was too busy with fear to

414

have any time left for disgust. But later, thinking about him, I kept wanting to vomit. I kept taking baths and douching, trying to get clean, and then I just declared myself clean and said the hell with it. Because there wasn't anything there to wash away, you know?'

I had a lot of visitors. TJ, of course, and Danny Boy, and Mick, who came alone a couple of times and showed up once with Kristin Hollander. ('I wonder,' Elaine said, after the two of them left, and I told her not to be silly. She gave me a look.)

A number of cops came, in addition to Sussman and Wentworth, and ex-cops like Joe Durkin and Ray Galindez. There were people I knew from AA and men from the Club of Thirty-one, and Ray Gruliow, who fit both categories. And friends and acquaintances from the building, and from all around the neighborhood.

Louise turned up, to see how I was and to let me know that she was continuing to spend time with David Thompson. 'Because I realized I was being an idiot,' she said. 'Here's this really nice guy who's fun to be with, in and out of bed, and he likes me. *And* he smokes. And I'm gonna get on my high horse because he's had a run of bad luck and has to sleep in his car? My God, a few years ago I was getting pig-drunk and puking on my shoes and going home with strangers, and where do I get off looking down on a decent guy like David?'

It was a lot better between them, she said, now that everything was out in the open, and he didn't have to keep his guard up, and she could stop worrying that he was hiding something. He wasn't moving in, they both agreed that wouldn't be appropriate yet, but at least he could stay over on nights when they went to bed together.

'Assuming he's got a good parking place,' Elaine said.

'And enough cigarettes,' Louise said.

And I said, 'Look, maybe I shouldn't mention this, but it's a big thing with you so you probably ought to know. He's planning on saving money, one way or the other, so that he can afford an apartment. And one thing he intends to do, partly to save money and also for long-term health reasons, involves smoking.'

She looked at me. 'He's gonna quit?'

'That's what he says.'

'Oh,' she said, and thought about it. 'Oh, what the hell,' she said. 'Nobody's perfect.'

I'm home now, and if I spend most of my time in bed with a book or in a chair in front of the television set, I manage to stay active enough to keep my blood circulating and my doctors happy. More often than not, I'll join TJ for breakfast at the Morning Star and hear about his adventures in the market. And twice a week I walk the few blocks up Ninth Avenue to St Paul's and go to a meeting in the basement. I used a walking stick at first, a splendid one of blackthorn with a great knob to hold on to and a brass ferrule at its tip. Mick had brought it back from Ireland for me, years before I had any use for it. I still use it sometimes, but only when I remember.

My insides seem to be working reasonably well, although every once in a while something reminds me that I'd had a knife stuck in there not too long ago. But the other night Elaine made a pot of chili, spiced the way I like it, so that it was as much a religious experience as a meal. And I did just fine.

Three mornings a week, I have a ninety-minute physical therapy session with a resolutely cheerful blonde named Margit, who shows up at the appointed hour with a sack of hand weights and pulleys and other implements of torture. I'm always pleased when she shows up, and even happier when she leaves. I'm making steady progress, she says, which is great to hear. And I'm really doing remarkably well for a man my age, she adds, which isn't.

And in a few weeks Elaine and I will be taking a cab to JFK and a plane to Lauderdale, where we'll get on a ship for a cruise through the West Indies and up the Amazon. Elaine says we won't have to do anything, we'll pack and unpack once and just sit back and relax. And eat six times a day, she says, and sit on the deck in the sunshine, and watch pink dolphins in the river and listen to the howler monkeys on its banks.

'We'll be fine,' she says, and I think she's probably right.

In the meantime, one or the other of us is often to be found standing at the south window, staring off into the distance. I'm not sure what Elaine sees, or even what I myself am trying to glimpse out there. We're gazing out at the past, perhaps, or into the future. Or, I sometimes think, at the uncertain present.